PENGUIN CLA

THE SIXTEEN SATIRES

ADVISORY EDITOR: BETTY RADICE

Not much is known about the life of JUVENAL, but he was probably born in A.D. 55, the son of a well-to-do Spanish freedman who had settled in Aquinum. In 78 he obtained the command of a cohort of Dalmatian auxiliaries and saw service in Britain under Agricola (there are several references in his *Satires* to Britain which indicate a first-hand knowledge). He was welcomed home with honour in 80, dedicated a shrine to Helvine Ceres, and was made an honorary priest of the deified Vespasian. When the Emperor Titus died in 81 and Domitian came to power, Juvenal probably spent the next ten years cultivating his position in society. He was writing satirical sketches privately and in about 93 a lampoon of his became known to the authorities and he was exiled to the Great Oasis in Upper Egypt. Recalled after Domitian's assassination in 96, he issued Book I of the *Satires* during 110–12. His material condition improved and he had a small farm at Tivoli and a house in Rome, where he entertained in a modest way. Books IV and V appeared in 123–5 and 128–30 and it is likely that he survived the Emperor Hadrian by a year or two, dying in about 140.

PETER GREEN, M.A., Ph.D. (Cantab), F.R.S.L., was born in London in 1924, and educated at Charterhouse and Trinity College, Cambridge, where he took first-class honours in both parts of the Classical Tripos (1950), winning the Craven Scholarship and Studentship the same year. After a short spell as a Director of Studies in classics at Cambridge he worked for some years as a freelance writer, translator and literary journalist, and as a publisher. In 1963 he emigrated to Greece with his family. From 1966 until 1971 he lectured in Greek history and literature at Athens; he is now the Dougherty Centennial Professor of Classics at the University of Texas at Austin. His publications include *Essays in Antiquity* (1960), *Alexander the Great* (1970), *Armada from Athens: The Failure of the Sicilian Expedition, 415–413 B.C.* (1971), *The Year of Salamis, 480–479 B.C.* (1971), *The Shadow of the Parthenon* (1972), *A Concise History of Ancient Greece* (1973), three historical novels, *Achilles his Armour* (1955),

The Sword of Pleasure (1957), *The Laughter of Aphrodite* (1965), a historical biography, *Alexander of Macedon 356–323* B.C. (1974), *Classical Bearings: Interpreting Ancient History and Culture* (1989) and, most recently, *Alexander to Actium: The Historical Evolution of the Hellenistic Age* (1990). He has also translated Ovid's *The Erotic Poems* and *The Poems of Exile* for the Penguin Classics.

Juvenal

THE SIXTEEN SATIRES

TRANSLATED WITH AN
INTRODUCTION AND NOTES BY
PETER GREEN

PENGUIN BOOKS

PENGUIN BOOKS

Published by the Penguin Group
Penguin Books Ltd, 27 Wrights Lane, London W8 5TZ, England
Penguin Books USA Inc., 375 Hudson Street, New York, New York 10014, USA
Penguin Books Australia Ltd, Ringwood, Victoria, Australia
Penguin Books Canada Ltd, 10 Alcorn Avenue, Toronto, Ontario, Canada M4V 3B2
Penguin Books (NZ) Ltd, 182–190 Wairau Road, Auckland 10, New Zealand

Penguin Books Ltd, Registered Offices: Harmondsworth, Middlesex, England

This translation first published 1967
Reprinted with revisions 1974
15 17 19 20 18 16 14

Printed in England by Clays Ltd, St Ives plc
Set in Monotype Bembo

CONTENTS

Acknowledgements   7
Preface to the 1974 edition   8
Introduction   9

SATIRE I   65
SATIRE II   75
SATIRE III   87
SATIRE IV   105
SATIRE V   117
SATIRE VI   127
SATIRE VII   163
SATIRE VIII   177
SATIRE IX   195
SATIRE X   205
SATIRE XI   227
SATIRE XII   241
SATIRE XIII   249
SATIRE XIV   263
SATIRE XV   281
SATIRE XVI   293

Select Bibliography   299
Additional Bibliography   303
Index   307

ACKNOWLEDGEMENTS

I FIRST became acquainted with Juvenal through the good offices of Mr A. L. Irvine, my late sixth-form master, who – with what I took at the time, wrongly, to be pure sadistic relish – set us to translate Satire X aloud, *unseen*, and afterwards made us learn long stretches of it by heart, together with parallel passages from Dr Johnson's *The Vanity of Human Wishes*. But in fact, of course, this was by far the best introduction to a notoriously difficult poet that one could hope for. Sink or swim, one stumbled through the unfamiliar vocabulary and allusions; and only those who have committed, say, the passage on the fall of Sejanus to memory can really begin to appreciate Juvenal's technical virtuosity: his subtle control of rhythm and sound-effects, his dense, hard, verbal brilliance. This book is, in a sense, the belated fruit of a seed sown some twenty-five years ago, and I am happy to acknowledge my debt to an inspired and inspiring teacher.

No student of Juvenal can afford to ignore two remarkable works published since the war. Ulrich Knoche's text presents the fullest, most thorough *apparatus criticus* Juvenal has ever possessed; and even when they differ from his judgement, scholars owe a vast debt of gratitude to Knoche for his devoted and meticulous industry. The same is true of a very different book, Professor Gilbert Highet's *Juvenal the Satirist* – virtually the only general study of Juvenal in existence, and an arsenal of recondite material which future commentators will ignore at their peril. Like any such study it is open to criticism; but the spiteful virulence with which it was received on publication by some of Professor Highet's fellow-classicists must be regarded as one of the less creditable episodes in modern scholarship, and the extent of its influence can only be measured by the mark it has left on all subsequent studies. My own task has been made incalculably lighter by it: my gratitude to Professor Highet is profound.

I would also like to thank Dr Michael Coffey and Professor J. P.

Sullivan, both of whom read early drafts of the first two satires and made most valuable comments on them; Dr Coffey also very kindly sent me an offprint of his exhaustive survey of modern Juvenal studies, published in *Lustrum*, which has been of inestimable service to me. I am grateful to Dr E. J. Dingwall for clearing up several (in every sense) arcane points, especially in Satires II and IX, and to Miss Sylvia Moody for undertaking some highly specialized research-work on my behalf at a time when I was unavoidably isolated from major classical libraries. But perhaps my greatest debt of gratitude is owed, jointly, to Dr E. V. Rieu, who originally invited me to translate Juvenal, and from whose wise comments my version benefited more than I can say; and to Mrs Betty Radice, his editorial successor, whose patience with my snail-like rate of progress has only been equalled by her vigilance in saving me from my own worst errors. Neither they, nor those other helpers I have named, should be held responsible for any mistakes which still remain; such anomalies can be safely ascribed to my own carelessness or obstinacy.

PREFACE TO THE 1974 EDITION

In the present edition I have brought my bibliography up to date by the selective addition of useful and significant items published since 1967; occasionally, as a result, I have changed my opinions about Juvenal's text, and at such points I have therefore revised my translation. I have also, here and there, where space permitted, inserted brief additional notes.

I would like to express my thanks to my colleagues in the Department of Classics at the University of Texas, and to the graduate students with whom I conducted a seminar on Juvenal, for doing so much, in class or private discussion, to clarify my ideas about this most perennially enigmatic of all Roman poets. I also owe a great debt of gratitude to Mrs Anne Vanderhoof, Librarian of the Battle Collection, whose help in tracing and obtaining recondite material has gone far beyond the call of duty.

Austin, Texas, September 1973   P.G.

INTRODUCTION

In the whole of Roman literature there is no more personally elusive character than Juvenal. His work – in marked contrast to the satires of his predecessors Horace and Persius – contains almost no autobiographical material. Of his contemporaries, only the epigrammatist Martial ever refers to him. It has been argued that he was a pupil of Quintilian's, and that the *Institutio Oratoria* alludes to him among 'contemporaries of promise', but this is pure speculation. After his death – it is unlikely that he survived long after the accession of Antoninus Pius in A.D. 138 – the *Satires* drop out of sight absolutely for about a century. Since both the vices and the literary fashions which Juvenal castigated became increasingly popular with the Imperial Court towards the close of the Antonine period, this neglect is understandable. Marcus Aurelius would scarcely have relished Juvenal's xenophobic attitude to all things Greek any more than his son, Commodus, would have tolerated a satirist who attacked nobles with a penchant for appearing as gladiators. No critic or grammarian in the second and third centuries A.D., though they make frequent references to other Roman poets, ever mentions Juvenal.

Ironically (since Juvenal's view of foreign religions was something less than respectful), his earliest rediscoverers seem to have been the Christian apologists, who raided his arsenal of moral invective for their own sectarian purposes. Tertullian (*c.* A.D. 160–220), though he does not mention the satirist by name, had clearly absorbed some of his more pithy tags. The first direct reference to Juvenal by a Christian writer comes early in the fourth century A.D. Lactantius quotes with approval the last lines of Satire X ('Fortune has no divinity, could we but see it: it's we,/We ourselves, who make her a goddess, and set her in the heavens'), and foreshadows the traditional view of Juvenal as a distinguished pagan moralist with a genius for crisp epigrams. The first non-Christian interest in the *Satires* hardly pre-dates the fourth century,

9

and may have been stimulated by the work of two Christian poets, Ausonius and Prudentius, who adapted and imitated them. Perhaps soon after 350 the first ancient commentary was produced; by 390 the historian Ammianus Marcellinus could observe that certain contemporary aristocrats, who had no time for literature in general – Juvenal's attraction has always been at least as much moral and political as artistic – were devouring him with some enthusiasm. At the same period Servius, the great commentator on Virgil, was at work in Rome: he alludes to the *Satires* on more than seventy occasions, thus breaking the complete silence of his predecessors. The bitter old man from Aquinum had reached a wide public at last, after centuries of neglect; from then on his fame never wavered.

But the years of darkness left a legacy of ignorance and neglect behind them which still bedevils any attempt to establish exactly what Juvenal wrote, let alone the details of his life. When the *Satires* were resurrected, it was natural that those who studied and admired them should want to know something about their author. But if, as seems probable, they had nothing to go on but one manuscript lacking its final pages, biographical details could only be sought from the *Satires* themselves. There are some thirteen late Lives extant, mostly derived from that preserved in the commentary of Probus; with the exception of the first sentence, all the details look as though they were manufactured after a study of Juvenal's own text. The first sentence tells us that Decimus Junius Juvenalis was either the son, or the adopted son, of a wealthy freedman, and 'practised rhetoric till about middle age, more as an amusement than as a serious preparation for teaching rhetoric or pleading in the courts.' The Lives generally agree that his birthplace was Aquinum, a hill-town near Monte Cassino, some eighty miles south-east of Rome; that he was exiled for attacking an actor with influence at court; and that this exile was spent in Egypt, though some Lives opt for Scotland. The emperor who banished him is variously given as Trajan or Domitian. There is one incredible tradition that his exile to Egypt took place when he was eighty years old, and was combined with a military command. Apart from the actual fact of exile, there is nothing here that could not have been invented in the fourth century by some scholar who simply read the *Satires* and then looked through his history-books for an appropriate context.

Only one of these Lives attempts to supply the date of his birth, and none tells us when he died. The year A.D. 55 may be a guess, but it is a plausible one, and fits the rest of our evidence: moreover, if the compiler of the Life had intended to fabricate evidence of this sort, he would in all likelihood have added a suppositious date of death as well. There is a tradition that he survived, worn out with old age, for some time (but we are not told how long) after the death of Hadrian in A.D. 138. Some sources believe that he died in exile, others that he returned to Rome, but pined away because his friend Martial had returned to his native Spain in A.D. 98. (This last assertion is obviously based on the evidence of Martial's poem to Juvenal from Bilbilis (12.18) and reinforces the suspicion that the biographers were making bricks with such straw as they had.) One, unfortunately, asserts that he 'amplified his satires in exile and made many changes in them,' a claim which may well have derived from the confused state of the text, and which has provided a splendid loop-hole for adventurous modern editors. The biographies do not tell us whether Juvenal ever married or had children; indeed, apart from the persistent tradition of his exile, and its cause, there is hardly anything in them – e.g. his military service, or his supposed presence in Britain and Egypt – which could not have been inferred from his own words. The variants on the story of his exile suggest that even this was preserved without any explanatory facts, and that Egypt or Britain may have been selected as its locale simply because he shows knowledge of them both in the *Satires*.

An examination of Juvenal's writings tends to confirm such a view. The biographical or chronological evidence which the *Satires* yield is singularly small. The first Book, consisting of Satires I–V inclusive, contains allusions to the banishment of Marius Priscus,

a corrupt provincial governor, whose trial was held in A.D. 100
(I 40–50); to the death of Domitian in 96 (IV 153); and perhaps to
the publication of Tacitus's *Histories*, between 104 and 109
(II 102–3). Satire II contains further allusions to Agricola's cam-
paign in the Orkneys and his plan for reducing Ireland (159–61),
and to Domitian's assumption of the office of Censor (30, 63, 161).
Both of these events can be dated to A.D. 84/5, and yet Juvenal
treats them as recent and topical. The impression conveyed by the
Book as a whole is that some of the material (especially Satires II
and IV) may well have been composed in private draft during the
reign of Domitian, and circulated more freely after his murder in
96, when Nerva called off the Terror and brought back the
political exiles. If the reference to Tacitus is upheld, the publication
of Book I will have taken place about 110/112.

Book II consists entirely of one work, the gigantic and virulent
Sixth Satire directed against women. Here we find (407 ff.), as a
specifically topical allusion, mention of floods and earthquake in
the East, and a comet 'presaging trouble/For some eastern prince,
in Armenia, maybe, or Parthia'. Just such a comet was visible at
Rome in November 115, the year before Trajan's Parthian
campaign; and in December of the same year there was a famous
earthquake at Antioch, which endangered the life of the Emperor
himself. This provides us with a plausible *terminus post quem*. Once
again there are earlier datable references which suggest that parts
of the draft had been written, or sketched, some time before: the
mention of Trajan's German and Dacian victories in 97 and 102/3,
the allusion to the Capitoline Games founded in 86, the lovingly
accurate description of a complicated feminine hairstyle which
had vanished for twenty years when Satire VI appeared (VI
204–5, 387 ff., 486 ff.: for Flavian coiffures see Paoli p. 111 and pl.
35).

Book III consists of Satires VII–IX. Satire VII begins with some
twenty lines praising 'Caesar' as the one hope for the arts, the
only patron writers and literature can depend on in these troubled
and philistine times. The introduction has every appearance of an

afterthought or revision, tacked on to an already existing draft: the bulk of the satire is devoted to a survey of the poverty and humiliation which not only writers, but lawyers, rhetoricians and schoolteachers have to endure. There is, moreover, a distinct flavour of ironic ambiguity about the compliment Juvenal pays his Imperial patron. On every count it seems likely that the Emperor in question was Hadrian, and that the publication of Book III took place between his accession in 118 and his departure for a tour of the provinces in 121 (see below, p. 172, n. 1). Satire VII is the first occasion on which Juvenal refers to an Emperor in anything but disparaging terms; Satire VIII, even more surprisingly, is dedicated to a young nobleman just going out to govern a province, and is a lecture on the theme of 'Virtue the one true nobility'. Satire IX, the sad tale of a discarded male gigolo, looks very much as though it had been rescued from Juvenal's bottom drawer and added as a makeweight (so Highet p. 212: see also below, p. 201, n. 2).

Book IV (Satires X–XII) contains no evidence which would enable us to guess its date of publication with any accuracy. In Satire XII there is a description of the inner harbour basin which Trajan constructed for the port of Ostia (XII 75–81). We know that this basin was built in 104; the knowledge, however, does no more than give us an obvious *terminus post quem* for the date of the satire's composition. But in Satire XI Juvenal speaks of himself as an old man with wrinkled skin – too old, indeed, to stand the noise and dust and heat of the Games – who prefers to sit quietly at home and sun himself. Also, his material circumstances have clearly changed. The nightmare obsession with poverty and degradation that permeates his earlier work has disappeared, and much of his lethal invective with it: now, he reveals, he is the owner of a modest competence – a farm near Tivoli, at least three slaves. It is not much, and he is conscious that snobbish guests might despise his bone-handled cutlery and frugal menu (XI 129 ff., 203 ff.); but he is no longer the snarling, indigent, chip-on-the-shoulder flay-all of the First Book. Indeed, Satire XII, a poem which celebrates the safe return of a friend after near-shipwreck, suggests that he has begun to take on a few of the characteristics he previously despised. When he slips into the grand manner one is no longer always quite sure that he is parodying it; and his periphrastic mythological allusions become less mocking, more turgidly Alexandrian.

With Book V we are on slightly firmer ground. This contains Satires XIII–XVI, and seems to have been the last work Juvenal published. Satire XIII can be dated to A.D. 127 by a reference to the addressee, who is described as sixty years old, and whose birth took place in the consulship of Fonteius Capito, A.D. 67. The events described in Satire XV are dated by Juvenal to the consulship of Aemilius Juncus – that is, to 127; and are described as having taken place 'lately', though the word *nuper* was capable of much stretching. Highet further argues, very ingeniously, that the reference in Satire XIV (96–106) to young Romans becoming Jewish converts and undergoing circumcision provides us with a *terminus ante quem* for Book V's publication. In 131/2, largely as the result of Hadrian banning the practice of circumcision, a violent Jewish rebellion broke out. 'Therefore,' Highet argues, 'Juvenal could not have brought out a book complaining about the custom as being too easy and too common, if it had been made illegal and difficult before the book was published.' There is, then, a fair presumption that Book V appeared between 128 and 130. If this is so, we have a consistent and plausible chronological sequence of publication, as follows: Book I, c. 110–12; Book II, c. 116; Book III, c. 118–20; Book IV, ?c. 123–5; Book V, c. 128–30.

Now this picture assumes an unnaturally short creative span, and thus confirms the late biographical tradition that Juvenal only began his career as a satirist when already middle-aged: he himself, in the programmatic First Satire (25), speaks of his youth as something over and done with. If the birth-date of A.D. 55 represents something fairly near the truth, as I believe it does, then Book I will not have appeared till Juvenal was in his mid-fifties, and Book V when he was well over seventy. If he was still alive after

Hadrian's death, he must have been about eighty-three or eighty-four when Antoninus Pius assumed the purple. Such a life-span fits in very well with his special preoccupations. Born a year after Nero's accession, he would have been an impressionable fourteen during the terrible 'year of the four emperors' (A.D. 69), when, after Nero's assassination in July 68, Galba, Otho and Vitellius were successively toppled and murdered, leaving Vespasian the undisputed occupant of the Imperial throne. Twenty-six at the time of Domitian's accession in 81, he would have just turned forty when a Palace conspiracy finally removed the tyrant in 96. The pattern is not susceptible of complete proof; but it makes consistent sense.

At some time during this period Juvenal made the acquaintance of the epigrammatist Martial, a man some fifteen years older than himself, whose first eleven books of *Epigrams* appeared between A.D. 85/6 and 98, at which point he left Rome for Spain. There is at least a possibility that Juvenal himself was a Spaniard. Sir Ronald Syme has pointed out that there were a large number of Junii in Spain, and that many of them settled – like our Juvenal – at Tivoli; the cognomen 'Iuvenalis' suggests either foreign or lower-class antecedents, and in fact two owners of it were freedmen from towns near Aquinum. (There was also one consul during the period, in A.D. 81, who had this cognomen: I have sometimes wondered whether 'Iulius Iuvenalis' should not in fact be 'Iunius Iuvenalis'.) Martial twice refers to Juvenal in Book VII of his *Epigrams*, published in the autumn of 92; then there is a gap of about ten years, until 101/2, when Martial sends his old friend a rather gloating little sketch of Bilbilis and its rural pleasures (XII 18), prefaced by a contrasting picture of what Juvenal himself may be assumed to be doing: pushing through crowds in the noisy Subura, or trudging uphill, sweating under the folds of a full-dress toga, to kick his heels in the ante-rooms of the great. The earlier poems had described Juvenal as *facundus*, or 'eloquent', a term regularly applied to barristers and speech-makers, and one which confirms the tradition that he practised *declamatio* as a young man. The later epigram, composed during the gestation of Book I of the *Satires*, agrees in detail with the picture Juvenal draws there of the squalid and humiliating life endured by the 'client', or retainer, of some wealthy patron.

Now the passage I have quoted from the Life specifically emphasizes that Juvenal's practice of rhetoric till 'about middle age' was not dictated by the necessity of earning a living; it was an *amusement*, the pastime of a *rentier* living on a gentleman's income. The tone of Martial's two earlier epigrams are quite consistent with such a supposition: Juvenal is a man to whom he sends little presents, whose friendship he is determined not to lose. But the note from Spain contains an unmistakable note of spiteful triumph: one gets the impression that Fortune (Juvenal's favourite bugbear) has reversed their positions.

There is one more piece of evidence, tantalizingly fragmentary, which both confirms the tradition that Juvenal's family came from Aquinum (we have his own word for it, too: see III 318–21), and suggests that the poet, in his youth, may have been relatively well-off. Two inscriptions (recorded in the eighteenth century but now lost) were found near the modern Aquino, both dealing with a certain [Ju]nius Juvenalis. The first commemorated his gift of an altar or shrine to Ceres, the second was a vote of thanks from the citizens of Aquinum to 'their benefactor', and a resolution to set up a tablet and statue of him to put his generosity on record. This Juvenal was a man of parts: commanding officer of a cohort of Dalmatian (Yugoslav) auxiliaries, joint-mayor of Aquinum during the census year (which implied extra responsibilities), and 'Priest of the deified Vespasian'. We cannot be certain – since the stone was broken, as so often with inscriptions, at the crucial point – whether this [Ju]nius Juvenalis was, in fact, the author of the *Satires*; but if he was not, he must have been a close relative, since he came from the poet's home-town, and was similarly associated with the cult of Helvine Ceres. (Ceres, incidentally, as Highet acutely points out, is almost the only Roman deity whom Juvenal consistently treats with anything like respect.)

The auxiliary command recorded here could be held either by a veteran centurion before retirement, or by a young man of the Equestrian Order, as the first step in 'the regular pattern of upper-middle-class service by which a man with some money could, without entering politics, make his way up through army appointments and governorships and administrative jobs until, with luck, he might become one of the most powerful officials in the empire' (Highet p. 34). The plum jobs in this field were the Prefecture of Egypt and the command of the Praetorian Guard, Rome's Household Brigade. If the man who dedicated this offering had been a veteran, he would surely have mentioned the fact; it seems reasonable to assume that he was a young *eques* (and thus of reasonable means) at the outset of his career in the Imperial administration. He was joint-mayor of Aquinum, a person of some standing: the office tended to go to men of about twenty-five, with some commissioned army service behind them. Vespasian died in 79 and was deified in 80 – but his son Titus also died and was similarly deified in 81: it seems a fair assumption that this Juvenal became Priest of the Deified Vespasian in 80, though the dedication itself may have been made later.

There is nothing here that is inconsistent with what we know about Juvenal the satirist, and much that suggests a very close connexion between the poet and the municipal careerist. If [Ju]nius Juvenalis of Aquinum was twenty-five when he was appointed Priest of the Deified Vespasian, he will have been born in A.D. 55, the precise date given in the Life. If he saw active service with his Dalmatian cohort, it was almost certainly during Agricola's campaign in Britain, between 78 and 84. Now one curious fact about the *Satires* is the number of times Juvenal alludes to Britain. Besides such public events as the campaign to capture the Orkneys, or the border warfare against the Brigantes, he brings in various odd incidental details: the short northern nights, the oysters of Richborough, whales off the Atlantic coast, the spread of civilization among the natives (a point also picked up by Tacitus in the *Agricola*), and chariot-fighting techniques.

It is at least a possibility that he saw service in Britain during 78–80, and was appointed to his honorary priesthood on his return, dedicating a shrine to Ceres for having brought him safely through the campaign in which he fought.

There still remains the enigmatic problem of his exile. The ancient commentators, and the Lives which follow them, agree that Juvenal was banished – 'on the pretext of military promotion', one remarks – to a military station in Upper Egypt, either at the Great Oasis or the frontier post of Syene. The reason for his relegation is always the same: three lines which are preserved in Satire VII (90–92):

What nobles cannot bestow, you must truck for to an actor.
Why bother to haunt the spacious ante-rooms
Of the great? Colonels and Governors, the ballet appoints
Every man jack of them.

These lines form the climax, in their present position, to a swinging diatribe against Domitian's favourite, the ballet-dancer and actor Paris, who seems to have had enormous influence in the distribution of honours and appointments. It is generally assumed that what sent Juvenal into exile was his specific reference to Paris: but there are weighty objections to this, the most telling of which is Domitian's pattern of behaviour during the last four or five years of his life. In 83 he had had Paris executed on suspicion of being the Empress's lover (see below, n. 8 to Satire VII, p. 173), and had divorced his wife. Ten years later he was still brooding over the affair. He executed one young aristocrat, Helvidius Priscus, merely for producing a farce in which Paris of Troy deserted the nymph Oenone, and thus obliquely reminding Domitian of the Imperial divorce. He put a young ballet-dancer to death because of a supposed facial resemblance to his former favourite, and even killed those who dropped flowers on the site of Paris's execution. It is inconceivable that Juvenal's gross attack could have been punished with the lesser penalty of exile. As Michael Coffey points out (with a horrific list of examples) 'the pattern of punishment especially in [Domitian's] later years suggests that death not exile was the fate of those who seemed to smirch the imperial dignity.'

But did Juvenal in fact refer to Paris at all? The lines described as having brought about his banishment are general, they name nobody. It is lines 87-9 that would have earned him instant execution, and would surely have been quoted by any scholar trying to manufacture a good case. No commentator mentions them in this context, and there is no proof that they even existed when Juvenal's original lampoon was in circulation. Now since Martial's two flattering epigrams were composed in 91/2, Juvenal's disgrace must have come later: as Highet rightly says, 'Martial was so subservient to Domitian that during the emperor's reign he would never have expressed affection for a condemned man.' If Juvenal was exiled, it will have been during the years of terror between 93 and Domitian's assassination in 96 – a fact which has led some scholars to dismiss the entire story of exile as a late fabrication. But if Juvenal made no specific reference to Paris at all, and was in fact (since Paris had been dead for a decade) merely expressing irritation at some obnoxious jack-in-office of the moment, the story of exile becomes far more plausible. We know from various sources – including Juvenal himself in Satire IV – that Domitian had a peculiarly macabre sense of humour. It would have been very much in character for him to inform this importunate and indiscreet person that he was being transferred to some command in the Oasis as a mark of promotion (see Suetonius, *Domitian* 11, pp. 302-3*; cf. Dio Cassius 67.1-3) – and for Juvenal to discover, the following day, that what this meant was *deportatio*, the harshest form of exile, involving loss of civil rights, confiscation of property, and severe limitation on movement.

If we accept this theory, Juvenal will have been exiled to Upper Egypt in 92/3, and returned to Rome in 96/7, after the accession of Nerva and the recall of the political exiles. We know, on his own

* Page references are to the Penguin Classics translations unless otherwise stated.

testimony, that he had visited Egypt, and loathed the Egyptians, with a xenophobic ferocity that eclipses even his distaste for the Greeks. His knowledge of the country is extensive and peculiar: it includes, again, a collection of vivid details – the negresses of Meroë whose breasts are bigger than their babies, the earthenware skiffs used on the Delta canals, the chap-fallen, wrinkled, elderly female baboon. But even three years of exile here could leave its mark on a man. Gregory Nazianzen saw Hero, the philosopher, when he was released after a four-year sentence in the Oasis, and said that he looked like Lazarus come back from the tomb. And this exile was only the culmination of fifteen nightmare years under Domitian. The psychological effect on such men was brilliantly described at the time by Tacitus, in his *Agricola* (3, pp. 52–3), in terms that recall Dostoyevsky's *House of the Dead*:

Now at long last our spirit revives . . . Public security, ceasing to be merely something hoped and prayed for, is as solid and certain as a prayer fulfilled. Yet our human nature is so weak that the cure lags behind the disease. Our bodies, which grow so slowly, perish in a flash; and so too the mind and its interests can be more easily crushed than brought to life again. Idleness develops a strange fascination of its own, and we end by loving the sloth that at first we loathed. Think of it. Fifteen whole years – no mean fraction of our human life – taken from us. Many have died a natural death, all the most irrepressible have fallen victims to the cruelty of the Emperor. Even we few that survive seem to have outlived, not only our fallen comrades, but our very selves, in those years stolen from our manhood that have brought us from youth to age, from age to the far end of life's journey – and no word said.

Penniless, his position and career smashed, seared by exile and the Terror, Juvenal came back, turned forty, to a Rome of jumped-up guttersnipes and decadent aristocrats: too proud to work, conditioned by his upbringing beyond any hope of adaptation, resigned to the humiliation of a client's life. Who in such circumstances – as he himself asked – could help writing satire? And who could refrain from making the various instruments of his downfall the main targets for his invective?

We can now summarize the main outline of Juvenal's life – always bearing in mind that most of the evidence is circumstantial, and that very little is susceptible of proof.* He was probably born in A.D. 55, the son of a well-to-do Spanish freedman who had settled at Aquinum, and who was determined to see that his son had a successful career in the Imperial civil service (I have often thought that XIV 190 ff. might be an autobiographical reminiscence). Perhaps in 78 he got his foot on the first rung of the ladder by obtaining the command of a cohort of Dalmatian auxiliaries, and serving in Britain under Agricola. In 80 he was welcomed home with honour by his fellow-townsmen, made joint-mayor of Aquinum, and dedicated a shrine to Helvine Ceres in thanksgiving for his safe return. His career was proceeding very much according to plan. He was made an honorary priest of the Deified Vespasian. But in 81 Titus died, and Domitian came to power. For the first two years of his reign preferment lay in the hands of an odious Greek actor, and even after the actor's downfall Juvenal's promotion continued to hang fire. For ten years he divided his time between the capital and his home-town, practising declamation, cultivating influential friends, and – very privately – trying his hand at satirical sketches to relieve his feelings. He made the acquaintance of another literary Spaniard, Martial, and was much influenced by his outlook and subject-matter. If he married, there is no evidence for it. His published work suggests that he was fond of children, but disliked smart society women and coterie homosexuals.

Late in Domitian's reign, probably about 93, a lampoon of his

* With various modifications and additions, the pattern of this reconstruction more or less follows that worked out by Highet in *Juvenal the Satirist*. Much criticism – especially over the matter of Juvenal's exile – has not succeeded in denting its general outlines, or in proposing any more plausible alternative. Even where I differ from Highet's findings, my debt to his research is incalculable, and I am glad to acknowledge it here.

on the sale of commissions became known to the authorities, and he was exiled to the Great Oasis (or Syene) in Upper Egypt, with loss of property and civil rights. Recalled by Nerva after Domitian's assassination, he fell into the squalid and humiliating life of a *déclassé* hanger-on – an existence which supplied incomparable material for the first three books of the *Satires*. Soon after his return, in 98, Martial abandoned the urban rat-race and went back to Spain (borrowing his fare off the Younger Pliny), from where he sent Juvenal a short poetic epistle of the *suave mari magno* variety, contrasting his own rustic relaxation with Juvenal's barren and obsequious daily round. During this period Juvenal was working at, and polishing, what he finally issued (*c.* 110–12) as Book I of the *Satires*. Book II followed about five years later, and Book III shortly after the accession of Hadrian. From now on the tone of Juvenal's work underwent a marked change, and this may well have been due to the improvement in his material circumstances. He seems to have had a small farm at Tivoli, and a house in Rome where he could entertain friends to a modest but pleasant meal. It is very likely that he benefited in some way by Hadrian's patronage of the arts; perhaps the Emperor gave him a pension and a small estate, as Augustus had done for Horace. If so, it is not hard to see why Juvenal thereafter dropped his stringent attacks on bad literature; Hadrian's taste was far from impeccable, and his touchiness over aesthetic matters notorious. Two more books of *Satires* appeared, in 123/5 and 128/30. By now Juvenal was a septuagenarian, who must have recalled, with some irony, his own vivid descriptions of old age in Satire X. He probably survived Hadrian by a year or two, to die, leaving few friends and little reputation, about A.D. 140 – in the middle of what Gibbon described as 'the period in the history of the world during which the condition of the human race was most happy and prosperous'.

*

'On the death of Domitian,' the Younger Pliny wrote, with characteristic candour, 'I reflected that here was a signal and glorious opportunity to punish guilt, to avenge misfortune, and to bring oneself into notice.' The reader of Juvenal's *Satires* cannot help but feel that their author (who may have been on bad terms with Pliny) envisaged an identical programme. Satire I, his manifesto, and probably the latest composition in the First Book, announces *indignatio* as his driving motif, and the world at large as his subject-matter:

> All human endeavours, men's prayers,
> Fears, angers, pleasures, joys and pursuits, these make
> The mixed mash of my verse.

But in fact this programme is never carried out. Juvenal writes from a very limited viewpoint, and the traverse of his attack is correspondingly narrow. Throughout his life, so far as we can tell, he never once questioned the social structure or the moral principles of the regime which had treated him so shabbily. (Any crypto-Republicanism one can detect in his work is no more than a reflection of the fashionable Stoic shibboleths current throughout his lifetime.) All that he asked of the Imperial administration was that its rulers should behave according to the dictates of virtue and morality; as for the upper classes, he seems to have hoped for no more from them than that they should set a good public example and avoid activities liable to tarnish their image with the plebs. His approach to any social problem is, basically, one of static conservatism. He may have thought that the client-patron relationship was fundamentally degrading, but he never envisaged its abolition. He attacked wanton cruelty to slaves, but did not query the concept of slavery itself (another characteristically Stoic attitude). His most violent invective, whether borrowed from the common rhetorical stockpot or the fruit of his own obsessions, is reserved for those who, in one way or another, threaten to disrupt the existing pattern of society, to inject some mobility and dynamism into the class-structure. It follows, *a fortiori*, that he will display especial animus against those who have robbed him, and his kind, of their chance to achieve what they regard as their birthright *within that framework*. This is one of the main keys to an understanding of the *Satires*.

Satire I is rightly regarded as a programme-piece: in it Juvenal deploys most of the main themes to which he afterwards returns – vapid, cliché-ridden literature and rhetoric; various kinds of social and sexual obnoxiousness; above all, the corrupting power of wealth. But the attack is both calculated and highly selective: in each case there is a special, and revealing, motive behind it. Juvenal's main point about mythological platitudes, acute enough in itself, is that they served as a handy refuge for writers anxious to avoid dangerous contemporary issues: that their unreality is due to deliberate escapism. The reader must draw his own conclusions: Juvenal neither attacks the rhetorical system of education *en principe*, nor the civilization which produced it. Instead he works through a cumulative list of significant illustrations. But his main thesis, developed with passionate intensity through the first three books, is (to put it in economic terms) the appalling influence which mobility of income can have on a static class-structure.

The actual figures whom Juvenal presents on the stage, both here and in subsequent satires, fall into three broad stylized categories. First, and most interesting as a pointer to Juvenal's own preoccupations, there is the decadent aristocrat – of either sex – who has in some way or other betrayed the upper-class code, whose conduct fails to reach those well-defined social and moral standards imposed on the governing classes as a complement to their privileges. This scapegoat figure is accused of many things, from extortion to miscegenation, from outrageous homo-sexuality to public appearances in the gladiatorial arena: what is common to each case is the *abrogation of responsible behaviour* which it implies. A governing class that lowers its standards and neglects its traditional duties constitutes a positive danger to the social structure over which it is set. This is what lies behind Juvenal's occasional blurring of social and moral criticism, as when the consul who demeans his office by driving his own gig in public is bracketed with forgers and adulterers, while Nero's crimes rise from mere murder to the climactic horror of his appearances on the stage. The rhetorical anticlimax is a device which Juvenal (like De Quincey in 'On Murder as One of the Fine Arts') employs to some effect: but it is hard not to feel the real and passionate animus behind examples of this sort. Juvenal flays upper-class shortcomings all the harder because he sees his world in peril: his terror of social change made him treat infringements of accepted manners or conventions on a par with gross major crimes. In a sense his instinct was sound. Collapsing social standards are as sure a sign of eventual upheaval as the ominous drying up of springs and wells which heralds a volcanic eruption. In the famous Sixth Satire against women, what Juvenal really objects to is not so much licentiousness *tout court* as the breaching of class and convention. All his examples are chosen from ladies of high society; and what most arouses his wrath against them is that they contract liaisons with *lower-class* persons such as musicians, actors, or gladiators. (One gets the feeling that he would have no particular objection to a little in-group wife-swopping provided it was done discreetly.) These great ladies are several times compared, disadvantageously, to their social inferiors, who bear children instead of having abortions, and would never indulge in such unfeminine pursuits as sword-play or athletics.

Balancing this picture, and in sharply dramatic contrast to it, is that of the wealthy, base-born *parvenu*, a figure whom Juvenal clearly found both sinister and detestable – with good reason, since as a phenomenon he directly threatened Juvenal's own social position, and that of the whole *rentier* class in Rome. The rise of the freedman class forms one of the most significant elements in the history of the early Empire. These coarse, clever, thrusting ex-slaves, most often of foreign extraction, suffered from none of the crippling conventions and moral beliefs that every upper-class Roman inherited as part of his emotional luggage. What enabled them to amass such gigantic fortunes, and to force their way into positions of immense political power, was by no means only

their native ability. They were cashing in on their masters'
ignorance of, and contempt for, a world ruled by commerce and
industry. Since the middle-class Equestrian Order, to which
Juvenal aspired, was mainly a matter of the right property
qualification, freedmen and their descendants began to monopo-
lize all the best posts which it offered. It is no accident that
Juvenal, in Satire I, draws so blistering a portrait of the Com-
mander of the Praetorian Guard and the Prefect of Egypt. These
were the supreme prizes of any Equestrian's career: in Juvenal's
poem they are both held by Egyptians – a jumped-up fish-
hawker called Crispinus, and a Jew, Tiberius Julius Alexander,
whose statue, Juvenal suggests, should be used as a public latrine.
He is always referring, enviously, to the capital sum of 400,000
sesterces which was required for admission to the Order. He and
his shabby-genteel friends are kept out of the seats reserved for
Equestrians while the sons of panders, auctioneers and gladiators
are entitled to them. He attacks those who are irresponsible
enough to fritter away their capital and become *déclassé* – a charge
he also brings against the aristocrats, but for a different reason:
since wealth now is the sole criterion of acceptance and power,
they are imperilling their position of authority by destroying the
de facto foundation on which it rests.

Yet though Juvenal regarded enough capital to qualify for
Equestrian status as the *summum bonum*, he never indicates in any
way that he would consider working to obtain it. He vaguely
hopes for it as a gift from God, or 'some godlike human', which
presumably is a periphrasis for Imperial patronage. Here we hit
on a central and vital factor in his attitude to life. Juvenal was a
bred-in-the-bone *rentier*, with all the characteristics of his class:
contempt for trade, indifference to practical skills, intense political
conservatism, with a corresponding fear of change and revolution;
abysmal ignorance of, and indifference to, the economic realities
governing his existence; a tendency to see all problems, therefore,
in over-simplified moral terms, with the application of right
conduct to existing authority as a kind of panacea for all ills. His

particular dilemma, like that of many another *laudator temporis acti* yearning for some mythical Golden Age, is that he is living by a set of moral and social assumptions that were obsolete before he was born. The only occupations he will recognize are those of the army, the law, and estate-farming. He is as rigidly and imperceptively snobbish about trade as any nineteenth-century rural squire – and with even less justification. As Highet says,

Since his ideal is the farm which supports its owner in modest comfort (or the estates which make a man a knight), he does not realize that Italy now lives by imports. And he will not understand that the Greco-Roman world was built up by the efforts of the shrewd, energetic, competent men who made harbours, highways, aqueducts, drainage-systems, and baths; who cleared the forests and set up the trade-routes; who exchanged the products of the far parts of the globe and ventured on innumerable dangerous voyages.

All he can see in the immense commercial activity of his day is a frantic scrambling after quick profits, stupid luxuries, or wheat to keep the rabble quiet. He is ready to admire Trajan's splendid new harbour at Ostia, but the socially inferior men who built and planned it elicit nothing from him but a quick, dismissive gibe about making money out of privy-contracts – 'These are such men as Fortune, by way of a joke,/ Will sometimes raise from the gutter and make Top People.' His ideal is not so far from that of Naevolus, the ageing homosexual gigolo: a small country home bestowed by some wealthy patron; 'a nice little nest-egg at interest/ In gilt-edged stock'; a life of cultivated idleness, the Victorian 'genteel sufficiency'. 'What can I do in Rome?' cries Juvenal's friend Umbricius, in a famous and much-quoted section of Satire III; and the reader is so carried away by the rhetorical brilliance of the passage that it never occurs to him to answer, briefly: 'A useful job of work.' Nor, indeed, does it occur to Juvenal.

It is sometimes said that Juvenal is a very modern figure, and this is true; but in ways he is far more like a nineteenth-century phenomenon such as Dickens. Indeed, it could be argued, without stretching the paradox too far, that George Orwell's essay on

Dickens is the most illuminating introduction to Juvenal in existence. The social parallels are so numerous and striking that they cannot be ignored. Again and again it might be the Roman poet rather than the English novelist that Orwell is analysing. Juvenal, like Dickens, 'displays no consciousness that the *structure* of society can be changed.' Like Dickens again, he lived in 'a city of consumers, of people who are deeply civilized but not primarily useful.' He too records 'pretentious meals and inconvenient houses, when the slavey drudging fourteen hours a day in the basement kitchen was something too normal to be noticed.' He too 'knows very little about the way things really happen. . . . As soon as he has to deal with trade, finance, industry or politics he takes refuge in vagueness, or satire.' He too sees revolution as a monster, and is acutely aware of the irrational bloodlust and opportunism of the mob, the *turba Remi*. He too has a special compassion for children: like Dickens he attacks bad education without proposing a better alternative. His xenophobia may be closer to Thackeray: but what he shares with Dickens more than any of Dickens' own contemporaries – and for much the same reasons – is that special horror of slums and poverty, that ignorance of, and distaste for, the urban proletariat which stand high among 'the special prejudices of the shabby genteel'. Like Dickens, he frowns – as we have seen – on social miscegenation: he objects to Eppia running off with her ugly gladiator for exactly the same reason that Dickens objects to Uriah Heep's passion for Agnes Wicklow. He too is a caricaturist; and as we know, it is fatal when a caricaturist sees too much. He too (like every urban Roman of his age) was 'out of contact with agriculture and politically impotent'. He too 'only succeeds with [the landowning-military-bureaucratic] class when he depicts them as mental defectives.' He too (and this is both his strength and his weakness as a satirist) in the last resort 'sees the world as a middle-class world, and everything outside these limits is either laughable or slightly wicked.'

The *rentier* and the caricaturist combine to produce a comic yet nightmarish *reductio ad absurdum* of the dole-queue at some great man's house which in fact is the core and centre of Satire I. It is a vivid and brilliant piece of work, memorable – Dickensian echoes again – for its 'turns of phrase and concrete details': wildly exaggerated, yet embodying social truths along with the personal fears and obsessions. The *sportula* ('dole' is an inadequate translation) has degenerated from a friendly *quid pro quo* into an impersonal soup-kitchen hand-out: one of Juvenal's most valid points against excessive money-grubbing is the way it corrupts personal relationships. In this Kafka-like crowd of greedy and obsequious hangers-on, impoverished aristocrats on the way down (including a consul and a praetor) jostle for precedence with a Syrian chain-store magnate on the way up, who remarks, unanswerably from his own point of view: 'What's in a senator's purple stripe, if true-blue nobles/ Are reduced to herding sheep up-country, while *I* have more/ Stashed away in the bank than any Imperial favourite?' Juvenal's comment is one of dejected and cynical resignation. *So let the Tribunes wait, and money reign supreme,* he remarks, adding that though the Romans – who were much addicted to deifying abstractions – had not as yet raised an altar to Cash, *still it is Wealth, not God, that compels our deepest reverence.*

But this, of course, was just as true of Juvenal and his class of cultured *rentiers* as of anyone else: once again he provides us with that nice touch of moral ambiguity which makes him so enjoyable to read. However much he might inveigh against the corrupting influence of money, he would never have admitted for one moment that it could possibly corrupt *him.* He not only yearned with fervent and frustrated longing for the financial portion that would admit him to the company of the elect, but regarded it as his moral prerogative – a not uncommon phenomenon among individuals or groups who lack the ability to obtain what they want by native talent. The idea that financial acumen should dictate the size of one's bank-balance seemed to him not only outrageous but quite irrelevant. He seethed with impotent fury – as did many of his class – to find himself shouldered aside and outsmarted by the kind of shrewd, vulgar millionaire that Petronius depicts so memorably in the *Satyricon*; worse still was the sinister political influence wielded over successive Emperors by Greek freedmen, to whom men of parts were forced to kowtow in the most humiliating manner. His introductory Satire, with its forgers, gigolos, informers and crooked advocates, is a threnody on the theme of collapsing social values, on the impotence of the old middle classes when confronted by a ruthless, unprincipled, and commercially talented opposition.

It is significant that Juvenal's programme-satire hinges round the caricature of a patron–client relationship because, fundamentally, it was the only relationship – certainly the only business relationship – that he was capable of understanding. At one level, the *quid pro quo* concept was built into Roman manners as a basic principle: it permeated the formalized structure of *amicitia* (which means both more and less than the English word 'friendship'), and was extended to men's relationships with the Gods. Here, as so often, Juvenal betrays his inability to see beyond the *status quo*. This was not really his fault, and Orwell, again, makes us see why: '*Given the fact of servitude,*' he remarks, '*the feudal relationship is the only tolerable one.*' If any single statement can illuminate and resolve the whole social content of Juvenal's work, this is it. He saw the feudal relationship everywhere: between master and slave, between patron and client, between the jobber of army commissions and the hopeful military careerist. Roman society formed a vast pyramid, with the Emperor – the most powerful patron of all – at the top, and the rabble roaring for bread and circuses at the bottom; in between came an interlinked series of lesser pyramids, where one man might play both roles, patronizing his inferiors and toadying to those above him. This is one of the points which Juvenal brings out and exaggerates in his caricature, and refers to again later (V 137–8) when describing Trebius's ultimate ambition – 'to be a magnate yourself/ And a patron of magnates.'

It is curious that all Roman writers of this period, Juvenal included, should so despise the *captatores*, the professional legacy-hunters, because, in a sense, legacy-hunting was the only occupation of the leisured classes: sinecure appointments, the *sportula*, a 'modest competence' on retirement – it all came to the same thing in the end. Petronius recognized this: he remarked that in Croton there were only two sorts of people, the rich and their sycophants. Perhaps the *captatores* were despised – in a way like the merchant-freedmen – for being efficient professionals, in whom the cold and obsessional pursuit of wealth had destroyed all human feeling. This is certainly what Juvenal felt.* He believed in the feudal relationship; it was the only one he knew, and he was aware that it had originally expressed, in formal terms perhaps, a personal, human relationship that contained a good deal more than mere reciprocal expressions of obligation. But what he now saw was the systematic reduction of this feudal concept into pure financial huckstering, at all levels, where both parties – without any thought of personal contact, let alone affection – were angling to secure the biggest possible profit. When Juvenal writes, as he so often does, about the corrupting effect of wealth, this notion is never very far from his mind. Money corrodes sexual relationships by encouraging, not only infidelity, but knowing complaisancy in the cuckolded husband; money destroys social stability by turning ex-slaves into titular middle-class gentlemen; money excuses vulgarity, buys favourable discrimination, corrupts true friendship, procures false sycophancy, leads to perjury, murder, fraud; money has become the criterion for winning professional respect; we mourn its loss with more heartfelt tears than we would the death of a friend or a lover.

Once client and patron had a genuine mutual relationship, based on trust, obligation and service: now all we see are 're-tainers whose friendship was bought/ With the meal-ticket

* He regards it as necessary to emphasize, when celebrating the survival of his friend after a storm, that his motives are altruistic – not those of the legacy-hunter (XII 93–130).

stashed in their wallets.' What is more, the whole idea of altruistic obligation is now actively despised, with dire effects on society as a whole:

> When you tell a young man that only fools give presents
> To friends, or relieve the debts of a poverty-stricken relation,
> It simply encourages him to rob and cheat, to descend
> To any criminal act . . .

Juvenal devotes three entire satires to demonstrating the way in which, at various levels, this relationship has become a corrupt parody of its original self. In Satire IV we see it from the apex of the pyramid, where Domitian and his Imperial Privy Council are on show: cold sadist and cowardly sycophants, discussing, not the situation on the frontiers, but what to do with a giant turbot. In Satire V it is the same story, but the props have been changed: the sadist is now a wealthy patron giving a dinner-party for his hangers-on, and deliberately torturing them with the contrast between what he is given and their own insultingly cheap entertainment. In Satire IX the principle is applied to the field of sexual relationships (it is also apparent at intervals during Satire VI) and taken to the ultimate point in human degradation, with a homosexual patron who grudges every penny he pays his gigolo, and puts sex on an exclusively cash basis:

> 'I paid you so much *then*,'
> He says, 'and a bit more later, and more that other time –'
> Working it out by piece-rates.

The homosexual's name is Virro; so is that of the host at the dinner-party. Whether Juvenal was pointing at a real person or not, he clearly intended his readers to link the two characters – and with good reason. But the pessimism goes further, since – as Juvenal so clearly sees – it takes two to make, or corrupt, a relationship; and those grovelling courtiers, those greedy free-loaders, that professional male prostitute, have all encouraged the intolerable situation in which they find themselves by abandoning their self-respect, their basic *humanitas*. Vicious host and decadent parasite, both are equally to blame.

The moral dilemma which Juvenal presents, here and elsewhere, lies at the heart of his position as a satirist, and has a very personal application to his life. Like his friend Umbricius, like all decent, educated *rentiers* of the middle class, who stick by their moral principles and expect certain traditional privileges and monopolies in return, Juvenal finds that the historical process is threatening to sweep him into oblivion. 'There's no room in this city for the decent professions,' Umbricius laments, before retiring to rural Cumae; and a study of Books I–III of the *Satires* shows us exactly why. Lawyers with principles are being ousted by cheap, flashy shysters, as crooked as the clients they defend. Posts in the army or the civil service are handed out by Greek freedmen, and obtained by former Egyptian fishmongers. Writers are at the mercy of ignorant, contemptuous patrons. Teachers are despised, bullied, and paid a miserable pittance. The traditional ruling classes are frittering away their money and their authority, and a new class of greasy and unprincipled upstarts is threatening to replace them. Worst of all, the 'humane professions' have been invaded by a flood of sedulous, slippery, quick-witted Greeks,

> All of them lighting out for the City's classiest districts
> And burrowing into great houses, with a long-term plan
> For taking them over. Quick wit, unlimited nerve, a gift
> Of the gab that outsmarts a professional public speaker –
> These are their characteristics. What do you take
> That fellow's profession to be? He has brought a whole bundle
> Of personalities with him – schoolmaster, rhetorician,
> Surveyor, artist, masseur, diviner, tightrope-walker,
> Magician or quack, your versatile hungry Greekling
> Is all by turns. Tell him to fly – he's airborne. [III 72–8]

Juvenal's xenophobia is not so much of the old-fashioned nationalist variety as that which we find in a trade unionist who sees his job threatened by immigrant labour. In this new urban rat-race he and his kind had either to compromise their principles, and beat the Greeks and freedmen at their own game, or go under. He could no longer rely on the benefits of Imperial preference.

The classic example of survival by compromise is, of course, Juvenal's elder contemporary Martial, the fashionable social pornographer, Rome's equivalent of a scandal-sheet gossip-columnist. His gross adulation of Domitian was only matched by the neat *volte-face* he performed after that Emperor's assassination, when he flattered Nerva, in equally lavish terms, for being above flattery. Juvenal felt unable to take this way out: perhaps, in any case, his specialized talent would have made heavy weather of Martial's feather-light political insincerities. At all events, he preferred to endure the grinding and humiliating indigence of a client's life, attending upon great men, stomaching snubs and insults, in return for a bare subsistence dole and the occasional dinner-invitation. Perhaps, with luck, a patron might sometimes lend him a peeling hall in the outer suburbs for a public recitation of his work-in-progress. The tragedy was that no conceivable alternative existed for him. He knew, all too well, the degradation involved: but a *déclassé* gentleman had to make his choice between subservience and the gutter:

> . . . are there no sidewalks
> Or bridges, no quarter-share in a beggar's mat
> For you to make your pitch from?* Is your hunger quite
> So all-devouring? Is dinner worth every insult
> With which you pay for it? Wouldn't your self-respect
> Be better served if you stuck it out where you are,
> Shivering cold, on a diet of mouldy dog's bread? [V 8–11]

Pity the poor *rentier*: robbed of his perquisites by clever foreigners, despised and humiliated by the upstart *nouveaux-riches* who have

---

* Echoes of Dickens are always cropping up in Juvenal. Just as his attitude to contractors much resembles that of Dickens to the ironmaster in *Bleak House*, or the dust-contractor in *Our Mutual Friend*, so here I am reminded of Scrooge's famous question: 'Are there no prisons? Are there no workhouses?'

replaced his traditional patrons both in the professions and at court, caught between the twin horrors of beggary and moral self-abasement. What we hear from Juvenal, in the earlier satires at least, is the *cri de cœur* of a doomed class. Later, the tone sheds its hysteria and asperity: once Juvenal has achieved the *rentier's* 'modest competence' much of the impulse for his satirical invective fades away. Though this does not make it any the less forceful or valid, his moral indignation had highly personal motives behind it; and these – as is inevitable – both modify and illuminate his moral, religious, and philosophical outlook.

*

Like so many writers who feel that the world they inhabit is out of joint, Juvenal is continually harking back to the distant past: the Golden Age before Saturn's fall, the semi-mythical period that followed Rome's foundation by Romulus, the early Republic of Livy's zealously Imperial propaganda. He never loses an opportunity to contrast the thrift, abstemiousness, simplicity, patriotism and moral rectitude of the good old days with the selfish hedonism and social flux he sees all around him. This well-worn rhetorical device had been done to death by almost every Roman poet since the close of the Republic; but Juvenal's handling of it deserves attention on at least two counts. To begin with, from his point of view there was a great deal of truth in it. The trouble with literary commonplaces, especially when they are sedulously imitated from one generation to the next, is that we tend to write them off as mere stage-properties. But the two or three centuries before Juvenal's lifetime *had* radically transformed Roman civilization and *mores*; a vast and sudden influx of wealth *had* corrupted former standards of behaviour and promoted reckless ambition; the Republic, however venal and inefficient, *had* been replaced by a despotism, however benevolent and enlightened; the average Roman citizen *had* lost effective political power; foreign upstarts *had* obtained a stranglehold on some of the most influential positions in the Empire; such members of the old aristocracy as

had survived the Civil Wars and subsequent Imperial purges
were, very often, taking refuge in hellraking or philosophical
quietism. Juvenal, as they say, had a case.

What he has been most often criticized for is the way he pro-
posed to present it. Towards the close of the first Satire he
remarks that the blunt outspokenness of a satirist such as Lucilius
would be impossible today: put the finger on a successful murderer,
let alone an Imperial favourite, and you are liable to end as a
human torch in the arena. Therefore the oblique approach must
be cultivated:

> It's too late for a soldier
> To change his mind about fighting when he's armed in the
>   battle-line.
> For myself, I shall try my hand on the famous dead, whose
>   ashes
> Rest beside the Latin and the Flaminian Ways.

This disclaimer has produced a whole host of interpretations.
Juvenal is being flippantly evasive, and refusing to commit him-
self; he is covering his line of retreat against possible libel actions,
and in fact has every intention of attacking contemporary figures;
his indignation is the synthetic flourish of the mere rhetorician,
and his disclaimer a clumsy imitation of similar stock apologias by
Horace and Persius. Such historical instances as he presents – and
there are fewer of them than one might suppose – are mostly
taken from the reigns of Claudius, Nero and Domitian. What is
more, his *Satires* were published – whatever the date of their
original composition – under emperors whose humane and
liberal attitude would, surely, have made such elaborate pre-
cautions unnecessary. The arbitrary despotism of the Terror, with
its police spies and informers, had been swept away. Why, we
ask ourselves, does the fellow keep hedging in this pusillanimous
fashion?

The answer seems to be, as Kenney shrewdly pointed out, that
Juvenal does not so much make specific attacks against the dead
(except in Satire IV, which is an isolated, and probably early,

exception) so much as use them as *exempla*, pegs on which to hang a moral generalization. This was a common practice among satirists and rhetoricians, and had the specific authority of Quintilian to back it. But Juvenal's use of it also throws light on his attitude to the Imperial civilization under which he is forced to live. Again, he does not criticize the structure of his society as such; all he sees is a steady decline in moral integrity from the Golden Age to his own day. If his solution – let men pursue virtue and all will be well – seems to us intolerably naïve, at least he saw the crucial flaw at the heart of his society, and expressed it in memorable terms. Highet's summing-up of his position is excellent:

> One evil emperor to him was like another. Every corrupt nobleman resembled his ancestors, having merely grown worse. Over a century earlier, Horace had pointed to this process, and said, in one of the gloomiest of his poems, that the morals of his countrymen were growing worse from father to son, uninterruptedly. Now, looking gloomily back, Juvenal saw the long slope reaching to his feet. He realized (although perhaps his audience did not) that it would be trivial to satirize only the men and women of his own time. They were end-products of a process which began with the lash of Julius Caesar and the wet sword of Augustus, which ran on through the lunatic Caligula, through Nero and the civil wars, to the fiendish emperor of yesterday and perhaps another monster tomorrow. This realization was one of his chief contributions to satire.

It was indeed: despotism has no guarantee of benevolence (though the Stoics tried to make their moral precepts a kind of inoculation against excess) and Juvenal at his gloomiest hardly foresaw some of the Imperial horrors in store for posterity. (It is an ironical gloss on his theory of parental influence that such a philosophical paragon as Marcus Aurelius should have produced, in his elder son and successor Commodus, precisely the kind of brutalized gladiatorial thug whom Juvenal most detested.) But the satirist's pessimism is prescient: he knows, only too well, that one good emperor does not bring the millennium. The central problem remains unchanged, and must be treated *sub specie aeternitatis*. This realization is one of his major claims to be treated as a classic.

It is also very relevant when we examine his attitude to religion, in particular to the concept of Fortune or Destiny. Stoic orthodoxy identified Fortune with God, and Nature, and Reason: this uneasy compromise reflected a prevalent mood of fatalism, which felt that the world must be ruled either by blind and random chance or else by immutable destiny. At the lowest level this trend was exemplified by the common passion for astrology and fortune-telling: for thinking people, especially those living within the shadow of the Imperial throne, it posed some very disturbing questions on the existence of free will. Tacitus felt the dilemma acutely. Is it true, he wonders, that 'the friendships and enmities of rulers depend on destiny and the luck of a man's birth'? May not our personalities play some part in determining our lives? Under Augustus it had been easy enough to believe in a benevolent Destiny directing the affairs of Rome and her citizens; by the time Lucan came to write his *Pharsalia* Fortune looked far less appealing. Juvenal accurately reflects this ambivalent attitude. At times he portrays Destiny as a capricious, immutable deity, playing hopscotch with our careers; but he also, with great emphasis and some shrewdness, declares at the end of Satire X:

> Fortune has no divinity, could we but see it: it's we,
> We ourselves, who make her a goddess, and set her in the heavens.

Ethically, Juvenal feels, as did most Stoics, that man must pursue virtue by his own efforts: though uncommitted to any specific philosophy, he had mopped up, in a piecemeal fashion, most of the most popular intellectual attitudes of the day. These included a briskly flippant cynicism towards the myths and ritual of traditional Roman religion, and a creed of moral self-help which by implication left little scope for divine interference.

What he never seems to have realized is that this detached urban sophistication of his struck at the very roots of the high-minded Republican *pietas* which he professed to find so admirable. Even when lauding his rude forefathers to the skies, he cannot help sneering wittily at their shaggy, acorn-belching primitivism: all his descriptions of the Golden Age have an unmistakable note of civilized latterday mockery running through them. There is, in ·fact, a radical split detectable between Juvenal's moral ideals, and the fashionable intellectual scepticism which he shared with most educated Romans of his day and age. This dichotomy sets up tensions and cross-currents throughout the *Satires*: it is nowhere so obvious as in Juvenal's dealings with Roman deities or mythology. In the old days, he tells us, the numinous power of the gods was nearer to Rome, and no one ever dared to scoff at divine power. It does not seem to occur to him that he never loses an opportunity of scoffing at it himself. He pokes fun at Jupiter's sexual escapades, and Numa's assignation with Egeria: he mocks Mars for being unable to keep robbers out of his own temple, and offers us a hilarious glimpse of life on Olympus before King Saturn 'exchanged his diadem/ For a country sickle, when Juno was still a schoolgirl'; he pooh-poohs anyone who is naïve enough to believe in Hades, and repeatedly debunks traditional mythology, which he sees, in his superior middle-class fashion, as a collection of mildly ridiculous and unedifying *contes drôlatiques*. In short, he falls into an error very common among intellectual moralists, that of proclaiming a social ideal with his rational mind, and then destroying any hope of its fulfilment by the emotional attitudes he brings to it. He, and those like him, who upheld *sapientia* – a word which embodies both the reasoning faculty, formal logic, and moral philosophy – against Fate, superstition, and all the messy irrational magma which bedevils men's minds everywhere, made one cardinal error. They totally ignored the cohesive social binding power of irrational and emotional factors on the human mind; they genuinely believed that men could be made wise and good by taking thought, and needed no other stimulus. There are, in any age, some people of whom this is true: but they always remain a small, if articulate, minority. By mocking religious traditionalism, the Stoics were undermining the very foundations of those antique virtues they sought to promote. Cash may have been a despicable deity; but it was hardly more despicable than the collection of blind, arbitrary, indifferent or bloody-minded figures of fun which Juvenal presents in the *Satires*. Philosophical self-help has always been a dubious substitute for religion; and as a rallying-cry for a national regeneration of morals it is laughable. One suddenly realizes what a tiny proportion of Rome's population Juvenal was addressing, how narrow his terms of reference were.

In this connexion, I think the significance of his penchant for satirical parody has received less attention than it deserves. Juvenal uses this device, not only to point the contrast between heroic past and degenerate present by decking out the latter in borrowed antique plumes, but also as an escape-valve for his own highly ambivalent feelings about the past. The parody kicks both ways. At one point in Satire IX Juvenal makes a male prostitute the recipient of an address which echoes Virgil's exhortation to a similarly orientated, but somewhat more genteel, literary shepherd. 'The unlovely reality of Naevolus,' as Mr Lelièvre demurely remarks, 'placed alongside a romanticized conception of the passion in which he deals, may be felt to represent an astringent comment on the conventions of pastoral poetry.' Perhaps it is even more than that. Juvenal parodies a number of authors – Horace, Ovid, Statius, Homer and Lucretius among them – but I do not think it accidental that his favourite target is grandiloquent epic, nor that the author he makes more fun of than all the rest put together is Virgil, the mouthpiece of Augustus, the singer of Rome's imperial destiny. Virgil announced, in the *Georgics*, that mythological themes were obsolete, and that 'Caesar' (i.e. Augustus) would be his theme; Juvenal makes a similar declaration, but – significantly – chooses vice and crime as his alternative topic. Where Virgil glorifies, Juvenal belittles: with symbolic appropriateness, he uses more diminutives than almost any other

Roman poet. He delights in transferring a heroic phrase to a mundane context. The cannibalistic Egyptian riot of Satire XV is a kind of anti-epic battle, and I have often wondered whether the spear-flinging ape on goatback at the end of Satire V was not meant to recall the equestrian manoeuvres of the *lusus Troiae* in Book V of the *Aeneid*. Juvenal may think that Rome has been rotted by long peace, but the glories of battle and conquest held singularly little appeal for him either.

I have said that he had no concept of altering the structure of his society, and this is true: on the other hand he was very prone to indulge in the backward-looking wish-fulfilment dream – something very different. *If only* is the keynote of his fantasy: *if only* Rome had never acquired an empire, *if only* we were still the small, simple, agricultural community that we were in the days of the Kings, *if only* there had not been that dreadful influx of wealth and clever foreigners to corrupt our morals, tempt us with luxury, give us the appetite for power! When Juvenal looks back to the Golden Age, he is lamenting the loss of innocence. His real hero is not so much Cicero – though the career of that provincial-made-good must have whetted his own ambitions in more ways than one – as Cato the Censor. Cato was a walking embodiment of the old semi-mythical virtues: husbandry, piety, service to the State. His xenophobia was at least as marked as Juvenal's, and as a moral Jeremiah he left the satirist standing. He even, more appropriately than perhaps he knew, went to the length of giving the Roman sewerage system a radical overhaul. (So, in a sense, did Juvenal.) His official post as Censor was one to which every satirist unofficially aspired.

But what made Cato particularly interesting to the intellectuals of a politically impotent age was the fact that he offered an almost unique example of morality, without any strings attached, actually controlling and changing the course of political events. Seneca had argued that only differences of character and behaviour distinguished the king from the tyrant: it followed as a necessary corollary that the one safeguard against despotism was the inculcation of moral virtue in the ruler. Under the early Emperors there was an obvious political explanation for this alarmingly *simpliste* attitude. What one cannot abolish, one must take steps to improve. Besides, no one had forgotten the bloody chaos and anarchy that had accompanied the death-throes of the Republic. The Romans might have sacrificed their freedom, but they had won peace, prosperity, and stable government in exchange. It was not difficult for the Emperor's supporters to argue that any show of independence, any talk of 'liberty', directly threatened the *pax Romana*. We have seen such arguments in our own day. The only alternative was the complete political quietism of thinkers such as the ex-slave Epictetus, who openly stated that Caesar could be left to guarantee men's social security, but that personal problems and emotions were the domain of philosophy. (This did not stop Domitian banishing him in 89: there were three purges of 'philosophers' at this period, by Vespasian in 71, and by Domitian in 89 and 93.) This was the intellectual legacy which Juvenal inherited. It would, I think, be true to say of him, as Professor Clarke says of Tacitus, that 'his heart was on the side of the republican past, his head on the side of the imperial present.'

If we try to pin down any coherent philosophy in Juvenal's work, we soon find ourselves forced to admit defeat. Juvenal himself (XIII 120–24) expressly denies allegiance to any of the three major groups of his day, the Stoics, Epicureans and Cynics – which does not mean that he refrained from raiding their commonplaces, in an eclectic fashion, whenever it happened to suit his book. His attitude to marriage resembles that of the Cynic, his cultivation of friendship has an Epicurean flavour, his aphorisms on such topics as virtue and fortitude and destiny are forceful expressions of Stoic doctrine, often more striking than anything composed by more professional thinkers. But he had little formal knowledge of philosophy as such, and scant aptitude for sustained rational argument: like A. E. Housman, one surmises, he found abstract thought irksome. His attitude to the whole business,

fundamentally, was that of the caricaturist who formed so large
an element in his creative personality: he saw life as a series of
vivid, static, distorted snapshots.* The 'intellectual image', as Mr
W. S. Anderson rightly reminds us, does not exist in Juvenal:
it would be very strange if it did, since the cast of mind which it
implies is wholly alien to Juvenal's method of exposition. Philoso-
phers, for Juvenal, were primarily eccentric individuals, who spent
their time laughing, weeping, living in tubs, or avoiding beans.
When he came to deal with contemporary upper-class Stoics, it
was in the same personal terms. He shows us a group of hypo-
critical crypto-homosexuals with crew-cuts, aping Cato's stern-
ness and shagginess, but in fact corrupt shams, whose knowledge
of the philosophers is limited to the plaster busts they have on
display in their houses. Juvenal does not work out a coherent
ethical critique of institutions or individuals: he simply hangs a
series of moral portraits on the wall and forces us to look at them.

*

Le style, as Buffon said, *c'est l'homme même*; and when we examine
the style, imagery, and structure of Juvenal's *Satires*, we find an
almost uncanny congruence between the author's personality and
the form of self-expression he chose. Satire had, originally, been a
literary medley, a loose sequence of isolated scenes. Intellectual
exponents of the art such as Horace and Persius had tightened
up its structure a good deal: but for a writer of Juvenal's tempera-
ment, who worked through images rather than by logic, the old
form was far more congenial. He picked a theme, and then

* This has caused much argument as to whether his general picture of
Rome under the Flavians is truth or rhetorical fiction. My own feeling is
that it is limited, selective, and often prejudiced; that it leaves out a great
deal – the happy, virtuous, hard-working majority are not alas, the stuff
which inspires great satire – and exaggerates much of what it includes;
but that ultimately it is based on fact, and presents a truly observed if highly
partial portrait both of Rome itself and of aberrant upper-class *mores*
during Juvenal's lifetime. A satirist may resort to caricature; but he seldom
tilts at exclusively paper windmills.

proceeded to drive it home into his reader's mind by a vivid and often haphazard accumulation of examples. Juvenal's sense of overall structure – as so often with an artist who dislikes abstract concepts – is sketchy, to say the least of it. Very often his work reads like a series of paragraphs that bear only a token relationship to each other, written at different times and stitched together without much concern for tidiness or coherence. If Juvenal ever read Quintilian's remarks about the need for economy and order in one's presentation of a subject, they cannot have made much impression on him. He announces a topic for later treatment, and then forgets all about it. He is full of abrupt jumps (some of them probably due to *lacunae* in our text) and splendidly irrelevant digressions. He prowls all round his subject, with the purposeful and disjunctive illogicality of a monkey exploring its cage. The cumulative effect is impressive: at times Juvenal seems to forestall the techniques of cinematic montage, and if he had been alive today it is a fair bet he would be making his living as a script-writer at Cinecittà. This is especially apparent in Satire III, with its fast-moving, well-edited shots – arranged, we may note, in chronological sequence – of street-scenes in the City. We can almost hear the cutting-room shears at work as we move from the fatal accident (pedestrian crushed under waggonload of marble) to the victim's home, and from there to Hades' bank, for a glimpse of the brand-new ghost awaiting Charon the ferryman; or from the bedroom of an insomniac bully to the dark street where he picks his quarrel with an innocent passer-by.

But since Juvenal was well acquainted with the rules of rhetoric – and since (perhaps more important) classical scholars are themselves tidy-minded intellectuals with a great gift for logical analysis – it has too often been assumed that the *Satires* must follow a *rational* structure and pattern if only we had the wit to see it. 'An abrogation of form,' says Mr W. C. Helmbold, 'is unthinkable for a professional writer of Juvenal's attainment.' This seems a very dubious assertion, besides begging the question of what can be defined as 'form'. Behind it one glimpses that old ghost which still haunts classical studies, however often right-minded scholars may exorcise it: the feeling that ancient authors achieved a perfection which somehow places them above common literary error, that they cannot be criticized, only explained and justified. *Tu nihil in magno doctus reprehendis Homero?* Horace asked – 'Tell me, do you, a scholar, find nothing to cavil at in mighty Homer?' Such an attitude, besides betraying a fundamental misconception of the way Juvenal worked, has had unhappy consequences for his text. When the German scholar Ribbeck argued that the second half of the *Satires* was so different in tone from the first that it must be the work of a late forger, he was only half in jest. Any passage which fails to measure up to an editor's preconceived standards of Juvenalian perfection, from the standpoint of aesthetics, rhetoric, structure, content, or even – on occasion – of decency, is liable to be excised from the canon as an interpolation, on the grounds that 'Juvenal could not possibly have written it.' So of recent years the *Satires* have been laid on a Procrustean bed of structural analysis: this has produced some useful insights, and a great deal of disagreement.

In Satire II, for instance, Juvenal has two loosely related themes, homosexuality and hypocrisy, which he develops by something not very short of random association. Our philosophers are hypocrites because they mask their homosexuality behind a pretence of virtue. They are aristocrats, and therefore doubly reprehensible. Domitian is the arch-hypocrite: despite his, and his relatives', sexual excesses he assumes the role of Censor. In any case, homosexuality is progressive and contagious, a symptom of our corruption: if a man joins the philosophical coterie he will end up at drag-parties and homosexual 'marriages'. Our conquests abroad contrast shamefully with the canker at the core: Rome corrupts all who live there. Now there is no overall logical pattern about this development, but it remains remarkably effective nevertheless: the apparent inconsistencies which some writers have found (e.g. between the supposedly unrelated topics of hypocrisy and perversion) melt away on inspection. Satire III is so splendidly orchestrated that the lack of logical sequence seems not to have bothered critics as much as one might expect. It falls loosely into two halves, on the vicissitudes of a poor but honest *rentier* and the discomforts and actual dangers of city life; but even so, Juvenal moves from one train of thought to another exactly as the fancy pleases him. As always, he obtains his effects by the piling up of visual effects, paradoxical juxtaposition rather than step-by-step development, a series of striking contrasts between the decent, innocent Roman (a kind of Candide-like observer) and the crooks, Greeks, draymen or other *canaille* who push ahead of him, bang him in the ribs, splash him with mud, beat him up at night, steal his job, drop slops on his head, and leave him to beg in the gutter when his apartment burns out.

If Juvenal can confine himself to a single theme, and then expand it by means of one extended dramatic illustration, his form is neat and logical enough: what Mr Anderson calls a 'frame' presentation, with the *exemplum* topped and tailed by introduction and coda. Two good instances of this are Satires V and XV, where in each case the dramatic illustration – a clients' dinner-party, a grisly fight in the desert – forms a simple core or *maquette* round which the entire poem is articulated. It is no coincidence that the most satisfying satires, structurally speaking, tend to be the shortest. Juvenal's only idea of structural enlargement is repetition, adding one 'frame' to another until he runs out of material. His dilemma bears some resemblance to that of Russian composers when endeavouring to make use of traditional themes: as Constant Lambert said, 'the whole trouble with a folk song is that once you have played it through there is nothing much you can do except play it over again and play it rather louder.' (Anyone who doubts this should look at Tchaikovsky's Fourth Symphony and see what he does with the Little Fir Tree motif.) But – and this is equally significant – there is no correlation between regularity of form and literary excellence in the *Satires*. The most dramatically vivid of them, that little *tour de force* Satire IV, is a broken-backed affair which has defied even the most ingenious attempts to unify its parts. Once again we see the principle of random selection at work, a train of thought which proceeds from one enticing image to another like a man leaping from tussock to tussock across a bog. Juvenal begins with an anecdote about his favourite *bête noire* Crispinus, the commander of the Praetorian Guard. Crispinus has bought a giant mullet for 6,000 sesterces – about £120. But the mention of one giant fish reminds Juvenal of another; he drops Crispinus and sails into a spoof-epic sketch of Domitian and his Cabinet solemnly debating what should be done with a giant turbot presented to the Emperor by an Ancona fisherman. Some scholars have found 'connecting ideas between the two parts in the ways in which Crispinus and Domitian use their big fishes and in the similarities of the two men's characters', which is little more than a ratification of the free-association principle. Juvenal, I cannot help feeling, would have been the ideal candidate for a Rorschach test.

This is nowhere more apparent than in what is arguably Juvenal's greatest, as well as his longest, achievement: the enormous diatribe against women and marriage which forms Satire VI, and was published by itself as Book II of his complete works. There have been innumerable attempts to extract a coherent pattern from this unwieldy monster, but all have broken down on points of detail. Highet describes the overall theme as the futility of marriage, and claims that the poem has a 'good bold simple structure, ending in a powerful climax'. But even he admits that 'the chief difficulty in it is to find some reason for the arrangement of the various types of married women's folly, in 352–591, and here the manuscripts appear to have been badly disturbed.' (When in doubt, blame the text.) Anderson, on the other hand, declares that 'the structure of Satire 6 is conclusively against an interpretation of the central theme as that of marriage. The subject of the satire is Woman, Roman Woman, and her tragedy. She has lost her womanhood . . .; in its place she had adopted viciousness.' Both are right, both wrong: the two themes co-exist in the satire, and Juvenal moves between them as the fancy takes him. He opens with a semi-ironic portrait of the Golden Age, when Chastity had not yet retired from earth: adultery, he reflects, is man's longest-established vice. Why marry, he asks, when so many handier forms of suicide are available? You'll be lucky to find a virgin, and even a virgin will soon change her ways when she starts moving in the society of young upper-class Roman matrons. From voyeuristic orgasms at the theatre she'll soon graduate to liaisons with actors, musicians or gladiators. Two cautionary illustrations follow: the senator's wife who ran off with a swordsman, Messalina's activities in the brothel.

So far the sequence has been orderly enough. But Juvenal's powers of concentration never seem to extend much beyond a hundred lines, and here, as usual, free association begins to creep in. After a couplet on sex crimes so irrelevant that some critics think they should be transferred to the end of the poem, Juvenal observes that the peccadilloes of rich wives are condoned because of the dowry they bring: the cash-motif has appeared again. There follows a cutting little sketch which illustrates Juvenal's favourite theme, the corruption of personal relationships, and – as in Satires IV, V, and IX – attacks both parties with equal vigour. This episode has never, I think, had quite the attention it deserves. Sertorius and Bibula are a cynical *reductio ad absurdum* of the marriage of pure self-interest. Bibula may be a mercenary gold-digger who takes Sertorius for all he's got; but Sertorius, equally, is a cold sensuous hedonist whose only interest in Bibula is a physical one, and who dumps her, ruthlessly, the moment her charms begin to fade. The marital relationship has been pared down to pure calculating self-interest: no human emotion remains in it. Here we have the same psychological theme that reappears in the commination on legacy-hunters at the end of Satire XII:

So long live legacy-hunters, as long as Nestor himself!
May their possessions rival all Nero's loot, may they pile up

Gold mountain-high, may they love no man, and be loved by
none.

Selfish greed, selfish indulgence are, between them, destroying all
human intercourse and affection. The individual now stalks
through life as though it were some sort of no-man's-land, in
armoured isolation, out solely for what he can get, giving no
quarter and expecting none. Even marriage has become the same
battleground in miniature. Hell, as Sartre said, is other people; but
it is also oneself.

Nevertheless, Juvenal goes on, there is no way out for a prospec-
tive husband: if the corrupt woman is a bitch, the virtuous woman
is a bore. Who would want to marry such a highminded noble
prig as Cornelia, 'Mother of the Gracchi', and burden himself with
that insupportable legacy of noble rectitude? (Here, for once, the
urban sophisticate shows through the moralist's mask: I suspect
that this represented Juvenal's basic attitude to the whole Re-
publican myth.) Virtuous pride is far from easy to live with, and
brings its own retribution – look what happened to that sow-like
breeder Niobe. With which reflection, Juvenal suddenly switches
to an attack on Greek fashions. From this point the *montage*
technique comes increasingly into play, and the pace quickens
with a kind of hysterical frenzy. Women torment you and run
your life, forcing you to discard old friends and make bequests to
your wife's lovers. There are quick shots of a wife bullying her
liberal husband into torturing a slave, a mother-in-law pandering
to her daughter's adultery. A preamble on female litigiousness
and quarrelsomeness leads into some vivid glimpses of upper-
class ladies practising swordplay. Women nag in bed, we are told,
and talk their way out of anything. At this juncture Juvenal stops
and asks what produced the decline in morals: wealth, he con-
cludes, and too many years of peace (this is rather like the pre-
1914 journalism of Belloc and Chesterton and W. E. Henley).
Then he is off again on alcoholism, orgies, and queer go-betweens
who turn out to be strongly heterosexual in bed. The final
sections of the poem present a series of stylized portrait-sketches:

the woman who is mad on the Games, the well-informed busy-body who talks back to generals, the hearty drinker with her dog-whip and her obliging masseur, the tyrant in the boudoir, beating the slave-girl who dresses her hair, the astrology-fans and devotees of exotic cults. With some final sulphurous remarks about abortions, aphrodisiacs, and parricide for profit, the satire grinds to a snarling but essentially unresolved halt. The reader has been not so much reasoned into agreement as battered into submission.

This technique may indicate a defect in Juvenal's constructive powers: but it seems to me a fundamental part of his satirical equipment. If it is a weakness, the weakness has been turned to the best advantage, and with considerable ingenuity. Here Juvenal stands poles apart from a naturally architectonic poet such as Virgil or Horace. The writer he far more resembles, not only in his pessimism and sense of moral purpose, but also in style and technique, is Lucretius. Both have the same urgent, nagging, neurotic method of exposition; both use the hexameter as a weapon to bludgeon their audience. Both, we may note, share that odd preoccupation with the Golden Age of rural primitivism from which they themselves, by temperament and habitat, were so far removed. Source-hunting in literature is, on the whole, an unprofitable game: but Juvenal *was* a noticeably bookish writer, and his debts were more interesting than most, since he turned them to such good use. He must have known Martial's *Epigrams*, for instance, almost by heart, since there is scarcely one of the earlier satires but contains some echo of them; yet Juvenal's borrowings are far from indiscriminate, and reveal a keen sense of judgement. He saw, clearly, that Martial's supreme quality was his gift for direct observation, his *pointilliste* use of the occasional piece to build up a composite, Mayhew-like portrait of Roman life and manners. Juvenal took the technique (and some of the descriptions) but adapted it to his own purposes, changing not only the context but also the phraseology. Furthermore, as Mr Lelièvre has pointed out with some acuteness, Juvenal's deliberate echoes of earlier writers very often serve the same purpose as do

those employed by T. S. Eliot in *The Waste Land*: they are touch-
stones to intensify the sense of moral decadence.

Orwell, in the essay I mentioned earlier, remarked that Dickens'
genius emerged most clearly from 'turns of phrase and concrete
details'. Broadly speaking, the same is true of Juvenal, though
temperamentally he was far removed from Dickens, and alto-
gether lacked the novelist's generous scope and warmth. Juvenal
is, *au fond*, a miniaturist, and his greatest gift – whether in a
dramatized scene, a piece of invective, or a moral statement – is for
vivid and memorable concision. His language, however casual
and demotic it may appear, has been distilled, refined, crystallized.
Dubrocard (see Additional Bibliography) points out that, of the
4790 words in the *Satires*, no less than 2130 are *hapax legomena*,
i.e. occur here once only, and nowhere else. It is not surprising
that his whole lifetime's output barely exceeded 4,000 lines of
verse. Seldom can one man's body of work have had less spare
fat on it. We see this most clearly and obviously in the famous
aphorisms which, even in Latin, have become part and parcel of
the Western European inheritance: *panem et circenses, quis custodiet
ipsos custodes?*, *rara avis*, *mens sana in corpore sano*, and many others,
such as *maxima debetur puero reverentia*, which are less well known
since the decline of Latin as a pillar of secondary education. This
gift of Juvenal's extends to his invective, in particular to his cold,
quasi-clinical handling of sexual misdemeanours. He never once
uses the Latin equivalent of a four-letter word (in which he pro-
vides a striking contrast to Martial); but as Highet says, when it
comes to turning your stomach with a couple of well-chosen
phrases, there is almost no one to touch him. While lambasting
Domitian in Satire II he throws off the following couplet:

> ... *cum tot abortivis fecundam Iulia vulvam*
> *solveret et patruo similes effunderet offas.*
> (His niece, a fertile creature, had her row of abortions,
> And every embryo lump was the living spit of Uncle.)

I have printed the Latin here because no translation on earth could
do full justice to Juvenal's revoltingly skilful use of language and

rhythm. The first hexameter, with its predominantly spondaic feet, its repeated *v*'s, *o*'s and *u*'s, moves forward in a series of slow, sluggish heaves that irresistibly suggest uterine contraction; the second begins and ends with an explosive burst (*solveret, offas*) which represents the actual expulsion of the embryo. Finally, there is the vulgar term *offa*, which not only *sounds* disgusting, but carries unpleasant associations, since it is most commonly used in connexion with pigs or sows.

This is no isolated instance. Perhaps Juvenal's greatest poetical achievement is his ability to marry sound, sense and rhythm into one organic whole. His ear for the nuances of vowel-sounds and consonantal patterns is acute, and few Roman poets can equal his absolute control over the pace, tone, and texture of a hexameter. The garrulous bluestocking in Satire VI (434 ff.) elicits the comment: 'Such a rattle of talk,/ You'd think all the pots and bells were being clashed together.' In the Latin you can actually *hear* them: *verborum tanta cadit vis,/ tot pariter pelves ac tintinnabula dicas/ pulsari.* With apparently careless ease he catches the crackle of a fire, the cooing of doves on the roof-tiles, an old man greedily gulping his food, the belch and eructation of a gluttonous Palace trimmer, the drunken dancing of Egyptian villagers, a tittering Greek, the heave and lurch of seasickness, the harsh, abrupt, staccato rattle of a bully's questions suddenly fired at his victim, the scrannel, hen-like piping of a counter-tenor. Examples could be adduced from every satire. Verbal dexterity is reinforced by a sparing, but dramatic, use of simile and metaphor: the informer who could slit men's throats with a soft whisper; the lofty but gimcrack tower reared by ambition; the father who is destroyed by the son he has himself trained in vice, like a lion-tamer who vanishes into the maw of his own lion; the senator's wife who drinks and vomits like a big snake that has tumbled into a vat. Sometimes the implications are very subtle. It took Mr Anderson to make us see that 'the metaphors in VII 82 ff. transform the inanimate epic of Statius into a very attractive female, whose allure resides entirely in her sex' – the point being, of course, that

INTRODUCTION

Statius is prostituting his art by pandering to popular taste (and, we might add, compromising his integrity by selling ballet-scenarios to Paris in order to make a living). We have already seen something of Juvenal's penchant for the diminutive and the anticlimax as devices for satirizing contemporary littleness: here, too, the effect is prepared for with great verbal skill, so that the deflationary punch-line, or even word, catches a reader with his defences down and forces him to *think*:

> Squalor and isolation are minor evils compared
> To this endless nightmare of fires and collapsing houses,
> The cruel city's myriad perils – and poets reciting
> Their work in *August*!

A few shocks of this sort, and we begin to ask ourselves whether, socially speaking, the amateur gladiator of distinguished family, the muleteer-Consul, or the stage-struck Emperor are not symptoms of more deep-seated flaws in the body politic than might at first be supposed.

But for the modern reader, whose interest in Juvenal is to a very large extent antiquarian rather than moralistic, the prime quality of the *Satires* is their ability to project the splendour, squalor, and complexity of the Roman scene more vividly than the work of any other author, Horace and Cicero included. This, of course, is particularly true of Satire III, on which J. W. Mackail wrote a paragraph in his *Latin Literature* which I can no more resist quoting than could Duff:

The drip of the water from the aqueduct that passed over the gate from which the dusty, squalid Appian Way stretched through its long suburb; the garret under the tiles, where, just as now, the pigeons sleeked themselves in the sun and the rain drummed on the roof; the narrow, crowded streets, half choked with the builders' carts, ankle-deep in mud, and the pavement ringing under the heavy military boots of guardsmen; the tavern waiters trotting along with a pyramid of hot dishes on their heads; the flower-pots falling from high window-ledges; night, with the shuttered shops, the silence broken by some sudden street brawl, the darkness shaken by a flare

53

of torches as some great man, wrapped in his scarlet cloak, passes along from a dinner-party with his long train of clients and slaves: these scenes live for us in Juvenal, and are perhaps the picture of ancient Rome that is most abidingly impressed on our memory.

Yet this is only a fraction of the motley scene which Juvenal paints, with quick, bold, economic strokes: the 'smoke and wealth and clamour' of Rome which Horace described are here, and its smells too, and above all its colourful, polyglot inhabitants, caught in one vivid phrase after another, glimpsed for a moment and then gone – the African poling his felucca up the Tiber, with a cargo of cheap rancid oil; the plump smooth successful lawyer riding above the heads of the crowd in his litter; the homosexual fluttering his eyelids as he applies his make-up, or wearing a chiffon gown, near-transparent, to plead a case in court; the ageing gladiator, straight out of Hogarth or Rowlandson, 'helmet-scarred, a great wen on his nose, an unpleasant/ Discharge from one constantly weeping eye'; a lady of quality, her large thighs wrapped in coarse puttees, panting and blowing at sword-drill; the downtrodden teacher and his resentful pupils, conning lamp-blackened texts of Virgil before daybreak; the sadistic mistress who sits reading the daily gazette or examining dress-material while one of her slaves is being flogged in the same room; the would-be poet giving a recital in a cheap, peeling hired hall, with his claque of freedmen distributed at strategic points through the audience (only Juvenal would have added the realistic touch of placing them *at the ends of the rows*); the fat, horsy consul Lateranus, swearing stable oaths, untrussing his own hay, or boozing with matelots and escaped convicts in some dockside tavern; the contemptible trimmers hurrying down to boot Sejanus's corpse in the ribs ('and make sure our slaves watch us') while sneering at the rabble for its opportunism; the miser hoarding fish-scraps in September; the squad of slaves with fire-buckets guarding a millionaire's *objets d'art*; the court-martial presided over by a group of hobnailed old colour-sergeants; the temple-robber

scraping gold leaf from the statues of unprotesting deities; the
sizzle of sacrificial offerings, the roar of the crowd at the races,
beggars blowing kisses, the carver flourishing his knives, fortune-
tellers, whores, confidence-men, politicians – it is an endless and
kaleidoscopic panorama. But it was not so much human en-
deavours that obsessed him – he had always been rather hazy
about what people actually *did* – so much as humanity itself, that
marvellous ant-hill which he hated and loved with equal fervour,
and from which he never succeeded in tearing himself away.

*

It is a curious and infuriating paradox that we possess, probably,
more manuscripts of Juvenal than of any other classical author,
including Homer, but that only one of these – P, the Codex
Pithoeanus-Montepessulanus, preserved in the Medical School of
Montpellier – derives from a relatively sound and intelligent
tradition. We know that an edition was prepared between 350
and 400 by a pupil of the great grammarian Servius: it is on this
that P (itself of the ninth century A.D.) depends, and the worst
omissions and corruptions which P repeats are likely to have been
already embodied in the text on which that editor worked. But
at about the same time as Servius's pupil was preparing his edition,
another and far less intelligent scholar also set about the text of
Juvenal. Repeatedly he 'introduced changes which he thought
would make Juvenal more intelligible and orderly, and usually
made him much stupider. It is a common fault of strong-willed
editors to assume that their author had no more imagination and
less sense of style than they themselves' (Highet p. 187). As one
of C. P. Snow's characters has reminded us, in the world of
scholarship we needs must choose the dullest when we see it; and
with an infallible instinct posterity pounced on the inferior
edition, which was disseminated in something like 500 manu-
scripts. Only P (apart from some anthology snippets preserved
at St Gall) represents the relatively uncontaminated 'Servian' text;
and P mysteriously vanished for several centuries after the

Renaissance, only reappearing about 1840, when it served as the foundation for Otto Jahn's edition of 1851.

But P (as Housman pointed out, with acid wit, in the preface to his own edition) though the best manuscript is by no means free from corruption, and in many places inferior manuscripts supply a correct reading where P does not. Since then the German scholar Ulrich Knoche has produced a text based on the widest collation of manuscripts yet undertaken, and his *apparatus criticus* is an essential tool for any future student of Juvenal. It was largely utilized by W. V. Clausen in his Oxford Classical Text edition of 1959; Clausen had the further advantage of personally collating P, which Knoche did not do, and as a result was able to correct a number of traditional mis-statements about its readings. My version of Juvenal is based, broadly speaking, on Clausen's text, though I have diverged from it on a number of occasions. Wherever I have done so the fact is attested in a footnote. The most important passages, for those who wish to consult them, are the following: I 85–6, 131–2, 156–7; II 46, 81; III 109, 112–13, 187, 217–18; IV 4–5, 79, 121; VI 12, 107, 114–24, 135, 365–6 [O passage], 415, 454–5; VIII 7, 111–12, 124, 159–62, 241; IX 40–53, 76, 119–23; X 54–5, 196–7, 295, 312–13, 326–7; XI 18, 112, 156; XII 3–4; XIII 153; XIV 229, 269; XVI 18. I have also differed from Clausen on a number of occasions about what should be secluded in square brackets [ ] as spurious or interpolated matter; but since such differences do not affect the actual *content* of the text, I have not listed them here. The 'interpolation theory', as a convenient panacea for explaining textual difficulties, has been coming back into fashion again lately; Knoche expunged over a hundred lines from the text, and Clausen, with more caution, about forty. Here – as should be apparent from my notes – I stand more with Vahlen, Housman, Duff, Griffith and Highet. Though interpolations do exist in Juvenal, they are far fewer than critics such as Jachmann would have us believe; and all attempts to prove an interpolation on purely aesthetic or even logical grounds must be regarded with deep suspicion. It is no argument to say that because a line is weak, otiose, or inappropriate, *therefore* Juvenal could not have written it: the ghost of classical perfectionism walks in odd places. 'Moralists,' as Housman observed, 'are often flat, and poets of the silver age redundant; and although for Juvenal's sake we may hope that these lines are spurious, we are not entitled to believe them so.'

Normally, in the Penguin Classics, it is not necessary to go into textual matters at such length. But Juvenal is something of a special case when it comes to translation. To begin with, his text, even after the labours of many editors, still contains many dubious or unresolved readings. Now in the nineteenth century it was the fashion to emend a corrupt passage by hook or by crook; but today scholarly caution is the watchword. Editors may be ready to throw out passages as spurious on what seem fairly flimsy grounds; but if they are confronted by a textual crux which, for one reason or another, cannot be submitted to this treatment, they are prone to advertise their critical restraint by obelizing the passage – that is, by isolating it within daggers († †) like some infectious case of illness, and leaving it as it stands. Whatever one's feelings about this editorial practice in principle, one can scarcely regard it as a help to the translator. The one thing no one can do with an obelized passage, almost by definition, is to translate it. Unlike a cautious editor, the translator is bound to produce some sort of coherent sense: he is not allowed to hedge his bets. This awkward fact must serve as a partial excuse for the number of occasions on which I have either accepted emendations proposed by others, or – when all other recourses failed – have tentatively supplied my own.

Another awkward textual hurdle for any translator is the problem of lacunae. If critics have been overwilling to find interpolated matter in Juvenal, they have also tended to underestimate the number of occasions on which passages from the interior of the *Satires* may have been lost in transmission, or deliberately excised, at a very early period. Here we must move with caution, since disjointed abruptness or illogical switches of topic in a poet with Juvenal's temperament may be evidence of creative idiosyncrasy rather than a defective text. But there are many passages where it is reasonable to assume a lacuna of one or more lines: for examples see Satires I 131–2, 156–7, III 112–13, IV 4–5, VI 118–19, 510–11, VII 205–6, XII 3–4, XVI 2–3. It is interesting, and may not be wholly coincidental, that with two exceptions all these lacunae are to be found in Books I–III, and that of the exceptions one is an obvious scribal error, while the other occurs in a satire on a politically explosive subject. Throughout these first three books, as we have seen, Juvenal was working at white heat: it is at least possible that the lacunae were the result of deliberate censorship – perhaps at least as much on moral as on political grounds.

Considerable support for such a thesis appeared in 1899, when a young student named E. O. Winstedt, examining an eleventh-century manuscript of Juvenal in the Bodleian Library, discovered, to his astonishment, that it contained 36 lines – 34 of them one continuous passage – which existed in no other text, and the absence of which had never been so much as suspected. The lines in question occur in Satire VI: they were inserted between lines 365–6 and 373–4. To complicate matters still further, they were obscure, corrupt, and of such sophisticated obscenity that Housman could write, truthfully, in his preface that 'until I translated and emended this fragment . . . no one had any notion what it meant'. His account (pp. xxix–xxx and xxxix–xl) of how this fragment was preserved in one Beneventan manuscript, and the process by which the text was battered into some sort of shape after the passage had been lost or excised, is still the *locus classicus* on the subject. As soon as the lines were published, there was a strong movement among certain scholars to prove them a spurious insertion or forgery. Until the last war this opinion more or less held the field. Since then intensive work on the 'O passage', as it is generally known, has reversed the position, and the case for these lines being Juvenal's work may be regarded as sound. They certainly are stamped with his authentic tone and technique: if he did not write them, it is hard to conceive who else could have done so. But the whole episode sheds a lurid light on the concealed pitfalls which Juvenal's text may contain at any point. 'I should not be surprised,' Highet wrote in 1954, 'if a new manuscript of Juvenal turned up tomorrow with half a dozen new passages (several of them shocking) and with a totally irregular provenance and descent.' So far this interesting event has not taken place; but it well might.

Textual problems apart, the translator of Juvenal is hampered by two main difficulties in achieving a version which will both convey the force and flavour of its original, and have immediate relevance for a modern, non-Latinate audience. One of these difficulties I have already discussed above.* No translator can hope to capture the condensed force of Juvenal's enjambed hexameters, his skilful rhythmic variations, his dazzling displays of alliteration and assonance and onomatopoeia: here I can claim no more than that I have recognized the problem, and done what I could to surmount it in a wholly different medium. It is hard to estimate the gulf which lies between an inflected, mosaic language such as Latin, and an uninflected language like English, with its plethora of controlling particles. Furthermore, the vowel-lengths in Latin are fixed quantities, whereas those in English are variable according to stress and context: we may say, broadly speaking, that whereas Latin verse is ruled by metre, English verse adapts itself elastically to rhythm. Therefore the first casualty in any version of Juvenal (or Virgil, or Lucretius) will be the strict hexameter. All attempts to acclimatize this growth on English soil (even such a brilliant *tour de force* as C. S. Calverley's experimental fragment of Book I of the *Iliad*) have ultimately failed, for one simple and insurmountable reason. A stress-hexameter, lacking the counter-tensions set up by the metrical framework of its Latin or Greek original, produces such a cumulative effect of dead, clumping monotony that two or three pages will normally be enough to send the reader to sleep – or in search of something

* pp. 51-2.

less stultifying. On the other hand, translating Juvenal into blank verse, let alone elegiac couplets, sets up alien associations which one should be at pains to avoid (I have treated this topic at some length in *Essays in Antiquity*, 1960, pp. 185–215, and interested readers can pursue the argument there). Prose is out of the question: despite Juvenal's chatty, discursive technique he is, first and foremost, a poet, a master of language and rhythm, who exploits the hexameter with a virtuosity perhaps only rivalled by Virgil.

The only solution, it seems to me, is the variable six-stress line first employed (so far as I know) by Mr Cecil Day Lewis in his admirable version of the *Georgics*, and since developed by Professor Richmond Lattimore in translations of Hesiod and the *Iliad*. It has been applied to Juvenal, with excellent results, by Professor Highet in the illustrative quotations which are scattered through his *magnum opus*. By allowing great latitude over the position of the caesura (the natural rhythmic break in a line), and the stresses governing the six 'feet', that dead monotony can be broken up to a surprising extent, while at least something of the hexameter's overall form can be retained. English falls naturally into iambic rhythms rather than into the dactylo-spondaic pattern of the hexameter (which may be why English translators have always succeeded comparatively well with Greek tragedy); it follows that many of the six-stress lines which Day Lewis, Lattimore and I employ to represent hexameters are really iambic Alexandrines in disguise. This seems to me the lesser of two evils. Any solution to the hexameter problem is bound to be a compromise; and at least the present one can reproduce one vital device – enjambement – which Juvenal uses constantly and with striking effect.

But there still remains another hazard, historical rather than literary. If English translators have succeeded with Greek tragedy, they have almost always come a dreadful cropper over Greek comedy – not so much on technical or aesthetic grounds, as because of the unfamiliar names, the obscure topical or historical allusions that they are for ever having to break off in mid-passage and explain to the layman. Nothing is calculated to annoy a reader more – or indeed to produce a stiffer, more pedantic flavour – than a text where every other line requires, and gets, some detailed marginal gloss before it can be understood. In this respect Juvenal must be counted a translator's nightmare. He is full of recondite references that he takes it for granted his reader will understand; he is writing for educated Romans who knew their own myths and history, and were at least as familiar with prominent public figures of the day – both at leader-page and gossip-column level – as an assiduous newspaper-reader or TV-scanner would be nowadays. I cannot pretend to have eliminated this difficulty altogether, but I have reduced it as far as possible by the use of two simple devices. One of these I call the 'silent gloss'. If a difficulty can be made clear by the addition of a brief phrase, I insert that phrase in the text of my version, without comment. For example, at VI 440–2 (an example we have already studied in another context) the bluestocking's jabber, Juvenal says, would make you 'think all the pots and bells were being clashed together'; there follows a baffling reference to one woman acting 'as lunar midwife'. Here I have tacitly inserted the phrase 'when the moon's in eclipse': just enough (I hope) to remind the average educated reader of a widespread primitive superstition – making a loud noise to scare demons during the moon's 'rebirth' – without his needing to hunt down the allusion in a footnote.

The other device is what might be termed 'functional substitution'. Juvenal is very fond of citing well-known names from history, not for any specific purpose, but as *representative types* of some virtue, vice, occupation, or personal characteristic. This is a regular practice among Roman writers, and was taught as part of the rhetorician's stock-in-trade. But for its effectiveness it depends on one's audience being familiar with the various touchstones employed. To a modern reader most of the names would mean nothing at all, and the device, far from calling up clusters of mental associations as it was meant to do, would become a baffling private code to which they lacked the key – thus totally defeating its own ends. For instance, at I 35–6 we read of an informer '*quem Massa timet, quem munere palpat/ Carus et a trepido Thymele summissa Latino*'. Who, the bewildered reader well may ask, are Massa and Carus? What is the relation of Thymele and Latinus, and just what is Latinus making her do? With the help of the ancient commentaries, and an acquaintance with the historical context, a specialist can, more or less, tease out the answer to this puzzle: but what Juvenal was aiming for when he packed these lines with – to him and his contemporaries – highly charged proper names was the delighted shock of instant recognition, and such an emotion is not liable to be induced by explanatory footnotes. Now in fact Massa and Carus were type-figures of the small-time informer, the minnows who circled round the big fish Juvenal is sketching here; and Latinus was an actor who saved his own skin by pushing his wife into this sinister creature's arms. This is the sense which Juvenal is conveying, and he means it as a perennial generalization: I therefore translate accordingly. We lose the associative image, but at least we gain unhampered clarity: 'Lesser informers dread him, grease/ His palm with ample bribes, while the wives of trembling actors/ Grease him the other way.' Another, slightly different, instance occurs in Satire II 24–8:

> *quis tulerit Gracchos de seditione querentes?*
> *quis caelum terris non misceat et mare caelo*
> *si fur displiceat Verri, homicida Miloni,*
> *Clodius accuset moechos, Catilina Cethegum,*
> *in tabulam Sullae si dicant discipuli tres?*

Here we have a whole battery of historical allusions without any purpose except to provide type-figures and point a contrast. The Gracchi are brought in, simply and solely, as radical revolutionaries, Verres as the classic rapacious governor, Milo as a political assassin, Clodius as an adulterer, Catiline and Cethegus as traitors, and Sulla as a dictator. There is no other reason whatsoever for their presence in this passage, and, once again, I have preferred to substitute the function for the name.

Perhaps my understanding of Juvenal has been deepened by the sheer discipline involved in translating him, however imperfect the final result of that discipline may be. But I do not think my *opinion* of him has really changed one iota since the summing-up which I first wrote over ten years ago, and published, with modifications, in 1960 (*Essays in Antiquity*, p. 184). That paragraph, then, will serve as an appropriate coda to this Introduction:

'Yes; Juvenal is a writer for this age. He has (in spite of his personal preoccupations) the universal eye for unchanging human corruption; he would be perfectly at home in a New York dive or a rigged political conference, ready to pillory the tycoons or degenerates who were elbowing him out of an easy job in some international organisation. Bureaucrats have taken over from aristocrats, but his cry still goes up; and if we finally weary of its savage brilliance, it is simply because the thought underlying it is so utterly negative, and, in the last resort, so ignoble in its purpose. The writer must compel our respect; but the man can never command our affections. Nevertheless, Juvenal is an historical no less than a literary landmark. He crystallizes for us all the faults and weaknesses we have watched gaining strength at Rome through the centuries; when his minatory voice dies away there is nothing left but to sit in silence, and listen to Gibbon's great rhetorical epitaph on a nation that sold its soul to win the fruits of the known world.'

PETER GREEN

Harlton – Redgrave –
Methymna – Pholegandros – Athens
1958–66

NOTE TO THE 1974 EDITION

New additional passages where I have further diverged from Clausen's Oxford text are: I 70, X 175, 202, XII 32, XV 85–6, XVI 18.

SATIRE I

Must I *always* be stuck in the audience at these poetry-readings,
    never
Up on the platform myself, taking it out on Cordus
For the times he's bored me to death with ranting speeches
From that *Theseid* of his? Is X to get off scot-free
After inflicting his farces on me, or Y his elegies? Is there
No recompense for whole days wasted on prolix
Versions of *Telephus*? And what about that *Orestes* –
Each margin of the roll crammed solid, top and bottom,
More on the back, and *still* it wasn't finished!
I know all the mythical landscapes like my own back-room:
The grove of Mars, that cave near Aeolus' island
Belonging to Vulcan. The stale themes are bellowed daily
In rich patrons' colonnades, till their marble pillars
Crack with a surfeit of rhetoric. The plane-trees echo
Every old trope – what the winds are up to, whose ghost
Aeacus has on his hellish rack, from what far country
The other fellow is sneaking off with that golden sheepskin,
The monstrous size of those ash-trees the Centaurs used for
    spears:
You get the same stuff from them all, established poet
And raw beginner alike.[1] I too have winced under the cane
And concocted 'Advice to Sulla': *Let the despot retire
Into private life, take a good long sleep*, and so on.[2] When you
    find
Hordes of poets on each street-corner, it's misplaced kindness
To refrain from writing. The paper will still be wasted.
Why then have I chosen to drive my team down the track
Which great Lucilius[3] blazed? If you have the leisure to listen
Calmly and reasonably, I will enlighten you.
    When a flabby eunuch marries, when well-born girls go
    crazy

For pig-sticking up-country, bare-breasted, spear in fist;
When the barber who rasped away at my youthful beard has
    risen
To challenge good society with his millions; when
    Crispinus[4] –
That Delta-bred house-slave, silt washed down by the Nile –
Now hitches his shoulders under Tyrian purple, airs
A thin gold ring in summer on his sweaty finger
('My dear, I couldn't *bear* to wear my *heavier* jewels') –
Why then, it is harder *not* to be writing satires; for who
Could endure this monstrous city, however callous at heart,
And swallow his wrath? Look: here comes a brand-new litter,
Crammed with its corpulent owner, some chiselling advocate.
Who's next? An informer. He turned in his noble patron,
And soon he'll have gnawed away that favourite bone of his,
The aristocracy. Lesser informers dread him, grease
His palm with ample bribes, while the wives of trembling actors
Grease him the other way. Today we are elbowed aside
By men who earn legacies in bed, who rise to the top
Via that quickest, most popular route – the satisfied desires
Of some rich old matron. Each lover will get his cut,
A twelfth share in the estate, or eleven-twelfths, depending
On the size of his – services rendered. I suppose he deserves
Some recompense for all that sweat and exertion: he looks
As pale as the man who steps barefoot on a snake – or is waiting
His turn to declaim, at Lyons, in Caligula's competitions.[5]

    Need I tell you how anger burns in my heart when I see
The bystanders jostled back by a mob of bravos
Whose master has first debauched his ward, and later
Defrauded the boy as well? The courts condemned him,
But the verdict was a farce. Who cares for reputation
If he keeps his cash? A provincial governor, exiled
For extortion, boozes and feasts all day, basks cheerfully
In the wrathful eye of the Gods; it's still his province,
After winning the case against him, that feels the pinch.

Are not such themes well worthy of Horace's pen? Should I
Not attack them too? Must I stick to the usual round
Of Hercules' labours, what Diomede did, the bellowing
Of that thingummy in the Labyrinth, or the tale of the flying
Carpenter, and how his son went splash in the sea?[6]
Will *these* suffice in an age when each pimp of a husband
Takes gifts from his own wife's lover – if she is barred in law
From inheriting legacies – and, while they paw each other,
Tactfully stares at the ceiling, or snores, wide awake, in his
    wine?
Will *these* suffice, when the young blade who has squandered
His family fortune on racing-stables still reckons to get
Command of a cohort? Just watch him lash his horses
Down the Flaminian Way like Achilles' charioteer,
Reins bunched in one hand, showing off to his mistress
Who stands beside him, wrapped in his riding-cloak!
Don't you want to cram whole notebooks with scribbled
    invective
When you stand at the corner and see some forger carried past
On the necks of six porters, lounging back like Maecenas
In his open litter? A counterfeit seal, a will, a mere scrap
Of paper – these were enough to convert him to wealth and
    honour.
Do you see that distinguished lady? She has the perfect dose
For her husband – old wine with a dash of parching toad's blood.
Locusta's a child to her[7]; she trains her untutored neighbours
To ignore all unkind rumours, to stalk through angry crowds
With their black and bloated husbands before them on the
    hearse.
If you want to be someone today you must nerve yourself
For deeds that could earn you an island exile, or years in gaol.
Honesty's praised, but honest men freeze. Wealth springs from
    crime:
Landscape-gardens, palaces, furniture, antique silver –
Those cups embossed with prancing goats – all, all are tainted.

Who can sleep easy today? If your greedy daughter-in-law
Is not being seduced for cash, it'll be your bride: mere
      schoolboys
Are adulterers now. Though talent be wanting, yet
Indignation will drive me to verse, such as I – or any
      scribbler –
May still command. All human endeavours, men's prayers,
Fears, angers, pleasures, joys and pursuits, these make
The mixed mash of my verse.[8]

                              Since the days of the Flood,
When Deucalion anchored his ship on a mountain peak
To search for a sign, the days when hard stones quivered
To living softness and warmth, and Pyrrha confronted
The first men with their naked mates, has there ever
Been so rich a crop of vices? When has the purse
Of greed yawned wider? When was gambling more frantic
Than it is today? Men face the table's hazards
Not with their purse but their strong-box open beside them.
Here you'll see notable battles, with the croupier for squire,
Holding stakes instead of a shield. Is it not plain lunacy
To lose ten thousand on a turn of the dice, yet grudge
A shirt to your shivering slave? Which of our grandfathers
Would have built himself so many country houses, or dined
Off seven courses, *alone*? Clients were guests in those days.
But now Roman citizens are reduced to scrambling
For a little basket of scraps on their patron's doorstep.[9]
He peers into each face first, scared stiff that some imposter
May give a false name and cheat him: you must be identified
Before you get your ration. The crier has his orders:
Each man to answer his name, nobility included –
Oh yes, our Upper-Ten are scrounging with the rest.
'The praetor first, then the tribune –' But a freedman blocks
Their way. '*I* got here first,' he says, 'why shouldn't I keep
My place? I don't give *that* for you. Oh, I know I'm foreign:
Look here, at my pierced ears, no use denying it – born

68

Out East, on the Euphrates. But my five shops bring in
Four hundred thousand, see? So I qualify for the gentry.[10]
What's in a senator's purple stripe, if true-blue nobles
Are reduced to herding sheep up-country, while I have more
Stashed away in the bank than any Imperial favourite?'
So let the Tribunes wait, and money reign supreme;
Let the Johnny-come-lately, whose feet only yesterday were
    white
With the chalk of the slave-market, flout this sacrosanct office![11]
Why not? Though as yet, pernicious Cash, you lack
A temple of your own, though we have raised no altars
To Sovereign Gold (as already we worship Honour,
Peace, Victory, Virtue, or Concord – whose roosting storks
Rattle and flap on the roof when you salute their nest),
Still it is Wealth, not God, that compels our deepest reverence.

   When the Consul himself tots up, at the end of his year,[12]
What the dole is worth, how much it adds to his income, how
Are we poor dependents to manage? Out of this pittance
We must pay for decent clothes and shoes – not to mention our
    food
And the fuel for heating. But plenty who can afford
A litter still queue up for their bob-a-day; some husbands
Go the rounds with a sick or pregnant wife in tow,
Or better (a well-known dodge) pretend she's there when she
    isn't,
And claim for both, displaying a curtained, empty sedan.
'My Galla's in there,' he says. 'Come on, let us through! You
    doubt me?
Galla! Put out your head, girl! I'm sorry, she must be asleep –
No, don't disturb her, please –!'
                   And so the day wears on
With its prescribed routine, its fascinating round.
Dole in pocket, we next attend my lord to the Forum;
Stare, bored, at all those statues – Apollo beside the Law
    Courts

(He must be an expert by now) or that jumped-up Egyptian
Pasha[13] who's had the nerve to gate-crash Triumph Row:
His effigy's only fit for pissing on – or worse.
[Experienced clients follow their patron home again],[14]
Hoping against hope for that dinner-invitation
Which never comes: worn out, they drift away to purchase
(Poor souls) their cabbage and kindling. But *he* meanwhile will
    loll
Alone at his guestless meal, wolfing the choicest produce
Of sea and woodland. These fellows will gobble up
Whole legacies at one course, off fine big antique tables:
Soon there won't be a parasite left. But who could stomach
Such measures in gourmands? What a grossly ravening maw
That man must have who dines off whole roast boar – a beast
Ordained for convivial feasting! But you'll pay the price
All too too soon, my friend, when you undress and waddle
Into the bath, your belly still swollen with undigested
Peacock-meat – a lightning heart-attack, with no time
To make your final will. The story circulates
As a dinner-table joke, the latest thing. But no one
Cares about you. Your corpse is borne out to ironical
Cheers from your cheated friends. Posterity can add
No more, or worse, to our ways; our grandchildren will act
As we do, and share our desires. Today every vice
Has reached its ruinous zenith. So, satirist, hoist your sails,
Cram on every stitch of canvas! But where, you may ask,
Is a talent to match the theme? and where our outspoken
Ancestral bluntness, that wrote what burning passion dictated?
'Show me the man I dare not name,' Lucilius cried,
'What odds if the noble Consul forgive my libel or not?'
But name an Imperial favourite, and you will soon enough
Blaze like those human torches, half-choked, half-grilled to
    death,
Those calcined corpses they drag with hooks from the arena,
And leave a broad black trail behind them in the sand.[15]

But what, you may ask, about the man who has poisoned
Three uncles with belladonna – are we to let *him* ride
In his feather-bedded litter, and look down his nose at us?
Yes; and when he approaches, keep mum, clap a hand to your
    mouth –
Just to say *That's the man* will brand you as an informer.
It's safe enough to retell how Aeneas fought fierce Turnus;
No one's a penny the worse for Achilles' death, or the frantic
Search for Hylas, that time he tumbled in after his pitcher.
But when fiery Lucilius rages with satire's naked sword
His hearers go red; their conscience is cold with crime,
Their innards sweat at the thought of their secret guilt:
Hence wrath and tears. So ponder these things in your mind
Before the trumpet sounds. It's too late for a soldier
To change his mind about fighting when he's armed in the
    battle-line.
For myself, I shall try my hand on the famous dead, whose
    ashes
Rest beside the Latin and the Flaminian Ways.[16]

Notes to Satire I

1. Cordus was an unknown writer of epics: the *Theseid* (analogous to the *Aeneid*) was the work he gave at public recitations. *Telephus* and *Orestes* are tragedies – Euripides wrote two plays with these names – composed for a platform performance rather than the stage. In this whole catalogue J. is emphasizing the derivative, artificial, cliché-ridden nature of contemporary literature – a point also made by the list of hackneyed mythological references, which he takes obvious pleasure in debunking: a swipe at the allusive poets in the Alexandrian tradition, who dragged them in on every page, and were especially fond of obscure periphrasis.

2. Pupils at school were often given the task of composing declamations, either to be put in the mouth of, or directed at, some great man of history. These exercises were known as *suasoriae*: examples by the Elder Seneca have survived. Sulla was Dictator from 82 to 78 B.C.

3. Gaius Lucilius (*c.* 180–*c.* 102 B.C.) was one of the earliest – and one of the greatest – Roman satirists. Protected by Scipio, he indulged in extremely outspoken social criticism, though his strictures, like J.'s, lacked moral coherence. Only fragments of his work survive.

4. Crispinus began his career as a fishmonger and was made an *eques* by Domitian. J. appears to have had some special grudge against him: see below, Satire IV, *passim*. He was from Memphis or Canopus in Egypt.

5. Sexual excess was commonly supposed in antiquity to produce an anaemic, washed-out appearance. For 'Caligula's competitions' see Suetonius, *Caligula* 20 (p. 159*): 'Caligula gave ... miscellaneous Games at Lyons, where he also held a competition in Greek and Latin oratory. The loser, it appears, had to present the winners with prizes and make speeches praising them; while those who failed miserably were forced to erase their entries with either sponges or their own tongues – at the threat of being thrashed and flung into the Rhone.'

* See footnote on p. 19.

6. The reference is to the Fall of Icarus: another sneer at ancient mythology, which in J.'s day had become no more than the lifeless stock-in-trade of every third-rate poet.

7. Locusta was a famous poisoner in Nero's reign. She dispatched the Emperor Claudius at Agrippina's orders, and also poisoned Britannicus for Nero himself. She was executed by Galba. See Suetonius, *Nero* 33 (pp. 226–7) and Dio Cassius 64.3.

8. Professor J. P. Sullivan has reminded me of Harrison's argument that the removal of lines 85–6 from their present position in the MSS leaves a far more logical sentence structure behind. He is not, however, responsible for the decision to insert them after line 80. Such 'slipped-position' lines are by no means rare in Juvenal.

9. Originally clients were entertained by their patrons; later there was substituted the *sportula*, or little basket of food to carry away. Later still this was commuted to a financial dole.

10. The minimum property qualification for admission to the Equestrian Order was 400,000 sesterces. Originally a body of cavalry, the *equites* in Imperial times were largely identical with the rich non-senatorial business community: 'burghers' or 'magnates' would be a fair equivalent. They held important posts in the civil service: the Prefecture of Egypt, for instance, was reserved for an *eques*.

11. Foreign slaves just imported had their feet chalked white by the dealer to distinguish them from *vernae*, or home-bred slaves.

12. The consuls held office for a year, and under the Empire, as *consul suffectus*, for a few months only. The position carried no salary (though there was an inadequate expense account) and most consuls reckoned on recouping from their subsequent appointment to a provincial governorship.

13. The 'Egyptian pasha' was Tiberius Julius Alexander, a Jew who became a Roman *eques;* he rose to the rank of Prefect of Egypt, and may have become Praetorian Prefect as well (see E. G. Turner, *Journal of Roman Studies* 44 (1954), 54 ff.). J. manages to symbolize in him both the contempt he felt for the Jews and his perennial dislike of Egyptians – a not unnatural feeling, since Egypt was his place of exile.

14. Housman suggested, almost certainly correctly, that a line had dropped out of the text here, after line 131, in which the clients

would be taken back to their patron's house. I have translated in accordance with this suggestion.

15. The text here is difficult. I follow Housman (who supposes a line to have been lost after 156) and translate his conjectural restoration.

16. The Via Flaminia was, at it were, the Great North Road from Rome; the Via Latina branched off from its southern counterpart, the Via Appia. The aristocracy often had tombs beside the major arterial roads, and the closing lines hint clearly at the main target of J.'s satire. The tomb of the actor Paris lay beside the Via Flaminia; Domitian himself was buried by the Via Latina. Yet – and coming after the reference to Lucilius this cannot but strike us as bathetic – J. is only going to attack those who are already dead. Highet (*Juvenal the Satirist* 56–8) points out (a) that most of his subjects are timeless; (b) that he may have been lying in order to protect himself; and (c) that he felt the past was truly important; that he 'saw the empire as one long continuous process of degeneration.'

ADDITIONAL NOTE

Baldwin (Additional Bibliography) suggests that J. may in fact have been attacking contemporaries under cover-names, though his theory of an unknown 'Tigillinus' lacks plausibility. Griffith sees a close rhetorical connexion between the ending of this Satire and Book XXX of Lucilius. Martyn argues that the main programme-theme, developed more specifically in later Satires, is that of perversion (sexual anomalies, the *clientela* paradox). Bertman goes hunting for fire-symbolism, and finds rather more of it (I suspect) than J. ever put there, even in his more Stoic moments. As a programme-piece, Satire I remains as elusive as ever.

At line 70 I now read, with Griffith, *rubeta* (Par. 8072, Montpell. 125, Vind. 111/107) for *rubetam* (*rell.* and all modern editors), and have changed my translation accordingly. Griffith is, however, wrong in saying that Harrison's plea to remove lines 85–6 left no one with any idea where to insert them: they go well (*pace* Martyn) after line 80, as I pointed out in 1967. At that time I also gratefully accepted Harrison's suggestion of *ecquando* for *et quando* in the same passage, so that it is not true, either, to claim that this proposal has been 'quietly forgotten'. See Additional Bibliography for all these references.

SATIRE II

Northward beyond the Lapps to the world's end, the frozen
Polar ice-cap – there's where I long to escape when I hear
High-flown moral discourse from that clique in Rome who
    affect
Ancestral peasant virtues as a front for their lechery.
An ignorant crowd, too, for all the plaster busts
Of Stoic philosophers on display in their houses:
The nearest they come to doctrine is when they possess
Some original portrait – Aristotle, or one of the Seven Sages –
Hung on the library wall. Appearances are deceptive:
Every back street swarms with solemn-faced humbuggers.
You there – have *you* the nerve to thunder at vice, who are
The most notorious dyke among all our Socratic fairies?[1]
Your shaggy limbs and the bristling hair on your forearms
Suggest a fierce male virtue; but the surgeon called in
To lance your swollen piles dissolves in laughter
At the sight of that well-smoothed passage. Such creatures talk
In a clipped, laconic style, and crop their hair crew-cut fashion,
As short as their eyebrows. I prefer the perverted
Eunuch priest of the Mother Goddess: at least he's open
And honest about it. Gait, gestures, expression, all
Proclaim his twisted nature. He is sick, a freak of fate,
Not to be blamed. Indeed, his wretched self-exposure,
The very strength of his passion, beg pity and forgiveness.

  Far worse is he who attacks such practices with hairy
Masculine fervour, and after much talk of virtue
Proceeds to cock his dish like a perfect lady. 'What?
Respect *you*?' screams the common-or-garden queen,
'When you're in the trade yourself? There's nothing to choose
Between us. It takes a hale man to mock a cripple,
And you can't bait niggers when you're tarred with the same
    brush.'

75

True enough: who would stand for a radical deploring
The latest revolution? Wouldn't you think the world
Had turned upside-down if rapacious provincial governors
Condemned extortion, or gangsters repudiated murder?
Supposing a co-respondent clamped down on adultery,
Or some arch-conspirator flayed his henchman in treason
With a patriotic lecture, or dictators inveighed
Against purges and proscriptions – wouldn't it turn your wits?
Such was the case, not so long since, when you-know-who
Was busy reviving those stern decrees against
Adultery: even Mars and Venus blushed. But all
The while he himself was flouting the law – and spiced
His crime with a dash of incest, in the proper tragic tradition.
His niece, a fertile creature, had her row of abortions,
And every embryo lump was the living spit of Uncle.[2]
Then isn't it right and proper for even the worst of men
To despise these bogus moralists, cast their censure
Back in their teeth? 'Where now are our marriage-laws?'
Was the daily complaint of one such sour-faced pussy,
Till a courtesan, maddened, took up the cudgels against him:
'How lucky we are today,' says she with a grin, 'in having
You to look after our morals! Rome had better behave –
A real oldfashioned killjoy has dropped on us out of the skies.
Do tell me, darling – where did you buy that divine
Perfume I can smell on your bristly neck? Come, come:
Don't be ashamed to tell me the name of the shop!
If we *must* rake up old laws, surely our list should be headed
By the Sodomy Act. What's more, you should first examine
The conduct of men, not women. Men are the worse by far,[3]
But their numbers protect them. They all back each other up,
And queers stick together like glue. Besides, you will never find
Our sex indulging in such detestable perversions:
All of us know our roles, from famous courtesan
To randy amateur harlot; *we* would not dream of giving
Tongue to each other's parts. But your lawyer-philosopher

76

Obliges young men both ways, his versatile efforts
Turning him doubly anaemic.4 Do *we* ever rob you of briefs,
Or set ourselves up as legal experts, or deafen
The Bench with shyster speeches? A female wrestler
Is a rarity in Rome: not many women can stomach
The athlete's diet – huge mouthfuls of raw mutton.
But *you* spin your yarn with a will, and come back home
With baskets crammed; you twist the swelling spindle
Like Penelope, or the spider-girl Arachne, or
That unkempt drab in the play, astride her stool.5
You remember that actor they called "the Danube Basin"?
Everyone knows why during his married life
He showered gifts on his wife – yet left both house and fortune
To a favoured freedman. Girls can do well for themselves
If they don't mind sleeping third in the marriage-bed. Get wed,
Keep mum: discretion spells diamond ear-bobs. How
Can *you* take a high moral line against women with such
A record? You censure the dove, yet absolve the perverted
     raven.'6
   When they heard these sharp home-truths the pseudo-
     philosophers
Fled in confusion. Not one count of the indictment
Could they refute. But where will men draw the limit
When they see a high-born advocate dress in transparent
     chiffon
To prosecute loose-living women, while the public stare
     pop-eyed?
If the women are whores, condemn them: yet even a proven
     whore
Wouldn't rig herself out like *that*. 'But it's mid-July,' he
     complains,
'I'm sweltering hot –' Then plead your case stark naked:
It's crazy, but less disgraceful. Do you think these suitable
     clothes
In which to expound the law to our victorious troops,

Their battle-scars still fresh, or to mountain peasants
Hot from the plough? If you saw a judge attired
In such a fashion, you'd be the first to cry scandal:
Imagine a *witness* in chiffon! Things have reached a pretty pass
When the keen, untiring defender of Roman law and freedom
Is a walking transparency. Infection spread this plague,
And will spread it further still, just as a single
Scabby pig in the field brings death to the whole herd,
Or the touch of one blighted grape will blight the bunch.7
   Sooner or later your chiffon gown will lead you
To worse things still. Corruption comes by degrees.
After a while you will find yourself taken up
By a very queer fraternity. In the secrecy of their homes
They put on ribboned mitres and three or four necklaces,
Then disembowel a pig and offer up bowls of wine
To placate the great Mother Goddess. Their ritual's all
      widdershins:
Here it is *women* who may not cross the threshold8: none
But males can approach this altar. 'Away, away, profane
Women!' they cry, 'no flute-girls here, no booming conches!'
(Such secret torch-lit orgies were known in Athens once,
When the randy Thracian priests outwore the Goddess herself.)
You'll see one initiate busy with eyebrow-pencil, kohl
And mascara, eyelids aflutter; a second sips wine
From a big glass phallus, his long luxuriant curls
Caught up in a golden hairnet. He'll be wearing fancy checks
With a sky-blue motif, or smooth green gabardine,
And he and his slave will both use women's oaths.9
Here's another clutching a mirror – just like that fag of an
      Emperor
Otho, who peeked at himself to see how his armour looked
Before riding into battle. A fine heroic trophy
That was indeed, fit matter for modern annals and histories,
A civil war where mirrors formed part of the fighting kit!10
To polish off a rival *and* keep your complexion fresh

Demands consummate generalship; to camp in palatial
     splendour
On the field of battle, *and* give yourself a face-pack
Argues true courage. No Eastern warrior-queen,
Not Cleopatra herself aboard that unlucky flagship[11]
Behaved in such a fashion.
                              Here you will find no
Restraint of speech, no decent table-manners;
These are the Goddess's minions, here shrill affected voices
Are quite in order, here the white-haired old rogue of a priest
Who conducts the rites is a rare and memorable
Glutton for meat, a teacher worthy of hire.
Yet one thing they omit: true Phrygian devotees
Would by now have slashed away that useless member: why
Draw the line at self-castration? And what about
That noble sprig who went through a 'marriage' with some
     common
Horn-player or trumpeter – and brought him a cool half-
     million
As a bridal dowry? The contract was signed, the blessing
Pronounced, and the blushing bride hung round 'her' husband's
     neck
At a lavish wedding-breakfast. Shades of our ancestors!
Is it a moral reformer we need, or an augur
Of evil omens? Would *you* be more horrified, or think it
A more ghastly portent, if women calved, or cows
Gave birth to lambs? Here is a man who once
Was a priest of Mars, who walked in the solemn procession
Sweating under the thongs of his nodding sacred shield;[12]
And now he decks himself out in bridal frills, assumes
The train and veil! O Father of our City,
What brought your simple shepherd people to such a pitch
Of blasphemous perversion? Great Lord of War, whence came
This prurient itch upon them? A wealthy, well-born
Man is betrothed in marriage to another man

79

And you do nothing! Not a shake of the helmet, no pounding
The ground with your spear, not even a complaint
To your father! Away with you then, remove yourself
From the broad Roman acres that bear your name,¹³ and suffer
Neglect at your hands! This is the kind of talk
We soon shall hear: 'I must go down-town tomorrow
First thing: a special engagement.'
                              'What's happening?'
                                                  'Need
     you ask?
I'm going to a wedding. Old So-and-so's got his boy-friend
To the altar at last – just a few close friends are invited.'
We have only to wait now: soon such things will be done,
And done in public: male brides will yearn for a mention
In the daily gazette. But still they have one big problem
Of a painful kind: they can't keep their marriage solvent
By producing babies. Nature knows best: their desires
Have no physical issue. In vain they sample foreign nostrums
Guaranteed to induce conception, or hold out eager hands
To be struck by the wolf-boys' goatskins.¹⁴ But the very worst
Remains to be told: our male bride took a trident,
Put on the net-thrower's tunic, and dodged about the arena
In a gladiatorial act.¹⁵ Yet this was the man whose blood
Was the truest of blue, whose Republican family tree
Outshone them all – privileged ringside spectators,
Even the noble patron in whose honour the show was staged.

    Today not even children – except those small enough
To get a free public bath¹⁶ – believe all that stuff about ghosts,
Or underground kingdoms and rivers, or black frogs croaking
In the waters of Styx, or thousands of dead men ferried
Across by one small skiff. But just for a moment
Imagine it's true – how would our great dead captains
Greet such a new arrival? And what about the flower
Of our youth who died in battle, our slaughtered legionaries,
Those myriad shades of war? If only they had

Sulphur and torches in Hades, and a few damp laurel-twigs
They'd insist on being purified. Yes: even among the dead
Rome stands dishonoured. Though our armies have advanced
To Ireland, though the Orkneys are ours, and northern Britain
With its short clear nights, these conquered tribes abhor
The vices that flourish in their conquerors' capital. Yet
We hear of one Armenian who outstripped our most effeminate
Young Roman pansies: *he* surrendered his person
To the lusts of a *tribune*. A good deal more than the mind
Is broadened by travel: he came to Rome as a hostage,
But Rome turns boys into men. If they stay here long enough
To catch her deadly sickness, there's never a shortage
Of lovers for them. Trousers, sheath-knives, whips
And bridles are cast aside, and so they carry back
Upper-class Roman habits to distant Ardaschan.[17]

Notes to Satire II

1. This is a variant on the classic gibe of antiquity (derived largely from Plato's *Symposium* and Aristophanes' *Clouds*) which assumes that all 'philosophers' are homosexuals. Juvenal inverts the cliché: in his day many homosexuals pretended to be philosophers.

2. The unnamed adulterer was the Emperor Domitian, who seduced his niece Julia, got her with child, and then forced her to have an abortion as a result of which she died (Suetonius, *Domitian* 22, p. 309). As Homer tells us, Aphrodite (Venus) cuckolded Hephaestus (Vulcan) with Ares (Mars): see *Odyssey* 8.266–366. Ares, in Greek mythology, had Eos, the Dawn, as mistress – Venus, in revenge, made her permanently in love with someone else – besides fathering children on Aglauros and other favoured heroines and maidens. Aphrodite also had an affair with Anchises (which resulted in Aeneas) and an Argonaut, Butes.

3. In line 46 I accept Buecheler's emendation *faciunt peiora*. The 'marriage laws' referred to in line 30 must be the *lex Iulia de adulteriis et stupro vel pudicitia* passed by Augustus in 18 B.C. and revived by Domitian in A.D. 90. The Sodomy Act, the *lex Scantinia de nefanda venere*, of uncertain date, was sternly enforced by Domitian. See Suetonius, *Domitian* 8 (p. 300).

4. For this 'double anaemia' see n. 5 to Satire 1. The scholiast attributes his pallor to his habit *inguina lambentis et stuprum patientis* (Wessner p. 21), a diagnosis which, though probably correct, is perhaps better left untranslated.

5. The term for the athlete's meat-ration, *colyphium*, is also slang for the penis: there were phallic-shaped bread rolls similarly called *colyphia*. This whole passage is packed with sexual *double-entendre*: it is a fair presumption that any reference to meat-eating in J. will also hint at *fellatio*. Arachne, the 'spider-girl', was a mythical Lydian who challenged Athena to a spinning competition, and was turned into a spider for her presumption. The 'drab astride her stool' is Antiope, in a play by Pacuvius: she was brought on-stage in chains, bedraggled and unkempt, and shown performing menial domestic

tasks at the bidding of her cruel captress Dirce, wife of Lycus of Thebes. See Propertius 3.15.11ff., and Graves, *The Greek Myths* 1.256–7.

6. This aphorism about ravens and doves contains an appropriately obscene allusion, since ravens were popularly supposed to both copulate and bring forth their young by the mouth. In his *Natural History* Pliny takes this notion one step further, and suggests (10. 12.32) that a woman who eats a raven's egg will likewise enjoy an oral birth.

7. At line 81 I now (1973), though with some misgivings, accept the reading of the main MSS, *conspecta*. Martyn (Additional Bibliography) opts for the reading of *V 10, contacta*, which he supports by the argument that J. was deliberately echoing, with satirical intent, the plague-imagery in Virgil's *Georgics* (3.440–566). He could just be right, though the proverbial *uva uvam videndo varia fit* militates against him, and in favour of the traditional reading.

8. As opposed to the Roman rites of the *Bona Dea*, where it was men who were debarred from participation. In 62 B.C. Clodius caused a great scandal by attending this goddess's rites disguised as a woman. See below, Satire VI 335–41.

9. Women swore by Juno. Though J. throughout is harping solely on sexual implications, this passage gives a fairly precise description of the ritual involved in the worship of the Asiatic Great Mother-Goddess, Ma or Cybele. In Imperial times her cult was assimilated to that of the Roman war-goddess Bellona. The Thracian goddess Cotys or Cotytto was worshipped in Athens as early as the fifth century B.C.: her cult was orgiastic and included effeminate elements. There is a striking parallel in Josephus's *Jewish Wars* (4.9.10) where similar practices – transvestism, elaborate make-up, perverse eroticism – are described as characteristic of certain Galilaeans in Jerusalem. See Colin, 'Juvénal et le mariage mystique de Gracchus' (Bibliography), and for phallic-shaped drinking-vessels, cakes, lamps, etc., and their popularity in Rome, G. R. Scott, *Phallic Worship* (1941) pp. 154 ff., with pls. xii, xxi, and xxiv.

10. Marcus Salvius Otho (A.D. 32–69) was married to Nero's mistress Poppaea; he also appears to have been an active homosexual, who had unnatural relations with Nero himself (Martial 6.32.2; Suetonius *Otho* 2, p. 256). Lines 99–100 parody Virgil's *Aeneid* (3.286

and 12.93–4): Otho bears the mirror as the heroic Abas bore his shield. He was defeated in April A.D. 69 by the legions of Vitellius, and committed suicide. See Lelièvre (Bibliography). It is very probable that the phrase *novis annalibus atque recenti/historia* ('modern annals and histories', as I now translate) carries a not-too-covert allusion to the *Annals* and *Histories* of J.'s friend Tacitus – that it formed, in fact, a literary puff, private joke, or advertisement.

11. Cleopatra was defeated, with Antony, at the naval battle of Actium in 31 B.C.

12. The Salii, or priests of Mars, had to be of patrician birth, with both parents living. On certain days in March and October they went through the City, performing ritual dances and singing traditional hymns. The 'figure-of-eight' shields they carried were supposedly modelled on the *ancile* (in all likelihood a meteorite) which Jupiter threw down from heaven as a gift to King Numa.

13. i.e. the Campus Martius, or Field of Mars, once used for army parades and exercises, but also (which lends irony to J.'s peroration) for the celebration of foreign cult rituals. By J.'s own time it was almost entirely covered with public buildings. In point of religious protocol there was no reason why the Salii should not worship Bellona; the two cults had many links (see Colin, *op. cit.*). But J. identifies foreign cults with sexual licence amongst the aristocracy – just as Livy, somewhat earlier, had associated the introduction of the Bacchanalia into Rome, not only with promiscuity, but also with perjury, forgery, and murder! See Bk 39.8–18.

14. The festival of the Lupercalia, or 'Wolf-feast', was held annually on 15 February, and clearly dated back to the fertility magic of a small 'primitive agricultural community. Youths ran round the city limits, striking any woman they met with strips of sacrificial goatskin, to promote conception.

15. To a modern reader this final indictment may come as a crashing anti-climax, and it is possible that J. (like De Quincey in his famous essay 'On Murder as One of the Fine Arts') was deliberately aiming at unexpected bathos. But for an aristocrat to appear in the arena clearly *was* a peculiar disgrace. See below, Satire VIII 199–210. Both Juvenal and Seneca make a close connexion between homosexuality and the arena. The net-fighter was despised by his more

orthodox fellow-gladiators. Cf. below, Satire VI O 7–12.

16. Below a certain age children were admitted free to the public baths: the normal fee was a *quadrans*, the rough equivalent of a farthing. For some reason women were charged more than men. See Carcopino, *Daily Life in Ancient Rome* (Pelican edition) pp. 253 ff. and 316–17.

17. Ardaschan, the ancient Artaxata, was the capital of Armenia: it stood on a tongue of land on the R. Araxes. Hannibal, as an exile at the court of King Artaxias, helped to supervise its construction (see below, Satire X 160 ff.); in A.D. 58 it was destroyed by Corbulo, and rebuilt by Tiridates, who renamed it Neronia in honour of the Emperor who had ceded it to him. Juvenal may have in mind the 'exchange-visits' which took place on this occasion.

SATIRE III

Despite the wrench of parting, I applaud my old friend's
Decision to make his home in lonely Cumae – the poor
Sibyl will get at least *one* fellow-citizen now!
It's a charming coastal retreat, and just across the point
From our smartest watering-spot.[1] Myself, I would value
A barren offshore island more than Rome's urban heart:
Squalor and isolation are minor evils compared
To this endless nightmare of fires and collapsing houses,
The cruel city's myriad perils – and poets reciting
Their work in *August*!

                While his goods were being loaded
On one small waggon, my old friend lingered a while
By the ancient dripping arches of the Capuan Gate, where once
King Numa had nightly meetings with his mistress. (But today
Egeria's grove and shrine and sacred spring are rented
To Jewish squatters, their sole possession a Sabbath haybox.[2]
Each tree must show a profit, the Muses have been evicted,
The wood's aswarm with beggars.)

                        From here we strolled down
To the nymph's new, modernized grotto. (What a gain in
    sanctity
And atmosphere there would be if grassy banks
Surrounded the pool, if no flash marble affronted
Our native limestone!) Here Umbricius[3] stood, and
Opened his heart to me.

                 'There's no room in this city,'
He said, 'for the decent professions[4]: they don't show any profit.
My resources have shrunk since yesterday, and tomorrow
Will eat away more of what's left. So I am going
Where Daedalus put off his weary wings,[5] while as yet
I'm in vigorous middle age, while active years are left me,
While my white hairs are still few, and I need no stick

87

To guide my tottering feet. So farewell Rome, I leave you
To sanitary engineers and municipal architects, men
Who by swearing black is white land all the juicy contracts
Just like that – a new temple, swamp-drainage, harbour-works,
River-clearance, undertaking, the lot – then pocket the cash
And fraudulently file their petition in bankruptcy.
Once these fellows were horn-players, stumping the provinces
In road-shows, their puffed-out cheeks a familiar sight
To every country village. But now they stage shows themselves,
Of the gladiatorial sort, and at the mob's thumbs-down
Will butcher a loser for popularity's sake, and
Pass on from that to erecting public privies. Why not?
These are such men as Fortune, by way of a joke,
Will sometimes raise from the gutter and make Top People.
What can I do in Rome? I never learnt how
To lie. If a book is bad, I cannot puff it, or bother
To ask around for a copy; astrological clap-trap
Is not in my stars. I cannot and will not promise
To encompass any man's death by way of obliging his son.
I have never meddled with frogs' guts[6]; the task of carrying
Letters and presents between adulterous lovers
I resign to those who know it. I refuse to become
An accomplice in theft – which means that no governor
Will accept me on his staff. It's like being a cripple
With a paralysed right hand. Yet who today is favoured
Above the conspirator, his head externally seething
With confidential matters, never to be revealed?
Harmless secrets carry no obligations, and he
Who shares them with you feels no great call thereafter
To keep you sweet. But if Verres[7] promotes a man
You can safely assume that man has the screws on Verres
And could turn him in tomorrow. Not all the gold
Washed seaward with the silt of tree-lined Tagus
Is worth the price you pay, racked by insomnia, seeing
Your high-placed friends all cringe at your approach – and

For what? Too-transient prizes, unwillingly resigned.
    'Now let me turn to that race[8] which goes down so well
With our millionaires, but remains *my* special pet aversion,
And not mince my words. I cannot, citizens, stomach
A Greek-struck Rome. Yet what fraction of these sweepings
Derives, in fact, from Greece? For years now Syrian
Orontes has poured its sewerage into our native Tiber –
Its lingo and manners, its flutes, its outlandish harps
With their transverse strings, its native tambourines,
And the whores who hang out round the race-course.[9]
        (That's where to go
If you fancy a foreign piece in one of those saucy toques.)
Our beloved Founder should see how his homespun rustics
Behave today, with their dinner-pumps – *trechedipna*
They call them – not to mention their *niceteria*
(Decorations to you) hung round their *ceromatic* (that's
Mud-caked) wrestlers' necks. Here's one from Sicyon,
Another from Macedonia, two from Aegean islands –
Andros, say, or Samos – two more from Caria,
All of them lighting out for the City's classiest districts
And burrowing into great houses, with a long-term plan
For taking them over. Quick wit, unlimited nerve, a gift
Of the gab that outsmarts a professional public speaker –
These are their characteristics. What do you take
That fellow's profession to be? He has brought a whole bundle
Of personalities with him – schoolmaster, rhetorician,
Surveyor, artist, masseur, diviner, tightrope-walker,
Magician or quack, your versatile hungry Greekling
Is all by turns. Tell him to fly – he's airborne.
The inventor of wings was no Moor or Slav, remember,
Or Thracian, but born in the very heart of Athens.[10]
    'When such men as these wear the purple, when some
        creature ·
Blown into Rome along with the figs and damsons
Precedes me at dinner-parties, or for the witnessing

Of manumissions and wills[11] – *me*, who drew my first breath
On these Roman hills, and was nourished on Sabine olives! –
Things have reached a pretty pass. What's more, their talent
For flattery is unmatched. They praise the conversation
Of their dimmest friends; the ugly they call handsome,
So that your scrag-necked weakling finds himself compared
To Hercules holding the giant Antaeus aloft
Way off the earth. They go into ecstasies over
Some shrill and scrannel voice that sounds like a hen
When the cock gets at her. We can make the same compliments,
     but
It's they who convince. On the stage they remain supreme
In female parts, courtesan, matron or slave-girl,[12]
With no concealing cloak: you'd swear it was a genuine
Woman you saw, and not a masked performer.
Look there, beneath that belly: no bulge, all smooth, a neat
Nothingness – even a hint of the Great Divide. Yet back home
These queens and dames pass unnoticed. Greece is a nation
Of actors. Laugh, and they split their sides. At the sight
Of a friend's tears, they weep too – though quite unmoved.
If you ask for a fire in winter, the Greek puts on his cloak;
If you say "I'm hot", *he* starts sweating. So you see
We are not on an equal footing: he has the great advantage
Of being able on all occasions, night and day,
To take his cue, his mask, from others. He's always ready
To throw up his hands and applaud when a friend delivers
A really resounding belch, or pisses right on the mark,
With a splendid drumming sound from the upturned golden
     basin.[13]
   'Besides, he holds nothing sacred,[14] not a soul is safe
From his randy urges, the lady of the house, her
Virgin daughter, her daughter's still unbearded
Husband-to-be, her hitherto virtuous son –
And if none of these are to hand, he'll cheerfully lay
His best friend's grandmother. (Anything to ferret

Domestic secrets out, and get a hold over people.¹⁵)
    'And while we are on the subject of Greeks, let us consider
Academics and their vices – not the gymnasium crowd
But big philosophical wheels, like that Stoic greybeard
Who narked on his friend and pupil, and got him liquidated.
He was brought up in Tarsus, by the banks of that river
Where Bellerophon fell to earth from the Gorgon's flying
        nag.¹⁶
No room for honest Romans when Rome's ruled by a junta
Of Greek-born secret agents, who – like all their race –
Never share friends or patrons. One small dose of venom
(Half Greek, half personal) dropped in that ready ear
And I'm out, shown the back-door, my years of obsequious
Service all gone for nothing. Where can a hanger-on
Be ditched with less fuss than in Rome? Besides (not to
        flatter ourselves)
What use are our poor efforts, where does it all get us,
Dressing up while it's dark still, hurrying along
To pay our morning respects to a couple of wealthy
Maiden aunts? But the praetor's really worked up, his
Colleague may get there before him, the ladies have been
        awake
For hours already, the minions catch it – "Get
A *move* on there, can't you?" Here a citizen, free-born,
Must stand aside on the pavement for some wealthy tycoon's
        slave:
He can afford to squander a senior officer's income
On classy amateur harlots, just for the privilege
Of laying them once or twice. But when *you* fancy
A common-or-garden tart, you dither and hesitate:
Can I afford to accost her? With witnesses in court
The same applies. Their morals may be beyond cavil, and yet
If Scipio took the stand (and he was selected
To escort the Mother Goddess on her journey to Rome) or
        Metellus

Who rescued Minerva's image from her blazing shrine, or even
King Numa himself, still the first and foremost question
Would be: "*What's he worth?*"[17] His character would
    command
Little if any respect. "How many slaves does he keep?
What's his acreage? What sort of dinner-service
Appears on his table – how many pieces, how big?"
Each man's word is as good as his bond – or rather,
The number of bonds in his strong-box. A pauper can swear
    by every
Altar, and every god between Rome and Samothrace, still
(Though the gods themselves forgive him) he'll pass for a
    perjuror
Defying the wrath of heaven. The poor man's an eternal
Butt for bad jokes, with his torn and dirt-caked top-coat,
His grubby toga, one shoe agape where the leather's
Split – those clumsy patches, that coarse and tell-tale stitching
Only a day or two old. The hardest thing to bear
In poverty is the fact that it makes men ridiculous.
"Out of those front-row seats," we're told. "You ought to be
Ashamed of yourselves – your incomes are far too small, and
The law's the law. Make way for some pander's son,
Spawned in an unknown brothel, let your place be occupied
By that natty auctioneer's offspring, with his high-class
    companions
The trainer's brat and the son of the gladiator
Applauding beside him." Such were the fruits of that pinhead
Otho's Reserved Seat Act.[18] What prospective son-in-law
Ever passed muster here if he was short on cash
To match the girl's dowry? What poor man ever inherits
A legacy, or is granted that meanest of sinecures –
A job with the Office of Works? All lower-income citizens
Should have marched out of town, in a body, years ago.
Nobody finds it easy to get to the top if meagre
Resources cripple his talent. But in Rome the problem's worse

Than anywhere else. Inflation hits the rental
Of your miserable apartment, inflation distends
The ravenous maws of your slaves; your humble dinner
Suffers inflation too. You feel ashamed to eat
Off earthenware dishes – yet if you were transported
To some rural village, you'd be content enough
And happily wear a cloak of coarse blue broadcloth
Complete with hood. Throughout most of Italy – we
Might as well admit it – no one is seen in a toga
Till the day he dies. Even on public holidays,
When the same old shows as last year are cheerfully staged
In the grassgrown theatre, when peasant children, sitting
On their mothers' laps, shrink back in terror at the sight
Of those gaping, whitened masks, you will still find the whole
Audience – top row or bottom – dressed exactly alike;
Even the magistrates need no better badge of status
Than a plain white tunic. But here in Rome we must toe
The line of fashion, living beyond our means, and
Often on borrowed credit: every man jack of us
Is keeping up with his neighbours. To cut a long story short,
Nothing's for free in Rome. How much does it cost you
To salute our noble Cossus (rare privilege!) or extract
One casual, tight-lipped nod from Veiento the honours-
    broker?[19]
X will be having his beard trimmed, Y just offering up
His boy-friend's kiss-curls: the whole house swarms with
    barbers,
Each of them on the make.[20] You might as well swallow
Your bile, and face the fact that we hangers-on
Have to bribe our way, swell some sleek menial's savings.
  'What countryman ever bargained, besides, for his house
    collapsing
About his ears? Such things are unheard-of in cool
Praeneste, or rural Gabii, or Tivoli perched on its hillside,
Or Volsinii, nestling amid its woodland ridges.[21] But here

We live in a city shored up, for the most part, with gimcrack
Stays and props: that's how our landlords arrest
The collapse of their property, papering over great cracks
In the ramshackle fabric, reassuring the tenants
They can sleep secure, when all the time the building
Is poised like a house of cards. I prefer to live where
Fires and midnight panics are not quite such common events.[22]
By the time the smoke's got up to your third-floor apartment
(And you still asleep) your heroic downstairs neighbour
Is roaring for water, and shifting | his bits and pieces to safety.
If the alarm goes at ground-level, the last to fry
Will be the attic tenant, way up among the nesting
Pigeons with nothing but tiles between himself and the
    weather.
What did friend Cordus own? One truckle bed, too short
For even a midget nympho; one marble-topped sideboard
On which stood six little mugs; beneath it, a pitcher
And an up-ended bust of Chiron; one ancient settle
Crammed with Greek books (though by now analphabetic mice
Had gnawed their way well into his texts of the great poets).
Cordus could hardly be called a property-owner, and yet
What little the poor man had, he lost. Today the final
Straw on his load of woe (clothes worn to tatters, reduced
To begging for crusts) is that no one will offer him lodging
Or shelter, not even stand him a decent meal. But if
Some millionaire's mansion is gutted, women rend their
    garments,
Top people put on mourning, the courts go into recess:
Then you hear endless complaints about the hazards
Of city life, these deplorable outbreaks of fire;
Then contributions pour in while the shell is still ash-hot –
Construction materials, marble, fresh-gleaming sculptured nudes.
Up comes A with bronzes (genuine antique works
By a real Old Master) acquired, as part of his booty,[23]
From their hallowed niche in some Asiatic temple;

B provides bookshelves, books, and a study bust of Minerva;
C a sackful of silver. So it goes on, until
This dandified bachelor's losses are all recouped –
And more than recouped – with even rarer possessions,
And a rumour (well-founded) begins to circulate
That he fired the place himself, a deliberate piece of arson.

   'If you can face the prospect of no more public games
Purchase a freehold house in the country. What it will cost
     you
Is no more than you pay in annual rent for some shabby
And ill-lit garret here. A garden plot's thrown in
With the house itself, and a well with a shallow basin –
No rope-and-bucket work when your seedlings need some
     water!
Learn to enjoy hoeing, work and plant your allotment
Till a hundred vegetarians could feast off its produce.
It's quite an achievement, even out in the backwoods,
To have made yourself master of – well, say one lizard, even.

   'Insomnia causes more deaths amongst Roman invalids
Than any other factor (the most common *complaints*, of course,
Are heartburn and ulcers, brought on by over-eating.)
How much sleep, I ask you, can one get in lodgings here?
Unbroken nights – and this is the root of the trouble –
Are a rich man's privilege. The waggons thundering past
Through those narrow twisting streets, the oaths of draymen
Caught in a traffic-jam – these alone would suffice
To jolt the doziest sea-cow of an Emperor[24] into
Permanent wakefulness. If a business appointment
Summons the tycoon, *he* gets there fast, by litter,
Tacking above the crowd. There's plenty of room inside:
He can read, or take notes, or snooze as he jogs along –
Those drawn blinds are most soporific. Even so
He outstrips us: however fast we pedestrians hurry
We're blocked by the crowds ahead, while those behind us
Tread on our heels. Sharp elbows buffet my ribs,

Poles poke into me; one lout swings a crossbeam
Down on my skull, another scores with a barrel.
My legs are mud-encrusted, big feet kick me, a hobnailed
Soldier's boot lands squarely on my toes. Do you see
All that steam and bustle? The great man's hangers-on
Are getting their free dinner, each with his own
Kitchen-boy in attendance. Those outsize dixies,
And all the rest of the gear one poor little slave
Must balance on his head, while he trots along
To keep the charcoal glowing, would tax the strength
Of a musclebound general. Recently-patched tunics
Are ripped to shreds. Here's the great trunk of a fir-tree
Swaying along on its waggon, and look, another dray
Behind it, stacked high with pine-logs, a nodding threat
Over the heads of the crowd. If that axle snapped, and a
Cartload of marble avalanched down on them, what
Would be left of their bodies? Who could identify bits
Of ownerless flesh and bone? The poor man's flattened corpse
Would vanish along with his soul. And meanwhile, all unwitting,
The folk at home are busily scouring dishes,
Blowing the fire to a glow, clattering over greasy
Flesh-scrapers, filling up oil-flasks, laying out clean towels.
But all the time, as his houseboys hasten about their chores,
Himself is already sitting – the latest arrival –
By the bank of the Styx, and gawping in holy terror
At its filthy old ferryman. No chance of a passage over
That mud-thick channel for him, poor devil, without so much
As a copper stuck in his mouth to pay for the ride.

   'There are other nocturnal perils, of various sorts,
Which you should consider. It's a long way up to the rooftops,
And a falling tile can brain you[25] – not to mention all
Those cracked or leaky pots that people toss out through
      windows.
Look at the way they smash, the weight of them, the damage
They do to the pavement! You'll be thought most improvident,

A catastrophe-happy fool, if you don't make your will before
Venturing out to dinner. Each open upper casement
Along your route at night may prove a death-trap:
So pray and hope (poor you!) that the local housewives
Drop nothing worse on your head than a pailful of slops.

   'Then there's the drunken bully, in an agonized state
For lack of a victim, who lies there tossing and turning
The whole night through, like Achilles after the death
Of his boy-friend Patroclus. [This lout is doomed to insomnia
Unless he gets a fight.] Yet however flown with wine
Our young hothead may be, he carefully keeps his distance
From the man in a scarlet cloak, the man surrounded
By torches and big brass lamps and a numerous bodyguard.
But for me, a lonely pedestrian, trudging home by moonlight
Or with hand cupped round the wick of one poor guttering
    candle,
He has no respect whatever. This is the way the wretched
Brawl comes about (if you can term it a brawl
When you do the fighting and I'm just cast as punchbag).
He blocks my way. "Stop," he says. I have no option
But to obey – what else can one do when attacked
By a huge tough, twice one's size and fighting-mad as well?
"Where have *you* sprung from?" he shouts. "Ugh, what a
    stench
Of beans and sour wine! I know your sort, you've been round
With some cobbler-crony, scoffing a boiled sheep's head
And a dish of spring leeks. What? Nothing to say for yourself?
Speak up, or I'll kick your teeth in! Tell me, where's your
    pitch?
What synagogue do you doss in?" It makes not a jot of
    difference
Whether you try to answer, or back away from him
Without saying a word, you get beaten up just the same –
And then your irate "victim" takes *you* to court on a charge
Of assault and battery. Such is the poor man's "freedom":

After being slugged to a pulp, he may beg, as a special
Favour, to be left with his last few remaining teeth.

'Nor is this the sum of your terrors: when every house
Is shut up for the night, when shops stand silent, when bolts
Are shot, and doors on the chain, there are still burglars
Lurking around, or maybe some street-apache will settle
Your hash with a knife, the quick way. (Whenever armed
      detachments
Are patrolling the swamps and forests, Rome becomes
A warren for this sort of scum.) Our furnaces glow, our anvils
Groan everywhere under their output of chains and fetters:
That's where most of our iron goes nowadays: one wonders
Whether ploughshares, hoes and mattocks may not soon be
      obsolete.
How fortunate they were (you well may think) those early
Forbears of ours, how happy the good old days
Of Kings and Tribunes, when Rome made do with one prison
      only!

  'There are many other arguments I could adduce: but the
      sun
Slants down, my cattle are lowing, I must be on my way —
The muleteer has been signalling me with his whip
For some while now. So goodbye, and don't forget me —
Whenever you go back home for a break from the City, invite
Me over too, to share your fields and coverts,
Your country festivals: I'll put on my thickest boots
And make the trip to those chilly uplands — and listen
To your *Satires*, if I am reckoned worthy of that honour.'

1. Cumae was the oldest Greek colony in Italy; it lay on the coast of Campania, six miles north of Cape Misenum. The rise of nearby Puteoli had turned it into a backwater. It was the Sibyl of Cumae who (as Petronius and T. S. Eliot remind us) hung in a bottle and, when asked her wishes, replied that she wanted to die. The inhabitants of Cumae were known as her 'citizens' – perhaps because she gave her oracles from a high, throne-like seat. The 'smartest water-spot' was Baiae, on the east coast of the Misenum peninsula.

2. The Porta Capena (now the Porta S. Sebastiana) stood close to the public fishmarket on the Appian Way: an aqueduct passed over it, hence the 'dripping arches'. Numa, the semi-mythical early King of Rome, was supposed to have got his laws through the divine inspiration of the nymph Egeria. J., following Livy, suggests that this was simply a cover for illicit intercourse. After the sack of Jerusalem by Titus in A.D. 70, many Jews made their way to Rome and eked out a scanty living as fortune-tellers or beggars. The 'Sabbath haybox' was for keeping food hot on a day when cooking was forbidden.

3. It is possible, though unlikely, that this Umbricius was the soothsayer mentioned by Tacitus and Plutarch as having predicted Galba's death, and who, according to the Elder Pliny, was the most distinguished *haruspex* of his age. The name is Etruscan, and not known elsewhere from our literary sources; but a tombstone has been found, in near-by Puteoli, commemorating the daughter of one A. Umbricius Magnus, who may have been J.'s friend.

4. The Romans made a firm distinction between the 'liberal arts and professions' which a free citizen might practise, and those 'sordid' or 'illiberal' occupations reserved for slaves, foreigners, and the lower orders generally.

5. Daedalus, as we learn from Virgil, ended his flight at Cumae. The periphrastic description is typical not only of J. – who has, as Duff observes, 'a great liking for describing places and persons by a periphrasis giving some historical or mythological details about

them' – but of Augustan and post-Augustan poets in general: it is an inheritance from the Alexandrian tradition.

6. i.e. practised maleficent magic against an enemy: the reference is not, as is generally supposed, either to divination or to poisoning, but to magical spells. The frog was commonly employed in such formulae, perhaps on account of its uncanny squamousness; the parts most commonly utilized were the tongue and the gut.

7. The Governor of Sicily against whom Cicero delivered his famous prosecution speeches on charges of embezzlement and extortion. The names passed into the language: Verres became the type and emblem of the rapacious provincial administrator.

8. J.'s violent dislike for the Greeks had good literary antecedents. Cato and the Elder Pliny, among others, detested them: in particular they were prejudiced against Greek doctors, whom they regarded as quacks and profiteers. Cf. below, Satire VI 187–93, 295 ff.

9. The Orontes, now the Nahr el-Asi, was the largest river in ancient Syria; it rose in the hills near Damascus and flowed northwards by Epiphania and Apamea, turning sharply south-west by Antioch to the sea. Syrian slaves were at a premium; and Syrian girl-harpists and timbrel-players were known in Rome as early as 189 B.C. Inevitably, they also became prostitutes. For the race-course or Circus Maximus as a whores' beat, see below, Satire VI 582–91.

10. Daedalus was traditionally supposed to have been a well-born Athenian: J.'s main objection to him (apart from his nationality) seems to have been that he was, in every sense of the phrase, flying in the face of nature.

11. Purple robes were only worn by certain senators on specific official occasions, under both Caesar and Augustus. Nero forbade the sale of Tyrian purple altogether. Romans asked their friends to witness such documents as wills, marriage-contracts, and slave-manumissions. The order of witnessing was dictated by social status.

12. The three types of feminine role in Greek-style comedies (*palliatae*) at Rome were (a) courtesans, e.g. Thais in Terence's *Eunuch*; (b) *matrones*, i.e. ladies of a household; (c) maids or slave-girls, *ancillae*. These parts were played by men: Columella also comments on the homosexual's ability to imitate women.

13. The two most common explanations of line 108 have to assume (a) that a drinking-cup gurgles as the last drop leaves it; or

(b) that most chamber-pots have false bottoms. It is, surely, easier to take lines 107-8 in conjunction: the basin or ladle (*trulla*) was placed upside-down on the floor, and the dinner-guests urinated at it in competition. The Greek applauds when his Roman patron hits the target squarely, 'with a splendid drumming sound'.

14. I follow Jacoby in reading *nihil huic* here, but substitute *vel* for his *et*: most MSS read *nihil aut*. I assume *huic* to have dropped out by false reading and haplography after *nihil*, and *aut* then to have been substituted for *vel* by a stupid scribe trying to mend matters.

15. Most editors take the words within brackets as an interpolation. I believe they are genuine: the unexplained change from singular to plural suggests rather that a line has been lost after 112, the sense of which would be: 'But such creatures do not even desire sexual pleasure for its own sake', etc.

16. The Stoic informer was Publius Egnatius Celer; Tacitus gives a graphic account (*Annals* 16.23.33, pp. 378 ff.) of how his victim, Barea Soranus, was accused and met his death at Nero's hands. Celer's birthplace is here identified as Tarsus on the River Cydnus; Dio Cassius claimed that he was born in Beirut and only educated at Tarsus, where Bellerophon's fall from Pegasus was supposed to have taken place. *Pinna* (*tarsos* in Greek) is either a feather or a hoof: hence the town's name. Pegasus was traditionally supposed to have sprung from the Gorgon Medusa's blood after decapitation by Perseus. 'Nag' is a deliberately derogatory, debunking term for the mythical flying steed.

17. In 205 B.C. a Sibylline prophecy foretold that foreign invasion could only be averted by bringing to Rome the cult-image of the Ideaean Mother from Pessinus in Phrygia. The following year P. Cornelius Scipio Nasica – though not yet even a quaestor – was chosen, on account of his purity and virtue, to convey the image from the ship to the matrons who were to guard it. In 241 B.C. the temple of Minerva was burnt, and L. Caecilius Metellus was blinded while rescuing the Palladium, or statue of Minerva, from the flames. For Numa see above, n.2. His wisdom and virtue (despite the Egeria episode, and an interesting weakness for primitive electrical experiments) were proverbial.

18. The first fourteen rows of seats behind the *orchestra* in a Roman theatre were reserved for the *equites*, or 'knights': this privilege was

established by the tribune L. Roscius Otho in 67 B.C. As the rank of *eques* carried a property qualification of 400,000 sesterces, poor men were automatically excluded from good seats. Technically, the *eques* also had to prove free birth for two generations on his father's side – which clearly does not apply in these instances. J.'s point is that the rich can flout the law with impunity, whereas the poor can't. The wealth of auctioneers was proverbial; but the profession was despised. Cf. below, Satire VII 5–12.

19. The name Cossus (a very ancient and distinguished one) is used to symbolize the aristocracy; cf. below, Satire VIII 21. Our Cossus was an advocate (VII 144) and a legacy-hunter (X 202). Veiento we shall meet again: see below, Satire IV 113 ff. and VI 82–113. An honours-broker (and praetor) under Nero, he was expelled from Italy in A.D. 62 for perpetrating a libellous mock-will. Under Domitian he was an informer, but (to many people's disgust) contrived to remain on good terms with Domitian's successor Nerva, even occupying a prominent position in the Senate, and becoming consul three times. He had a curious hobby of training dogs to pull go-carts, like horses.

20. At line 187 for *libis* of the MSS, which makes no satisfactory sense (witness the number of explanations it has elicited), I conjecture *Licinis*. Some kind of *venal person* (rather than a cake for sale) is demanded by the context: Licinus was a celebrated freedman of Augustus, a barber – peculiarly apt in this context – famous for the wealth he amassed. J. refers to him at Satire I 109.

21. Praeneste (the modern Palestrina), Gabii (Castiglione) and Tibur (Tivoli) are all in J.'s part of Latium, between 10 and 30 miles from Rome. Volsinii (Bolsena) lies about 80 miles north-west of Rome, in Etruria, on the lake of the same name. All were quiet rural retreats: Gabii (cf. below Satire X 100) was almost deserted.

22. The double danger of fire and collapsing houses became almost proverbial under the Empire. Jerry-built apartment blocks were run up to considerable heights in an effort to combat over-crowding: the upper storeys were usually constructed of wood. Fires were frequent and (since both water-supplies and fire-services were ill-regulated) tended to be devastating. See Carcopino 34 ff.

23. Lines 217–18: I read *praedarum* and *aera* with Housman. Giangrande (see Bibliography, p. 300) retains the reading *phaecas-*

ianorum, rather than *haec Asianorum*, and suggests (on the principle of *lectio difficilior*) that J. was referring to the gods of local *Greek* officialdom, the *phaecasium* being a special white shoe affected by – among others – Athenian gymnasiarchs.

24. No wheeled traffic was permitted in the streets of Rome for ten hours after dawn: the night, as many writers from Horace to Martial testify, was constantly disturbed by rumbling carts and shouting drovers. The worst sufferers were the poor, who lived in tenements above the main thoroughfares. The 'doziest sea-cow of an Emperor' was probably Claudius, who had a habit of cat-napping in public: see Suetonius, *Claudius* 8 (p. 186; cf. p. 201). The connexion with sea-cows or seals is explained in Seneca's *Apocolocyntosis* 5, where Claudius's voice is described as 'a kind of hoarse inarticulate bark, like a sea-beast'. Seals were also believed – as Pliny's *Natural History* shows – to have curious sleepy habits: so the joke was doubly appropriate.

25. Cf. above, n. 22. Even after the Great Fire of A.D. 64, and despite repeated legislation on the subject (Trajan, for instance, imposed a limit of 60 feet on the height of frontages), 'skyscrapers' continued to be built well above the safety margin. Only the upper storeys had windows looking out on the road.

ADDITIONAL NOTE

At line 68 I have revised my translation of *ceromatico* in accordance with Reinmuth's cogent remarks (Additional Bibliography) about the new fad, under the Empire, of wrestling in mud: see also below, Satire VI 246, and additional note ad loc.

SATIRE IV

Here's Crispinus again,[1] and I shall have frequent occasion
To parade him before you – a monster of wickedness
Without one redeeming virtue, a sick voluptuary
Strong only in his lusts, which draw the line at nothing
Except unmarried girls . . .[2]

                    . . . So what are all his possessions
Worth in the end – those mile-long colonnades[3]
And shady parks where he drives with his carriage and pair,
His countless mansions, his property just off the Forum?
No evildoer can flourish, least of all the seducer, whose crime
Is compounded with sacrilege, for whom not so long ago
A priestess, a Vestal Virgin, broke her vows, and was doomed
To be buried alive, the blood still hot in her veins.[4]
But now to a lighter topic – though if any other man had done
The same, he'd have had the authorities on his tail:
For what would be reprehensible in Citizen A or B
Was quite all right for Crispinus. What's to be done
When the man himself is so much more revolting
Than any charge you can bring against him? He bought a red
Mullet for sixty gold pieces – ten to each pound weight,
To make it sound more impressive. A shrewd investment,
    perhaps,
If he'd used it to make some childless dotard name him
A principal legatee; or, better, presented it
To his expensive mistress, the kind who goes abroad
In a grotto-like sedan, blinds drawn. But no, he bought it
For his own consumption. We see things done today
Undreamed-of by that pinchpenny gourmet Apicius.[5]
Did *you* pay so much for a fish, Crispinus, you who once
Went around in a loin-cloth of your native papyrus? Why,
You could have bought the fisherman for less than the fish,
    cash down,

Or a nice provincial estate, or a regular ranch in Apulia
Where land goes at knock-down prices. What kind of menu
    was it
That the Emperor guzzled himself, I wonder, when all that
    gold –
Just a fraction of the whole, the merest modest side-dish –
Was belched up by this purple-clad Palace nark, this
Senior Knight who once went bawling his wares
(Job-lots of catfish from some wholesaler's auction)
Through the Alexandrian back-streets? O Muse of Epic, begin! –
You can sit down for the job, by the way, and singing's out –
This is real life, the truth. Say on then, Pierian virgins,
(And I hope that calling you 'virgins' will work to my
    advantage).
    In the days when the last Flavian was flaying a half-dead world,
And Rome was in thrall to a bald Nero,[6] there swam
Into a net in the Adriatic, hard by Ancona,
Where the shrine of Venus stands on her headland, a monstrous
Turbot, a regular whopper, as huge as those tunny that spend
All winter under the frozen Sea of Azov, and at last,
Torpid with sloth, fat from long hibernation,
When the spring sun melts the ice, are borne down-current
To the mouth of the Black Sea. This splendid catch the owner
Of boat and trawl has earmarked for Rome's High Priest,[7]
His Imperial Majesty – since who would dare put up
Such a fish to auction, or buy it, when the very seashore
    swarms
With narks and informers? Every Inspector of Seaweed
From miles around would pounce on this wretched boatman,
All quoting law, to wit, that the fish had strayed from Caesar's
Imperial stews, and must at once be restored to
Its former master. If X and Y the legal pundits
Are to be trusted, everything rare and beautiful
That swims in the ocean, wheresoever, remains
Crown property. So, rather than spoil such a turbot,

Let it be given away, a royal present.
                                    Now autumn
With its pestilential winds was yielding to winter's frosts;
Now patients were hopeful for milder, third-day fevers,
And icy blasts helped keep the turbot refrigerated.
On sped the fisherman, as though blown by a south wind,
Till below him lay the lakes where Alba, though in ruins,
Still guards the flame of Troy and the lesser Vestal shrine.[8]
A wondering crowd thronged round him, blocking his way for
     a little
Till the doors on their smooth hinges swung inward, the
     crowd gave way,
And the Senators – still shut out – saw the fish admitted to
The Imperial Presence. 'Accept,' the fisherman said, 'this
     oblation
Too large for a private kitchen. Keep holiday today,
Purge your stomach forthwith of its last square meal
And prepare to eat a turbot saved to adorn your reign –
It insisted on being caught.' Most palpable flattery, yet
The imperial plumage rose: there is nothing godlike power
Will refuse to believe of itself in the way of commendation.
But alas, no big enough dish could be found for the fish. A
     summons
Went out to the Privy Council, each of whom quailed beneath
The Emperor's hatred, whose drawn white faces reflected
That great and perilous 'friendship'.[9] First there in response
To the chamberlain's call of 'Hurry! His Majesty is seated!'
Was Pegasus,[10] clutching his cloak all anyhow, Pegasus
The bewildered City's lately-appointed bailiff –
For what else, in those days, could you call the City Prefect
But a bailiff? Still, Pegasus made as devoted
And righteous a jurist as any – although he held in practice
That those troubled times were warrant for Justice pulling her
     punches
On every occasion.[11] Next came the aged, genial Crispus,[12]

Whose manners – like his morals – were mild and pliable.
 No one
Could better have served to advise a monarch with absolute
 sway
Over seas and lands and nations – if only he had been free,
Under that scourge, that plague, to tender honest counsel,
Speak out against cruelty. But what could be more capricious
Than a tyrant's ear, when the fate of his so-called friends and
 advisers
Hung on his word? Best play safe, stick to the weather –
How rainy or hot it's been, how spring showers are here again.
So Crispus never struck out against the current, never
Uttered his private opinions, or staked his life on the truth;
And so he survived many winters, to reach his eightieth year,
Safeguarded, even in *that* Court, by such defensive techniques.
 After him hurried in another elderly statesman,
Acilius, with his son, a youth who ill-deserved
The harsh, too-imminent fate in store for him, cut down
By Authority's sword.[13] Longevity and breeding
Are so rare a conjunction today, so portentous, I'd rather be
A son of the soil, a shrimpling brother to giants.[14]
Poor wretch, the trouble he took – stripped off and sticking
 bears
In that private country arena! No good. Such patrician gambits
Are common knowledge today, the tricks old Brutus knew
Take no one in. Too easy to gull a bearded monarch.[15]
Next, no more cheerful-looking, despite his plebeian blood,
Came Rubrius,[16] years ago found guilty of an offence
Best not referred to, yet still more shameless than some queer
Satirist knocking queers. Montanus'[17] belly next
Hove into view, that slow gross paunch, and – reeking
With pre-noon scent, worse than a brace of funerals –
Crispinus; then Pompeius,[18] his match in ruthlessness,
Whose whisper slit men's throats; Fuscus,[19] who dreamed of
 battle

Lolling in marbled halls, his guts a predestined
Feast for Rumania's vultures; Veiento the trimmer,[20]
And deadly Catullus,[21] burning for love of a girl
He had never seen, a monster – even by current standards –
In a class of his own, blind fawner and ominous underling
Whose department was Roads and Bridges: none better suited
To beg at carriage-wheels outside Ariccia, blowing
Kisses to every coach as it lumbered down the hill.
His double-take at the turbot was unsurpassed, he went on
And on about it, staring left – though the creature
Happened to be on his right. (In similar fashion
He would give a running commentary, blow by blow,
On a boxer's[22] ringcraft, or the ascent of the hoist
That whisks boy-acrobats up to the awnings.) But now
Veiento, intent on holding his own, like some frenzied
Priest of the Mother-Goddess, burst out in prophetic
Utterance. 'A mighty omen!' he cried, 'a sign
Of great and glorious victory! You will capture
Some king – perhaps Arviragus of the Britons[23]
Will tumble out of his chariot: he's a foreigner
And so is the fish. Just look | at that row of spines protruding
Along its back.' All that Veiento left out was
The creature's age and birthplace.
                                    'Then what is your advice?
Shall we cut him up?' '*Him?*' Montanus cried, 'no, no –
Spare him that last indignity! Let a deep casserole
Be procured, large enough to contain his massive bulk
Within its fragile walls! Some mighty Prometheus
Must be found, at once, for the making of such a dish –
Quick, fetch clay and a wheel – but henceforward, Caesar,
Let potters always be numbered among your retinue.'
    Motion carried – and worthy of such a proposer. He'd known
The old Imperial Court and its luxuries, Neronian
Banquets that sharpened dull appetites at midnight
A second time, when guests were awash with vintage wine,

Their veins on fire. No man in my day was a greater
Gourmet: he knew, at the very first bite, what bed
An oyster came from, Circeii, Lake Lucrinus
Or Richborough: sea-urchins he placed with a single glance.

   All rose. The meeting was over, the Councillors dismissed.
Yet their mighty master had sent an emergency summons
Which brought them all posthaste, in a lather of terror,
To his country castle. He could have had fresh news
Of trouble across the Rhine, or among the hairy Prussians;
Panic-stricken dispatches might have been pouring in
From all parts of the empire. Yet would that such nonsense
Had absorbed all his savage instincts! He robbed Rome
Of her best and noblest sons, unopposed. No hand was raised
To avenge them. He could welter in noble blood. But
Once the commons began to fear him, then he was done for.[34]

1. See above, Satire I 26, with n. 4. These are, in fact, the only two satires where Crispinus is mentioned; so either J. changed his mind, or some of his work is lost.

2. It seems clear that at least one line, and possibly much more, has fallen out between lines 4 and 5. The whole passage from 5–10 clearly refers to a previous description of Crispinus's downfall, or mortality, or both, and comes as a complete *non sequitur* after the introductory sketch. Neither emendation (e.g. Housman's desperate *cum sit* for *minime*) nor the removal of line 8 as an 'interpolation' will really do. There are, I believe, many more sins of omission than commission in J.'s text (the 'O passage' in Satire VI is only the best-known example); and though – as the scholiast reveals – that text has, on occasion, been tampered with, most of the more obvious alterations seem to have been made in an attempt to cobble together broken fragments where something had been lost.

3. These enormous covered colonnades, in which the wealthy could ride or drive protected from the weather, are referred to again in Satire VII 178 ff., and also by Martial. There were no less than three of them in Nero's Golden House, each 1,000 feet long (Suetonius, *Nero* 31, pp. 224–5).

4. Domitian revived the ancient punishment of burying unchaste Vestal Virgins alive: this allusion is almost certainly to the death of the Virgin Cornelia in A.D. 91 for intercourse with various lovers – including an unnamed Roman *eques* who may, but need not, have been Crispinus.

5. M. Gabius Apicius lived in the reigns of Augustus and Tiberius, and was renowned both for his *gourmandise* and his extravagance. It is said that after he had spent the rough equivalent of £1,000,000 he balanced his books, found he had no more than 100,000 gold pieces left, and poisoned himself, on the grounds that no gourmet could be expected to live on such a pittance. The cookery-book associated with his name is a late compilation.

6. The 'bald Nero' was Domitian, who lost his hair in middle age and 'took as a personal insult any reference, joking or otherwise, to

bald men, being extremely sensitive about his own appearance'
(Suetonius, *Domitian* 18, p. 308). The whole passage, including the
invocation, is a deliberate parody of the epic convention, in particu-
lar of a lost poem by Statius on Domitian's German wars. (On this,
and the *consilium Principis* of Domitian in general, with a useful
prosopographical analysis, see now Griffith, Additional Biblio-
graphy.) Four lines of this poem survive: it is interesting that they
mention no less than three of the *amici Principis* (Privy Councillors)
whom J. goes on to satirize by name.

7. All the Emperors, from Augustus onwards, assumed the title of
Pontifex Maximus.

8. The two lakes were the *lacus Albanus* and the *lacus Nemorensis*.
Alba Longa was supposedly founded by Ascanius son of Aeneas,
who removed his seat of government thither from Lavinium. Its
destruction was due to the Roman king Tullus Hostilius, but the
temples were spared (some were still standing in Augustus's day)
and a sacred flame alleged to have been brought from Troy still
burnt there. Domitian resided permanently at his villa on the site;
the fisherman must have brought the turbot to Rome from Ancona,
and thence along the Via Appia to Alba.

9. The Imperial *consilium Principis*, or Privy Council, was instituted
by Augustus, more formally established by Tiberius, and continued
by subsequent Emperors. This quasi-Cabinet seems to have consisted
of the leading senators, such as the Consuls and City Prefect, and the
Equestrians with key posts – e.g. the Prefect of Egypt and the
Commander of the Praetorian Guard. A member of the Council
was known as *amicus Caesaris*, or 'friend of Caesar'. Other writers
beside J. (such as Pliny and Tacitus) allude to the irony of this term
under Domitian, and the terror which such an Imperial summons
might induce. Certain *amici* had the additional and still more
honourable title of *comes*, 'companion' – just as some of their
modern equivalents are Privy Counsellors.

10. He had been *consul suffectus* in Vespasian's reign, and after-
wards was governor of several provinces before becoming City
Prefect under Domitian. He acquired great fame as a jurist: his
learning was such, we are told, that men thought him a walking
book rather than a human being. He was the son of a trireme-

commander, and derived his name from the figurehead on his father's pinnace.

11. I read, and punctuate, *sanctissimus – omnia quamquam* at line 79.

12. Q. Vibius Crispus was from Vercellae; three times consul, including a spell as *consul suffectus* under Nero in 61, and probably for the last time in 83, with Veiento as his colleague. He held a pro-consulship in Africa between 71 and 75, and was also Inspector of Aqueducts. He was a drinking companion of Vitellius, and Quintilian describes him as a witty man: his standard of wit may be judged from an anecdote in Suetonius (*Domitian* 3, p. 297): 'At the beginning of his reign Domitian would spend hours alone every day catching flies – believe it or not! – and stabbing them with a needle-sharp pen. Once, on being asked whether anyone was closeted with the Emperor, Vibius Crispus answered wittily: "No, not even a fly." '

13. Acilius Glabrio the elder is only mentioned here: he would be about eighty at the time, and we can place his *floruit* under Claudius or Nero. His son was consul, together with the future Emperor Trajan, in 91. Why he fought bears (and a huge lion too, it seems) in Domitian's private arena is doubtful. He may have wanted to convince the Emperor he was mad, and therefore harmless; he may have hoped to impress him with a display of gladiatorial expertise; or he may have been forced to perform by Domitian, who sus-pected him of treason, but could not prove his suspicions. At all events, he was afterwards exiled as a revolutionary, and in 95 executed, the charge being augmented with one of 'atheism and ... Jewish customs'. The name Acilius Glabrio is found in the catacomb of Priscilla, and it seems likely that this Acilius was in fact a Christian convert.

14. All giants were supposed to be 'earth-born', like Antaeus; but the Latin term, *terrae filius*, also meant 'a son of the soil' in the sense of 'a nobody'.

15. The reference is to L. Junius Brutus, who by feigning feeble-mindedness persuaded his uncle, Tarquinius Superbus, that he did not constitute a threat to the throne. A 'bearded king' symbolizes old-fashioned simplicity. Africanus Minor first set the fashion for daily shaving, and it was not till Hadrian's day that the beard

returned. I have sometimes wondered whether the whole passage may not contain a sly reference to Hadrian's weakness for 'advanced' literature, and his consequent gullibility where fraudulent *avant-gardisme* was concerned; there is, similarly, something very ambiguous about the opening of Satire VII, on Imperial patronage for the arts.

16. Rubrius Gallus was a veteran military commander: he fought for Nero against Galba and Verginius Rufus in 68, and later for Otho against Vitellius, perhaps as commander of the Praetorian Guard. He sided with Vespasian, who appointed him governor of Moesia. According to the scholiast, his 'unspeakable crime' was the seduction of either Domitia Longina or Titus's daughter Julia, in either case while the girl was still a minor.

17. Perhaps T. Junius Montanus, *consul suffectus* in 81 and a friend of Nero's. The Curtius Montanus expelled from the Senate in 66 for lampooning Nero may have been his son.

18. This unpleasant character is otherwise unknown.

19. Cornelius Fuscus supported Vespasian against Vitellius in 69, and is highly praised by Tacitus for his qualities of leadership. He lived in retirement on his estate during Nero's reign, but was appointed procurator of Pannonia by Galba. The fleet at Ravenna elected him commander in the campaign against Vitellius, and Vespasian rewarded him with the rank of praetor. Domitian appointed him Praetorian Prefect, and sent him out as general in the second Dacian War of 86/7, during which his army was annihilated and he himself killed. Dacia was roughly equivalent to the modern Rumania.

20. For A. Didius Gallus Fabricius Veiento see above, Satire III 185 and n. 19. His wife may have been the Eppia who ran off with a gladiator: see below, Satire VI 113.

21. The blind informer Catullus – L. Valerius Catullus Messalinus – was consul in 79 with Domitian, and did not outlive him, though he seems to have been active and influential as late as 93. Lines 116–19: Beggars traditionally had their 'stands' or 'pitches' on bridges or at the bottom of hills, to catch the traffic as it slowed down. Ariccia – a favourite haunt of beggars in Martial's and Juvenal's day – is in a hollow on the Via Appia, about twenty miles south of Rome. The

phrase *a ponte* (116) perhaps parodies the titles of the Imperial Secretaries: *ab epistulis, a secretis,* etc.

22. I accept Hirschfeld's emendation of *pugnos* for *pugnas.*

23. According to Caesar, the British in battle habitually ran out along the pole of their chariot and fought from the yoke. The name Arviragus is mentioned by Geoffrey of Monmouth: Shakespeare borrowed it for *Cymbeline.* But nothing substantial is known of him.

24. Domitian's murderers were his niece Domitilla's steward Stephanus, an officer called Clodianus, a freedman named Maximus, a chamberlain, Satur, and an unnamed Imperial gladiator (Suetonius, *Domitian* 17, p. 307). So far some sort of justification for J.'s gibe about 'the commons' can be made out. But in fact all these were Palace retainers, and the plot was a Palace conspiracy instigated by Domitian's wife. The working-classes had no more to fear from him than from any other Emperor. J.'s knowledge of the proletariat is almost as deficient as his sympathies for them.

SATIRE V

If you claim your mind is made up still, Trebius,[1] if you
    remain
Unashamed of the life you propose, and count it the highest
Good to scrape crumbs from another man's board; if you swear
You can swallow iniquities such as the lowest wits and jesters
Of Augustus's court would have gagged on, I'll doubt your
    word
Even on oath. True, I know nothing more cheaply
Satisfied than a belly. Yet suppose the bare subsistence
Needed to fill its void is lacking — are there no sidewalks
Or bridges,[2] no quarter-share in a beggar's mat
For you to make your pitch from? Is your hunger quite
So all-devouring? Is dinner worth every insult
With which you pay for it? Wouldn't your self-respect
Be better served if you stuck it out where you are,
Shivering cold, on a diet of mouldy dog's bread?

   Get one thing clear from the start: a dinner-invitation
Settles the score in full for all your earlier
Services. This great 'friendship' produces — food. Each meal,
However infrequent, your patron reckons against you
To square his accounts. So if, after two months' neglect,
With the bottom place to be filled at the lowest table,
He says 'Be my guest' to you, his forgotten retainer,
You're beside yourself with joy. What more could Trebius
Hope for? Now at last he has his reward — though it means
Cutting his sleep short, hurrying out in the dark with
Shoelaces trailing, all in a pother for fear lest
Everyone's done the rounds already, paid their respects
Before the stars have vanished, while the chill constellations
Are circling the heavens still.

                  Yet — heavens! — what a dinner!
The wine's so rough sheep-clippings wouldn't absorb it,

And turns the guests into raving madmen. At first
It's only insults – but soon a regular battle
Breaks out between you and the freedmen, cheap crockery flies
In all directions, you're slinging cups yourself
And mopping the blood off with a crimsoned table-napkin.
The wine that Virro,³ your host, is drinking has lain in its
    bottle
Since the consuls wore long hair: those grapes were trodden
During the Social Wars⁴ – yet never a glassful
Will he send to a friend with heartburn. Tomorrow he'll
    choose
Some other vintage, the best, a jar so blackened with smoke,
So ancient, that its source and date are illegible:
Such wine our Stoic martyrs would toss down, garlanded,
On the birthday of Brutus or Cassius.⁵ The goblets Virro
Drinks from are regular tankards, amber-encrusted,
Studded with beryl. But *you* get no golden vessels –
Or if you do, a waiter is stationed by you
To count the jewels, check your sharp fingernails.
You must forgive him: that jasper of his is widely
Admired, a collector's piece. Virro, like many others,
Has switched his gems from his fingers to his wine-cups.
(Our ancient heroes – Aeneas for instance – kept such
Gauds for their scabbards.) No, the cup *you* drink from
Will be the sort with four big nozzles – named
After Nero's long-nosed cobbler from Beneventum⁶ –
Shoddy and cracked, crying out for cement to mend it.

    If my lord's stomach is heated by wine and food, then
Ice-water, sterilized, chiller than mountain snow-drifts
Is brought him at once. Just now I complained of the difference
Between your wine and his – but the same applies
To the very water you drink. *Your* cups are proffered
By some Saharan groom, or in the bony hand
Of a blackavised Moor, whom you'd much prefer *not* to meet
    while

Driving uphill, at night, past the tombs on the Latin Way.
But himself has the flower of Asia before him, a youth
Purchased for more than those early Roman kings could
Scrape up between them, cash and chattels together –
Warrior Tullus, Ancus, the lot.⁷ So when you're thirsty
Catch your black Ganymede's eye. A boy whose price-ticket
Ran into thousands won't mix drinks for a bum –
Though such youth, such beauty excuse his disdain. Will he
    ever
Get round to you? If you ask him for hot or cold water
Do you suppose he will fetch it? Not likely: it's beneath him
To serve some crumbling dependent, he fiercely resents
The smallest request, even the fact that you're seated
While he's on his feet. Great houses are always crammed
With these supercilious minions. Here comes another:
Look how he grumbles as he hands out the bread, although
It's so hard you can scarcely break it, solidified
Lumps of old mouldy dough that crack your grinders
Sooner than let you bite them. But the loaf reserved for my
    lord
Is snowy-white, fresh-baked from the very finest flour.
And remember, please, to keep your hands to yourself, to
    show
A proper respect for the bread-pan. Yet if by chance you
    presume
And reach for a slice, someone is bound to make you
Drop it at once: 'The impertinence! Keep to your own
Basket *if* you please, learn the colour of your bread!'
'Was it for this,' you wail, 'that day after day
I left my wife so early, went hurrying up the steep
And chilly Esquiline streets,⁸ while violent springtime
Hailstorms bombarded me, or some sudden cloudburst
Beat through my sodden cloak? Was it for this?'
    Just get the size of that crayfish: it marks out a platter
Reserved for my lord. See the asparagus garnish

Heaped high around it, the peacocking tail that looks down
On the other guests as it's brought in, borne aloft
By some strapping waiter. But *you* get half an egg
Stuffed with one prawn, dished up in a little saucer
Like a funeral offering.9 Himself souses his fish
With the finest oil, but *your* colourless boiled cabbage
Will stink of the lamp; the stuff you use as a dressing
Came to town in some native felucca. One good sniff,
And you know why Africans always get plenty of clearance
At the public baths. Rub it on as a prophylactic
Against venomous snakes – they won't come anywhere near you.
     My lord will have his mullet, imported from Corsica or from
The rocks below Taormina: home waters are all fished out
To fill such ravening maws, our local breeding-grounds
Are trawled without cease, the market never lets up –
We kill off the fry now, close seasons go by the board.
Today we import from abroad for domestic consumption:
     these
Are the luxury fish which legacy-hunters purchase,
And which their spinster quarries sell back to the retailer.
Virro is served with a lamprey: no finer specimen
Ever came from Sicilian waters. When the south wind lies low,
Drying damp wings in his cell, then hardy fishermen
Will dare the wrath of the Straits. But what's in store for you?
An eel, perhaps (though it looks like a water-snake), or
A grey-mottled river-pike, born and bred in the Tiber,
Bloated with sewage, a regular visitor to
The cesspools underlying the slums of the Subura.10
     A word with himself now – if he will deign to listen.
'No one expects such generous gifts today
As the old Republican gentry11 once bestowed on
Their humbler friends. In those times such largesse
Brought more honour than title or office. All we ask
Is – dine with us as an equal. Do this, and no one cares
If you follow the current fashion, keep your wealth for yourself,

Act poor to your friends. Go ahead.'
                              What comes in next?
Himself is served with a force-fed goose's liver,
A capon as big as the goose itself, and a spit-roast
Boar, all piping hot, well worthy of fair-haired
Meleager's steel. Afterwards, if it's springtime,
And there's been sufficient thunder to bring them on,
Truffles appear. 'Ah, Africa!' cries the gourmet,
'You can keep your grain-supply, unyoke your oxen,
So long as you send us truffles!' Meanwhile, to ensure that
No cause for resentment is lacking, behold the carver
Prancing about, with flourishes of his knife,
Obedient to all his master's instructions: no
Small matter to make a nice distinction between the
Carving of hares and hens!
                              If you ever dare
To hold forth as though you were someone, a man with a
      double
Handle to his name, you'll find yourself being dragged
Out of there by the heels, and bounced from the front-door
Like one of Hercules' victims, the badman of the legend.¹²
When will Virro toast *you*, or offer to drink from the cup
Your lips have touched? Which of you is so reckless,
So desperate-bold as to call to the Lord of the Feast
'A health with you, sir'? No, there are plenty of privileges
Which out-at-elbows men are forbidden to exercise. *But*
If some god, or mere godlike human, one kindlier than the
      Fates,
Capitalized you for knighthood¹³ – then see how you'd jump
From nowhere to the position of Virro's dear, dear friend!
'Give Trebius this! A helping of that for Trebius!
Will you try some tenderloin, brother?' But it's your cash
That earns his respect, your cash that's truly his brother.
If you're aiming right for the top, though – to be a magnate
      yourself

And a patron of magnates – don't have a small heir playing
Soldiers around the house with his young, enchanting sister:
Barrenness in your wife makes for cheerful, attentive friends.
But as things are now, even should your wife present you
With triplets, still Virro will offer congratulations
On your squalling brood, send each a green baby-coat,
And later play uncle to them with peanuts and pennies
Whenever the little freeloaders turn up at dinner-time.

    For the lower-income guests, some dubious toadstools:
For my lord, a dish of such mushrooms as Claudius guzzled
(Until that one prepared by his wife, after which
He never touched food again). To himself, and his fellow-
    tycoons,
Virro has choice fruits served, their scent a feast in itself,
Fruit such as grew in Phaeacia's eternal autumn,[14]
Or might, you feel, have been rifled from the Hesperides.
For yourself, a rotten apple, only fit to be munched
By those performing monkeys you see along the
    Embankment,[15]
Dressed up with shield and helmet, cringing beneath the whip
As they learn to hurl a spear from the back of some shaggy
    she-goat.

    You imagine Virro's a chiseller? Hardly. He does it to
Make you suffer, for kicks. What farce or pantomime
Could be a bigger joke than your empty, rumbling belly?
So – in case you didn't get it – his whole idea's to reduce you
To tears of rage, an endless grinding of teeth.
You see yourself as a free man, guest at the magnate's banquet;
But *he* assumes you've been hooked by his kitchen's delectable
Odours – and not far wrong. No self-respecting person,
Whether born to purple or homespun, however
    down-and-out –
Would endure *that* twice. It's the hope of a good dinner
That lures you on. 'Surely he'll give us a picked-over
Hare, some scraps from the boar's haunch? Surely a chicken's

Carcase will come our way?' So you sit there, dumb
And expectant, all of you, clutching untasted rolls.
He's no fool to abuse you like this. If you can swallow
The whole treatment – why, you deserve no better. Some day
You'll find yourself meekly bending your shaven pate to be
    cuffed,
Like a public buffoon,[16] well inured to the whip, a worthy
Companion for such a feast – and for such a friend.

1. A Trebius Sergianus was consul in A.D. 132, under Hadrian; it is pleasant to think that this might conceivably be the same man, and that Fortune, after his early humiliations, smiled on him in his later years. The name also occurs several times in inscriptions from J.'s birthplace, Aquinum.

2. See above, Satire IV, n. 21.

3. The name Virro is uncommon. J. uses it once again, in Satire IX, to portray a homosexual, who may possibly be the person referred to here. The best-known historical holder of the name, Vibidius Virro, was in A.D. 17 expelled from the Senate by Tiberius for dissolute behaviour. Professor Syme has suggested that the family was Paelignian: if so, it came from within forty miles of Aquinum.

4. The 'Social Wars' – perhaps 'Wars with the Allies' would be a better translation, but 'Social Wars' has been canonized by long usage – lasted from 91 to 88 B.C. They were, essentially, a general rebellion against Rome by her Italian allies, who, after the assassination of their champion, the tribune Livius Drusus, saw no hope of obtaining full Roman enfranchisement by peaceful means.

5. The 'Stoic martyrs' were Thrasea Paetus and his son-in-law, Helvidius Priscus, who both lost their lives as a result of aggressive Republicanism under Emperors who did not care overmuch for the memory of the Republic. Thrasea was executed by Nero in A.D. 66, and Helvidius by Vespasian. Observing the birthdays of Brutus and Cassius was only one among many ways in which they proclaimed their attitude.

6. The 'long-nosed cobbler from Beneventum' was a deformed shoemaker's apprentice who rose to power and wealth under Nero, first as court buffoon, then as a professional informer against the great. J. might almost have put in the reference to him here as a contrast to the 'Stoic martyrs', since he made his unsavoury career at the expense of the Senatorial opposition.

7. Tullus Hostilius was Numa's successor as King of Rome, about 670 B.C.; he embarked on a series of wars which fully justify his epithet here. Ancus Marcius, the fourth of the Kings, came to the

throne about 638: he is supposed, among other achievements, to have founded the port of Ostia and built the first prison in Rome.

8. The Esquiline Hill was the richest and most fashionable residential quarter of the city.

9. Nine days after a funeral offerings of eggs, salt and lentils were left on the grave of the deceased.

10. Lines 103–6 have always presented a puzzle, both textual and interpretative. What kind of fish was the *Tiberinus*? How was it spotted, and what was its connexion with ice (*glacie*)? Professor D. S. Robertson's attractive theory was that the fish is rotten, and the marks of putrefaction are hidden by lumps of ice. For long I accepted this theory; now I am not so sure. The context deals with the live fish in its natural habitat; then, by transition, with the cooked fish served up to the guests. A fish on its slab in the shop would be out of place here. Hesitantly I accept Clausen's emendation, *glaucis* for *glacie*, which gives us a 'grey-spotted' *Tiberinus*: but this can scarcely be – as he supposes – the sea-bass (*lupus*), which was a noted delicacy. The river-pike, a habitual foul feeder, fits the context far better, and I have translated accordingly. However, the latest critic to tackle this crux, Bradshaw (see Bibliography), keeps the text as it stands, arguing ingeniously that the *Tiberinus was* the sea-bass (*lupus*), which came upriver and contracted the disease known as saprolegnia: this both produced the patches on its skin – wrongly attributed to the effect of ice – and made the fish sluggish and easily caught. Giangrande (see Bibliography, p. 300) similarly upholds the reading of the manuscripts. He cites Galen and Macrobius to show that the Romans avoided – if they could afford to – any fish that fed in the tainted waters of the Tiber, and specifically the *lupus*. But his attempt to justify *glacie* by a reference to Satire IV 41–4 (above, p. 106) is less convincing.

11. 'The old Republican gentry' once again refers to the Republican-minded senatorial opposition group under the early empire: J. names Gaius Calpurnius Piso and Seneca (both of whom lost their lives as the result of the famous 'Conspiracy of Piso' against Nero in A.D. 65), together with Cotta, who was a patron of the poet Ovid.

12. The 'badman' is Cacus, whose story is told by Virgil in Bk VIII of the *Aeneid*, lines 193–270 (pp. 206–9).

13. i.e. provided the minimum sum of 400,000 sesterces needed to qualify for the Equestrian Order.

14. The allusion is to the eternally productive orchard of Alcinous, the King of Phaeacia who figures in Homer's *Odyssey*; Bk VII, lines 114–21 describe it.

15. The 'Embankment' was originally a defensive earthwork constructed by Servius Tullius to protect the eastern side of Rome: it stretched from the Esquiline Hill to the Colline Gate, and later became a favourite spot for citizens to take a constitutional, being both high and breezy, and very like the modern promenade. Not only performing animals, but also fortune-tellers were often found there: see below, Satire VI 588.

16. A certain type of professional buffoon – the 'fall-man', the eternal he-who-gets-kicked – always had his head shaved: this applies equally to the *stupidus* of the mimes and the idiot clown (*morio*) who performed at private parties. Professor Highet (as so often) has the perfect modern parallel: 'A clown act called "The Three Stooges", which used to appear in short film farces during the 1940s, had a perfect *stupidus* in it, a burly man with a head clipped or shaven smooth, who was always being slapped on it by his quicker and cleverer fellow stooges.'

SATIRE VI

During Saturn's reign I believe that Chastity still
Lingered on earth, and was seen for a while, when draughty
Caves were the only homes men had, hearthfire and household
Gods, family and cattle all shut in darkness together.
Wives were different then – a far cry from Cynthia,
Or the girl who wept, red-eyed, for that sparrow's death.[1]
Bred to the woods and mountains, they made their beds from
Dry leaves and straw, from the pelts of savage beasts
Caught prowling the neighbourhood. *Their* breasts gave suck
To big strong babies; often, indeed, they were shaggier
Than their acorn-belching husbands. In those days, when the
  world
Was young, and the sky bright-new still, men lived differently:
Offspring of oaks or rocks,[2] clay-moulded, parentless.
Some few traces, perhaps, of Chastity's ancient presence
Survived under Jove – but only while Jove remained
A beardless stripling, long before Greeks had learnt
To swear by the other man's head, or capital; when no one
Feared thieves in the cabbage-patch and orchard, when
  kitchen-gardens
Were still unwalled. Thereafter, by slow degrees,
Justice withdrew to heaven, and Chastity went with her,
Two sisters together, beating a common retreat.

   To bounce your neighbour's bed, my friend, to outrage
Matrimonial sanctity is now an ancient and long-
Established tradition. All other crimes came later,
With the Age of Iron; but our first adulterers
Appeared in the Silver Era. And here you are in *this*
Day and age, man, getting yourself engaged,
Fixing up marriage-covenant, dowry, betrothal-party;
Any time now some high-class barber will start
Coiffeuring you for the wedding, before you know it the ring

Will be on her finger. Postumus, are you *really*
Taking a wife? You used to be sane enough – what
Fury's got into you, what snake has stung you up?
Why endure such bitch-tyranny when rope's available
By the fathom, when all those dizzying top-floor windows
Are open for you, when there are bridges handy
To jump from? Supposing none of these exits catches
Your fancy, isn't it better to sleep with a pretty boy?
Boys don't quarrel all night, or nag you for little presents
While they're on the job, or complain that you don't come
Up to their expectations, or demand more gasping passion.
    But no: you staunchly uphold the Family Encouragement
        Act,³
A sweet little heir's your aim, though it means foregoing
All those pickings – fat pigeons, bearded mullet, the bait
Of the legacy-hunter's market. Really, if *you* take a wife, I'll
Credit anything, friend. You were once the randiest
Hot-rod-about-town, you hid in more bedroom cupboards
Than a comedy juvenile lead. Can this be the man now
Sticking his silly neck out for the matrimonial halter?
And as for your insistence on a wife with old-fashioned
Moral virtues – man, you need your blood-pressure checked,
        you're
Crazy, you're aiming over the moon. Find a chaste
And modest bride, and well may you sacrifice
Your gilded heifer to Juno, well may you go down flat
And kiss the stones before the Tarpeian altar!
Few indeed are the girls with a ritual qualification
For the feast of the Corn-Goddess – nine whole days'
        abstinence! –
Or whose fathers wouldn't prefer, if they could, to avoid
Such tainted filial kisses.⁴ Hang wreaths on your doorposts,
Strew your threshold with ivy! Tell me, will Hiberina
Think one man enough? You'd find it much less trouble
To make her agree to being blinded in one eye.

But *you* maintain that a girl who's lived a secluded
Life on her father's estate, way out in the country,
Can keep a good reputation. Just put her down
In the sleepiest outback town you can think of – and if she
    behaves
As she did back home, then I'll believe in that country
Estate of yours. But don't tell me nothing ever
Came off in caves, or up mountains – are Jove and Mars *that*
    senile?

  Look around the arcades, try to pick out a woman
Who's worthy of your devotion. Check every tier of seats
At all the theatres in town: will they yield one single
Candidate you could love without a qualm? When pansy
Bathyllus5 dances Leda, all *fouettés* and *entrechats*,
Just watch the women. One can't control her bladder,
Another suddenly moans in drawn-out ecstasy
As though she was coming. Your country girl's all rapt
Attention, she's learning fast.
                              But when the theatrical
Season is over, the stage-props all packed away,
The playhouses closed and empty, in those summer
Dogdays when only the lawcourts go droning on,
Some women relieve their boredom by taking in
Low-down vaudeville farces – and their performers.
Look at that fellow who scored such a hit in the late-night
Show as Actaeon's mother, camping it up like mad –
Poor Aelia's crazy about him. These are the women
Who'll pay out fancy prices for the chance to defibulate
A counter-tenor, to ruin a concert performer's voice.
One has a kink for ham actors. Are you surprised? What else
Do you expect them to do? Go ape on a good book?
Marry a wife, and she'll make some flute-player
Or guitarist a father, not you. So when you erect
Long stands in the narrow streets, and hang your front-door
With outsize laurel wreaths, it's all to welcome an infant

Whose face, in that tortoiseshell cradle, under its canopy,
Recalls some armoured thug, some idol of the arena.
    When that senator's wife, Eppia, eloped with her fancy
        swordsman
To the land of the Nile, the Alexandrian stews,
Egypt itself cried out at Rome's monstrous morals.
Husband, family, sister, all were jettisoned, not
One single thought for her country; shamelessly she forsook
Her tearful children, as well as – this will really surprise you –
The public games, and her favourite matinée star.
Luxury-reared, cradled by Daddy in swansdown,
Brought up to frills and flounces, Eppia nevertheless
Made as light of the sea as she did of her reputation –
Not that our pampered ladies set any great store by *that*.
Boldly she faced this long and arduous voyage,
The chop and toss of Tuscan waters, the loud
Ionian swell. When a woman endures danger and hardship
In a good cause, her conscience clear, then chill
Terror ices her heart, her knees turn to water,
She can scarcely stand upright; but wicked audacity
Breeds its own fortitude. To go aboard ship is torture
Under a husband's orders: then the smell of the bilges
Is sickening, then the sky wheels dizzily around.
But a wife who's off with her lover suffers no qualms. The one
Pukes on her husband, the other sits down to a hearty
Meal with the crew, takes a turn round the quarter-deck,
Helps to haul on the sheets, and enjoys it.
                                        What was the
        youthful
Charm that so fired our senator's wife? What hooked her?
What did Eppia see in him to make her put up
With being labelled 'The Gladiatress'? Her poppet, her Sergius
Was no chicken, forty at least, with a dud arm that held
        promise
Of early retirement. Besides, his face looked a proper mess –

Helmet-scarred, a great wen on his nose, an unpleasant
Discharge from one constantly weeping eye.[6] What of it?
He was a gladiator. That name makes all the breed
Seem handsomer than Adonis; this was what she preferred
To her children and her country, her sister, her husband: steel
Is what they all crave for. Yet this same Sergius,
Once pensioned off, would soon have bored her as much as
    her husband.

  Do such private scandals move you? Are you shocked by
    Eppia's deeds?
Then look at the God's rivals, hear what Claudius
Had to put up with. The minute she heard him snoring,
His wife – that whore-empress – who dared to prefer the
    mattress
Of a stews to her couch in the Palace, called for her hooded
Night-cloak and hastened forth, alone or with a single
Maid to attend her. Then, her black hair hidden
Under an ash-blonde wig, she would make straight for her
    brothel,
With its odour of stale, warm bedclothes, its empty reserved
    cell.[7]
Here she would strip off, showing her gilded nipples and
The belly that once housed a prince of the blood.[8] Her
    door-sign
Bore a false name, Lycisca, 'The Wolf-girl'. A more than
    willing
Partner, she took on all comers, for cash, without a break.
Too soon, for her, the brothel-keeper dismissed
His girls. She stayed till the end, always the last to go,
Then trailed away sadly, still with a burning hard on,
Retiring exhausted, yet still far from satisfied, cheeks
Begrimed with lamp-smoke, filthy, carrying home
To her imperial couch the stink of the whorehouse.

    What point in mentioning spells, or aphrodisiac potions,
Or that lethal brew served up | to stepsons? Sexual compulsion

Drives women to worse crimes: lust is their strongest motive.*
  'Censennia's husband swears she's the perfect wife: why
    so?'
Because she brought him three million. In exchange he calls
    her chaste.
The shafts that waste him, the fires that burn him up
Have nothing to do with desire. That torch was lit
By cash; it was her dowry that fired those arrows,
And purchased her freedom. She can make come-hitherish
    signs
Or write billets-doux in front of her husband; your wealthy
Woman who marries a miser has widow's privileges.
  'Then why does Sertorius burn with passion for Bibula?'
When you get to the root of it, what he loves isn't his wife
But merely her face. When the first few wrinkles appear,
When her skin goes dry and slack, when her teeth begin
To blacken, when her eyes turn lustreless, then: 'Pack
Your bags!' his steward will tell her. 'Be off with you! You've
    become
A nasty bore, always blowing your nose. Be off,
And double quick: there's another wife due to arrive,
Without that eternal sniffle.' But now she's riding high,
She's the new princess, wheedling ranches and vineyards,
Prize sheep, herdsmen and all from her husband. Yet that's
    nothing:
She demands all his slave-boys, his field-gangs: if a neighbour
Owns any item they don't, it has to be purchased.
In wintertime, when the arcades are crammed with
Canvas market-stalls, and the mural of Trader
Jason is blocked from view, armed sailors and all,9
She goes on a shopping spree: huge crystal vases, outsize
Myrrh-jars of finest agate, and, lastly, a famous
Diamond ring, once worn by Queen Berenice –

  * Reading *summum* for the contradictory *minimum* of the MSS. I owe
this interpretation to Courtney (see Bibliography) pp. 39-40.

Which adds to its price. (She had it from her brother,
That barbarous prince Agrippa, as a token
Of their incestuous love, in the land where kings
Observe the Sabbath barefoot, where – by long-established
Tradition – pigs are suffered to attain a ripe old age.)[10]
　'Not one woman, out of so many, who meets your
　　requirements?'
Assume one with beauty and charm, fertile, wealthy, her hall
A museum of old ancestral portraits, grant her
Virginity more stunning than all those dishevelled Sabine
Maidens who stopped the fighting could raise between them,[11]
Make her a *rara avis*, a black swan or the like – still
Who could stomach such wifely perfection? I'd far far sooner
Marry a penniless tart[12] than take on that virtuous
Paragon Cornelia, Mother of Statesmen, so haughty,
So condescending a prig, her dowry weighted down
With famous triumphs. As far as I'm concerned
You can take your battle-honours – Hannibal, Syphax,
The whole Carthaginian myth – and get lost with them,
　　madam.[13]
　'Apollo, be merciful; Artemis, lay by your shafts,'
Amphion prayed. 'The children are not to blame –
Strike down their mother!' But Apollo, unheeding,
Drew back the bowstring. So Niobe lost, at one stroke,
Her quiverful and her husband – all through the fatuous pride
That made her boast she was nobler in her offspring
Than Leto – and more prolific than the white Alban sow.[14]
　What beauty, what decorum are worth having thrown in
　　your face
Day in day out? What pleasure remains in such rare
And lofty perfection, when pride of spirit has turned it
From honey to bitter aloes? What man is so besotted
That for half the day, or more, the wife he lauds to the skies
Doesn't give him cold shivers? Often it's trivial faults
That offend a husband most. What could be more repulsive

Than the way no modern girl will believe her looks
Are worth a damn till she's tarted up *à la grecque?*
Our provincial dollies ape Athenian fashion, it's smart
To chatter away in Greek – though what should make them
    blush
Is their slipshod Latin. All their emotions – fear,
Anger, happiness, anxiety, every inmost
Secret thought – find expression in Greek, they even
Make love Greek-style. It might be all right for schoolgirls
To behave this way; but when you're well over eighty,
And go round in public using such phrases as *Zoé*
Kai Psyché – 'My life, my soul!' – real bedroom language,
It's most unbecoming. Such naughty, caressing endearments
Have fingers, they'd start a twitch in any man's groin.
But don't go preening yourself, dear: even if your voice
Were softer and more seductive than any matinée idol's,
Your age is still scored on your face.

                  So, man, if you're not
  going to love
Your lawfully wedded spouse, why marry at all? Why waste
Good money on a reception, or those cakes handed out at the
    end
To your well-gorged guests, when the party's breaking up?
Why lose a salver of mint-new golden guineas –
Victory issues, too[15] – on the first-night bridal offering?
But if your mind is set, with uxorious obsession,
On one woman and one only, then bow your neck to the yoke
In voluntary servitude.

                No woman spares any lover;
She may be on fire herself, but that doesn't lessen
Her gold-digging itch, her sadistic urges. So
The better you are as a man, the more desirable
Your husbandly virtues, the less you get out of your wife.
Want to give someone a present? Buy or sell property? *She*
Has the veto on all such transactions; she even controls

Your friendships: lifelong companions, visitors since boyhood,
May find the door slammed in their faces. Pimps and ring-
  masters,
The toughs of the arena – these, when they make their wills,
Have a free hand. But you are compelled to include
Two or three of her lovers amongst your legatees.
  'Crucify that slave!'
                          'But what is the slave's offence
To merit such punishment? Who has brought charges against
  him?
Where are the witnesses? You must hear his defence: no
Delay can be too long when a man's life is at stake.'
'So a slave's a *man* now, is he, you crackpot? All right, perhaps
He didn't do anything. This is still my wish, my command:
Warrant enough that I will it.'
                                So she imposes
Such whims on her husband. But soon enough she moves on
To another kingdom, switching establishments
Till her bridal veil's worn out; then, finally, back she comes
To the bed she scorned and abandoned, leaving behind her
A freshly garlanded house, the bridal hangings
Not yet removed, the boughs still green on the threshold.
Score up another husband: that makes eight
In under five years: it ought to go on her tombstone.

    While your mother-in-law still lives, domestic harmony
Is out of the question. She eggs her daughter on
To run through your capital and enjoy it. She gives advice
On the subtlest, least obvious way to answer billets-doux
From would-be seducers. It's she who hoodwinks or fixes
Your servants, she who takes to her bed when she's well,[16]
Who lies tossing and turning under the sheets till the doctor
Makes his visit. Meanwhile, all hot impatience,
Hidden behind the scenes, her daughter's lover
Keeps mum, and pulls his wire. Do you really believe
Any mother will pass on a loftier set of morals

Than she learnt herself? Besides, it's profitable
For an old whore to bring up her daughter to the trade.

   There's scarcely one court hearing in which the litigation
Wasn't set off by a woman. Defendant or plaintiff, if
She's not one she's the other, ready to deal with a brief
Single-handed, and full of advice to Counsel –
How to open his case, or present individual points.

   And what about female athletes, with their purple
Track-suits, and wrestling in mud? Not to mention our lady-
      fencers –
We've all seen *them*, stabbing the stump with a foil,
Shield well advanced, going through the proper motions:
Just the right training needed to blow a matronly horn
At the Floral Festival[17] – unless they have higher ambitions,
And the goal of all their practice is the real arena.
But then, what modesty can be looked for in some
Helmeted hoyden, a renegade from her sex,
Who thrives on masculine violence – yet would not prefer
To *be* a man, since the pleasure is so much less?
What a fine sight for some husband – *it might be you* – his wife's
Equipment put up at auction, baldric, armlet, plumes
And one odd shinguard! Or if the other style
Of fighting takes her fancy, imagine your delight when
The dear girl sells off her greaves! (And yet these same women
Have such delicate skins that even sheer silk chafes them;
They sweat in the finest chiffon.) Hark how she snorts
At each practice thrust, bowed down by the weight of her
      helmet;
See the big coarse puttees wrapped round her ample hams –
Then wait for the laugh, when she lays her weapons aside
And squats on the potty! Tell me, you noble ladies,
Scions of our great statesmen – Lepidus, blind Metellus,
Fabius the Guzzler[18] – what gladiator's woman
Ever rigged herself out like this, or sweated at fencing-drill?
   The bed that contains a wife is always hot with quarrels

And mutual bickering: sleep's the last thing you get there.
This is her battleground, her station for husband-baiting:
In bed she's worse than a tigress robbed of its young,
Bitching away, to stifle her own bad conscience,
About his boy-friends, or weeping over some way-out
Fictitious mistress. She keeps a copious flow
Of tears at the ready, awaiting her command,
For any situation: and you, poor worm, are agog,
Thinking this means she loves you, and kiss her tears away –
But if you raided her desk-drawers, the compromising letters,
The assignations you'd find that your green-eyed whorish
Wife has amassed! Suppose, though, you catch her in bed with
A slave, or some businessman? *Quick, quick, Quintilian,*
Find me a pat excuse, she prays.[19] *I'm stuck,* says the Maestro,
You can get yourself out of this one.

                                 And she does. 'We agreed
    long ago
To go our separate ways – you were at liberty
To do as you pleased, and I | could have my fun on the side.
It cuts no ice with me if you bawl the house down –
I'm only human too.'

                        For sheer effrontery, nothing
Can beat a woman caught in the act; her very
Guilt adds fresh fire to her fury and indignation.
  What was it (you well may ask) that bred such monsters,
    how
Do they come about? In the old days poverty
Kept Latin women chaste: hard work, too little sleep,
These were the things that saved their humble homes from
    corruption –
Hands horny from carding fleeces, Hannibal at the gates,
Their menfolk standing to arms. Now we are suffering
The evils of too-long peace. Luxury, deadlier
Than any armed invader, lies like an incubus
Upon us still, avenging the world we brought to heel.

Since Roman poverty perished, no visitation
Of crime or lust has been spared us. Sybaris, Rhodes,
Miletus, shameless Tarentum, drunk and garlanded[20] – all
Come pouring in upon our Seven Hills. But filthy
Lucre it was that first brought these loose foreign
Morals amongst us, enervating wealth that
Destroyed us, over the years, through shameless self-indulgence.
    What conscience has Venus drunk? Our inebriated beauties
Can't tell head from tail at those midnight oyster suppers
When the best wine's laced with perfume, and tossed down neat
From a foaming conch-shell, while the dizzy ceiling
Spins round, and the tables dance, and each light shows double.
Why, you may ask yourself, does the notorious Maura
Sniff at the air in that knowing, derisive way
As she and her dear friend Tullia pass by the ancient altar
Of Chastity? and what is Tullia whispering to her?
Here, at night, they stagger out of their litters
And relieve themselves, pissing in long hard bursts
All over the Goddess's statue. Then, while the Moon
Looks down on their motions, they take turns to ride each
        other,
And finally go home. So you, next morning,
On your way to some great house, will splash through your
        wife's piddle.
    Notorious, too, are the ritual mysteries
Of the Good Goddess,[21] when flute-music stirs the loins,
And frenzied women, devotees of Priapus,
Sweep along in procession, howling, tossing their hair,
Wine-flown, horn-crazy, burning with the desire
To get themselves laid. Hark at the way they whinny
In mounting lust, see that copious flow, the pure
And vintage wine of passion, that splashes their thighs!
Off goes Saufeia's wreath, she challenges the call-girls
To a contest of bumps and grinds, emerges victorious,
But herself is eclipsed in turn – an admiring loser –

By the liquid movements of Medullina's buttocks:[22]
So the ladies, with a display | of talent to match their birth,
Win all the prizes. No make-belief here, no pretence,
Each act is performed in earnest, and guaranteed
To warm the age-chilled balls of a Nestor or a Priam.
Delay breeds itching impatience, boosts the pure female
Urge, and from every side of the grotto a clamorous
Cry goes up, 'It's time! Let in the men!' Supposing
One lover's asleep, another is told to get dressed
And hustle along. If they draw a blank with their boy-friends
They rope in the slaves. If enough slaves cannot be found
The water-carrier's hired. If they can't track him down, either,
And men are in short supply, they're ready and willing
To cock their dish for a donkey. Would that our ancient ritual
(At least in its public aspect) was uncontaminated
By such malpractices! But every Moor and Hindu
Knows the identity of that 'lady'-harpist
Who brought a tool as long as both anti-Catonian
Pamphlets by Caesar into the sanctuary where
All images of the other sex must be veiled, where even
A buckmouse, ball-conscious, beats an embarrassed retreat.[23]
    Once, no man would have dared to make light of divine
        power,
Or sneer at the earthenware bowls, black pots, and brittle
        platters
Of Vatican clay that sufficed King Numa. But nowadays
What altar does not attract its Clodius in drag?[24]
    In every house where there's a practising Master
Of Obscene Arts installed – that occupational
Twitch in his right hand hints at unlimited prospects –
You'll find a disgusting crowd, camp if not actually queer.
They let these creatures defile their meals, admit them
To the sacred family board. Glasses that should be broken
When La Courgette's drunk from them, or The Bearded Cowrie,
Are washed up with the rest. The *lanista*[25] runs

A cleaner, more decent establishment than yours:
He quarters the fag targeteers and the armoured heavies
Well away from each other; net-throwers aren't required
To mess with convicted felons, nor are shoulder-guards
And the light-armed fighter's trident found in the same cell.
Even the lowest riff-raff of the arena
Observe this rule; even in prison they chain them
With separate gangs. But the creatures your wife allows
To share your cup! A dyed-blonde washed-up whore
On the graveyard beat would gag at drinking from it,
Whatever the vintage. Yet these are the advisers
On whose say-so their mistress will marry – or suddenly
Decide to beat a retreat; with whom she relieves
Her flagging spirits, the boredom of daily existence;
Under whose expert guidance she learns to shimmy
Her hips and pelvis. What other tricks she acquires
Only the teacher knows – and he's far from reliable
In every case. He may line his eyes with kohl,
And wear a yellow robe and a hairnet – but adultery
Is the end in view. That affected voice, the way
He poses, one arm akimbo, and scratches his bottom, shouldn't
Lull your suspicions. He'll be a champion performer
When he gets into bed, dropping the role of Thais
For that of the potent Triphallus.
                                        Hey there, *you*,
Who do you think you're fooling? Keep this masquerade
For those who believe it. I'll wager that you're one hundred
Per cent a man. It's a bet. So will you confess,
Or must the torturer rack the truth from your maids?
I know the advice my old friends would give – 'Lock her up
And bar the doors.' But who is to keep guard
Over the guards themselves? They get paid in common coin
To forget their mistress's randy little adventures;
Both sides have something to hide. Any sensible wife,
Planning ahead, will first turn the heat on them.

High and low alike, all women nowadays
Share the same lusts. The peasant trudging barefoot
Over black cobbles is no whit superior to
The lady who rides on the necks of tall Syrian porters.
    Ogulnia's mad on the Games. To see them she'll hire
Dresses, attendants, a carriage, a baby-sitter,
Cushions, lady companions, and a cute little blonde
To carry her messages. Yet whatever remains
Of the family plate, down to the very last salver,
She'll hand out as a present to some plausible athlete.
Many such women lack substance – yet poverty gives them
No sense of restraint, they don't observe the limits
Their resources impose. Men on the other hand
Sometimes at least show providence, plan for the future
In a practical way, learn by the ant's example
To fear cold and hunger. But an extravagant woman
Never knows when she's overdrawn. None of them reckon
The cost of their pleasures, as though, when the strong-box
        was empty,
More money would grow there, the pile replenish itself.
    There are girls who adore unmanly eunuchs – so smooth,
So beardless to kiss, and no worry about abortions!
But the biggest thrill is one who was fully-grown,
A lusty black-quilled male, before the surgeons
Went to work on his groin. Let the testicles ripen
And drop, fill out till they hang like two-pound weights;
Then what the surgeon chops will hurt nobody's trade but the
        barber's.
(Slave-dealers' boys are different: pathetically weak,
Ashamed of their empty bag, their lost little chickpeas.)
Look at that specimen – you could spot him a mile off,
Everyone knows him – displaying his well-endowed person
At the baths: Priapus might well be jealous. And yet
He's a eunuch. His mistress arranged it. So, let them sleep
        together –

Yet I wouldn't bet on a handsome, passionate youth
With his first beard sprouting to better *that* performance.

  If your wife has musical tastes, she'll make the professional
Singers come when she wants. She's forever handling
Their instruments, her bejewelled fingers sparkle
Over the lute, she practises scales with a vibrant
Quill once employed by some famous virtuoso –
It's her mascot, her solace, she lavishes kisses on it,
The darling object.

                    A certain patrician lady,
Whose lutanist protégé was due to compete in
The Capitoline Festival,²⁶ made enquiry of Janus
And Vesta, offering wine and cakes, to find out
If her Pollio could aspire to the oakwreath prize
For the best performance. What more could she have done
If her husband was sick, or the doctors shaking their heads
Over her little son? She stood there at the altar,
Thinking it no disgrace to veil her face on behalf of
This cheapjack twangler. She made the proper responses
In traditional form, and blanched as the lamb was opened.
Tell me now, I beg you, most ancient of deities,
Old Father Janus, do such requests get answered? There must
Be time and to spare in heaven. From what I can see
You Gods have nothing on hand to keep you occupied.
One woman's mad on comedians, another's pushing some
      tragic
Ham of her choice: the diviner will soon get varicose veins.

  Yet a musical wife's not so bad as some presumptuous
Flat-chested busybody who rushes around the town
Gate-crashing all-male greetings, talking back straight-faced
To a uniformed general – *and* in her husband's presence.
She knows all the news of the world, what's cooking in Thrace
Or China, just what the stepmother did with her stepson
Behind closed doors, who's fallen in love, which gallant
Is all the rage. She'll tell you who got the widow

Pregnant, and in which month; she knows each woman's
Pillow-endearments, and all the positions she favours.
She's the first to spot any comet presaging trouble
For some eastern prince, in Armenia, maybe, or Parthia.[27]
She's on to the latest gossip and rumours as soon as
They reach the city-gates, or invents her own, informing
Everyone she meets that Niphates[28] has overflowed
And is inundating whole countries – towns are cut off,
She says, and the land is sinking: flood and disaster!
   Yet even this is not so insufferable
As her habit, when woken up,[29] of grabbing some poor-class
Neighbour and belting into him with a whip. If her precious
Sleep is broken by barking, 'Fetch me the cudgels,'
She roars, 'and be quick about it!' The dog gets a thrashing,
But its master gets one first. She's no joke to cross,
And her face is a grisly fright. Not till the evening
Does she visit the baths: only then are her oil-jars and
The rest of her clobber transferred there. First she works out
With the weights and dumb-bells. Then, when her arms are
    aching,
The masseur takes over, craftily slipping one hand
Along her thigh, and tickling her up till she comes.
Lastly she makes for the sweat-room. She loves to sit there
Amid all that hubbub, perspiring. Meanwhile at home
Her unfortunate guests are nearly dead with hunger.
At last she appears, all flushed, with a three-gallon thirst,
Enough to empty the brimming jar at her feet
Without assistance. She knocks back two straight pints
On an empty stomach, to sharpen her appetite: then
Throws it all up again, souses the floor with vomit
That flows in rivers across the terrazzo. She drinks
And spews by turns, like some big snake that's tumbled
Into a wine-vat, till her gilded jordan brims
Right over with sour and vinous slops. Quite sickened,
Eyes shut, her husband somehow holds down his bile.

Worse still is the well-read menace, who's hardly settled for
    dinner
Before she starts praising Virgil, making a moral case
For Dido (death justifies all), comparing, evaluating
Rival poets, Virgil and Homer suspended
In opposite scales, weighed up one against the other.
Critics surrender, academics are routed, all
Fall silent, not a word from lawyer or auctioneer –
Or even another woman. Such a rattle of talk,
You'd think all the pots and bells were being clashed together
When the moon's in eclipse. No need now for trumpets or
    brass:
One woman can act, single-handed, as lunar midwife.³⁰
But wisdom imposes limits, even on virtue, and if
She's so determined to prove herself eloquent, learned,
She should hoist up her skirts and gird them above the knee,
Offer a pig to Silvanus (female worshippers banned) and
Scrub off in the penny baths.³¹ So avoid a dinner-partner
With an argumentative style, who hurls well-rounded
Syllogisms like slingshots, who has all history pat:
Choose someone rather who doesn't | understand *all* she reads.
I hate these authority-citers, the sort who are always thumbing
Some standard grammatical treatise, whose every utterance
Observes all the laws of syntax, who with antiquarian zeal
Quote poets I've never heard of. Such matters are men's
    concern.³²
If she wants to correct someone's language, she can always
Start with her unlettered girl-friends. A husband should be
    allowed
His solecisms in peace.

                                There's nothing a woman
Baulks at, no action that gives her a twinge of conscience
Once she's put on her emerald choker, weighted down her
    ear-lobes
With vast pearl pendants. What's more insufferable

Than your well-heeled female? But earlier in the process
She presents a sight as funny as it's appalling,
Her features lost under a damp bread face-pack,
Or greasy with vanishing-cream that clings to her husband's
Lips when the poor man kisses her – though it's all
Wiped off for her lover. She takes no trouble about
The way she looks at home: those imported Indian
Scents and lotions she buys with a lover in mind.
First one layer, then the next: at last the contours emerge
Till she's almost recognizable. Now she freshens
Her complexion with asses' milk. (If her husband's posted
To the godforsaken North, a herd of she-asses
Will travel with them.) But all these medicaments
And various treatments – not least the damp bread-poultice –
Make you wonder what's underneath, a face or an ulcer.

   It's revealing to study the details of such a woman's
Daily routine, to see how she occupies her time.
If her husband, the night before, has slept with his back to
      her, then
The wool-maid's had it, cosmeticians are stripped and flogged,
The litter-bearer's accused of coming late. One victim
Has rods broken over his back, another bears bloody stripes
From the whip, a third is lashed with a cat-o'-nine-tails:
Some women pay their floggers an annual salary.
While the punishment's carried out she'll be fixing her face,
Gossiping with her friends, giving expert consideration
To the width of the hem on some gold-embroidered robe –
Crack! Crack! – or skimming through the daily gazette;
Till at last, when the flogger's exhausted, she snaps 'Get out!'
And for one day at least the judicial hearing is over.
Her household's governed with all the savagery
Of a Sicilian court. If she's made some assignation
That she wants to look her best for, and is in a tearing hurry
Because she's late, and her lover's waiting for her
In the public gardens, or by the shrine (bordello

Might be a more accurate term) of Isis – why then, the slave-
    girl
Arranging her coiffure will have her own hair torn out,
Poor creature, and the tunic ripped from her shoulders and
    breasts.
'Why isn't this curl in place?' the lady screams, and her
    rawhide
Lash inflicts chastisement for the offending ringlet.
But what was poor Psecas's crime? How could you blame an
    attendant
For the shape of your own nose? Another maid
Combs out the hair on her left side, twists it round the curlers;
The consultative committee is reinforced by
An elderly lady's-maid inherited from Mama,
And now promoted from hairpins to the wool department.
    She
Takes the floor first, to be followed by her inferiors
In age and skill, as though some issue of reputation
Or life itself were at stake, so obsessionally they strive
In beauty's service. See the tall edifice
Rise up on her head in serried tiers and storeys!
See her heroic stature – at least, that is, from in front:
Her back view's less impressive, you'd think it belonged
To a different person. The effect is ultra-absurd
If she's lacking in inches, the sort who without stilettos
Resembles some sawn-off pygmy, who's forced to stand
On tiptoe for a kiss.
                        Meantime she completely
Ignores her husband, gives not a moment's thought
To all she costs him. She's less a wife than a neighbour –
Except when it comes to loathing his friends and slaves,
Or running up bills . . .33
                        . . . And now in comes a procession,
Devotees of the frenzied Bellona, and Cybele, Mother of
    Gods,34

Led by a giant eunuch, the idol of his lesser
Companions in obscenity. Long ago, with a sherd,
He sliced off his genitals: now neither the howling rabble
Nor the kettledrums can outshriek him. His plebeian cheeks
Are framed in a Phrygian mitre. With awesome utterance
He bids her beware of September and its siroccos –
Unless, that is, she lays out a hundred eggs
For purificatory rites, and makes him a present
Of some old clothes, russet-coloured, so that any calamity,
However sudden or frightful, may pass into the garments –
A package-deal expiation, valid for twelve whole months.
In winter she'll break the ice, descend into the river,
And thrice, before noon, let the eddies of Tiber close
Over her timorous head;³⁵ then crawl out, naked, trembling,
And shuffle on bleeding knees, by way of penance,
Across the Field of Mars. Indeed, if white Io so orders,
She'll make a pilgrimage to the ends of Egypt,
Fetch water from tropic Meroë for the aspersion
Of Isis's temple, that stands | beside those ancient sheep-pens
The public polling-booths.³⁶ She believes that she's summoned
By the voice of the Lady herself – just the sort of rare
Mind and spirit, no doubt, that a god *would* choose to talk to
In the small hours! That's why high praise and special honours
Go to her dogheaded colleague, Anubis, who runs through the
       streets
With a shaven-pated crew dressed in linen robes, and mocks
The people's grief for Osiris. He it is who intercedes
For wives who fail to abstain from sex on the prescribed
And ritual days, exacting huge penalties
When the marriage-bed is polluted, or when the silver
Serpent appears to nod. His tears and professional
Mutterings – after Osiris has been bribed with a fat goose
And some sacrificial cake – will guarantee absolution.
    No sooner has *he* pushed off than a palsied Jewess,
Parking her haybox outside, comes round soliciting alms

In a breathy whisper. She knows, and can interpret,
The Laws of Jerusalem: a high-priestess-under-the-trees,
A faithful mediator of Heaven on earth. She too
Fills her palm, but more sparingly: Jews will sell you
Whatever dreams you like for a few small coppers.

    Then there are fortune-tellers, Armenians, Syrians,
Who'll pry out the steaming lungs of a pigeon, predict
A young lover for the lady, or a good fat inheritance
From some childless millionaire. They'll probe a chicken's
Bosom, unravel the guts of a puppy: sometimes
They even slaughter a child. The seer can always
Turn informer on his client.

                      Chaldaean astrologers
Will inspire more confidence: their every pronouncement
Is a straight tip, clients believe, from the oracular fountain
Of Ammon.37 (Now that Delphi has fallen silent
The human race is condemned to murky unknowing
Of what the future may bring.) The most successful
Have been exiled on several occasions – like you-know-who
With his venal friendship and rigged predictions, who settled
The hash of that great citizen dreaded by Otho . . .38
                              . . . Nothing
Boosts your diviner's credit so much as a lengthy spell
In the glasshouse, with fetters jangling from either wrist:
No one believes in his powers unless he's dodged execution
By a hair's breadth, and contrived to get himself deported
To some Cycladic island like Seriphos, and to escape
After lengthy privations. Your wife, your Tanaquil,39
Is for ever consulting such folk. Why does her jaundice-ridden
Mother take so long dying? When will she see off
Her sister or her uncles? (She made all enquiries
About *you* some while back.) Will her present lover
Survive her? (What greater boon could she ask of the Gods?)
Yet she at least cannot tell what Saturn's gloomy
Conjunction portends, or under which constellation

Venus is most propitious; which months bring loss, which gain.
When you meet such a woman, clutching her well-thumbed
Almanacs like a string of amber worry-beads,
Keep very clear of her. *She* isn't shopping around
For expert advice; she's an expert herself, the sort
Who won't accompany her husband on an overseas posting –
Or even back home again – if the almanac forbids it.
When she wants to go out of town, a mile even, or less,
She computes a propitious time for her tables. If she rubs
One corner of her eye, and it itches, she must never
Put ointment on it without first consulting her horoscope; if
She is ill in bed, she will only take nourishment
At such times as Petosiris, the Egyptian, may recommend.[40]

 Women of lower rank and fortune learn their futures
Down at the racecourse, from phrenologist or palmist,
With much smacking of lips against evil influences.[41]
Rich ladies send out to hire their own tame Phrygian
Prophet, they skim off the cream of the star-gazers, or
Pick one of those wise old parties who neutralize thunderbolts:
The Circus and the Embankment preside over more
Plebeian destinies. Here, by the dolphin-columns
And the public stands, old whores in their off-shoulder
Dresses and thin gold neck-chains come for advice –
Should they ditch the tavern-keeper? marry the rag-and-bone
  man?
Yet these at least endure the dangers of childbirth, all
Those nursing chores which poverty lays upon them:
How often do gilded beds witness a lying-in
When we've so many sure-fire drugs for inducing sterility
Or killing an embryo child? Our skilled abortionists
Know all the answers. So cheer up, my poor friend,
And give her the dose yourself. Things might be worse – just
  suppose
She chose to stay pregnant, to swell her belly with frolicsome
Infants: you might become some piccaninny's Papa,

And find yourself making your will on behalf of a son and heir
Whose off-black face was better not seen by daylight.

    I say nothing of spurious children, changelings picked up
Beside some filthy cistern, and passed off as nobly-born –
False hopes, deluded prayers! – our future priesthood,
Our bluest patrician blood. Fortune by night
Is shameless, smiles on these naked babes, enfolds them
One and all in her bosom: then, for a private joke,
Deals them out to great families, loves and lavishes
Her care upon them, makes them her special favourites.

    Here comes a peddler of magic spells and Thessalian[42]
Philtres. With these any wife can so befuddle
Her husband's wits that he'll let her slipper his backside.
If you get mental blackouts, gross amnesia
About yesterday's doing, plain softening of the brain,
This is your trouble. Yet even these tricks can be endured
Provided you aren't driven raving mad by the kind
Of knock-out mixture Caesonia once brewed up
For her husband, Nero's uncle.[43] When an Empress sets fashions
What woman won't follow suit? Established certainties
Went up in flames then, mere anarchy ruled the world:
Had it been Juno herself who drove her husband crazy
The shock could have been no greater. Why, Agrippina's
Mushroom turned out less lethal: *that* only settled the hash
Of one old dotard, saw off his tremulous headpiece
And beslobbered, drooling chops to some nether heaven.[44]
    But
Caesonia's potion brought fire and sword and the rack,
Mowed down Senate and burghers in one mangled, bloody
    heap:
Such was the cost of one philtre, a single poisoner.

    Wives loathe a concubine's offspring. Let no man cavil
Or call such hatred abnormal: to murder your step-son
Is an old-established tradition, perfectly right and proper.
But wards with rich portions should have a well-developed

Sense of self-preservation. Trust none of the dishes at dinner:
Those pies are steaming-black with the poison Mummy put
    there.
Whatever she offers you, make sure another person
Tries it out first: let your shrinking tutor sample
Each cup you're poured. Do you think this is melodrama?
Am I making the whole thing up, careless of precedents,
    mouthing
Long-winded bombast in the old Sophoclean manner
That's quite out of place here under Italian skies?
How I wish that it *was* all nonsense! But listen to Pontia's⁴⁵
Too-willing confession: 'I did it, I admit I gave aconite
To my children. Yes, they were poisoned, that's obvious –
But *I* was the one who killed them.'

                    'What, you viper,
Two at one meal? The brutality of it! *Two*
You did away with?'

                'Indeed; and if there'd been seven
I'd have polished *them* off, too.'

                   Whatever the tragic poets
Tell us about Medea and Procne⁴⁶ may well have happened:
I won't dispute that. Such women were monsters of daring
In their own day – but not from the lust for cash.
We find it less freakish when wrath provides the incentive
For a woman's crimes, when whitehot passion whirls her
Headlong, like some boulder that's carried away by a landslide,
What *I* can't stand is the calculating woman
Who plans her crimes in cold blood. Our wives sit and watch
Alcestis⁴⁷ undertaking to die in her husband's stead:
If they had a similar chance, *they'd* gladly sacrifice
Their husband's life for their lapdogs'. Take a morning stroll,
You'll meet Danaids galore; an Eriphyle
Or Clytemnestra turns up in every street.⁴⁸ The only
Difference is this: whereas Clytemnestra used
A clumsy great double-axe, nowadays an ounce of toad's lung

Is just as effective. But cold steel may have a comeback
If our modern Agamemnons take a hint from old Mithridates,
And sample the pharmacopeia till they're proof against every
   drug.[49]

1. 'Cynthia' was the pseudonym which Propertius used to describe his mistress Hostia in the poems he wrote about her; the girl who wept for her sparrow was 'Lesbia', the mistress of Catullus, whose real name was Clodia, and who was the sister of Publius Clodius, referred to below in lines 335–45. The point, of course, is that both these women were neurotic, sophisticated creatures with the loosest of sexual habits. Hostia was chronically unfaithful. Cicero accuses Clodia of incest with her brother; one of her later lovers described her as a 'two-bit Clytemnestra'.

2. I accept Scholte's emendation *rupe et robore* in line 12.

3. In A.D. 9 Augustus passed a law, the *Lex Papia Poppaea*, which gave special privileges to those with three or more children, and restricted the rights of bachelors, spinsters or childless couples to inherit property.

4. The 'feast of the Corn-Goddess' (Ceres) took place in August, and somewhat resembled a Harvest Festival: it included a ceremonial procession of white-clad women bearing first-fruits. One condition of participation in this ceremony was nine days' previous abstention from sexual intercourse. The scholiast, with typical blunt accuracy, explains the point about fathers fearing their daughters' 'tainted kisses': *quia et irrumantur mulieres, dicit.*

5. Bathyllus seems to have been a *pantomimus*, or ballet-dancer, under Domitian. The most famous Bathyllus, however, who was, broadly speaking, the Diaghilev of the Imperial ballet, lived much earlier, under Augustus, and was a favourite of Maecenas: it was customary to repeat the names of 'stars' in successive generations, and we shall find the same thing happening with Paris the actor. It is hard to realize the influence which the Roman ballet exerted on Roman citizens. It was not only immensely popular, but formed a centre for violent factions like those of the various racing-colours (there were two rival schools of ballet), and was sometimes the cause of riots and bloodshed.

6. At line 107 I accept Nisbet's ingenious emendation *sulcus* (for

sicut): the only way so far suggested of making this passage into tolerable Latin.

7. Lines 113–24 are a textual nightmare. The general sense is clear: the Latin is in many places quite hopeless. I do not agree with attempts by various editors to solve the problem on a basis of wholesale linear transposition (for the latest attempt see Courtney, p. 39) and have kept the text in the line-order given by the MSS. Again, it seems clear that several lines must have fallen out: possibly after 117, certainly after 118. To avoid the first loss we must take *meretrix augusta* in apposition to *uxor*, which is awkward, but just possible. To make 119 follow on 118 we have to get rid of *linquebat*, which, despite editorial claims, cannot be anything but a transitive verb. I have sometimes wondered whether *linquebat* was not a corruption of *iam properat*; but it seems more sensible to assume a lacuna after 118, perhaps of one line only, something such as *iussit, et amplexus subito cubitusque seniles . . .* etc.

8. The 'prince of the blood' was Britannicus, Messalina's son by Claudius. The boy's stepmother, Agrippina, persuaded Claudius to adopt her own son Lucius Domitius (Nero), who thus succeeded to the throne after Claudius's death by poisoning in 54. Britannicus himself was also murdered a year later, presumably as a potential rival to Nero. See below, lines 615–26.

9. During the Saturnalia (17–19 December) a fair and market were held in the Campus Martius, and the canvas stalls erected for this purpose made it impossible to see the frescoes in the Portico of Agrippa. One of the more famous of these frescoes depicted Jason and the Argonauts. Once again J. belittles a mythological theme, here by reducing the voyage of the Argonauts to a mere trading venture.

10. Berenice and Agrippa II are perhaps best known for St Paul's appearance before them at Caesarea in A.D. 62. Berenice, after two marriages, the second to her uncle, lived for many years with Agrippa, her brother, incestuously accordingly to general belief. The emperor Titus fell in love with her during his Jewish campaign (67–70), and had her as his mistress in 75, when she visited Rome. It is quite possible that she sold some famous ring during this visit.

11. Sabine women had a high reputation for chastity. Their role as peacemakers is described by Livy (1.13, p. 32). After their 'rape' Sabine troops under Mettius Curtius invaded Rome, and came very

close to capturing the Palatine Hill. As the battle raged in the valley between the Palatine and the Capitol, the women (for whatever motive) decided to intervene. 'With loosened hair and rent garments they braved the flying spears and thrust their way in a body between the embattled armies', etc. The whole passage makes me wonder whether scholars do not seriously under-estimate Livy's deadpan sense of humour.

12. Reading *Venustina*, which I take to be a piece of contemporary *argot* for a prostitute.

13. Cornelia, mother of the Gracchi, was the second daughter of Scipio Africanus, who conquered the Numidian prince Syphax in 203 and defeated Hannibal at the Battle of Zama in 202. She had twelve children (though only three survived to adult life, and of these three the two boys, Gaius and Tiberius, both suffered political assassination) – a fact which suggests that the next few lines, describing the fate of Niobe, may have something of a back-kick at Cornelia herself.

14. Niobe was the daughter of Tantalus and wife of Amphion. She, like Cornelia, had twelve children, six boys and six girls; she angered Leto by boasting that she was at least the equal of Leto, who had borne two children only, Apollo and Artemis. (Ovid tells us that she also disparaged Leto's ancestral connexions.) The two thereupon killed all Niobe's offspring; Amphion hanged himself; and Niobe, after one tearful meal, was turned to stone. The 'white Alban sow' may be found in the *Aeneid*, together with its farrow of thirty young: it marked the future site of Alba Longa (*Aeneid* 3.390 ff., pp. 86–7).

15. The coins were *aurei* (almost the exact equivalent of our guinea); the 'victory issues' were for Trajan's conquests in Germany (A.D. 97) and Dacia (A.D. 102/3). This detail provides a *terminus post quem* for the composition-date of Satire VI. We have no other reference to such a marriage-custom, but we know from Martial that successful gladiators in the arena were so rewarded: J. may simply be making a not uncommon joke, the transference of battle-imagery to the bedroom.

16. The scholiast points out, very sensibly, that the mother-in-law fakes illness in order to give her daughter a good excuse for frequent visits: the adulterous meetings take place in the mother-in-law's

house. The passage would not require a note were it not for the fact that modern scholars seem unanimous in agreeing that it is *the daughter* who feigns illness: a Kaufman and Hart notion hardly (one would have thought) conducive to peaceful infidelity.

17. The Floralia, or Festival of Flowers, took place between 28 April and 3 May. Games were held and farces performed: as Duff delicately puts it, 'custom sanctioned unusual freedoms on the part of the actresses'. Prostitutes played a large part in the proceedings, and some of the ritual – clearly of the old ithyphallic fertility-cult variety – was described as 'most improper'. Trumpets were blown at the beginning of all public shows.

18. For Metellus see n. 17 to Satire III. The Aemilii Lepidi were a most distinguished Roman family who produced numbers of statesmen (including the Triumvir). The Fabii were one of the most ancient patrician *gentes*, tracing their ancestry back to Hercules and the Arcadian Evander: Fabius the Guzzler, so named because of his youthful gourmandizing, was Q. Fabius Maximus Gurges, consul in 292 and 276 B.C.

19. Quintilian – M. Fabius Quintilianus (A.D. *c.* 35–*c.* 100?) was a Spanish rhetorician, educated in Rome, and appointed Professor of Latin Rhetoric by Vespasian. He is best known from his surviving work, the *Institutio Oratoria*, composed after his retirement in A.D. 90. The 'pat excuse' is the *color*, a frequent technical term among the rhetoricians for any approach that would present an action in the most favourable possible light.

20. There is a highly obscure allusion here. In 281 B.C. the Romans sent an embassy to Tarentum to complain of various outrages the Tarentines had been guilty of; the ambassador was insulted by a drunk in the theatre, who befouled his robe. 'It will,' said the ambassador, 'take much blood to clean'; and since the Tarentines called in King Pyrrhus to help them, it did.

21. The Bona Dea, or 'Good Goddess', was said to be either the daughter or wife of the Roman deity Faunus. Her worship, which appears to have been a mystic and orgiastic fertility cult, was strictly reserved for women. Men were not even supposed to know her real name. Her sanctuary – alluded to here – was a grotto on the Aventine. Her festival was celebrated annually in the house of the consul or praetor, since the offerings made then were on behalf of

the Roman people as a whole. During the ceremony no male could enter the building, and all male images had to be covered. It began with a sacrifice, and included dancing and the drinking of wine (which was referred to throughout as 'honey'). It generally took place at night.

22 'Saufeia' and 'Medullina' are names carefully chosen as representative of ancient Roman families. The latter was a family name of the Gens Furia; Claudius's first fiancée was called Livia Medullina Camilla.

23. It is hard to tell throughout this passage how far J. is giving a slanted and prejudiced account of a genuine – if by his day somewhat debased – ceremony, and how far what he says is mere malicious invention. But these details seem genuine enough: we may also note that women were required to prepare for the occasion by a period of sexual abstinence, which gives more point to J.'s climax.

24. Publius Clodius profaned the ceremony of the Bona Dea in December 62 B.C., when it was being held in Caesar's house. Caesar's wife Pompeia (to complicate matters) was Clodius's current mistress. This triggered off a sizable political crisis; it also adds to J.'s image of the 'two anti-Catonian pamphlets'. Clodius was brought to trial, but got off by bribing the jurors.

The following 34 lines, the so-called 'O[xford] Passage', were first discovered in a unique Bodleian MS in 1899, and have been much discussed since. (See introduction, pp. 58 ff.). They are inserted after line 365, where they seem singularly out of place. For many years I have thought that the logical point for their introduction was after line 345: recently Mr J. G. Griffith published an article, in Hermes 91 (1963), 104–14, saying precisely the same thing, and I have accordingly taken the liberty of transferring them in my translation.

25. The *lanista* was the director and trainer of a gladiatorial school. There is no precise equivalent in English without a cumbersome periphrasis.

26. A.D. 86 Domitian restored the great temple on the Capitol. To celebrate this he founded 'a festival of music, horsemanship and gymnastics, to be held every five years, and awarded far more prizes than is customary nowadays. The festival included Latin and Greek public-speaking contests, competitions for choral singing to the lyre

and for lyre-playing alone, besides the usual solo singing to lyre accompaniment . . .' (Suetonius, *Domitian* 4, p. 298). The prizes were oakleaf wreaths, and the competition lasted without interruption until the fifth century A.D.

27. Trajan invaded Armenia in 113 and Parthia, probably, in 116. In December 115 there was a great earthquake at Antioch. Highet (pp. 12–13) concludes from this that the Sixth Satire was composed and published at some time fairly soon after 116, and that these are the events which J. makes his gossip allude to.

28. The whole point is that Niphates was a mountain, not a river: in fact, the highest range in the Taurus, rising to over 10,000 feet. The lady, with typical feminine inaccuracy, fails to get her geography right. (On the other hand both Lucan and Silius Italicus make the same mistake, so perhaps J.'s pleasant effect here is unintentional.)

29. At line 415 I accept Duff's brilliant emendation *experrecta*, based on the scholium to line 417, which suggests that the true reading was ousted by a gloss, *exorta*, which was then changed, for metrical reasons, to *exortata*.

30. Eclipses of the moon were supposed to be caused by witchcraft: the witch's incantations, perhaps reinforced by the magic bird-wheel, or *iynx*, would torture and diminish the moon unless such a din was created that the spells were inaudible. The moon's waxing was not only connected in the popular mind with menstruation, but also regarded in itself as a kind of pregnancy. The beating on pots and pans also acted as an apotropaic against evil spirits. Witches were supposed to be able to 'call down' the moon, and obtain a curious magical foam from it.

31. Both these activities symbolize masculine status. Silvanus, a vague and numinous deity of all wild land beyond the tillage, was exclusively worshipped by men. The 'penny baths' were where men went; it is not certain whether women merely paid more, or used a different section of the building as well.

32. At lines 454–5 I read, and punctuate, as follows: . . . *antiquaria versus:/ haec curanda viris. opicae*, etc. Housman is responsible for the full stop after *viris*; *haec* (in my opinion an almost certain emendation for *nec*) was picked up by Postgate from one of Ruperti's MSS.

33. I strongly suspect that line 511 has been cobbled together, and

covers a considerable omission. The break in the sense is violent; we pass, with no real or logical transition, from the portrait of the sadistic mistress to that of a superstitious lady, rather akin to the *Superstitious Man* of Theophrastus; what is more, we appear to come in on it in the middle, where she is being visited by a series of quacks and diviners such as turn up in Aristophanes' Cloud-Cuckooland.

34. Bellona was originally a native Roman war-goddess; but by Imperial times her worship had been syncretized with that of the Cappadocian mother-goddess Ma. Cybele, the great mother-goddess of Anatolia, whose main shrine was at Pessinus in Phrygia, was also known as the Idaean or Dindymenian Mother; her cult was officially brought to Rome in 205/4 B.C. (see n. 17 to Satire III), together with that of her young consort Attis. The great spring festival, from 15–28 March, was probably developed after Claudius's day, and it seems to be this which is alluded to here.

35. The scholiast points out that this descent into the river took place after intercourse with a man.

36. The site of the Isaeum in the Campus Martius has been identified. So, more strikingly still, has the great temple of Isis on the Ethiopian island of Meroë, far up the Nile: it is clear, then, that what J. says here is no rhetorical exaggeration. For evidence of Greek and Roman pilgrimages to Meroë see Highet, pp. 242–3.

37. Ammon was originally the god of Thebes in Egypt. His fame in Hellenistic and Roman times was almost entirely bound up with his oracle in the oasis at Siwah, in Cyrene, which came to rival the oracles of Delphi or Dodona – especially after it was consulted by Alexander, who may have gone there with the object of being deified.

38. Lines 558–9 are omitted by several of the best MSS and not commented on by the scholiast; they are certainly J.'s, but seem out of place here, where the sense would run more smoothly if the text read '. . . on several occasions. Nothing,' etc. The astrologer in question was called either Ptolemaeus or Seleucus; the 'great citizen' whom Otho feared was the future brief-lived Emperor Galba. It seems that Ptolemaeus switched allegiance from one to the other with considerable dexterity – as anyone of his calling must have needed to do, not once but several times, in the 'Year of the Four Emperors' (A.D. 69).

39. The wife is given the sobriquet 'Tanaquil' (an Etruscan name) after the wife of Tarquinius Priscus, whose skill in magic and fortune-telling enabled her to learn the future destiny of Servius Tullius. She was also (and this point will not have been lost on J.) 'an aristocratic young woman who was not of a sort to put up with humbler circumstances in her married life than those she had been previously accustomed to' (Livy 1.34, p. 56),

40. Petosiris was joint author, with Nechepso, of an astrological treatise composed about 150 B.C. or a little later. The two names may be a double pseudonym for one author. The treatise is supposed to have first given the signs of the zodiac their astrological significance.

41. The *poppysma* was a sound made with the lips to avert the evil eye or similar maleficent influences: it may still be heard today in the 'po-po-po-po' of a Greek peasant woman when she is told bad news. Perhaps the implication here is that the fortunes given were, on the whole, far from flattering.

42. Thessalian women had a notorious reputation throughout antiquity for skill in magical arts of every sort: authors from Euripides to Lucian mention their uncanny powers.

43. Nero's uncle was the emperor Caligula. 'He was well aware,' Suetonius tells us (*Caligula* 50, p. 174) 'that he had mental trouble . . . Caesonia [his wife] is reputed to have given him an aphrodisiac which drove him mad.'

44. Claudius was poisoned with a dish of mushrooms prepared by his wife Agrippina, though the details of his death are confused, and Suetonius (*Claudius* 44, pp. 206–7) lists several variant accounts. For his physical peculiarities see *Claudius* 30 (p. 200), and Seneca, *Apocolocyntosis* 5.

45. Pontia's case was something of a *cause célèbre* during Nero's reign. According to the scholiast she was Petronius's daughter, and poisoned her children after her father had lost his life as a result of the 'Conspiracy of Piso'; on conviction she committed suicide by opening her veins after a sumptuous banquet – which was exactly what Petronius himself had done. Father-fixation, the Freudian might say, could scarcely go further.

46. Medea and Procne were both familiar instances from myth-ology of mothers who killed their children – but both, as J. emphasizes, acted out of passion.

47. Alcestis is familiar to us from Euripides' play of that name; she was the wife of Admetus of Pherae in Thessaly, and volunteered to die on his behalf, an offer which he willingly accepted. Later Heracles found Admetus grieving for his dead wife, and successfully forced either Hades or the incarnation of Death, Thanatos, to give Alcestis back.

48. The daughters of Danaus killed their husbands; so did Eriphyle; so did Clytemnestra. This is the only reason J. has for bracketing their names together in this context.

49. The anecdote by which Mithridates VI, King of Pontus (c. 120–63 B.C.) is best known – his diet of prophylactics, which made him immune to poison – has been immortalized in a poem by A. E. Housman.

ADDITIONAL NOTE

At line 246 I now interpret *femineum ceroma* as 'female mud-wrestling': see Reinmuth (Additional Bibliography). At line 477 I accept Durry's interpretation of *cosmetae* (Additional Bibliography), and translate accordingly.

SATIRE VII

All hopes for the arts today, all inducement to study, depend
Upon Caesar[1] alone. Who else spares a glance for the wretched
Muses in these hard times, when established poets lease
An out-of-town bath-concession or a city bakery
To make their living, when hungry historians are quitting
Helicon's vales and springs for the auction-rooms? No
    comedown,
They feel, no disgrace; if you can't turn an honest penny
In the shady grove of the Muses, you might as well
Accept the title – and income – of an auctioneer, join in
The saleroom battles, flog lots under the hammer
To a crowd of bidders – winejars, three-legged stools,
Bookcases, cupboards, remaindered plays by nonentities
On stale mythological themes. A better career, surely,
Than the perjuror's, telling a judge you saw what you didn't.
    Leave that
To our get-rich-quick crowd, the Asiatic burghers –
Galled ankles, revealed by low slippers, blow the gaff on *their*
    origins.[2]
But henceforth none who shape eloquent utterance
To tuneful measures, none who have bitten Apollo's
Laurel will be compelled to labour in fields that
Demean their craft. So at it, young men: your Imperial
Leader is urging you on, surveying your ranks for talent
That merits his support.
                    But if you had thoughts of obtaining
Patronage for your art from some other benefactor,
And it's in this hope that you continue to scribble
On your nice buff parchment, you might as well give up –
Order a bundle of firewood, make a burnt sacrifice
Of your works to Vulcan; or else just lock them away
And let the bookworms riddle them full of holes.

Break your pen, poor wretch, destroy all those battle-pieces
That kept you awake so late, the high-flown compositions
Hammered out in that cramped garret, the dreams of a laureate's
    wreath
On your gaunt and sculptured brow! Yet this is the best
You could ever hope for: our skinflint millionaires
May flatter artistic talent, may load it with compliments
(Like children admiring a peacock) – but nothing further.
So the prime of life slips by, the years when you might
Have been a sailor, soldier, farmer, until the spirit
Grows weary, until old age creeps up on your penniless
Gift of the gab and you hate yourself and your art.

  Your private patron, for whom you forsook the book-lined
    haunts
Of Apollo and the Muses,3 knows every dodge to avoid
Shelling out on you. Why, he's a poet himself, remember,
And in a thousand years – *he* thinks – there's been no one
But Homer to touch him. If the sweet itch for renown
Stirs *you* to give a recital, he'll fix you up with some peeling
Dump of a hall in the suburbs, its doors all barred
And bolted like the gates of a city under siege.
He'll lend you a claque of freedmen and other hangers-on
To sit at the end of each row, distribute the applause;
But none of these noble patrons will underwrite your outlay
On hiring seats and benches, the upper tiers and the framework
Of beams that supports them, the cushioned front-row chairs
That have to be returned, double-quick, when the performance
    is over.
Yet still we keep at it, ploughing a dusty furrow,
Turning up barren sand. You can't get out, you're hooked
By writer's itch; the craving for bookish renown
Becomes a sick obsession. But the outstanding poet,
Whose inspiration is rare and unique, who makes
Nothing from common stock, strikes no debased
Poetic currency, minted with platitudes – though

I can't think of one just now, still I'm sure they exist –
Such a paragon's life is bound to be free from anxieties,
Unclouded by bitterness; he's a woodland-lover,
And just the right sort to drink at the Muses' fountain.
     How can grim poverty grasp the enchanted wand
Of inspiration, how find that singing grotto
If you're forced to scrape and pinch to meet the body's
Unending demands for cash? When Horace cried 'Rejoice!'⁴   ~ *Ode*
His stomach was comfortably full. What room for true genius
Save in the heart that's devoted uniquely to poetry
And untroubled by other concerns, that's sustained by Apollo,
By Dionysus? It calls for a lofty temperament, not
Some petty mind scared stiff at the cost of a blanket,
To have visions of horses and chariots, of divine godhead,
To limn the Fury that once confounded Rutulian
Virgil —Turnus.⁵ If Virgil had not possessed at least one servant,
And a fairly comfortable lodging, how flat that scene
Would have fallen – no spark of life in the snakes entwined
Round the Fury's head, voiceless her deep and sounding
Trumpet. Can we expect a modern playwright to match
The ancient tragedians when, in order to finish his *Atreus*,
He must hock his coat, and the dishes?
                                        Numitor can't spare a
     penny
For a friend in need, though his mistress never goes short,
And he scraped up enough (remember?) to purchase that tame
     lion –
Not to mention the meat it scoffed. Of course it comes cheaper
To feed a lion than a poet: poets have bigger bellies.
     Fame may satisfy Lucan,⁶ lying at rest now
In his park with its statuary; but for epic poets
Less well endowed, poor starvelings, glory alone,
However great, must remain eternally insufficient.
The City is all agog when Statius⁷ agrees
To fix a recital-date. He's a sell-out, no one

Can resist that mellifluous voice, that ever-popular
Theban epic of his: the audience sits there spellbound
By such fabulous charm. Yet despite the cheers and the
    stamping
Statius will starve, unless he can sell a libretto
To Paris,[8] Director-in-Chief of Imperial Opera and Ballet,
Paris, the carpet-knight maker, the jobber of high commands.
What nobles cannot bestow, you must truck for to an actor.
Why bother to haunt the spacious ante-rooms
Of the great? Colonels and Governors, the ballet appoints
Every man jack of them. Yet you need not begrudge the living
A poet makes from the stage. Today the age
Of the private patron is over; Maecenas and Co.
Have no successors. Genius got its reward
In those days; many a poet found it worthwhile to sweat
At his desk, on the waggon, right through the December
    vacation.[9]
    What about writers of history? Do all their labours
Bring them a bigger return, or merely consume
More midnight oil? With unrestricted licence
They pile up their thousand pages – and an enormous
Stationery bill: the vast extent of the theme,
Plus their professional conscience, makes this inevitable.
But what will the harvest yield, what fruit will all your
    grubbing
Bring you? Does any historian pull down a newsreader's
    wage?
'Oh, they're an idle lot, though, too fond of their shady
    deck-chairs.'
How about barristers, then? How much do you think *they*
    extract
From all their work in court, all those bulging bundles of briefs?
They *talk* big enough – especially when there's a creditor
Listening, or, worse still, some dun with a weighty
Ledger comes nudging them in the ribs, and makes trouble

About a bad debt. Then they huff and puff like a bellows,
Pump out tremendous lies, spray spittle all over
    themselves –
Yet if you look at their incomes (real, not declared),
You'll find that a hundred lawyers scarcely make more than
    one
Successful jockey. The magistrates take their places,
And up you stand, a whey-faced poor man's Ajax,
To defend some case of contested | citizenship before
A clodhopping jury. Go on then, burst your lungs, talk till
    you drop,
Collect a green palm-wreath on your garret staircase[10] –
But what's the pay-off? One dried-up hock-end of ham
And a jar of pickled fish, or some mouldy onions –
African ration standard – or five quart bottles
Of the cheapest local wine. Four cases, let's say,
Bring you one gold piece between them – but by prior
    agreement
The solicitors take their cut. It's a different matter
With a blue-blooded advocate: *he* gets the maximum fee
Though we did a better job. Just look at that bronze group
He's got in his forecourt, that four-horse chariot
From some ancestor's triumph, and himself on a warlike
Charger, bow drawn, eye squinting along the arrow,
Stiffly upright, a dummy dreaming of battles.
This is the way they go bankrupt, this is what will happen
To that show-off Tongilius, who's such a bore at the baths
With his mob of muddy retainers and his outsize oilflask
Of rhinoceros-horn, who has eight stout Thracian slaves
Humping the poles of his litter through the Forum, to go
    shopping
For slaves or silver, glassware or country houses.
That pirated gown of his, with the Tyrian purple weave,
Backs up his credit. Such display has its uses:
A purple robe attracts clients. It pays these gentry to live

Above their means, to advertise, sell themselves high –
But spendthrift Rome sets no limits to their extravagance.
    Trust in our eloquence, can we? Why, Cicero himself
Wouldn't get tuppence these days without an enormous ring
To flash in court. When a litigant's picking a lawyer,
His first consideration will be, *Have you got eight slaves,*
A dozen freeborn retainers, a litter in attendance,
An escort of citizens? That was why one advocate
Hired a sardonyx ring to wear while pleading his cases –
And why he made more than his colleagues. Forensic skill
Seldom goes with shabby linen. How often, I ask you,
Does a down-at-heels barrister get the chance to produce
Some weeping mother in court? Who'll listen to *him*, however
Persuasive he was? If you really suppose your tongue
Can earn you a workable living, you'd better emigrate
To Gaul or Africa – lawyers are flourishing there.
    Or do you teach declamation? You must possess iron nerves
To sit through a whole large class's attack on 'The Tyrant'.
        Each boy
Stands up in turn, and delivers by rote what he's just
Learnt at his desk; all gabble off the same
Stale old couplets and catchphrases – bubble-and-squeak
Rehashed without end, sheer death for the poor master.
What type of case is involved, what's the best approach
And the clinching argument, what counter-shots will be fired
By the opposition party – these are things that everyone
Is desperate to learn, but won't pay for. 'What, *pay* you?' they
        exclaim,
'But what have you taught me?'
                                        'Of course, it's the teacher's
        fault
If some bumpkin pupil isn't thrilled to the marrow
Week after week, while dinning | his awful Hannibal speech
Into my wretched head, whatever the set theme
Up for discussion – should Hannibal march on Rome

From Cannae? And after that | torrential thunderstorm, should he
Play safe, and withdraw his rain-sodden, dripping troops?
What wouldn't I give – just name your figure, I'll pay it,
Cash on the nail – for any boy's father to hear him
As often as I do!'

                That's the stock complaint of our teachers
When they put aside classroom speeches such as 'The Rapist',
Or 'A Case of Poison', or 'The Wicked Ungrateful Husband',
Or the one about pounded drugs that can cure chronic
    blindness[11] –
And sue in the real-life courts for recovery of their fees.
So, if he takes my advice, the teacher who's emerged
From some academic retreat to do battle in the arena –
His peppercorn fees are the highest he can command
In this profession – will forthwith retire from the Bar
To some other walk of life. When you learn how much
Well-known musicians or singers are paid for giving lessons
To top people's sons, you'll cut down your *Manual of Public
    Speaking*
  To voice-production alone. For his private baths, a magnate
Will lay out thousands, and more, for a covered cloister to
    drive round
When it's wet – you couldn't expect him to wait till the
    weather clears,
Or let his pair get muddy. Better to ride
Where those polished hooves will keep | their lustre un-
    diminished.
Elsewhere he plans a banqueting-hall, with lofty
Numidian columns, so placed that it gets the best
Of the winter sunshine; and, whatever his mansion
May have set him back, he must still have a first-class chef
And a major-domo. With such expenses, a tenner
Is more than enough for Quintilian. There's nothing comes
    lower
Than a son on the list when Daddy is paying out cash.

                                'Then
how   169

Did Quintilian get all those vast estates?' Ignore
The exceptions.[12] Luck makes you handsome and brave, luck
    brings
Brains and breeding, a splendid pedigree, plus
The senatorial crescent to sew on your black shoestraps.
Luck makes a first-class speaker or javelin-thrower, luck
Means that you still sing well when you've caught a streaming
    cold.
It makes all the difference under just what conjunction
Of planets you utter your first thin squalls when you're
Still red from your mother's womb. If Fortune so pleases,
You may rise from teacher to consul; let her frown, and presto!
The consul's a teacher once more.[13] Look at self-made men
Such as Bassus and Cicero:[14] what brought *them* to the top
But the stars in their courses, the miraculous occult powers
Of Fate, who gives kingdoms to slaves, who lets captives
    triumph – although
Such lucky ones are as rare as the proverbial white raven.
Professorial chairs too often prove barren comfort,
Bring banishment or death. Cases abound: the wretch
Who hanged himself, or that other | penniless exile to whom
Athens dared give nothing but the cup of cold hemlock.[15]
Gods, grant the earth lie easy and light on our fathers' shades,
With crocus bloom: may their ashes enjoy eternal springtime,
Who held that the teacher stood in a parent's place,
And must be revered as such! Achilles, approaching manhood,
Still feared the rod, was still having singing-lessons
In his native mountains, would never have dared to laugh
At the music-master's tail.[16] But pupils nowadays
Will sometimes beat up their instructor – it happened to Rufus,
That professor they nicknamed 'Cicero of the Rhône'.

   What schoolmaster, even the most successful, commands
A proper return for his labours? Yet even this little,
However trifling – and any professor makes more –
Is further whittled away when the pupil's unfeeling

Attendant, and the cashier, have each taken their cut.
Better give in, then: bargain, be beaten down
For a lower fee, like a hawker peddling blankets
And winter rugs – so long | as you get *some* recompense
For presiding, before it's light, in a hell-hole any blacksmith
Or wool-carder would refuse to train apprentices in;
So long as you get *some* return for enduring the stink
Of all those guttering lanterns – one to each pupil,
So that every Virgil and Horace is grimed with lampblack
From cover to cover. Yet, nine times out of ten,
You need a court order to get even this small pittance.
In return, what's more, such parents demand quite impossible
Standards from any master: his grammar must be above cavil,
History, literature, he must have all the authorities
Pat at his fingertips. They'll waylay him *en route*
For the public baths, and expect him to answer their questions
Straight off the cuff – who was Anchises' nurse, what
Was the name of Anchemolus' stepmother, and where
Did she come from? How old was Acestes when he died?
How many jars of Sicilian wine did the Trojans
Get from him as a present?[17] They demand that the teacher
Shall mould these tender minds, like an artist who shapes
A face out of wax, with his thumb. He must, they insist,
Be a father to all his pupils, must stop them getting up to
Indecent tricks with each other (though it's no sinecure
To keep check over all those darting eyes – and fingers).
'See to it,' you're told, 'and when the school year's ended,
You'll get as much as a jockey makes from a single race.'

1. There has been much argument as to the identity of this Emperor, whom J. does not address by name. It is now generally, and plausibly, agreed that it must have been Hadrian. The occasion could have been either his accession in A.D. 118 (each new ruler, it was hoped, would prove a generous patron of the arts), or, as Highet suggests, his subsequent refoundation of the Athenaeum as a literary centre. The latter event will have taken place before 121, when Hadrian left Rome for a lengthy tour of the provinces. Highet also points out that Satire VII 'contains [J.'s] first dedication to any individual, and his first complimentary reference to any emperor.'

2. The *gallica* was some kind of Gaulish shoe or slipper which left the ankle bare, thus revealing the tell-tale scars left, on one of them (*altera*), by the slave-dealer's shackles. With all modern editors I omit line 15 ('Although Cappadocian burghers and Bithynians do such things . . .'), since it is clearly out of place here: it may have formed part of an alternative version of the passage, later discarded.

3. There seems to be an allusion here to the libraries which Augustus and his wife Livia established, respectively, in the temples of Apollo and the Muses on the Palatine.

4. The allusion is to Horace's *Odes*, 2.19.5, where he describes the excited cries of the Bacchanals. Horace, having a generous patron, could write poetry under ideal conditions: certainly he never went hungry.

5. See Virgil, *Aeneid* 7.445–46 (p. 189): for this episode the Fury Allecto appeared in a dream to Turnus, and when he mocked her prophecies she 'exploded into blazing anger. And even as he spoke the young prince found his limbs suddenly possessed by a trembling, and his eyes became fixed in a stare; so countless were the snakes which uttered the Fury's hiss, and so horrifying was the apparition which stood revealed . . .' etc.

6. The poet Lucan (Marcus Annaeus Lucanus) was born in Cordoba, in Spain, on 3 November A.D. 39, but spent most of his short life in Rome. His uncle was Seneca, the philosopher: the family had considerable wealth, which is the point of the reference

here. At first an intimate of Nero's, Lucan latterly passed out of Imperial favour: it may have been the veto on his literary activities which led him, in 65, to join the ill-fated Conspiracy of Piso, as a result of which he, his father, and both his uncles were forced to commit suicide. He left his epic poem *Pharsalia* (Penguin Classics translation by Robert Graves) unfinished at the time of his death.

7. Publius Papinius Statius (A.D. 45–96) was a Neapolitan who settled in Rome, and seems to have been on reasonably friendly terms with Domitian. His 'ever-popular Theban epic', the *Thebaid*, took twelve years to compose, and during this period Statius – like modern writers – gave occasional public recitals of 'work in progress'. He does not appear to have ever been quite so hard up as J. would have us believe.

8. The Paris referred to here was a well-known *pantomimus*, or ballet-dancer, of Domitian's reign, executed in A.D. 83 for a suspected liaison with Domitian's wife, the empress Domitia. 'Paris' was probably a stage-name, since it belonged to another *pantomimus* under Nero (this one too was executed, in 67), and recurs again in the following century (cf. n. 5 to Satire VI, p. 153). Military tribunes automatically became equestrians, or 'knights', after six months' service; the practice of appointing *honorary* tribunes, who were elevated without in fact holding a command, began with Claudius (see Suetonius, *Claudius* 25, p. 196, and Pliny, *Letters* 4.4). Martial obtained equestrian status in this manner, perhaps from Titus (3.95.9).

9. The 'December vacation' was the Saturnalia (17–19 December), a riotous carnival during which slaves had temporary licence to act as they pleased, and governed by a kind of 'Lord of Misrule', the *Saturnalicius princeps*.

10. As both Martial and Lucian tell us, a lawyer who won a case was entitled to advertise the fact by hanging up palm-branches outside his door.

11. The Roman passion for rhetoric is perhaps, more than any other characteristic, calculated to bewilder a modern reader. Public speaking was not only a practical skill, but also an art practised for its own sake in the schools, and often kept up afterwards. Many satirists, from Petronius to Juvenal, mock the unreality of the set themes traditionally employed. As Duff remarks, one of the stock exercises was to make attacks on tyrants or panegyrics on

tyrannicides: 'It might be supposed that the imperial government would not approve of this practice as a regular part of education; but the tyrant of the schools was too fantastic and unreal a creation to be taken seriously.'

12. For Quintilian see n. 19 to Satire VI. His official salary as Professor of Rhetoric under Vespasian was 100,000 sesterces *per annum*, and this was further augmented by a large and lucrative practice at the Bar.

13. J. has an actual case in mind: an ex-praetor and senator, Valerius Licinianus, who was also an excellent rhetorician, but found himself sent into exile after an alleged liaison with a Vestal Virgin. He accepted a Chair of Rhetoric in Sicily under Trajan, and, so Pliny tells us in his *Letters*, began his inaugural lecture with the words: 'What sport you make with men, Fortune: you turn senators into professors, and professors into senators!' The second translation applied, in a sense, to Quintilian, since he received consular honours through the good offices of Domitian's brother-in-law.

14. P. Ventidius [Bassus] was the stock example of the upstart who triumphed over both low birth and adverse circumstances. As a child he was captured at Asculum and exhibited in the triumph of Cn. Pompeius Strabo. He is contemptuously referred to as a 'muleteer', but may have been an army contractor. In 43 B.C. he attained the consulship (see below, Satire VIII 148, for another 'muleteer consul'), and in 38 himself celebrated a triumph over the Parthians. He died shortly afterwards.

15. Thrasimachus (or possibly Lysimachus) was, says the scholiast, an Athenian rhetorician who died by hanging. Secundus Carrinas was exiled by Caligula, according to Dio Cassius, for 'making derogatory remarks about tyrants in the gymnasium': so the practice did have its risks, after all. But Knoche thinks, and I am inclined to agree with him, that something has fallen out of the text after 205, and that the man to whom Athens gave nothing but a cup of cold hemlock must, surely, be Socrates.

16. Another of J.'s debunking side-swipes at mythological figures: Achilles' music-master was Chiron, the Centaur, half-man and half-horse.

17. 'What Songs the *Syrens* sang,' wrote Sir Thomas Browne,

'or what name *Achilles* assumed when he hid himself among women, though puzzling questions are not beyond all conjecture.' Another surprising thing about educated Romans is the habit, which they seem to have inherited from Greek Alexandria, of intense fascination with such *recherché* scraps of knowledge. The questions Browne lists are those which Tiberius asked his savants: see Suetonius, *Tiberius* 70 (p. 144); but the point about J.'s list seems to be that none of the answers are known. For Anchemolus and his stepmother see Virgil, *Aeneid* 10.388–9; for Acestes, *Aeneid* 1.195 5.73 ff.

ADDITIONAL NOTE

Griffith (Additional Bibliography) offers what is clearly the correct explanation of *stlattaria* at line 134: the gown is obtained by means of 'piratical' extortion, through bargaining with a desperate prospective client before accepting his case. This practice was well known in Rome, and frowned on by respectable jurists: see, e.g., Quintilian 12.7.11. I have also gratefully borrowed Griffith's ingenious reinterpretation of lines 126–8, presenting Aemilius as a horse-archer shutting one eye to aim his bow (*hastile*), as well as his neat gloss on *artem scindes Theodori* at line 177. For an alternative, but to me less convincing, interpretation of 126ff. see J. F. Killeen and Martyn in Additional Bibliography.

SATIRE VIII

What good are family trees? What point is there in being
    valued
For the length of your pedigree, Ponticus?[1] Where does it
    get you
Having the painted masks of your ancestors on display,
Or all those statues – an Aemilius in his chariot,
Half of a Curius, a Corvinus lacking one shoulder,
A noseless Galba? What is the object of boasting
About your high ancestry? Why trace back the ramifications
Of your kinship with dusty Pontiffs or Masters of Horse, if
    your own
Life is a public disgrace?[2] Why have so many portraits
Of generals around, if you spend the whole night gambling
Under their noses, if you're ready for bed
At daybreak – a time when *they* would be up and striking camp
And moving their forces off? Why on earth should a Fabius,
Though descended from Hercules, be entitled to any respect
For inherited honours – his rights at the Great Altar,
Being styled 'Of the Rhône'[3] – if he's a greedy numskull
And softer than any lambkin, if his backside
Is pumiced smooth, a caricature of his hairy
Ancestors, if he blots the family scutcheon by traffic
In illegal drugs, and his statue has to be broken up?
You may line your whole hall with waxen busts, but virtue,
And virtue alone, remains the one true nobility.
Model your conduct on that of patrician heroes,
A Paulus, a Cossus, a Drusus:[4] honour *their* images
Above all your ancestral portraits: when you are consul
Let *them* go before the lictors. Your foremost obligation
Lies with the spiritual virtues. Prove that your life
Is stainless, that you always abide by what is just
In word and deed – and *then* I'll acknowledge your noble status:

All hail to you, sir, whatever your birth! When Osiris
Is born again, the Egyptians cry: 'We have found him!
   Rejoice!'
So should his country greet so rare and distinguished a son.
Nobility cannot be claimed for one whose behaviour
Falls short of his breeding, whose sole claim to distinction
Lies in a name. But dwarfs get labelled 'Atlas',
A blackamoor's 'Snowball', some ugly misshapen girl
Is known as 'Miss Europe', while the scabbiest mongrel –
All bald and patched with mange, and lazily licking
The rim of an empty lamp – we call 'Pard' or 'Tiger'
Or 'Leo', or anything else (if there is) that roars more fiercely.
So be on your guard, friend: an old patrician title,
When assumed by you, may produce | very much the same
   effect.
  At whom is this warning aimed? I'm talking to you,
   Rubellius
Blandus.⁵ You give yourself airs because you can claim descent
From the House of Drusus – as though it were by some act
Of your own that you are a noble, that the bright Julian blood
Runs in your mother's veins, that she wasn't some weaving-
   woman
Who worked for hire beneath the windy Embankment!⁶
'You others are dirt,' you tell us, 'the rabble, the very dregs:
Not one of you knows his own father's parentage,
Whereas *I* claim descent from the Kings.'
                  Long life then, m'lord,
And much joy of your pedigree! Yet first-class advocates
May be found in this common herd, men used to handling
   briefs
For illiterate noblemen; if you're after a jurist
Who's expert at slashing through all legal knots and riddles,
Look among the plebeians. Where are our front-line troops
Recruited from, those brave professionals, always
Holding the fort in Germany, or the Middle East?⁷ But you,

With your blue blood and nothing else, resemble some limbless
Herm:[8] your one advantage is that the statue's noddle
Is marble, whereas you, you dummy, are alive.
    Tell me, O scion of Trojans, what's the first characteristic
Of a thoroughbred? Speed and strength. The horse we most
        admire
Is the one who romps home a winner, cheered on by the
        frenzied
Roars of the crowd. Good breeding doesn't depend on
A fancy pasturage; the thoroughbred earns his title
By getting ahead of the field, by making them eat his dust.
But if he's seldom victorious, the auction-ring will claim him,
Though his pedigree may be starred with every legendary
Name from the stud-book. No ancestor-worship here, no
Respect for the dead. Sold off at knock-down prices,
Constantly changing hands, these slow and plodding
        descendants
Of noble bloodstock will end up turning a mill-wheel,
Neck-galled from the collar, fit for no other work.
So, if we are to respect not your possessions but *you*,
Show me some personal act | of merit to set beside
Those honours we have paid, and pay still, to the forebears
Who endowed you with all you own.
                                        Yet this will suffice
For the youth who (rumour tells us) has let his kinship with
        Nero
Go to his head, who's puffed up with silly pride: but then
One seldom finds any decent respect for others
In the class he represents. I don't want to see *you* valued
By your ancestors' record, achieving nothing that's worthy
Of honour yourself. To lean on borrowed glory
Is a shabby expedient: the pillars may totter and fall,
The house collapse in ruin. The trailing vine-shoot
Yearns for its widowed elm. Be a good soldier, a faithful
Guardian; let all your judgements be made with integrity.

If you are called to bear witness in some ambivalent
And dubious case, though Phalaris should command you
To perjure yourself, though the brazen bull was being stoked
While he dictated the lies you were to repeat,⁹
The worst sin still is to choose survival before honour,
To lose what gives life its value for the sake of saving your skin.
Though he dine off ten dozen oysters, or fill the bathtub
With expensive essence, the man who deserves to die
Is already dead in his soul.

                So when you at last obtain
Your long-awaited reward, that provincial governorship,
Set some curb on your anger and greed, pity the destitute
Local inhabitants, whose very bones, you'll discover,
Have been sucked dry of marrow: observe what the law
    prescribes,
Respect the Senate's decrees, think what rewards
Await the good ruler, remember the thunderbolt
Of justice with which our parliament struck down those
    governors
Who outpirated the Cilicians.¹⁰ Yet what good ever came
Of their condemnation? Official B will deprive
Some wretched native of all that Official A has left him,
Until his only recourse is to peddle the threadbare
Clothes off his back. Yet he seldom complains. Why risk
Losing the last few coppers you need for your passage-money
To Rome – or Hades?

                Once, long ago, when our allies
Were newly conquered, and when their communities still
    flourished,
It was a different story. They grumbled, but could afford
To stand the loss. Their houses were stacked roof-high
With piles of bullion, scarlet cloaks from Sparta
And Coan purple. Paintings and statues and ivories
By the Old Masters, so vivid they seemed alive,
Were in every home; few sideboards but bore fine specimens

Of the engraver's art. Then came the conquistadors –
Antony, Dolabella, temple-plundering Verres[11] –
Carrying off whole shiploads of private loot, more trophies
In peace than in war. But today, when you confiscate
A provincial farmstead, what does it yield? A few yoke
Of oxen, one stallion kept for stud, a small
Herd of brood-mares. You're lucky if you can collect
A single valuable image from the shrine of the household gods:
Such are the choicest pickings today.[12] Perhaps you despise
The unwarlike Rhodians, the scented sons of Corinth –
And rightly so: what harm can ever befall you
From youths who put on perfume and shave their legs to the
    crutch?
But steer clear of rugged Spain, give a very wide berth
To Gaul and the coast of Illyria; don't touch those African
Labour-gangs sweating away in the wheatfields to supply
A Rome whose only concern now is racing and the stage.
(It's not so long, besides, since Marius skinned the niggers
Down to their loin-cloths: nothing to hope for there.[13])
But rule number one is this: Take care not to victimize
Courageous, desperate men. You may strip them of all
Their gold and silver, they still possess swords and shields,
Helmets and javelins: the plundered keep their weapons.[14]

    What I have just propounded is no mere rhetorical flourish,
Believe me, but sober truth, leaves from the Sibyl's book.[15]
If your staff are upright and honest – no long-haired catamite
Who can fix your verdicts for cash – if your wife is above
    suspicion,
And doesn't come round on circuit from town to town
Like a harpy with crooked talons, a regular gold-digger, then
You can trace your lineage back to the Woodpecker King –
    or if loftier
Names are what you're after, why not load your pedigree
With all those embattled Titans, and Prometheus for good
    measure?[16]

[Pick your own ancestry from any myth you like.]
But if ambition and lust dictate your headlong progress,
If you splinter the rods in blood across provincial backs, if
Blunt axes and weary headsmen are your prime delight,
Then you will find your noble ancestry beginning
To rebel against you, to hold | a bright torch to your
    shamelessness.
The higher a criminal's standing, the more public the obloquy
His vices call down on him. The habitual forger
Acquires no virtue by signing a fraudulent deed
In some temple his grandfather built, or beside his father's
Triumphal statue. What's all your blue blood worth
If you slip out by night, wrapped in a hooded cloak,
To commit adultery?
                There goes fat Lateranus,
Driving a gig flat out past his ancestors' bones and ashes,[17]
Locking the drag on the wheel himself – *himself!* – a Consul
Turned muleteer. It's night, but the moon can see him, the
    stars
Look down as witnesses – and when his term of office
Is ended, why then, Lateranus will flourish his whip
In broad daylight, quite shamelessly, flick a cheerful salute
To respectable elderly friends as he passes; he'll untruss
The hay-bales himself, and fodder his weary horses.
Meanwhile, official duties call him. But though he'll sacrifice
'A dun steer and eke a shearling', as ancient ritual prescribes,
The only goddess he swears by, even at Jove's high altar,
Is Epona, Our Lady of Horseflesh, whose picture you'll find
    daubed
On the doors of his reeking stables.[18] He's a familiar client
At the all-night taverns; when he shows up, mine host –
Some greasy Syrian from the Jewish quarter, with slicked-back
Pomaded hair – runs out, greets him obsequiously,
Calls him 'M'lord' and 'Your Honour', while the barmaid
    gives

A hitch to her skirts, and uncorks her bottle for action.[19]
  I can hear his supporters' comeback: 'Well, didn't we all
Behave like that as young men?' Perhaps, but you kicked the
    habit
Before you reached manhood. Wild oats should be sown and
    done with:
Some follies should not outlast your first official shave.
Youth rates a certain indulgence, agreed: but Lateranus
Was still boozing around – at the baths, or in low-class
    cabarets –
When old enough for Eastern campaigns, for garrison
Duty in Syria, maybe, or on the Rhine or Danube,
Old enough to protect the Emperor's person. Send down
To the docks for your general, Caesar: you'll find him sprawled
In the biggest, shadiest tavern, beside some hired killer,
With a bunch of thieves and matelots and fugitive criminals,
Among hangmen and coffin-makers and a castrated
Priest who's passed out on the job, still clutching his drums.
No social distinctions here: bed and board are in common,
Privilege is abolished, all men are free and equal.[20]
If you came across one of your slaves in such a den, Ponticus,
Wouldn't you pack him off for a spell of hard labour
On your country estate? But blue blood has special licence,
And gets away with behaviour that would shame a working
    man.
  Yet it's hard to plumb rock-bottom, produce such examples
That nothing worse could be thought of. When Damasippus
Had run through his capital, he hired himself out
To play in noisy farces, like *The Ghost* of Catullus, while
Lentulus made a hit as *The Crucified Bandit*. (A pity
He wasn't nailed up in earnest.)[21] The spectators must
Take part of the blame: they sit there, shamelessly gawping,
While barefoot patricians swop gags and buffooneries,
Stoogeing around with slapstick, getting the big laughs.
Does it matter what *price* they charge for their degradation?[22]

The point
Is, that they do it – and when there's no Nero to make them,
    either.
Their honour's for sale, to stage and arena alike. Suppose
You were faced with the choice, though – death, or a life on
    the boards –
Which would you opt for? Was there ever a man so scared
By the prospects of death that he'd rather play jealous husbands
Or be a clown's feed-man? Still, when Emperors turn harpist,
A blue-blooded comic lead isn't quite such a shock. What's left
After this but the arena? Here, too, gross public scandal
Awaits you: a Gracchus fighting, and not in full armour, either,
With target and falchion – such gear he can't abide,
No visor to cover *his* face. The weapon that catches his fancy
Is – a trident. Watch him gather the folds of his net
And throw it, and miss his cast, and bolt for dear life
Out of the ring, his features exposed, quite recognizable
To the whole audience. Who | could mistake that open-necked
Cloth-of-gold tunic, that mitre with dangling ribbons?²³
So the swordsman paired against Gracchus had perforce to
    endure
Worse ignominy than wounds.
                              On a free popular vote
Who could help but prefer a Seneca to a Nero,
Victim to parricide? If punishment was determined
By the number of deaths, you'd need more than one sack,
One snake, one monkey, to square off Nero's account.²⁴
Orestes' crime was the same, but circumstances made it
A very dissimilar case – *he* killed with divine sanction,
To avenge a father slain in his cups. Orestes never
Had Electra's blood on his head, he never murdered
His Spartan wife, or mixed up a dose of belladonna
For any close relative. *He* never sang on the stage
Or composed a Trojan epic – and what, in that bloody regime,
Cried out for vengeance more when the military took over?

Such were the acts of this prince of the blood, and such
His accomplishments – how he adored inflicting that ghastly
     voice
On audiences abroad, and winning Greek parsley-wreaths!
So deck his ancestral statues with concert-tour souvenirs,
Make offerings of the costumes he wore as Antigone
Or Thyestes, the mask in which he played Melanippe,
And hang up his harp on his own colossal marble likeness!
    Where could you hope to find men of loftier ancestry
Than Catiline or Cethegus?[25] Yet they planned a night attack
On the City, they were willing to fire Rome's houses and
     temples
(Like a bunch of trousered Gauls repeating the exploit
Of their warrior forebears) well though they knew what end
The attempt might bring them – to fry in the shirt of pitch.[26]
But the Consul was not caught napping: he beat their forces
     back,
Posted armed guards everywhere, stopped the panic, alerted
The Seven Hills – yet what was he? A raw provincial burgher,
No birth, no breeding, who'd just hit Rome from Arpinum.[27]
A civilian, maybe; and yet this Johnny-come-lately
Won as much fame and honour within the City walls
As Octavius' bloody sword brought *him* after Actium
And the massacre of Philippi.[28] But when Rome's citizens
Styled Cicero 'Sire of his country', they were still a free
     people.
    Another son of Arpinum once toiled as a ploughboy, for
     hire,
In the Volscian hills, and afterwards joined the army –
Centurion-bait, his brains half cudgelled out whenever
He leaned on his spade, took a breather from camp-entrenching.
Yet this was the same man who faced the threat of Teutonic
Invasion, who single-handed stood up in this mortal crisis
And saved the trembling City. So when the ravens
Swooped down to feast on those giant barbarian

Carcases, the largest they'd ever seen, his colleague
Shared in his triumph, but all | the cheers were for Marius.²⁹
   Plebeian by name, plebeian in spirit, the Decii still
Were accepted by the Earth-Goddess, by the underworld deities
As a worthy self-sacrifice, an oblation for the whole host
Of legions and allied troops, the flower of all Latium.
[So the Decii stood higher than those whose lives they
     preserved.]³⁰
   The last of our virtuous Kings to assume the mantle
Of old Quirinus, the diadem, rods and axes
Had a slave for a mother – whereas the Consul's sons (who
Should have done splendid deeds to rescue imperilled
Freedom, something Horatius holding the bridge, or
Mucius thrusting his hand in the flames, or the virgin
Cloelia swimming the Tiber would all applaud) instead
Plotted to open Rome's gates to her exiled tyrants. A slave
It was that forestalled them, revealing their criminal secrets
To the Senate (why not commemorate *him*?), and the sons
Of Brutus justly endured the scourge and the axes, then
For the very first time applied in due form by law.³¹
   I'd rather you had Thersites for father, so long as *you*
Resembled Achilles, and matched up to Vulcan's arms:
Suppose you'd been sired by Achilles, but proved a Thersites
     yourself?
Yet, in the last resort, however far back you may trace
Your ancestral line, whatever | the length of your pedigree,
Where did it all begin? In a kind of ill-famed ghetto.
Your first forefather, whatever his name, was either
A shepherd – or something I'd really better not mention.³²

1. The only person of this name we know from the period is Valerius Ponticus, who was banished during Nero's reign for complicated legal collusion and chicanery in the courts: see Tacitus, *Annals* 14.41 (p. 332 n. 4). It has been supposed that J.'s 'Ponticus' may be fictitious, a mere imaginary recipient of the author's lecture on titled snobbery. I rather doubt this; almost all J.'s characters can be run to earth somewhere, and the fact that we cannot trace some of them is no guarantee (in the fragmentary state of our evidence) that they did not exist.

2. It has been acutely pointed out that in this satire J. brings in the name of almost every distinguished Roman family, including such *gentes* as the Aemilia, Curia, Sulpicia, Valeria, Fabia, Cornelia, Claudia, Junia, Antonia, Sergia and Julia. The Emperor Galba boasted that he could trace his family back to Jupiter (Suetonius, *Galba* 2, p. 244) and Pasiphaë (a relationship, one might have thought, better hushed up). The Corvini were distinguished nobles under the Empire: see Friedländer's note, p. 401.

At line 7 I read *pontifices posse ac* with Housman: Clausen retains *Corvinum, posthac* and prints lines 6–8 in square brackets as an interpolation.

3. The Fabian *gens* was supposedly descended from Hercules and Vinduna, Evander's daughter. The 'Great Altar' was the *ara maxima* of Hercules, an extremely ancient shrine, between the Circus Maximus and the Tiber, close to the Aemilian Bridge. The title 'Of the Rhône' (*Allobrogicus*) was conferred in 121 B.C. upon Quintus Fabius Maximus after his defeat of the Allobroges, a Gallic tribe that dwelt between the Rhône and the Isère.

4. L. Aemilius Paulus Macedonicus concluded the Third Macedonian War in 168 B.C. with the defeat of Perseus: he was responsible for the settlement of Greece. The Cossus here referred to is probably Cn. Cornelius Lentulus Cossus, who in A.D. 6 defeated the Gaetuli in Africa, earning himself the title 'Gaetulicus'. On Tiberius's accession he was sent to deal with the mutineers in Pannonia: Tacitus says of him that he 'was honoured for poverty patiently

endured, followed by great wealth respectably acquired and modestly employed' (*Annals* 4.44, p. 175). His colleague in Pannonia was the Drusus referred to here, Tiberius's brother, and the father of both Germanicus and Claudius. All three examples are chosen for combining an illustrious military career with high moral character. Lentulus Cossus was about the only man of distinction to survive friendship with Sejanus (Tacitus, *Annals* 6.30, p. 209; and cf. below, Satire X 58 ff.).

5. Tiberius's son Drusus Caesar had a daughter, Julia, who in A.D. 33 married a C. Rubellius Blandus. Their son, C. Rubellius Plautus, the great-great-grandson of Augustus, was a man of Stoic principles and considerable moral courage, who could have led a successful revolt against Nero, but preferred to live in loyal retirement. Yet this did not safeguard him: he was finally executed, on Nero's orders, in A.D. 62. It is generally, and most improbably, supposed that one of these two is under discussion here: for some choice vagaries of interpretation see Highet, p. 273 n. 7. But J.'s whole point is that the man whom he is addressing is a nobody, whose blood is his one claim to distinction. Duff, as so often, hits the mark exactly when he writes (p. 300): 'Rubellius Blandus is taken as a type of noble birth and nothing more . . . Juvenal must mean one of this family, possibly a son or brother of Rubellius Plautus.'

6. For the 'Embankment' see n. 15 to Satire V: the weaving-women, we recall, had fortune-tellers and performing monkeys as their companions. Cf. Satire VI 588.

7. i.e. on the eastern and western frontiers of the Empire, the Euphrates and the Rhine.

8. A Herm was a quadrangular pillar of stone, topped by the head of the god Hermes: such pillars stood at most street corners and outside many private houses in Athens. Many of them (as J.'s readers would be well aware) were equipped with large erect phalluses, and the implication as regards this degenerate representative of the nobility is clear enough. The epithet 'scion of Trojans' is several times used by J., and always in the same sarcastically pejorative context: see Satire I, 100, and XI 95. It is the equivalent to our 'coming over with the Conqueror', and alludes, of course, to the settlement by Aeneas.

9. Phalaris was tyrant of Acragas (Agrigento) in Sicily, *c.* 570–554

B.C. He is mainly remembered today for two things: the hollow brazen bull in which he is said to have roasted his victims alive, a habit reminiscent of the Moloch cult, and one, as Grote put it, 'better authenticated than the nature of the story would lead us to presume'; and his supposed *Letters*, which Richard Bentley, in a memorable dissertation, showed not to be authenticated at all, but forgeries by some late sophist, perhaps a contemporary of Lucian.

10. One of these was Cossutianus Capito, who in A.D. 57, as Tacitus tells us (*Annals* 13.33, p. 289), 'was indicted by the Cilicians. This vicious and disreputable man believed he could behave as outrageously in his province as in Rome.' The other is only referred to as 'Tutor', and cannot be identified with certainty.

11. Cn. Cornelius Dolabella was Governor of Cilicia in 80/79 B.C., with Verres as his Legate. In 78 Dolabella was prosecuted for extortion in his province, and condemned. Another Dolabella was similarly charged with extortion in Macedonia, by Julius Caesar, in 77; and in 43 yet a third, P. Cornelius Dolabella, the most vicious of them all, was murdered after wholesale extortions in Asia Minor. (Hence I am inclined to read *Dolabellae* in the plural at 105, and to scan the line by hiatus.) The Antonius referred to here is not Mark Antony, but his uncle, whom Duff, scarcely exaggerating, describes as 'a monster of rapacity'. Caesar brought charges against him in 76 for extortion in Greece; he was finally exiled in 59 for plundering Macedonia, where he had been Governor in 62. For Verres see n. 7 to Satire III.

12. Clausen brackets lines 111-12 as an interpolation: this seems unnecessary.

13. Marius Priscus (not Gaius Marius) was prosecuted jointly by Tacitus and the Younger Pliny for extortion in North Africa, and sentenced to banishment from Rome and Italy, A.D. 100: see Pliny, *Letters* 2.11; he is the governor referred to in Satire I 49.

14. Clausen brackets line 124 as an interpolation: it is, to be sure, a striking pleonasm, but here I agree once more with Duff, who observes acutely of J. that 'it is quite in his manner to repeat in an epigrammatic form exactly what he has just said', and who, in his note on VIII 258, has the last word on the 'interpolation theory': '... the line is weak in itself ... but that Juvenal had better not have written it, is no proof that he did not.' Even a classic may nod.

15. 'Leaves from the Sibyl's book' were oracular utterance and therefore unquestioned truth. Her sayings, inscribed on palm-leaves, were preserved in the Capitol, and consulted by the Sacred College (*quindecemviri*). Cf. n. 1 to Satire III.

16. Picus, the 'Woodpecker King', was originally a woodpecker *tout court*, sacred to Mars; but afterwards became translated into one of the early Italian kings, son of Saturn and father of Faunus. The Titans and Prometheus, though not Roman by origin, are suggested as providing a more secure genealogy. J. recurs to the dubious origins of Rome's native nobility in the last lines of this satire.

17. It is generally agreed that this was Plautius Lateranus, who narrowly escaped execution in A.D. 48 for adultery with Messalina, lost his senatorial rank, was restored to it by Nero in 56, and perished through his implication in the Conspiracy of Piso (65): Tacitus confirms that he was of 'big build'. But there are difficulties. Plautius Lateranus was executed while still consul-designate; J.'s character is clearly in office. Also, Tacitus makes it clear that Plautius Lateranus joined the plot from patriotic motives; since J. disliked Nero intensely it is hard to see why he picked out one of his opponents for ridicule unless he considered that driving one's own gig was a worse crime – which he conceivably may have done: see Satire I 61, and below, lines 220 ff. The alternative candidate is T. Sextius Lateranus, consul in A.D. 94; he is generally excluded because of the specific reference to Nero at line 170–1. But the Emperor he served under was Domitian; and Domitian was often spoken of as a second Nero. (Nero's original name was Lucius Domitius Ahenobarbus.) It is impossible to make a clear decision in favour of either Lateranus, though my own inclination, on balance, is towards the second.

18. Epona is called, by the scholiast, 'the goddess of muleteers': modern research suggests that she was a Gallic nature-deity specially associated with horses, asses and mules. See Highet p. 273 n. 4 and refs. there cited.

19. Something is clearly amiss with the text of 159–62. Line 160 looks like a doublet of 159, and is omitted by some MSS; but it makes sense of a sort as it stands. Housman thought a line had dropped out after 160. Lines 161–2 read better with 160 omitted: otherwise 161 needs the insertion of *et* after *adfectu* to make it read smoothly (see Helmbold, *Mnemosyne* 4/5, 1952, 226 f.), and there is the

likelihood that more may have dropped out after 162: perhaps a line with a definite verb describing the activities of the barmaid Cyane. The reader should be warned that the sense here is admissible, but no more than approximate.

20. This looks like a cynical sideswipe at Stoic theories of equality.

21. Damasippus is unknown, but was probably chosen here, like Lentulus (who must have have been a member of the noble Lentuli Cornelii clan) as a typical patrician wastrel. Catullus was not the famous lyric poet, but a popular farce-writer under Nero: cf. below, Satire XIII 111. *The Ghost* (*Phasma*) must have been very like the *Mostellaria* of Plautus, which was based on a Greek original of this name. *The Crucified Bandit* described the life of a famous highwayman called Laureolus, and his execution: it had become a perennial favourite as early as Caligula's reign. Suetonius (*Caligula* 57, p. 177) says that 'the leading character . . . had to die while escaping, and vomit blood'; but Martial (7.4) clearly alludes to his crucifixion.

22. Line 192 has a rare puzzle in the phrase *sua funera*, variously rendered as 'their dead selves' (Duff) or 'their (*sc.* distinguished) dead, i.e. ancestry, not death or moral suicide' (Quincey, in Coffey, 193) or 'the "stage-deaths" of those who appeared in a notorious mime'(Griffith, ibid.). I prefer to take it in the sense of 'their degradation' (or ruin, or fall). J.'s (to us) somewhat heated feelings about well-bred persons appearing on the stage, especially in a professional capacity, is confirmed in detail by Tacitus, *Annals* 14.20–21, *passim* (pp. 312–13). For Nero's pressurizing in this field see *Annals* 14.14.10 (p. 310): ' . . . he brought on to the stage members of the ancient nobility whose poverty made them corruptible. They are dead, and I feel I owe it to their ancestors not to name them' – a reticence which J. clearly did not share.

23. The descendant of the Gracchi who appeared as a *retiarius* or net-man in the arena was obviously notorious: we have already met him in Satire II 143 ff., and previously as a homosexual 'bride'. J. Colin (in *Les études classiques* 23 see Bibliography) argues persuasively that the *galerus* worn by Gracchus was in fact the tall bonnet of a Salian priest, which, with a blasphemous flourish, he kept to wear for his gladiatorial activities. I have translated in accordance with this interpretation.

24. The traditional penalty for parricide was that the culprit,

after scourging, should be sewn in a sack with a dog, a cock, a snake and a monkey: the sack was then thrown into the sea (*Digest* 48.9.9). Nero's victims included his mother, his aunt Domitia Lepida (Suetonius, *Nero* 34, pp. 227–8), his adoptive sister Antonia, Britannicus, and his wife Octavia. His epic poem on the Fall of Troy was recited at the literary festival he founded in A.D. 65; his tour of Greece as a concert artiste took place in 67/8, and he brought home no fewer than 1808 crowns of victory.

25. Catiline was a member of the *gens Sergia* and Cethegus belonged to a patrician branch of the *gens Cornelia*. Their famous conspiracy took place in 63 B.C. The Gauls defeated Rome's armies at the Allia in 390 B.C. and afterwards sacked and burnt the city.

26. The 'shirt of pitch', or *tunica molesta*, was a punishment reserved for those guilty of arson, and probably first applied to the Christians in A.D. 64, when Nero convicted them of causing the Great Fire of Rome: see Tacitus, *Annals* 15.44 (p. 354). The victim was tied to a stake, clad in a shirt impregnated with pitch, tar, resin, and similar combustibles, and turned into a kind of human torch. Cf. above, Satire I 155. That some kind of actual garment was worn is also suggested by Martial (4.86.8), who applies the phrase to greaseproof paper used for frying fish in.

27. The consul of 63 B.C. referred to here was, of course, Cicero, who was born in Arpinum on 3 January 106, but in fact spent most of his life from childhood onwards in Rome. He was a 'provincial knight', and the first of his family to hold a high office of State. In November 63 he denounced Catiline in the Senate: the conspirators were executed (a decision which afterwards caused Cicero much trouble, since his opponents never admitted the legality of this step), and Catiline's rebel forces finally destroyed in the field on 5 January 62.

28. At line 241 I accept Jahn's emendation *sibi* for the corrupt † *in* of the MSS, rather than the palaeographically more attractive *vi*, proposed by de Ruyt (*Revue Belge de Philologie* 23, 1944, 246–50): *sibi* balances and contrasts with *illi*, just as *abstulit* does with *contulit*. Octavius, the future Augustus, defeated Antony and Cleopatra at Actium in 31 B.C., and Brutus at Philippi in 42.

29. Gaius Marius (157–86 B.C.) rose rather faster than J. suggests. He was Tribune in 119 and Praetor in 115; by 107 he held his first

consulship. The invasion by two Germanic tribes, the Cimbri and Teutones, took place in 102. Marius defeated them that year at Aquae Sextiae, and again in 101, together with his colleague Q. Lutatius Catulus, at Vercellae. His acclaim during his triumph was much enhanced by the fact that he was a 'man of the people' and the prospective instrument of democratic reform; whereas Catulus was very much an aristocrat.

30. P. Decius Mus and his son, of the same name, both gave up their lives in this manner to save a Roman army: the father in 340 B.C., while fighting against the Latins, and the son in 295, during the Battle of Sentinum, against the Samnites: see Livy 8.9.8 and 10.28.15. This was a piece of primitive magic, known as *devotio*, and accompanied by a *carmen* or spell: see Pliny, *Natural History* 28.12.3.

31. The sons of Brutus, Titus and Tiberius, joined a plot for the restoration of Tarquinius Superbus: their detection and execution – the latter approved and witnessed by their father – is strikingly described by Livy 2.3–6 (pp. 92–5). Horatius Cocles is too well known from Macaulay's *Lays of Ancient Rome* to need any explanation. Gaius Mucius entered the camp of Lars Porsena and made an unsuccessful attempt to assassinate him: on being threatened with torture unless he revealed the whole plot he thrust his right hand into the fire and let it burn, crying 'See how cheap men hold their bodies when they care only for honour!' Afterwards he was known as 'Scaevola', or 'The Left-handed Man', a title preserved by his descendants (Livy 2.12–13, pp. 102–3). The same source tells the story of Cloelia, a girl held as hostage by the Etruscans, who one day rallied her fellow-hostages to swim the Tiber under enemy fire, and brought them all safely back to Rome. 'Porsena,' we are told, 'was furious, and sent to Rome to demand Cloelia's return – adding that the loss of the other girls did not trouble him.'

32. The 'kind of ill-famed ghetto' was the Asylum, or sanctuary, which Romulus – 'to help fill his big new town', as Livy says – threw open to every kind of slave, debtor or criminal: 'that mob was the first real addition to the City's strength, the first step to her future greatness' (Livy 1.8–9, pp. 26–7). In other words, a Roman noble's forbears were either shepherds (like Romulus and his first small group) or else fugitive convicts.

ADDITIONAL NOTE

At lines 85–6 Brown (Additional Bibliography) objects that the sentence ending 'the man who deserves to die is already dead in his soul' is not only dubious Latin, but, as it stands, irrelevant, on the grounds that 'if you are urging a man to remain true to his principles even in the face of death, it is irrelevant to add that oysters and perfume will not save him from the moral death which results from turpitude.' This is perhaps to place too much faith in J.'s sense of consequential logic; but Brown's explanation – that a line containing an antecedent relative clause may have dropped out before line 85 – has much to commend it.

SATIRE IX

JUVENAL: Why do you look so gloomy, more down in the
    mouth than Marsyas
After his flaying,[1] each time we meet? What's that glum
    frown for,
Naevolus? Why should *you* walk around with an expression
Like Ravola's when he was caught in the act, damp-bearded,
Muff-diving on Rhodope? (If a slave takes a lick at a tart
We give *him* a licking.) Heavens, your face looks longer
Than a share-pusher's when he offers a triple rate of interest
And can't find one taker. What's produced all these sudden
Lines and wrinkles? You used to take life as it came –
The provincial squire in person, a dinner-table wit
Whose jokes had an edge of urban sophistication.[2]
What a change today – that sick-hound look, that unkempt
Bush of dry hair! Your complexion's lost all the glow
It once got from hot packs of depilatory bird-lime,
Coarse bristles sprout unchecked on your hairy thighs.
You've lost weight, too, you're as thin | as some chronic
    invalid
With quartan ague. A wasting body reveals
All moods in the mind it houses: anguish and pleasure
Stamp themselves on the face then. You seem to have
    transformed
Your way of life, to be on a completely different track.
It's not so long, I recall, since you used to hang around
The temples of Ceres and Isis, or Ganymede's little shrine
In the temple of Peace, or Cybele's secret grotto
On the Palatine Hill[3] – all such places are hot-spots for easy
    women.
You laid them by dozens then, and (something you don't
    mention)
More often than not you would have their husbands, too.

NAEVOLUS: Many have made a packet from my way of life,
    but it's never
Brought *me* any decent pickings. Sometimes I'll collect
A greasy street-cloak, coarse and crudely dyed,
Cut from a bolt of loose-woven Gallic cloth, or
Some silver-plated gewgaw, lacking a hallmark.
Mankind is ruled by the Fates, they even govern those
    private
Parts that our clothes conceal. If your stars go against you
The fantastic size of your cock will get you precisely nowhere,
However much Virro⁴ may | have drooled at the spectacle
Of your naked charms, though love-letters come by the dozen
Imploring your favours, though – quote – *A man is attracted*
*By the very sight of – a pansy.*⁵ Yet what could be lower
Than a close-fisted queer? 'I paid you so much *then*,'
He says, 'and a bit more later, and more that other time –'
Working it out by piece-rates.

                        'Well,' I say, 'fetch the
    accountant
With his reckoner and tables, tot up the total figure:
A miserable five thousand. Now list *my* services. Do you
Suppose it's easy, or fun, this job of cramming
My cock up into your guts till I'm stopped by last night's
    supper?
The slave who ploughs his master's field has less trouble
Than the one who ploughs *him*.'

                        'But you used to fancy yourself
As a pretty young boy,' he says, ' a latter-day Ganymede –'
'Can't your sort ever show kindness to your minions, your
    humble
Ploughboys of pleasure? Are you so tight in the purse
That you even grudge the expense of your peculiar vices?'
What a creature! But still you're obliged to send *him* presents –
A green parasol, maybe, or big amber worry-beads –
On every birthday, or early in showery spring

When he lolls around on his sofa, examining the private
Tributes that he's been given to celebrate Ladies' Day.[6]

 'Tell me, you sparrow,[7] who are you keeping all those
Estates and mountains for? To traverse your pasturelands
Would tax the strength of a kite. Your Campanian vineyards
Yield you a rich return – who lays down more casks
Of first-class vintage wine? Would it cost you so much
To spare a few acres on which yours truly, after retirement,
Might rest his exhausted loins? Would you honestly rather
Pass on that country cottage (the child with its peasant mama,
A puppy scampering round) to some cymbal-bashing boy–
     friend?'[8]

'You mustn't *ask*,' says he, 'it's so rude.' But my rent cries out
Ask him! and so does my single slave (as single
As the big eye of Polyphemus which crafty Ulysses exploited
To make his get-away.[9]) But one's not enough, a second
Will have to be bought, and both must be fed. Then what
Can I do in the winter gales? What on earth can I tell these two
When December's north winds blow freezingly round their
     shoulders
And naked feet? *'Hold on for summer and the cicadas'*?

 'You can hedge if you like, discount all the rest, but don't you
Think it worth *something*, Virro, that if I hadn't displayed
True dedication to duty, your wife would be virgin still?
You know very well how often you begged for my help,
And in just what way, and the promises you made me –
Often enough she'd be on the point of bolting
When I finally got her to bed, she'd have torn up her
     marriage-vows
And be leaving for good.[10] It'd take me a hard night's work
To fix *that* little crisis, with you boo-hooing outside.
Witnesses? Well, we've the bed – and you (who heard its
     creaking,
Not to mention the groans of your wife). There's many a
     household

Just on the point of break-up that's been saved by adultery.
How can you shuffle like this? Where's your sense of values,
    man?
I sired you a son and a daughter: doesn't that mean
Anything to you at all, you ungrateful bastard? Aren't you
Bringing them up as your own? You love to advertise
These proofs of your manhood by entries in the Gazette[11] –
Congratulations, Daddy! Hang a wreath on your door, you've
    got
Something – from me – to shut up the gossip-mongers.
You hold parental rights now, I've cleared your legal standing
As an heir. You receive the estate tax-free, plus extras.
But just think of the added benefits if I provide you with
Another child, and bring | the score up to three!'[12]

                              JUVENAL:
    Indeed,
You have a case for complaint here, Naevolus. But what
Does *he* say on the other side?

                        NAEVOLUS: Takes no notice at all,
He's so busy looking around for another two-legged donkey
As my replacement. But don't pass a word of this on –
Keep my complaints to yourself, they're for your ears only:
These pumice-smooth fags make the deadliest enemies. Once
I shared in his secrets, and now he just loathes my guts,
As though I'd told all I knew. He wouldn't scruple
To have me knifed or clobbered, to set my place on fire –
And don't underestimate one thing: for millionaires
Poison is never expensive. So treat this as top secret.
JUVENAL: Ah Corydon, Corydon dear,[13] what secrets do you
    suppose
A rich man can keep? If his slaves don't tattle, his horses
And dog will, his doorposts, his pillars – shut all the windows,
Pull the curtains tight, bar every door, turn out
The lamps, get rid of the guests, let no one sleep within
    earshot,

And *still* whatever he did at the second cock-crow
That barman down on the corner will know by dawn, together
With every rumour started by the great man's kitchen staff
From head cook to bottle-washer. Of course they'll slander
      him;
Gossip's their only weapon, their way of getting back
For whippings. Besides, there's always some drunk to button-
      hole you
At the crossroads, and pour his story in your unwilling ears.
These are the lot you should bind to silence about
What you were saying just now. Tattling a secret gives them
A bigger kick than pinching, and swilling, as much good wine
As Saufeia[14] did, while conducting a public sacrifice.
First among many reasons for decent living, surely,
Is the need to be proof against the malice of your slaves:
The tongue is a slave's worse part. Yet the master, in thrall
To those whom he supports with his own cash and bread
Is worse served still, is never truly free.[15]
NAEVOLUS: Useful advice, my friend, but a little too vague
      and general.
What's my best move *now*, after all these wasted years
And disappointed hopes? The bloom of life will wither
Too soon, our miserable span on earth is running out:
While we drink, while we're calling out for garlands and ·
      perfumes
And girls, old age creeps up on us, unregarded.
JUVENAL: Never fear: so long as these Seven Hills stand fast
You'll always have friends in the trade, they'll still come
      flocking
From near and far, by ship or by coach, these gentry
Who scratch their heads with one finger.[16] And here's another
      sound
Piece of advice: chew colewort, it's a fine aphrodisiac.
NAEVOLUS: Save that stuff for the lucky ones. *My* Fates are
      overjoyed

If cock can keep belly fed. Poor little household gods,
Whom I supplicate with a pinch of incense or barley-meal,
Or a tiny garland – when will I ever lay by
Enough to insure my old age against the beggar's
Crutch and mat? A nice little nest-egg at interest,
In gilt-edged stock; a small silver dinner-service
(Too large, even so, by old Republican standards[17]);
A pair of brawny porters, Bulgarians, to take me
By sedan, through the crowds, to my seat in the noisy Circus –
What else? A stooped engraver, and a portraitist with the
     knack
Of dashing off five-minute likenesses.[18] That's enough
For a poor man such as myself: not an ambitious programme,
But unlikely, even so, to materialize. Whenever
Fortune's invoked for my benefit, she plugs up her ears
With wax from Ulysses' ship, is deaf to all blandishments.[19]

Notes to Satire IX

1. Marsyas was a satyr who challenged Apollo to a musical contest on the flute, or oboe: Apollo, taking advantage of the agreement that the victor could do what he would with the loser, had Marsyas flayed alive. The scholiast suggests that 'Marsyas' here may also allude to some contemporary advocate of that name: perhaps this is no more than a guess. If so, there is probably a covert obscene allusion. The scholiast was alive to such nuances: he also points out that the name 'Ravola' was coined on etymological grounds, to suit his activity (*ravulus* means 'hoarse').

2. Highet suggests (p. 121) that this satire was a product of J.'s earlier days, rescued from his bottom drawer later: and the context here suggests that Naevolus was a provincial, which supports such a theory.

3. On the temple of Isis as a place of assignation cf. Satire VI 529: the scholiast suggests, further, that both this and the shrine of Ganymede – appropriately enough – were used as a rendezvous by male homosexuals. The temples of Ceres and Cybele, being reserved for the use of women, were obvious places to watch if a man wanted a pick-up.

4. Virro is the name of Naevolus's unpleasant employer: he was, we may assume, the same person as the sadistic host of Satire V. (See n.3 to Satire V, p. 124). He, too, appears to have been a provincial, from within forty miles of J.'s home town of Aquinum: perhaps the relationship was one that J. had observed in his youth.

5. This is a parody of Homer, *Odyssey* 16.294, 19.13: the original operative word was not 'a pansy' but 'cold steel'.

6. It is generally assumed that from lines 40–53 Naevolus is addressing J. directly: Clausen and Knoche and Housman all punctuate thus. But this raises serious difficulties. Lines 46–7 I cannot believe were addressed to Virro: they are surely far more applicable to Naevolus, and the real problem is whether they are spoken by Virro or J. himself. The use of *tu* and *vos* throughout is puzzling. I have assumed that lines 40–46 (*ponatur calculus ... quam dominum*) are addressed by Naevolus to Virro; that 46–7 form Virro's startled

reply; that 48-9 is Naevolus's final thrust in this reported discussion, all of which is now being retailed to J., dialogue included. In 50-53 Naevolus addresses J. direct; then he resumes his apostrophe of Virro. Punctuating dialogue in a classical text is always open to error, since MSS have a bare minimum in the way of distinguishing marks. I would say no more for my rearrangement than that it makes tolerable sense.

'Ladies' Day' was the festival known as the Matronalia, celebrated on 1 March, and associated with the cult of Juno as goddess of married women and childbirth.

7. The lechery of the sparrow was proverbial in antiquity: see Pliny, *Natural History* 10.107. Chaucer, too, had the same belief; he wrote of the Somnour: 'As hoot he was and lecherous as a sparwe'.

8. The 'cymbal-bashing boy-friend' was not simply (as the context might suggest) a hep homosexual musician, but, more specifically, a priest of Cybele, and, therefore, a eunuch: so the scholiast, followed by Friedländer (p. 440).

9. The reference is to the episode of the *Odyssey* in which Odysseus and his companions gouged out the Cyclops' one eye with a red-hot stake (*Odyssey* 9.106 ff.).

10. At line 76 I accept Highet's emendation *migrabat* for *signabat*: see *Classical Review* NS2 (1952), 70 f.

11. The 'Gazette', or *Acta Diurna*, contained a record of the acts of the Senate, the popular assemblies, and the various courts of justice, together with registrations of births, marriages, deaths, divorces and other such personal data.

12. See above, n. 3 to Satire VI, p. 153.

13. Another parody: this time of Virgil, *Eclogues* 2.69, where Corydon the shepherd is recounting his more genteel homosexual passion for his master's favourite Alexis, and asks himself 'Ah Corydon, Corydon, what madness has seized upon you?'

14. We last met Saufeia at Satire VI 320, during the ritual of the Good Goddess, bumping and grinding with the call-girls. It is likely that the swigging of sacrificial wine took place on the same occasion: see notes 21 and 22 to Satire VI, pp. 156-7.

15. Clausen follows Knoche in bracketing 120-3: I prefer, with Housman, to bracket 119 (surely the intrusive gloss, if there is one, or a discarded alternative version), and, with rather less confidence,

to accept his emendation *tum est his* for the impossible †*tunc est* at 118, in default of anything better.

16. The scholiast assumes that this gesture refers to their patting and fixing their hair like women: it seems more likely to have been a secret sign, easily recognized by the initiated.

17. In 257 B.C. C. Fabricius Luscinus, as Censor, had an ex-consul named P. Cornelius Rufinus removed from the Senate on the grounds that he possessed more than ten pounds' weight of silver plate, contrary to the existing sumptuary laws: see Livy *Epitome* 14 and Friedländer p. 449, who collects other references.

18. Why the modest requirements of Naevolus should include a tame engraver and portraitist – especially after his strictly limited intentions in the matter of silverware – is very hard to see. Friedländer remarks that Verres had such artists as his private employees (Cicero, *In Verrem* II, 4, 24, 54): we should expect Verres to, but not Naevolus. Yet he states that this will do 'for a poor man like myself'. Perhaps he hoped to establish them in a workshop and make a profit on their sales. Settis (Additional Bibliography) suggests that the 'five-minute likenesses' in fact refer to those *a macchia* designs first known from Nero's Golden House (*Domus Aurea*), and referred to by the Elder Pliny (*Natural History* 35.109) as *compendiariae picturae*, 'shorthand methods of painting': cf. Petronius, *Satyricon* 2.9. See also Plato, *Republic* 495E, and Claude Mossé, *The Ancient World at Work* (1969), 90.

19. This refers to the occasion on which Odysseus and his crew sailed past the Sirens' rocks, and Odysseus stopped the ears of the rest with wax to prevent them hearing the Sirens' seductive song, but himself listened, bound to the mast so that he could not jump overboard: see Homer, *Odyssey* 12.173 ff.

SATIRE X

Search every land, from Cadiz to the dawn-streaked shores
Of Ganges, and you'll find few men who can distinguish
A false from a worthwhile objective, or slash their way
    through
The fogs of deception. Since when were our fears or desires
Ever dictated by reason? What project goes so smoothly
That you never regret the idea, let alone its realization?
What you ask for, you get. The Gods aren't fussy, they're
    willing
To blast you, root and branch, on request. It's universal,
This self-destructive urge, in civilian and soldier
Alike. The gift of the gab, a torrential facility,
Has proved fatal to so many; so has excessive reliance
On muscle and physical beef.[1] But more are strangulated
By the capital they amass with such expense of spirit,
Those bloated fortunes that dwarf any normal inheritance
Till they look like some puny dolphin beside a British whale.
So during the Reign of Terror, at Nero's command,
Longinus was banished, Seneca – grown too wealthy –
Lost his magnificent gardens, storm-troopers besieged
Lateranus' ancestral mansion.[2] Garrets are very seldom
The object of military raids. When you go on a night journey,
Though you may have only a few small treasures with you
You'll take every stirring shadow, each moonlit reed
For a sword or a cudgel. But the empty-handed
Traveller whistles his way past any highwayman.

  The most popular, urgent prayer, well-known in every
    temple,
Is for wealth. *Increase my holdings, please make my deposit account
The largest in town!*[3] But you'll never find yourself drinking
Belladonna from pottery cups. The time you should worry is
    when

You're clutching a jewelled goblet, when your bubbly gleams
    with gold.
They had a point – don't you agree? – those two old
    philosophers:
One of them helpless with laughter whenever he set foot
Outside his house, the other a weeping fountain.⁴
The cutting, dismissive sneer comes easily to us all –
But wherever did Heraclitus tap such an eye-brimming
Reservoir of tears? Democritus' sides shook non-stop,
Though the cities *he* knew had none of our modern trappings –
Togas bordered or striped with purple, sedans, the tribunal,
The rods and axes.⁵ Suppose he had seen the praetor
Borne in his lofty carriage through the midst of the dusty
Circus, and wearing full ceremonial dress –
The tunic with palm-leaves, the heavy Tyrian toga
Draped in great folds round his shoulders; a crown so enormous
That no neck can bear its weight, and instead it's carried
By a sweating public slave, who, to stop the Consul
Getting above himself, rides in the carriage beside him.⁶
Then there's the ivory staff, crowned with an eagle,
A posse of trumpeters, the imposing procession
Of white-robed citizens marching | so dutifully beside
His bridle-rein, retainers whose friendship was bought
With the meal-ticket stashed in their wallets.⁷ Democritus long
    ago
Found occasion for laughter in all human intercourse,
And his wisdom reveals that the greatest men, those destined
To set the highest examples, may still be born
In a land with a sluggish climate, a country of muttonheads.
The cares of the crowd he derided no less than their pleasures,
Their griefs, too, on occasion: if Fortune was threatening,
'*Up you,*' he'd say, and give her the vulgar finger. So
If our current petitions are pointless – destructive, even –
What *should* we ask for, what message leave on the knees of the
    Gods?⁸

Some men are overthrown by the envy their great power
Arouses; it's that long and illustrious list of honours
That sinks them. The ropes are heaved, down come the statues,
Axes demolish their chariot-wheels, the unoffending
Legs of their horses are broken. And now the fire
Roars up in the furnace, now flames hiss under the bellows:
The head of the people's darling glows red-hot, great Sejanus⁹
Crackles and melts. That face only yesterday ranked
Second in all the world. Now it's so much scrap-metal,
To be turned into jugs and basins, frying-pans, chamber-pots.
Hang wreaths on your doors, lead a big white sacrificial
Bull to the Capitol! They're dragging Sejanus along
By a hook, in public. Everyone cheers. 'Just look at that
Ugly stuck-up face,' they say. 'Believe me, I never
Cared for the fellow.' 'But what was his crime? Who brought
The charges, who gave evidence? How did they prove him
    guilty?'
'Nothing like that: a long | and wordy letter arrived
From Capri.'¹⁰ 'Fair enough: you need say no more.'
                                  And what
Of the commons? They follow fortune as always, and detest
The victims, the failures. If a little Etruscan luck
Had rubbed off on Sejanus, if the doddering Emperor
Had been struck down out of the blue, this identical rabble
Would now be proclaiming that carcase an equal successor
To Augustus. But nowadays, with no vote to sell,¹¹ their motto
Is 'Couldn't care less'. Time was when their plebiscite elected
Generals, Heads of State, commanders of legions: but now
They've pulled in their horns, there's only two things that
    concern them:
Bread and the Games.
                    'I hear | that many are to be purged.'
'That's right, they're turning the heat on, and no mistake.'
                                      'My
    friend

Bruttidius looked somewhat pale when I met him in town
     just now[12] –
Our slighted Ajax, I fear, is out for blood: disloyal
Heads will roll.'
                    'Come on, then, quickly, down to the river –
Boot Caesar's foe in the ribs while his corpse is still on show.'
'Yes, and make our slaves watch us – eyewitnesses can't deny it,
Can't drag their wretched masters into court at a rope's end.'
That's how they talked of Sejanus, such was the private gossip
After his death. Would you really choose to be courted as
He was? To own his wealth? To hand out official
     appointments –
Consulships, army commands? To be known as the
     'protector'
Of an Imperial recluse squatting on Capri's narrow
Rocks with his fortune-tellers? You'd certainly enjoy
Having the Guards Brigade and the Household Cavalry
At your beck and call, and a barracks with you as
     Commandant.[13]
Why not? Even those who lack the murderer's instinct
Would like to be licensed to kill. Yet what fame or prosperity
Are worth having if they bring you no less disaster than joy?
Would you rather assume the mantle of the wretch who's
     being dragged
Through the streets today, or lord it over some sleepy
Rural backwater, an out-at-elbows official
Inspecting weights, giving orders for the destruction
Of short-measure pint-pots? Admit, then, that Sejanus
Had no idea what to pray for. His interminable pursuit
Of excessive wealth and honours built up a towering
Edifice, storey by storey, so that his final downfall
Was that degree greater, the crash more catastrophic.
Take men like Pompey or Crassus – and that other tyrant[14]
Who cowed Rome's citizens, brought them under the lash:
What proved their downfall? Lust for ultimate power

Pursued without scruple – and the malice of Heaven
That granted ambition's prayers. Battle and slaughter
See most kings off; few tyrants die in their beds.
  Eloquence, that's what they're after, all of them: even the
       schoolboy
– With one small houseslave to carry his satchel behind him,
And only a penny to spare for an offering to Minerva –
Spends all his holidays[15] praying that one day *he'll* become
As good – and successful – as Cicero, or Demosthenes. And yet
Both of these perished because of their eloquence, both
Were destroyed by their own overflowing and copious talent.
That talent alone cost Cicero his severed head and hand:
What third-rate advocate's blood ever stained the rostra?
O fortunate Roman State, born in my great Consulate –
Had he always spoken thus, he could have laughed Antony's
Swords to scorn. I prefer such ridiculous verses
To you, supreme and immortal Second Philippic.[16] And then
Violent, too, was the end of Demosthenes, who held
All Athens spellbound with his torrential oratory
In the crowded theatre. Under | an evil-fated star
He was born, and the Gods were against him, that ardent boy
Whom his father – swart and bleary with working red-hot
       ore –
Sent away from the coals and the pincers, the grime of the
       smithy,
The sword-forging anvil, to learn the rhetorician's trade.
  Consider the spoils of war, those trophies hung on tree-
       trunks –
A breastplate, a shattered helmet, one cheekpiece dangling,
A yoke shorn of its pole, a defeated trireme's
Flagstaff or figurehead, the miserable frieze of prisoners
On a triumphal arch – such things are coveted
As the zenith of human achievement. These are the prizes
For which every commander, Greek, barbarian, Roman,
Has always striven; for them he'll endure toil

And danger. The thirst for glory by far outstrips the
Pursuit of virtue. Who | would embrace poor Virtue naked
Without the rewards she bestows? Yet countries have come to
    ruin
Not once, but many times, through the vainglory of a few
Who lusted for power, who wanted a title that would cling
To the stones set over their ashes – though a barren
Fig-tree's rude strength will suffice to crack the stone asunder.
Seeing that sepulchres, too, have their allotted fate.
   Put Hannibal in the scales: how many pounds will that
    peerless
General mark up today? This is the man for whom Africa
Was too small a continent, though it stretched from the surf-beaten
Ocean shores of Morocco east to the steamy Nile,
To Ethiopian tribesmen – and new elephants' habitats.[17]
Now Spain swells his empire, now he surmounts
The Pyrenees. Nature throws in his path
High Alpine passes, blizzards of snow: but he splits
The very rocks asunder, moves mountains – with vinegar.
Now Italy is his, yet still he forces on:
'We have accomplished nothing,' he cries, 'till we have
    stormed
The gates of Rome, till our Carthaginian standard
Is set in the City's heart.'
                     A fine sight it must have been,
Fit subject for caricature, the one-eyed commander
Perched on his monstrous beast! Alas, alas for glory,
What an end was here: the defeat, the ignominious
Flight into exile, everyone crowding to see
The once-mighty Hannibal turned humble hanger-on,
Sitting outside the door of a petty Eastern despot
Till His Majesty deign to awake. No sword, no spear,
No battle-flung stone was to snuff the fiery spirit
That once had wrecked a world: those crushing defeats,
Those rivers of spilt blood were all wiped out by a

Ring, a poisoned ring. On, on, you madman, drive
Over your savage Alps, to thrill young schoolboys
And supply a theme for speech-day recitations![18]

One globe seemed all too small for the youthful Alexander:
Miserably he chafed at this world's narrow confines
As though pent on some rocky islet. Yet when he entered
Brick-walled Babylon, a coffin was measure enough
To contain him.[19] Death alone reveals the puny dimensions
Of our human frame. A fleet, we are told, once sailed
Through Athos (the lies those old Greek historians
Got away with!), the sea was spanned with a bridge of boats
And chariots drove across it: deep streams and rivers
Were drunk dry by the Persians at breakfast-time. (The rest
You can hear when some tame poet, sweating under the armpits,
Gives his wine-flown recital.[20]) Here was a barbarian
Monarch who flogged the winds with a rigour they'd never
     known
In Aeolus' prison-house, who clapped chains on Poseidon
And thought it an act of mercy, no doubt, to spare the God
A branding as well: what God would serve *this* master?
But mark his return from Salamis – the single unescorted
Vessel, the blood-red sea, the prow slow-thrusting
Through shoals of corpses. Such was the price he paid
For that long-cherished dream of glory and conquest.[21]

   '*Grant us a long life, Jupiter, O grant us many years!*'
In the bloom of youth it's this which, pale with anxiety,
You pray for, and this alone. Yet how grisly, how unrelenting
Are longevity's ills! Look first | at your face, you'll see an ugly
And shapeless caricature of its former self: your skin
Has become a scaly hide, you're all chapfallen, the wrinkles
Scored down your cheeks now make you resemble nothing so
     much
As some elderly female baboon in darkest Africa.
Young men are all individuals: A will have better looks
Or brains[22] than B, while B will beat A on muscle;

But old men all look alike, all share the same bald pate,
Their noses all drip like an infant's, their voices tremble
As much as their limbs, they mumble their bread with toothless
Gums. It's a wretched life for them, they become a burden
To their wives, their children, themselves; the noblest and best
    of them
Become so loathsome a sight that even legacy–hunters
Turn queasy. Their taste-buds are ruined, they get scant pleasure
From food or wine, sex lies in long oblivion –
Or if they try, it's hopeless: though they labour all night long
At that limp and shrivelled object, limp it remains.
What can the future hold for these impotent dodderers?
Nothing very exciting. Sex is a pretty dead loss –
The old tag's true – when desire outruns performance.

   Other senses deteriorate: take hearing, for instance.
How can the deaf appreciate music? The standard
Of the performance eludes them: a top-line soloist,
Massed choirs in their golden robes, all mean less than nothing.
What does it matter to *them* where they sit in the concert-hall
When a brass band blowing its guts out is barely audible?
The slave who announces the time, or a visitor, must bawl
At the top of his lungs before they take in the message.

   The blood runs thin with age, too: now nothing but fever
Can warm that frigid hulk, while diseases of every type
Assault it by battalions. (If you asked me their names
I'd find it less trouble to list all Oppia's lovers,
The number of patients Doc Themison kills each autumn,
The partners that X, the wards that Y has defrauded,
The times tall Maura goes down in a day, the pupils
Hamillus has off; I could sooner | list all the country-houses
Owned by the barber who shaved me when I was a lad.[23])
One has an arthritic hip, another sciatica,
Lumbago plagues a third, while the totally sightless
Envy the one-eyed. Here's a fellow whose jaws would open
Wide, once long ago, at the prospect of dinner – but now

Those leaden lips must mumble the tit-bits another hand
Feeds to him; when he gapes today, he's like a baby
Swallow that sees its mother approaching, her beak
Well-crammed with grubs. But worse than all bodily ills
Is the senescent mind. Men forget what their own servants
Are called, they can't recognize yesterday's host at dinner,
Or, finally, the children they begot and brought up. A heartless
Codicil to the will disinherits their flesh and blood,
And the whole estate is entailed to some whore, whose expert
     mouth
– After years in that narrow archway – earns her a rich reward.
  If he keeps his wits intact, though, a further ordeal awaits
The old man: he'll have to bury his sons, he'll witness
His dear wife's end, and his brother's, he'll see the urns
Filled with his sisters' ashes. Such are the penalties
If you live to a ripe old age – perpetual grief,
Black mourning, a world of sorrow, ever-recurrent
Family bereavements to haunt your declining years.
Nestor, the King of Pylos, if we can trust great Homer,
Lived longer than any creature save the proverbial crow –
Happy, no doubt, to have postponed his death for so many
Generations of men, to have sampled the new-made wine
So many times, to have passed | beyond his hundredth year.
But wait a moment – just look at the way he went on
About Fate's decrees, and his too-long thread of life, while
The funeral flames were licking up round his son,
His Antilochus: look how he asked all his fellow-mourners the
     reason
He'd survived till now, what crime he'd ever committed
To deserve such longevity.²⁴ So Peleus, mourning the dead
Achilles; and so his father at Odysseus the seafarer's passing.
If Priam had died at a different time, before
The building of those ships for Paris's reckless venture,
He might have gone down to the shades while Troy still stood,
     with

Magnificent obsequies – his coffin shouldered
By Hector and Hector's brothers, while Ilion's womanhood
Wept, and Cassandra keened, and Polyxena rent her garments.
So what did length of days bring him? He saw his world
In ruins, saw its destruction by fire and the sword;
Then put off his crown, took arms, and – a dotard, but a
    soldier –
Fell before Jove's high altar, like some ancient ox
Turned off from the plough, whose stringy neck is severed
By his master's knife. This at least was a manly death:
But Hecuba lived on, stark crazy, grinning and barking
Like a mad dog.[25]

                    I'll pass over Mithridates
And Croesus (warned by the wise and eloquent Solon
To beware of his final years):[26] let our own countrymen
Provide an example. What else brought great Marius
To exile and prison, to an outlaw's life in the marshes,
To begging his bread through the streets of conquered
        Carthage?
But suppose he'd expired at the climax of his triumphal
Procession, after parading those hordes of captured Teutons,
Just as he stepped from his chariot – what more fortunate
Paragon, men would say, had Rome, or the world, to show?[27]
Pompey's Campanian fever came as a providential
Blessing in disguise; but the public prayers of so many
Cities prevailed: Rome's destiny, and his own,
Kept him alive for defeat | and decapitation – a fate
Such as not even Catiline or his fellow-conspirators
Suffered: at least they died whole, without mutilation.[28]

    When a doting mother passes the shrine of Venus, she'll
        whisper
One prayer for her sons, and another – louder, more fanciful –
For her daughters to have good looks. 'And what's wrong with
        that?'
She'll ask you. 'Didn't Latona rejoice in Diana's beauty?'

Perhaps; but the fate of Lucretia should warn us against our
    urge
To pray for a face like hers; Virginia would be happy
To take on poor Rutila's hump, to give Rutila best.[29] A
    handsome
Son keeps his wretched parents in constant anxiety:
Good looks and decent behaviour too seldom are found
In the same person. However old-fashioned his background,
However strict the morality on which he was brought up –
And even if Nature, with generous, kindly hand has
Turned him out a pure-minded, modestly blushing
Youth (and what greater gift, being more powerful
Than any solicitous guardian, could she bestow?)
Manliness still is denied him. A seducer will not scruple
To lay out lavish bribes, corrupt the boy's very parents:
Cash always wins in the end. But no misshapen
Stripling was ever unsexed by a tyrant in his castle,
No Nero would ever rape a clubfooted adolescent –
Much less one with a hump, pot-belly, or scrofula.

    So you're proud of your handsome son? Fair enough –
      but don't ever forget
The extra hazards that face him. He'll become a notorious
Layer of other men's wives, always scared that some husband's
Hot on his tail for revenge. He'll have no better luck
Than Mars did, he can't expect to steer clear of the toils for ever[30] –
And sometimes an outraged cuckold will go far beyond
All legal sanctions, will horsewhip his rival to ribbons,
Stick a knife in his heart, or a mullet up his backside.
Maybe the first time your dream-boy goes with a married
Woman he'll really love her. But when she gets in the habit
Of giving him little presents, it won't be long before
He's become the perfect gigolo, taking them all for their
    eyeteeth –
And remember, there's nothing these women won't do to
    satisfy

Their ever-moist groins: they've just one obsession – sex.
'But what's wrong with good looks if you're chaste?' Try out
    that question
On Hippolytus or Bellerophon: did stern self-restraint
Benefit *them*? The women whose love they'd spurned,
Phaedra and Sthenoboea, both hot with shame, flared up
And lashed themselves into a fury.[31] Pure feminine ruthlessness
Thrives best on hatred and guilt.

                              What advice, do you suppose,
Should one give the young man whom Caesar's wife is
    determined
To marry?[32] This blue-blooded sprig of the higher nobility –
Wonderfully handsome, too – is raped and doomed by one
    glance
From Messalina's eyes. She sits there, waiting for him,
Veiled as a bride, while their marriage-bed is prepared
In the public gardens. A big traditional dowry
Will be handed over, the ceremony witnessed in due form,
The omens taken. Did you think these were secret doings
Known only to intimate friends? But the lady's determined
On a proper, official wedding. So what's your decision? If
You refuse her commands, you'll die before lighting-up time;
If you do the deed, you'll get a brief respite, until
Your liaison is so well known that it reaches the Emperor's
    ears:
He'll be the last to learn of this family scandal. Till then
Better do what you're told, if a few more days' existence
Matter that much. But whichever you reckon the quicker
And easier way, your lily neck still gets the chop.
  Is there nothing worth praying for, then? If you want my
    advice,
Let the Gods themselves determine what's most appropriate
For mankind, and what best suits our various circumstances.
They'll give us the things we need, not those we want: a man
Is dearer to them than he is to himself. Led helpless

By irrational impulse and powerful blind desires
We ask for marriage and children. But the Gods alone know
What they'll be like, our future wives and offspring!
Still, if you must have something to pray for, if you
Insist on offering up the entrails and consecrated
Sausages from a white pigling in every shrine, then ask
For a sound mind in a sound body, a valiant heart
Without fear of death, that reckons longevity
The least among Nature's gifts, that's strong to endure
All kinds of toil, that's untainted by lust and anger,
That prefers the sorrows and labours of Hercules to all
Sardanapalus' downy cushions and women and junketings.33
What I've shown you, you can find by yourself: there's one
Path, and one only, to a life of peace – through virtue.
Fortune has no divinity, could we but see it: it's we,
We ourselves, who make her a goddess, and set her in the
     heavens.

Notes to Satire X

1. J., as the scholiast makes clear, had a particular instance in mind here: that of the strong man Milo of Croton, who, while out for a walk one day, found an oak-tree in a field, split down the trunk and held with wedges. Milo decided to complete the job with his bare hands: he thrust the two halves further apart, the wedges dropped out, his strength failed, and he found himself trapped as the halves snapped together again. While in this helpless position he was eaten by wolves. See Valerius Maximus, 9.12, ext. §. 9.

2. C. Cassius Longinus, a famous jurist, was Governor of Syria in A.D. 50; in 66 he was exiled by Nero, on the trumpery excuse that he had in his house a statue of Cassius, the murderer of Caesar. His place of banishment was Sardinia: he is said to have been blind at the time. Vespasian recalled him. See Tacitus, *Annals* 16.7–9 (pp. 372–3); Suetonius, *Nero* 37 (p. 230). Seneca was forced to commit suicide as a result of the Conspiracy of Piso in 65: there was a rumour that Piso was to be dropped, and Seneca offered the purple instead of him: Tacitus, *Annals* 15.65 (p. 365); cf. Satire VIII 212. For Plautius Lateranus see Satire VIII, n. 17 (p. 190).

3. Rome's Exchange or Bourse was in the Forum: this was where the bankers operated, and where they kept their clients' deposits, in strong-boxes.

4. Democritus of Abdera (c. 460–c. 370 B.C.), known to later generations as the 'Laughing Philosopher', was a pupil of Leucippus, and from him inherited and developed the Atomist school of philosophy which so influenced Lucretius. Heraclitus of Ephesus (fl. c. 500 B.C.), an obscure but strikingly original thinker, conceived the world as a conflict of opposites, with fire as the agent of natural change. His Roman reputation as the 'weeping philosopher' is ill-deserved: it depended partly on a misinterpretation of the famous dictum that 'all things flow' like rivers, partly on Theophrastus's attribution to him of *melancholia* (here not so much melancholy as impulsiveness). See Kirk-Raven, *The Presocratic Philosophers* (Cambridge 1957), p. 184.

5. The *toga praetexta*, with purple border, was worn by senior

magistrates (consuls, praetors, curule aediles), who also had the rods, or fasces, and axes borne before them as a symbol of office. The tribunal was the elevated dais or platform on which the magistrates' inlaid chairs were placed. The toga striped with purple (*trabea*) was the ceremonial attire of the Equestrian Order, or 'Knights', who wore it on special parades. To ride in a sedan had been at first a privilege of Senators' wives, but in J.'s time, as we have seen, men also used them.

6. The occasion here described is the *pompa Circensis*, the procession which preceded the races in the Circus Maximus: it was presided over by a consul or a praetor, and bears some resemblance to the State opening of Parliament. The president headed the procession, robed as a triumphant general in ceremonial tunics (one embroidered with palms, the other with gold embroidery on purple) and a heavy cloak: these robes were kept, except when being used, in the treasury of Jupiter Capitolinus. The point of the slave riding beside the Consul was to placate Nemesis: we are told that he was required, at intervals, to murmur in the great man's ear: 'Remember you are mortal.'

7. The ivory staff was also part of a triumphing general's insignia. The retainers, or 'clients', have received their 'dole' before the ceremony – this time in the form of a cash payment, not food.

8. At lines 54–5 I read *aut si perniciosa petuntur,/ propter quae*, etc., and (with Clausen) a mark of interrogation after *deorum*. Votive wax tablets, inscribed with petitions, were left either on the wall of a temple or else on the knees of a divine image.

9. Sejanus (L. Aelius Sejanus) was born at Vulsinii in Etruria. His father was a Roman *eques*. On the accession of Tiberius he became joint Prefect of the Praetorian Guard with his father. As the reign progressed his power steadily increased. He may have had a hand in the death of Tiberius's son Drusus in 23; he certainly deported Agrippina and her son Nero in 29. By 31 he was consul, and had Tiberius (now a recluse on Capri) completely in his pocket: he judged the time had come to make a bid for the throne himself. But Tiberius, warned by his brother's widow of what was afoot, sent his 'long and wordy letter' to the Senate: Sejanus was arrested, and executed on 18 October 31.

10. Tiberius had withdrawn to Capri in 27: he never returned to Rome during his lifetime.

11. It was in A.D. 14 that Tiberius transferred the election of magistrates from the popular assemblies to the Senate – a most far-reaching constitutional change. See Tacitus, *Annals* 1.15 (p. 39), where it is remarked that 'the public, except in trivial talk, made no objection to their deprival of this right'.

12. Bruttidius Niger was aedile in A.D. 22: it is fairly certain that he is the man referred to here. Tacitus remarks of him that he 'was a highly cultured man who, if he had gone straight, would have attained great eminence' (*Annals* 3.66, p. 147). Instead he chose to curry Imperial favour as an informer. Seneca has preserved a passage from one of his historical works describing the death of Cicero (*Suasoriae* 6.20 f.).

13. After the appointment of his father as Prefect of Egypt, Sejanus was made sole commander of the Praetorian Guard. He also concentrated it in a single barracks near the Viminal Gate, a move contrary to the original intentions of Augustus (Suetonius *Augustus* 49 p. 79), and the object of which was all too clear: 'Orders could reach [the battalions] simultaneously, and their visible numbers and strength would increase their self-confidence and intimidate the population' (Tacitus, *Annals* 4.2, p. 153).

14. The 'other tyrant' is Julius Caesar, with Pompey and Crassus the third member of the First Triumvirate: he is portrayed as reducing Roman citizens to the status of slaves.

15. The holiday in question was a feast of Minerva's known as the Quinquatrus, and held over the five days 19–23 March: since Minerva was the goddess of wisdom, this feast was particularly observed by schoolmasters and their pupils.

16. Cicero's much-derided poem *On His Consulship* was composed in 60 B.C. After Caesar's murder he finally broke with Mark Antony in the late summer of 44, and delivered the First Philippic – so named after Demosthenes' speeches against Philip of Macedon – on 2 September, in reply to an attack that Antony had made on him the day before. Antony's next speech against Cicero was delivered in the Senate on 19 September, and it was this that elicited the Second Philippic here referred to. Curiously, the speech seems not actually to have been delivered, but circulated in written form after Antony left Rome late in November. Cicero was executed by Antony (with Octavian's connivance) on 7 December 43, and his

head and right hand cut off and impaled on the Rostra in the Forum.

J. is somewhat cavalier with the facts of Demosthenes' life. His father was no horny-handed blacksmith but a wealthy sword-manufacturer; and in any case he died when the boy was only seven. Demosthenes died in 322, a year after Alexander, when Antipater had finally defeated the Athenians at Crannon. A Macedonian garrison was installed in Athens, and a warrant issued for Demosthenes' execution. He took sanctuary in the temple of Poseidon at Calauria, and there committed suicide by sucking poison from his pen: an apt end for so vituperative an orator.

17. Much heavy weather has been made of 'Juvenal's other elephants' in the learned journals: but it seems clear enough to me that J. (as at the beginning of this satire) is simply taking in another panoramic sweep – from the elephants of Morocco (which Hannibal used to cross the Alps) to those of Ethiopia.

18. After his defeat at Zama in 202 by Scipio Africanus, Hannibal remained in Carthage till 193, a zealous and radical-minded statesman. At this point his right-wing political enemies convinced Rome that he was intriguing with Antiochus of Syria; and since, when a commission of inquiry arrived to investigate the matter, Hannibal fled to Syria, there may have been some truth in this charge. After Antiochus's collapse Hannibal first went to Crete, then sought refuge with King Prusias of Bithynia, the 'petty Eastern despot' here referred to. He took poison concealed in his ring in 183/2 when his extradition was demanded by the Roman authorities. For the popularity of Hannibal as a subject for stock declamation in the schools see Satire VII 161; cf. VI 291.

19. Alexander died of a fever at Babylon in 323 B.C.: the city's mud-brick walls, raised by Semiramis, were famous throughout antiquity.

20. For Xerxes' canal through the peninsula of Mt Athos (traces of which have been discovered by modern archaeologists) and his bridging and lashing of the Hellespont see Herodotus VII 21-5, 36-7 (pp. 425-6, 429-30). The 'tame poet' was one Sostratus, who may have been identical with the flashy rhetorician Sosistratus who declaimed on the defeat of Xerxes (J. O. Thomson, *Classical Review* NS1, 1951, pp. 3 ff.): J. says his recitation was made *madidis alis*, which can mean either 'with drunken inspiration' or 'with damp

armpits'. The *double entendre* is neat in Latin, but cannot be reproduced in English: I assume J. intended both meanings to be taken up, and have translated accordingly.

21. It is interesting to compare J.'s luridly dramatized account of Xerxes' plight after Salamis with that given by Herodotus (8.97, pp. 530–31) – or even with Aeschylus's *Persians*; Aeschylus, after all, fought in the battle himself.

22. At lines 196–7 most MSS read *pulchrior ille/ hoc atque †ille† alio*; P and O amongst others omit *ille* in line 197. The scholiast, interpreting this passage, remarks that all young men have different good qualities: some are handsomer than others, some *more eloquent*. Therefore we would expect, at the beginning of 197, a second comparative epithet. Tentatively I suggest the emendation *pulchrior ille/ hoc aut callidior*.

23. The *gens Oppia* was a family of some distinction under the early Republic, but seems to have sunk into obscurity under the Empire. A Vestal Virgin named Oppia was condemned for unchastity in 483 B.C. (Livy 2.42, p. 138): this suggests that Oppian women ran to form down the centuries, since J. is more likely to have had a contemporary in mind. Themison was a fashionable doctor in the time of Seneca and Celsus: perhaps, like the *pantomimi*, distinguished medical men assumed the names of their well-known predecessors as a form of advertisement. Fevers and other illnesses were most prevalent in autumn: cf. Satire IV 56. For Maura's sexual activities cf. Satire VI 307 ff. The pederastic schoolmaster Hamillus is otherwise unknown. J. seems to have borne a particular animus against his one-time barber: the line is repeated from Satire I 25.

24. Roman exaggeration went to work on Nestor, as on many other characters from Greek mythology. In the *Iliad* (1.250 ff.) he is only more than *two* generations old, i.e. something over sixty (cf. the scholiast here); by Ovid's day (*Metamorphoses* 12.187 f.) he was no less than two hundred! His son Antilochus was killed while defending his father in battle: Paris had killed one of Nestor's horses, and Nestor called out to Antilochus for help: see Homer *Odyssey* 3.111, Pindar, *Pythian Odes* 6.28 ff.

25. Priam's fate is not mentioned by Homer: J.'s account is taken more or less directly from Virgil, *Aeneid* 2.506–58, a moving and dramatic sequence. The myths concerning Hecuba's end are in-

teresting. Polymestor (whom she had blinded for the murder of her son Polydorus) prophesied that she would be metamorphosed into a bitch, and leap into the sea from the headland in the Hellespont (Dardanelles) later known as Cynossema, or 'The Bitch's Grave'. Other accounts say she wandered round Thrace for a long time, in the shape of a bitch, howling and being stoned by the inhabitants; or that she was made Odysseus's slave, and either committed suicide by drowning herself, or else was put to death because of her furious invectives against the Greeks. Surely it needs a minimum of aetiologizing to deduce from this that the sack of Troy and the deaths of her husband and children deranged her mind?

26. Croesus, the last King of Lydia, was overthrown and put to death by Cyrus in 546 B.C. Mithridates VI of Pontus (cf. n. 49 to Satire VI) was driven out by Lucullus in 72, finally defeated by Pompey in 67, and died in the Crimea, at the hands of a guard, when faced with rebellion by his son Pharnaces. Both men are chosen here as types of wealthy and powerful monarchs who finally lost all they had, including their lives.

27. For Marius's victory over the Teutones and Cimbri, see above, n. 29 to Satire VIII. In 88 B.C. his undignified struggle with Sulla for appointment to the post of supreme commander in the war against Mithridates led directly to Sulla's march on Rome. Marius fled to North Africa, enduring much on the way. He was several times captured and in danger of death, once after being dragged out of the stinking Minturnae swamps at a rope's end. When he finally reached Africa he is reported to have said: 'Tell the praetor that you have Gaius Marius sitting as a fugitive on the ruins of Carthage.' The appeal fell on deaf ears. But in 87 Marius returned to Rome, joined forces with Cinna and the 'popular party', and captured the city. Then the bitter old man, crazed by his sufferings in exile, took a bloody revenge. His slave-bodyguard conducted an indiscriminate *putsch* of all Marius's personal enemies, whatever their rank or status. Meanwhile Marius and Cinna elected themselves consuls for 86; but Marius died within three weeks of taking office, and his ashes were afterwards, on Sulla's orders, scattered in the River Anio.

28. After Pompey's defeat at Pharsalia (9 August 48 B.C.) he sailed to Egypt to seek asylum and protection, on the grounds that he had been instrumental in restoring the father of the present monarch to

his throne. But Ptolemy was only a boy of thirteen, and the power lay with Theodotus of Chios, Achillas, and the eunuch Pothinus, his advisers. Nervous of antagonizing Caesar, they had Pompey murdered as he stepped ashore from his boat. His head was cut off and sent to Caesar, who wept at the sight, though Pompey's death solved several awkward problems for him. The headless body was left lying on the seashore, and afterwards buried by Pompey's freedman Philippus. Pompey's murder seems to have inspired Roman writers with a special kind of horror and repugnance.

29. Lucretia and Virginia were the two classical instances in early Roman history of the dangers to which feminine beauty could lead. Lucretia was the wife of L. Tarquinius Collatinus, and her rape by Sextus Tarquinius is said to have been directly responsible for the overthrow of Tarquinius Superbus and the establishment of a Republic in Rome. (See Livy 1.57–60, pp. 81–5.) Virginia, the daughter of a centurion, caught the eye of the *decemvir* Appius Claudius, who tried every trick to get her, including a rigged court hearing in which a retainer of his claimed the girl as his slave. In the end, amid scenes of riot, the father stabbed his daughter to prevent her falling into Appius's hands (Livy 3.44–58, pp. 215 ff.).

At line 295, for the meaningless *accipere †atque suum† Rutilae dare* of the MSS I would suggest, as a possible emendation, *accipere et quaestum Rutilae dare*, i.e. 'give her the advantage', 'give her best'. Rutila is otherwise unknown: presumably she was some well-known hunchback of the day. The *gens Rutila* was an ancient plebeian family.

30. The allusion is to the trick by which Hephaestus contrived to catch Ares (Mars) and Aphrodite in the act of adultery: see Homer, *Odyssey* 8.266 ff. At 312–13 I accept Courtney's emendation *mariti/ irae debebit*.

31. At 326 there is another odd textual crux: the best MSS have *erubuit †nempe haec† ceu fastidita repulso* (or *repulsa*), for which I am tempted to substitute *erubuit nam Phaedra ut fastidita repulso*, an emendation which would explain the metrically unnecessary periphrasis *Cressa* at line 327. Phaedra was the daughter of Minos (and thus 'the Cretan woman'); she fell in love with her stepson Hippolytus, and slandered him when he rejected her advances. After his death, when Theseus, Hippolytus's father, learnt of his innocence,

Phaedra committed suicide. Stheneboea was the wife of Proetus, but killed herself through a hopeless passion for Bellerophon.

32. This extraordinary story is confirmed, at length and in detail, by Tacitus (*Annals* 11.12 and 26 ff., pp. 230–31, 238–43). The man in question was Gaius Silius, the consul-designate, whom Messalina forced to divorce his aristocratic wife Junia Silana. Both were subsequently executed. The only point in which the two accounts differ is that Tacitus makes Silius, rather than Messalina, the initiator and advocate of the marriage ceremony – which of course would spoil the point of J.'s rhetorical argument. The incident took place in A.D. 47.

33. Sardanapalus, more correctly known today as Assurbanipal, was King of Assyria 668–631 B.C. Famous in antiquity for his luxury and effeminacy, he is now immortalized by some famous reliefs in the British Museum (a lion hunt, a garden feast) and by Layard's discovery of his palace and library.

ADDITIONAL NOTE

At line 175 I now read *aequor* for the weak *isdem* of the MSS: see D. A. Kidd (Additional Bibliography). Reeve (see also Additional Bibliography) suggests excising 356, the famous *mens sana in corpore sano* line, on the grounds of illogicality and awkward syntax: if the only thing worth praying for is virtue (which lies in your own hands anyway), what becomes of sense and morality if you are then told to pray for health instead? I admit the awkward syntax, but find the logic a trifle disingenuous. Famous tags need more to dislodge them than that: and J. did not, it is clear, have the well-ordered and ruthlessly consistent mind of a professional academic (cf. above, p. 194, *Additional note*).

At line 202 I adopt Lafleur's emendation of *Cossus* for *Cosso* (see Additional Bibliography), and have revised my translation accordingly.

SATIRE XI

If Atticus dines in state, he's thought a fine gentleman;
If Rutilus does, he's crazy. What gets a bigger horse-laugh
From the man in the street than a gourmand | gone broke?
    Every dinner-party,
All the baths and arcades and theatre foyers are humming
With the Rutilus scandal.[1] He's young still, physically fit
To bear arms, and hot-blooded. Much more of this riotous
    living
And he'll sign his freedom away – with no official
Compulsion, but no official discouragement, either –
To some tyrant of a *lanista*, take the gladiator's oath.[2]
You'll find plenty more like him, men who live for their
    palate
And nothing else, whose creditors – bilked too often –
Now lie in wait for them at the entrance to the Market.[3]
The more hopeless their straits, when they're tottering to ruin
Like some tumbledown house with light glinting through its
    cracks,
The better they dine. They'll ransack earth air and water
For special delicacies: cost is no object – indeed,
The higher the price, you'll find, the better pleased they are.
So raising more money to squander presents no problem –
They'll hock the family plate, or pledge poor Mummy's
    portrait,[4]
And spend their last fiver on dainties – to eat off earthenware:
Thus they're reduced, in the end, to a gladiator's rations.
That's why it makes a difference who's host: what in Rutilus
Would be damned as spendthrift folly, gets his neighbour the
    name
Of a generous fellow. The verdict depends on their means.
  I've got no time for the man who can tell you by just how
    much

Atlas out-tops all the mountains of Libya, but isn't
Capable of distinguishing between a purse and an iron-bound
Strongbox. From heaven descends the maxim *Know Thyself* 5 –
To be taken to heart and remembered, whether you're choosing
A wife, or aiming to win a seat in that august body
The Senate. Thersites never laid claim to Achilles' armour:
Ulysses did – and look at the show *he* made of himself.6
If you decide to plead some touch-and-go case, where vital
Issues hang in the balance, take stock of yourself, get it clear
Just what you are – a talented, forceful speaker
Or a third-rate windbag. A man should know his own
    measure
In great things and small alike: when you're buying fish
Don't go hankering after salmon on a herring income.7 What sort
Of end awaits you if your appetite expands
As your funds contract, if you sink all Daddy's cash
And property into a belly capacious enough to swallow
Capital holdings, family silver, herds and estates
Ad infinitum? The last thing such *rentiers* ever part with
Is their ring: when the finger's bare, why, beggary follows.
    It's not
An untimely grave the extravagant have to fear:
Death holds less terror for them than lingering old age.
    The pattern is pretty constant. They raise a City loan
And squander it, publicly. When it's just about exhausted,
And the lenders are looking pale, these gentlemen skip out
To some smart watering-place, for a cure of oysters.8
To welsh on your debts these days is thought no worse an
    action
Than fleeing the stuffy Subura for a place on the Esquiline.
There's only one regret that moves these expatriates,
One thing they really miss – a whole year of the Games, and
    the Circus.
They've forgotten what blushing means: Shame has been
    driven out

Of Rome with catcalls, and few hands were raised to stop her.
    Today, dear friend,⁹ you'll discover whether the way I live
Really matches up to all my fine exhortations –
Whether, while praising beans, I'm a secret glutton, whether
I order porridge aloud, but privately whisper 'cheesecakes'
In the waiter's ear. Now you've promised to be my guest
You'll find me just like Evander: so you can be Hercules,
Or if you feel modest, Aeneas – not quite so classy, but still
Of divine descent (and both guests were raised to the heavens,
One by fire, one by water).¹⁰ Now here's what we're going
    to have –
All homegrown produce, nothing bought in the market.
First, a plump tender kid from my farmstead at Tivoli,
The pick of the flock, that's never cropped grass, or nibbled
Low-sprouting willow-shoots, whose veins hold more milk
    than blood;
Mountain asparagus, picked by my bailiff's wife
After she's finished her spinning; big straw-packed eggs
Still warm from the nest, and the pullets that laid them, and
    grapes
Preserved for six months, but as fresh as when they were
    gathered;
Baskets of Syrian pears and Italian bergamots, fragrant
Apples, the equal of any you'd find in an east-coast orchard –
Don't worry, winter's ripened them, the cold's dried out
Their green autumnal juices, made them quite safe for dessert.
    Time was when this would have seemed a luxurious banquet
To our greatest soldiers and statesmen. Curius¹¹ used to raise
Spring greens on a little allotment, and bring them in himself
To cook on his modest hearthfire. But today the scruffiest
Chain-gang ditcher disdains such fare, is nostalgic
For the smell of tripe in some hot and crowded cook-shop.
Once, as a special treat on feast-days, they'd bring down
A side of salt pork from its rack, or a flitch of bacon
For some relative's birthday, and maybe a little fresh meat

If they'd run to a sacrifice. You'd find some kinsman who'd
    been
Three times consul, perhaps, who'd commanded armies or held
The Dictatorship, knocking off work an hour or two early
On such an occasion, trudging down from the hillside
With his mattock over his shoulder. In the days when men
    quailed
Under the stern regime of leaders like Fabius, Cato,
Scaurus, Fabricius; when even a Censor in office
Might be censured himself by his more inflexible colleague,[12]
Then nobody thought it a matter for serious concern
What species of tortoise or turtle was swimming the seas, to
    provide
Fine and noble adornments for the bedheads of the *élite*,
Our scions of Trojan stock; couches were small in those days,
Their sides without inlaid work, their simple bronze headrest
Displaying, in bas-relief, a garlanded ass's head
With country children playfully romping round it –
Houses, furniture, diet were all of a piece throughout.
    Our early Republican troops were rough diamonds, they
        hadn't acquired
A taste for Greek *objets d'art*. When a city was sacked,
And their share of the loot consisted of silver-chased
Antique goblets, quite priceless, they'd break them up to make
Horse-trappings, or to emboss their helmets in relief
With the Wolf (grown tame as required by Imperial Destiny),
And the Quirinal Twins beneath their rock, and Mars
Swooping naked out of the sky with spear and shield – fit
    sight
For a dying foeman.[13] These troops ate their porridge from
    plain
Earthenware bowls: any silver they had was reserved
To display on their armour. (If you're jealous by nature,
The whole set-up in those days, I suppose, *could* arouse your
    envy.)

  Divine might, too, was closer: the voice of godhead echoed
Through the silent[14] midnight City, prophetic, revealing how
The Gauls were at hand, how they'd marched from Ocean's
        shores.
So Jupiter warned us, such was his care for our welfare
When his image was baked clay still, still undefiled by gold.
  Our tables were home-grown then, made out of local
        timber –
If a gale blew down some ancient walnut, its trunk
Was laid by for such uses. But your modern millionaire
Cannot enjoy his dinner – the turbot and venison
Are equally tasteless, the scent and the roses stink
Like garbage in his nostrils – unless that broad table-top[15]
Rests on an ivory leopard, rampant, snarling, a stand
Carved in the round from tusks such as Assuan exports,
And the slippery Moors, and the blacker-than-Moorish Hindu:
Tusks that those great beasts shed in some Arabian wadi,
So burdensome they'd grown, too big to support.[16] This makes
For *bon appétit* and a strong | digestion: to such a man
Table-legs of silver are like an iron signet-ring.
That's why I blacklist guests who make snobbish comparisons
Between their means and mine, who despise my non-affluence.
There isn't an ounce of ivory here, not even my dice
Or draughtsmen; knife-handles, too, are of bone. Yet this
        doesn't harm
The taste of the food, or make | a chicken harder to slice.
Nor will you find a server to whom the whole School of Carving
Has to defer, a pupil of the maestro, Trypherus,[17]
In whose classroom a splendid banquet – sow's paunch,
        pheasant, boar,
Antelope, hare, gazelle, not to mention the tall flamingo –
Is mock-carved with blunt knives on elmwood dummies: the
        clatter
Resounds through the neighbourhood. My own raw youngster
Has never had the chance to knock off a guinea-fowl's wing

Or the odd slice of venison: mixed scraps are the most *he* can
    hope for.
My cups, too, are the cheapest, picked up at bargain prices,
And the houseboy who hands them round is dressed for
    warmth,
An uncouth local, no smooth imported Asiatic
Bought for a fortune: when | you want something, ask in
    Latin.
My servants all dress alike, their hair's close-cropped
And straight – though they've combed it today, because of
    the party.
One is a shepherd's son; another a ploughman's, and he
Is homesick for the mother he's been away from so long,
He misses their little cottage, the pet kids that he played with.
His expression is frank, his manners decent and modest,
Such as one might expect from a free youth, born to the
    purple.[18]
He doesn't shave his armpits, or camp around[19] in the bath-
    house,
Nervously holding an oil-flask in front of his cute little balls
And oversized member. The wine he'll serve you was bottled
On the slopes of his native mountains, where he wandered as a
    child;
[Servant and wine both share a common fatherland.]
   Perhaps you may be expecting a troupe of Spanish dancers,
Gypsy girls with their wanton songs and routines, the climactic
Applause as those shimmying bottoms grind to floor-level – a
    sight
Which most brides enjoy when they've got their husbands
    beside them.
(Though to mention the fact in their presence would be a
    great *faux pas*,
Such shows arouse flagging passions, they're the tycoon's
    substitute
For Spanish fly.) Yet actually it's the ladies

Who get most worked up by these visual and auditory stimuli,
Who reach such a pitch of excitement that they wet themselves.
    No such
Follies as these in *my* modest home: I leave them
To the nabob who spits his wine on a floor of Spartan
    marble:²⁰
Let him have the lot – the clack and whirr of the castanets,
The language so foul that a whore all stripped for action
Under some stinking archway would blush to employ it;
Let him revel in all the arts and obscenities of lust –
The rich are forgiven such conduct. If middling folk commit
Adultery, or gamble, it's a shocking disgrace; but when
Such tricks are played by the smart set, they're chic and madly
    gay.
At my feast today we'll have very different entertainment:
We'll hear the Tale of Troy from Homer, and from his rival
For the lofty epic palm, great Virgil. It makes no difference
Whose is the voice that recites such immortal poetry.
    Now cast care aside, shelve all your business worries:
You've got the whole day free, so relax and treat yourself
To a welcome rest. Don't let's have any mention
Of money – and if your wife's in the habit of staying out
All night, if she comes home next morning with clothes
    suspiciously creased
And spotted with damp, if she's red in the face and ears,
If her hair-do's all anyhow, don't boil with throttled resentment,
Just forget all your troubles the moment you cross my
    threshold,
Your house, your servants, the losses and breakages
They cause you: forget, above all, the ingratitude of friends.
    Now the spring races are on: the praetor's dropped his
    napkin
And sits there in state (but those horses just about cost him
The shirt off his back, one way and another); and if
I may say so without offence to that countless mob, all Rome

Is in the Circus today.[21] The roar that assails my eardrums
Means, I am pretty sure, that the Greens have won – otherwise
You'd see such gloomy faces, such sheer astonishment
As greeted the Cannae disaster, after our consuls
Had bitten the dust. The races are fine for young men:
They can cheer their fancy and bet at long odds and sit
With some smart little girl-friend. But *I'd* rather let my
      wrinkled
Old skin soak up this mild spring sunshine than sweat
All day in a toga. Here nobody cares if you visit
The baths an hour before noon – though do so five days
      running
And you'll very soon find such a life can get just as boring
As any other: restraint | gives an edge to all our pleasures.

1. The Atticus here used as a symbol of wealth is probably Tiberius Claudius Atticus, father of the Athenian millionaire, rhetorician and public benefactor Herodes Atticus, and a near-contemporary of J.'s. He discovered a treasure on his estate in Attica. Rutilus cannot be identified with any certainty. He may have been related to the hump-backed Rutila of Satire X; we cannot tell. In any case he is here no more than the type of the self-beggared spendthrift. The 'gourmand gone broke' that J. alludes to is Apicius: see n. 5 to Satire IV (p. 111).

2. If a Roman citizen of means intended to hire himself out as a gladiator he had to notify one of the Tribunes of the People (*tribuni plebis*), who could, at discretion, approve or cancel the contract (hence the reference to 'official compulsion', etc.). The gladiators' oath to the *lanista*, or trainer, virtually stripped those who took it of their individual rights. See Petronius, *Satyricon* 117 p. 128: '... We swore an oath dictated by Eumolpus, that we would be burned, flogged, beaten, killed with cold steel or whatever else Eumolpus ordered. Like real gladiators we solemnly handed ourselves over, body and soul, to our master.'

3. The *macellum*, or Market, was where meat, fish, and vegetables were sold in bulk: it was like Smithfield, Billingsgate and Covent Garden rolled into one. An exact modern equivalent is the great open market in Piraeus. It was the obvious place for a gluttonous debtor to be caught and pinned down by his creditors.

4. At line 18 the MSS have *vel matris imagine fracta*. In order to explain why the mother's likeness is broken up, we have to assume (a) that it was a statue and (b) that it was of solid silver. But the spendthrift's need is to raise quick ready money: and the value of a silver statuette is not visibly appreciated by melting it down, though *fracta* can be used in this sense: see below, line 102. What the wastrel does, surely, is to *pawn* this family heirloom; and therefore I suggest the emendation *pacta*, which is also palaeographically plausible, since *fr* and *p* are barely distinguishable in many hands. The *imago* may then be any kind of portrait.

5. This was the famous aphorism inscribed on the temple at Delphi, and ascribed to Apollo himself, through the intermediary vehicle of one of the Seven Sages.

6. J. is here echoing the low opinion of Odysseus as expressed, e.g., by Ovid or Seneca. It looks as though his version of the contest over Achilles' arms is that given by Ovid in the *Metamorphoses*, 13.1 ff. (pp. 310–21), which illustrates the old and commonplace theme of the conflict between men of action and men of words: ' . . . it was evident from the result what eloquence could do: for the skilful speaker carried off the hero's arms.' Not only that; but as a crafty, devious, cowardly, lying poltroon he brought dishonour on them. See W. B. Stanford, *The Ulysses Theme* (Oxford 1954), pp. 138 ff.

7. The fish actually in question are mullet and gudgeon; but since the whole point of the comparison is a question of price, and to English-speaking readers the contrast might be blunted by unfamiliarity, I have taken the liberty of substituting more local varieties.

8. The 'smart watering-place' is Baiae, on the Bay of Naples: cf. above, Satire III 5 and n. 1 ad loc. Lucrine oysters, from the same area, were a famous delicacy: see above, Satire IV 140.

9. It is generally doubted whether J.'s friend Persicus, addressed here, can be the same as the rich, childless Persicus of Satire III 221, who is suspected of firing his own house in order to collect compensation. From Persicus's own point of view this seems probable; but it implies a degree of consistency in J. himself which I do not, I fear, feel able to infer from his published work. A Paulus Fabius Persicus was consul in A.D. 34, with L. Vitellius, and achieved notoriety for his licentiousness: perhaps J.'s friend was a descendant.

10. Evander was a king of Arcadia who, some sixty years before the Trojan War, led a colony to Italy, and built a town, Pallantium, on the Palatine Hill. This foundation was subsequently merged with Rome. Virgil, *Aeneid* VIII 358 ff., represents him as still being alive at the time of Aeneas's arrival, and as entertaining him. He is also supposed to have entertained Hercules. Aeneas's divine descent was through his mother, Aphrodite (Venus). Both he and Hercules were deified: Aeneas died by drowning in the R. Numicius, while Hercules was burnt on Mt Oeta. The passage which J. clearly has in mind at this point is *Aeneid* VIII 364–5, where Evander says: 'Guest

of mine, be strong to scorn wealth and so mould yourself that you also may be fit for a God's converse. Be not exacting as you enter a poor home.'

11. M. Curius Dentatus (the 'Dentatus' is supposed to derive from the circumstance of his having been born with teeth in his mouth) defeated the Sabines during his first consulship (290 B.C.), Pyrrhus during his second (275) and the Lucanians, Samnites and Bruttians during his third (274). His simplicity and honesty were proverbial. After the conquest of the Sabines he took no more land than any common soldier; his only booty from the defeat of Pyrrhus was a wooden sacrificial bowl. Afterwards he retired to his farm, though he held the Censorship in 272. One Samnite embassy to him found him sitting by the fire roasting turnips: when they tried to press costly presents on him Curius remarked that he preferred ruling the wealthy to possessing wealth himself.

12. For the *gens Fabia* see n. 3 to Satire VIII (p. 187). M. Porcius Cato Censorinus (234–149 B.C.) was a man of aggressive virtue, puritan instincts, and few manners, who hated foreigners, believed in traditional robust virtues, and had no hesitation about imposing his views on others. As Censor in 184 he taxed luxury, checked corruption, and, with poetic aptness, spent 1,000 talents on the sewerage system. A visit to Carthage in 157 or 153 convinced him that the city must be destroyed ('*Delenda est Carthago*'), and he lived just long enough to see war declared in 150. The Scaurus referred to here is probably M. Aemilius Scaurus, who supported Drusus's reforms in 90 B.C. For Fabricius (Censor 275 B.C.) see n. 17 to Satire IX (p. 203). The two quarrelling Censors were M. Livius Salinator and C. Claudius Nero (204 B.C.); see Livy 29.37. The latter defeated Hasdrubal at the Battle of the Metaurus in 207.

13. The 'Quirinal Twins' are Romulus and Remus, and the Wolf the one that suckled them, thus by its maternal instinct setting Rome on the path of empire. The god Mars is there as their father: Duff remarks that 'in the works of art depicting this myth [Mars] is always represented as naked (except for a *chlamys* floating behind him), armed with shield and spear, and generally as hanging in the air, on his way to visit Rhea Silvia.' There is a similar representation on the shield of Aeneas: see Virgil, *Aeneid* VIII 630 (p. 220). Cf. Friedländer pp. 499–500. Livy (25.40.2) dates Roman appreciation of

Greek art to the capture of Syracuse in 212 B.C., and the introduction of foreign luxuries to the defeat of the Asiatic Gauls in 187 (39.6.7). Sallust also sees Asia as the source of corruption, but dates it to Sulla's campaign there, 87–83 B.C. (*Catiline Conspiracy* 11.6).

14. At line 112 I accept Nisbet's suggestion of *tacitamque* for *mediamque* (made in his review of Clausen, *Journal of Roman Studies* 52, 1962, pp. 233–8).

15. The *orbis* was a table-top cut from a single tree-trunk, and roughly circular: the favourite wood was the *citrus*, or Moroccan cyprus. The curious passion which rich men had for this rather unlikely luxury, with its supporting leg of ivory or precious metal, is confirmed by Pliny in the *Natural History* (13.91–9), where there is a detailed description of its manufacture, together with the size of particular specimens and the prices paid for them. The largest, made from two invisibly joined semi-circular slabs, was four and a half feet in diameter and three inches thick; a single slab just under four feet in diameter is also recorded. Luxury tables could change hands for the price of a large estate, and women twitted by their husbands for excessive addiction to jewellery had an obvious retort to hand.

16. It hardly needs saying that there is no truth whatsoever in the belief (developed here by the scholiast) that elephants get rid of their over-heavy tusks by thrusting them into the ground, or by any other method. We have here yet another of those myriad myths concerning natural history which abound in ancient writers, yet which (one would have thought) even a minimal capacity for direct observation would suffice to dispel. The taste for them still flourishes in the Mediterranean. On the Greek island where I used to live swallows are firmly believed to hitch rides, during migration, on the backs of storks; and there is a local snake which is credited with the capacity to pick up stones with its tail and sling them in cows' faces.

17. Trypherus is diabolically well named, since *trypheros* is a Greek adjective meaning both 'delicate', 'dainty', or 'soft', especially of food, and 'voluptuous' or 'effeminate' of people.

18. The purple-bordered toga (*toga praetexta*) was worn, not only by curule magistrates (see n. 5 to Satire X, pp. 218–19), but also by all free-born adolescents until, at about the age of sixteen, they assumed the all-white *toga virilis* of manhood.

19. Despite Friedländer's ingenious explanation (p. 505), I prefer

to accept the reading *draucus* of some minor MSS for the more usually accepted *raucus*. The former has been well defended by R. Verdière, in *Latomus* 11 (1952) pp. 25 f.

20. It was the custom to sample the wine and then spit it out, after tasting, not into a receptacle but on the floor. Laconian or Spartan marble, particularly the green marble of the Eurotas Valley (Duff p. 375), was much admired.

21. When the image of Cybele, the Great Mother, was brought to Rome in 204 B.C. from Pessinus (see n. 17 to Satire III and n. 34 to Satire VI, pp. 101 and 159), the Megalesian Games (4–10 April) were instituted in her honour. On the last day of the festival races were held, at which the starting signal was given by the President of the Games dropping his napkin. For the procession and ceremony on such an occasion see n. 6 to Satire X (p. 219). The praetor had to pay the competing teams and the successful charioteers out of his own pocket: cf. Martial 5.25.7 and 10.41.4. In J.'s day the Circus could hold about 300,000 spectators: Rome's total population then was nearer 2,000,000. Of the four regular *factiones* or teams, the Red, the White, the Blue and the Green, only the last two were really important: partisan feelings ran unbelievably high. For Nero's passionate addiction to racing see Suetonius *Nero* 22 (pp. 219–20). Hannibal's victory at Cannae, in Apulia, took place in 216 B.C. The consul L. Aemilius Paullus fell on the battlefield; his colleague survived. Spectators in the Circus were required to wear the toga as a mark of formality.

SATIRE XII

My birthday, Corvinus?[1] No; a still happier occasion
Has called for this gay turf altar, on which I'll sacrifice
The beasts that I vowed to the Gods – a snowy lamb apiece
For Juno, Queen of Heaven, and the Fates, and fierce Minerva
With that blank-faced African Gorgon emblazoned on her
    shield.[2]
But the victim reserved for Tarpeian Jove is a mettlesome
Frisky young calf – just look at the way he flashes
Those half-grown horns, and strains on the rope – high time
He was weaned, he feels, as he butts the tree-trunks; but now
He's just right for the altar-stone and the ritual aspersion
Of unmixed wine. If my means matched up to my wishes
I'd have laid on a bull so big he could hardly move,
And bulkier than – Hispulla[3]; no locally-pastured beast
But a pedigree Umbrian, reared | among lush green water-
    meadows.
With a neck so massive that only the heftiest priest
Could slash it through at a stroke[4] – all this to celebrate
The return of my friend, still trembling after the horrors
He's undergone, and astonished to find himself safe and sound.
Small wonder: for he survived not deep-sea perils alone
But being struck by lightning. The heavens were blotted out
With one black mass of cloud: burning and sudden
Fire flashed down on the yards, each man believed that he
Had been hit – and, thunderstruck, very soon concluded the
    worst
Shipwreck was nothing to this | inferno of blazing sails.
(The whole thing resembled a storm in a poem, exactly the
    same
Horrors took place.) But more, and worse, let me tell you,
Was still to come. Though the rest is all of a piece,
An experience many have suffered – witness those countless

241

Votive plaques in the temples: our artists, as everyone knows,
Get their bread-and-butter from Isis[5] – still such vicissitudes
Should move you regardless. This | was just the fate that befell
My friend Catullus.[6] The hold was half-seas under,
Great waves pounded the vessel from either side, the mast
Yawed as she rolled, the grizzled | old captain's expertise
Could provide no solution. So he resolved to compound with
The winds, and jettison cargo – thus imitating the beaver,
That castrates itself when cornered, sacrifices its balls
For the chance of freedom: such | a valuable drug is secreted,
It knows, in its groin. 'Heave all my goods overboard,'
Catullus shouted, willing | to throw out even his rarest
Possessions – a purple robe, fine enough for any Maecenas,
And other fabrics made from that natural honey-golden
Wool that's only found on the sheep of the Guadalquivir:
A product of rich herbage, the Spanish climate, some special
Property in the water.[7] Out went his silverware, too,
Wrought salvers, three-gallon wine-bowls designed to satisfy
The thirst of a drunken Centaur – or Senator's wife;[8]
Baskets, thousands of dishes, chased goblets out of which
Philip the Crafty drank, the man who bought cities cash down.[9]
But where in the world would you find anyone else with the
    courage
To save his skin, not his silver, to set life above property?
Some are so blind with greed that they live for their fortunes
Rather than making their fortunes enhance their lives.[10]
    Even when most of the cargo and stores had gone overboard
The ship made no headway. So in his extremity,
As a last resort, the captain took down the mast – with cold
    steel:
Desperate straits indeed, when your vessel has to be saved
By such diminution! If you insist on trusting
Your life to the wind's mercy with only four fingers' breadth
– Or seven at most – of pitchpine planking between
Yourself and death, remember, next time, to look out for

Safety nets and iron rations, an emergency water-bottle,
And axes to chop off a spar with in case of
       shipwreck.
  But luck was with our traveller: after a time the sea
Fell calm, and his destiny triumphed over wind and waves
       alike.
The Fates, in cheerful mood, now spun him a yarn of whiter
Wool, and the mildest breeze sprang up, and the stricken
Vessel ran on before it, under her spritsail
And a clutter of bellying garments. As the sirocco
Dwindled, the sun shone through, bringing fresh hope; and
       soon
They glimpsed that lofty peak, so dear to Ascanius,
Aeneas' son, that he chose it for his abode, and deserted
His stepmother's city Lavinium: the White or Alban Mount,
So called from the white sow whose thirtyfold litter gladdened
Those Trojan wanderers' hearts, whose dugs won immortal
       fame.[11]
  At last the vessel entered the harbour of Ostia, passing
The Tyrrhenian lighthouse, gliding between those massive
Piers that reach out to embrace the deep, and leave
Italy far behind – a man-made breakwater
That no natural harbour could equal. The captain nursed his
       lame
Vessel through to the inner basin, its waters so still
That a rowboat could safely ride there: the crew, with shaven
       heads,[12]
Safe home at last, kept telling the tale of their adventures.
  So be off with you, boys: let your words and thoughts be
       tempered
By reverence as you garland the shrines, strew meal
On the sacrificial knives, and dress the fresh turf altars:
I'll follow you presently. Then, once the essential rite
Has been duly performed, I'll come back home, where my own
Small images are fresh-waxed and wreathed with flowers. Here

I'll make my private oblations to Jupiter, burn incense
For family and household gods, scatter nosegays of every hue.
The house is as bright as a pin, the gateway's decked
With branches in celebration; our early-lighted lamps
Join in the act of thanksgiving.

                              But don't mistake my motives,
I beg you, Corvinus: the friend | for whose safe return I've
    raised
These altars has three little heirs. Who'd bestow so much
As a croupy old chicken, its eyes just glazing over,
On such a barren acquaintance? Just think of the cost! Fat quails
Never go to the men with children.[13] But if some wealthy
Spinster or bachelor catches the mildest fever, you'll find
The whole of the temple cloister's soon hung with votive
    prayers
For the invalid's speedy recovery. Some promise a sacrifice
Of a hundred oxen: they'd make it elephants if they could.
(Such beasts, however, are not for sale here, nor do they breed
In Latium, or anywhere under Italian skies;
True, you will find them at pasture in the Rutulian forests
Once ruled by Turnus – but these | have been imported from
    darkest
Africa, and belong to the Emperor's private herd.[14]
They'll acknowledge no lesser master: their ancestors bowed
    the knee
To Hannibal, or King Pyrrhus, or our Roman generals;
Whole cohorts – no small part of an army – filled the turrets
They bore into battle.) A hardened legacy-hunter would not
Hesitate, if he could, to line up one of these tuskers
Before the altar, and slaughter it for some maiden lady's
Household gods, sole victim to match the full worth of such
Exalted divinities – or of those who covet their wealth.
Just say the word, and he'll vow | to sacrifice his tallest,
Most good-looking slaves, he'll deck his houseboys and
    chambermaids

With the ritual chaplet; and if he happens to have a nubile
Daughter like Iphigeneia, he'll offer *her* up – although
He could hardly hope she'd be switched for a doe, like her
      predecessor.[15]

   I agree with my fellow-citizen: a legacy far outweighs
Even a thousand ships.[16] If a dying man recovers,
He's properly hooked: he'll cancel his previous will, and
Leave all his possessions, maybe, to our legacy-hunting friend
In return for such shining devotion. Then watch the victor
Strut cock-a-hoop over his rivals: *now* do you understand
How well it paid off to butcher that Mycenaean maiden?
So long live legacy-hunters, as long as Nestor himself!
May their possessions rival all Nero's loot, may they pile up
Gold mountain-high, may they love no man, and be loved by
      none.

1. Corvinus is a regular cognomen of the gens Valeria: see above, VIII 5–7, and n. 2 ad loc.; cf. I 108. J.'s friend was therefore a well-connected person, but nothing else is known about him.

2. It looks very much as though a line has dropped out between vv. 3 and 4. It is stretching *reginae* somewhat to translate it as 'Queen of Heaven', though the scholiast explains that this was Juno (adding, significantly, that some authorities took it as Fortune). Pallas Athene can be identified from her attributes, but, again, is not named. Perhaps there was once another line here, something such as *Iunoni, Fatisque iterum; torvaeque Minervae*, and some early copyist's eye slipped from *Minervae* to *Maura*.

3. Highet plausibly suggests that J. had some kind of feud with the Younger Pliny, and lost no opportunity of denigrating him or his relatives. Calpurnia Hispulla was Pliny's wife's aunt; there were two other ladies of this name – both known to Pliny – and one of the three may well have been the fat person described here: not to mention the Hispulla of VI 74 who had an affair with an actor.

4. At line 14 I read *iret et a grandi cervix ferienda ministro*: see J. G. Griffith, *Classical Review* NS10 (1960), 189–92.

5. A shipwrecked person could use a painted picture of the storm he had escaped in two ways: he could hang it in the temple of a god or goddess as an ex-voto offering in gratitude for his deliverance, or display it as part of his stock-in-trade as a beggar (see below, XIV 301) to excite the sympathy of passers-by. Isis was supposed to be a most efficacious deity for the storm-tossed sailor to invoke: thus she provided artists with a steady source of income through the ex-voto offerings vowed to her.

6. Again, an unknown person: neither the famous poet, nor the informer of IV 113 (though the reference to blindness in those dubious lines 50–51 has sometimes made me wonder about this), nor the farce-writer of VIII 186 and XIII 111.

7. The last of these explanations seems the most likely one: there were rich iron deposits in Baetica (Guadalquivir) and a proportion

of iron oxide in the water might well have produced the effect on the sheep which J. describes.

8. The Senator in question was called Fuscus; he may have been the Cornelius Fuscus referred to at IV 112 (cf. n. 19 ad loc.).

9. This was Philip of Macedon, Alexander's father; and the specific occasion which J. has in mind is the capture of Olynthus in 347 B.C., which was achieved by bribing the city's leaders. Duff quotes Philip's justly famous dictum that 'no fort is impregnable into which an ass, laden with gold, could make its way.'

10. Lines 50–51 have been generally condemned by recent editors as a feeble interpolation: 'poverty of diction', 'vapid chiasmus', 'tame repetition' are only some of the insults hurled at them. They seem to me no worse than many of J.'s aphorisms, and their deletion yet another instance of that odd editorial belief that an ancient author is always self-consistent, and always writes at the top of his bent.

11. The white sow was to be the sign by which Ascanius would recognize the site of his new city: the number of piglings denoted the number of years before the founding of Alba Longa: see Virgil, *Aeneid* 3.389 ff. (pp. 86–7) and 8.43 ff. (pp. 202–3).

12. Ostia's first artificial harbour was begun by Claudius in A.D. 42. It had two curving moles and enclosed an area of some 850,000 square yards. Between the moles stood an artificial island with a lighthouse on it. But despite its size, this harbour was ill-protected against strong prevailing winds. In A.D. 62 a particularly violent storm wrecked some two hundred vessels lying at anchor there. It was not until 104 that Trajan constructed his hexagonal inner basin, with numbered berths and a right-angled channel that protected it against bad-weather hazards. There is an excellent and well-illustrated account of Ostia and its harbours in Paul Mackendrick's *The Mute Stones Speak* (London 1962), pp. 251–65; those who wish to pursue the topic in greater detail should consult Russell Meiggs' *magnum opus, Roman Ostia,* (Oxford 1960). J.'s description here clearly refers to Trajan's inner basin, and the Satire must, therefore, be dated after 104. The crew of Catullus's vessel shaved their heads in fulfilment of a vow made during the storm.

13. We have already had several glimpses of the legacy-hunters in action – as Highet (134–5) so well describes them, 'that strange class of schemers who would court the childless rich in the hope of being

left a substantial legacy' – see above, V 98, VI 40; cf. V 135–45. Horace has a biting picture of them in the *Sermones* (2.5). When Eumolpus, in Petronius's *Satyricon*, makes his will, he stipulates that 'those who come into money by the terms of my will shall inherit only upon satisfaction of the following condition: they must slice up my entire body into little pieces and swallow them down in the presence of the entire city.' 'Just close your eyes,' says one determined beneficiary, 'and pretend you are eating a million sesterces, not human offal . . .' (p. 163).

14. The keeping of elephants was an Imperial prerogative: the Emperor's herd, as we know from inscriptions, had its reserve at Laurentum, near Ardea, the city of the Rutuli. For Turnus see the *Aeneid, passim*, especially Bks 7–12. Ardea was near the modern town of Anzio.

15. The substitution of a doe or hind for Iphigeneia on the sacrificial slab at Aulis has all the marks of a late 're-write' designed to purge the original myth of its more barbarous elements. Neither Pindar, Aeschylus nor Sophocles allude to this incident: the earliest reference is that of Euripides, *Iphigenia in Tauris* 28.

16. A thousand ships was the traditional number of Agamemnon's pan-Hellenic fleet: the Homeric Catalogue of Ships gives a slightly larger figure, 1186.

ADDITIONAL NOTE

At line 32 the reading *arbore* <*et*> *incerta* proposed by Kilpatrick strengthens the sense considerably and should be seriously considered by editors. I am happy to accept Griffith's convincing interpretation of the much-obelized verb *aspice* at line 61 (Additional Bibliography), and retranslate accordingly.

On J.'s attitude to Trajan see now K. H. Waters (Additional Bibliography), who points out the near-total absence in the *Satires* of references to post-Domitianic imperial policy or administration. This – and the equally silent witness of Martial – he explains as natural caution in the face of Trajan's ruthlessly authoritarian régime.

SATIRE XIII

All deeds that set evil examples result in unpleasantness
For the doer himself. To begin with, no guilty person, although
He may have suborned some judge to award him a rigged
    verdict,
Can ever win acquittal at the bar of his conscience. Calvinus,[1]
Don't you think public opinion's unanimous over this recent
Outrage against you, this breach-of-trust case you've brought?
Yet you're not so poorly off that one modest financial
Setback would sink you. Besides, | your plight, as everyone
    knows,
Is by no means rare: many others have suffered a similar
Mishap – by now it's a cliché, just average bad luck.
Why not drop these excessive complaints? One's indignation
Should never get overheated, or disproportionate
To the size of one's actual loss. But you, my friend, can
    scarcely
Bear the smallest iota of trivial misfortune;
Your temper's red-hot, you've a burning pain in your guts,
And all because a friend won't refund the capital
You entrusted to him! Should this *really* surprise
Someone turned sixty, born | in Fonteius' consulship?[2]
Or has a lifetime's experience taught you nothing at all?
    Philosophy's fine, its scriptures provide you with precepts
For rising above misfortune: but those who have learnt the
    hard way,
In the school of life, to bear all vicissitudes
Without fret or resentment – don't we admire them, too?
What feast-day's so holy it never produces the usual quota
Of theft, embezzlement, fraud, all those criminal get-rich-
    quick schemes,
Glittering fortunes won by the dagger or drug-box?
    Good men come ráre: count up, you'll scarcely find as many

249

As there are gates in Thebes, or mouths to the rich Nile.³
We live in the world's ninth age, a period still worse
Than the age of iron: such evil defies Nature
To find a name that fits it, a metal sufficiently base.⁴
And yet we're always demanding good faith from Gods and
        mortals
With such noisy insistence, it's like | some lawyer's claque,
        applauding
His speech in court. You old booby, don't you know the kind
        of passion
Other folk's money arouses? Can't you see how naïve and
        comic
A figure you cut these days, with your adamant belief
That a man should stick to his word, that there's really
        something
In all this religious guff, the temples, the mess of blood?
That was how primitive man lived long ago, before
King Saturn was ousted, before he exchanged his diadem
For a country sickle, when Juno was only a schoolgirl,
And Jupiter – then without title – still dwelt in Ida's caves.⁵
No banquets above the clouds yet for Heaven's inhabitants,
With Hebe and Ganymede there to hand round drinks, and
        Vulcan,
Still black from the smithy, scrubbing the soot off his arms
With spirits of – nectar.⁶ Each God would breakfast in private;
There wasn't our modern rabble of divinities, the stars
Ran to far fewer deifications, the firmament rested lighter
On poor old Atlas' back. The throne of the nether regions
Stood vacant still – grim Pluto | and his Sicilian consort,
The Furies, Ixion's wheel, the boulder of Sisyphus,
The black and murderous vulture, all these were yet to come:
While they'd got no monarch, the shades could enjoy a high
        old time.⁷
    In those days it was regarded as a most heinous offence,
To be punished by death, if a young man failed to stand up

In his elders' presence; and he, though scarcely bearded, was
      still
Deferred to himself by a schoolboy. It made no odds
Whose strawberry-beds were bigger, which store-room held
      more acorns:
That four years' lead ensured him immutable respect,
And manhood's first fuzz shared equal | status with grizzled age.
   So dishonesty then was exceptional, something quite
      shocking;
But now it's just the reverse – if a friend *doesn't* disavow
The funds entrusted to him, if he returns your holdall
With its rusting specie intact, such honesty's a portent
Fit to be set on record, and marked by the sacrifice
Of a garlanded lamb. If ever I meet a decent
God-fearing man, I bracket him with such freaks as
A boy with a double member, or fishes turned up
Under the plough by some gawping bumpkin, or even
A pregnant mule. It worries me, just as though
The sky had rained stones, or a swarm of bees had settled
On some temple roof-top, or maybe | a river in spate had
      come
Roaring down to its outfall with torrents of blood or milk.[8]
   So your complaint is this, then: by a trustee's fraudulence
You've been robbed of a couple of hundred. Yet others may
      have been
Bilked just like you, have lost a secret deposit
Up to five thousand, or more [9] – such a pile that the biggest
      strong-box
Can scarcely contain it. The Gods | in Heaven may witness
      the theft,
And who cares – so long as no mortal finds out? Just listen
To those loud denials, observe | the lying brass of the man!
He'll swear by the Sun's rays, by Jupiter's thunderbolts,
By the lance of Mars, by the darts of Delphic Apollo,
By the quiver and shafts of Diana, the virgin huntress,

By the trident of Neptune, Our Father of the Aegean;
He'll throw in Hercules' bow and Minerva's spear, he'll ransack
The armouries of Olympus down to their very last item;
And when he's a father, he'll shed big tears, and exclaim:
'May I eat my own son's noddle, well boiled, with a sweet-
          sour sauce,
If I'm not telling the truth!'
                              Some think that Fortune governs
All mortal hazards: the world, they contend, has no prime
          mover,
But day and night and the seasons succeed each other
By some process of Nature. So they'll have no qualms about
          laying
Their forsworn hands on any altar you please. There are others
Who believe in the Gods, in retribution for evil, but still
Perjure themselves regardless. 'Let Isis,' they argue,
'Do what she likes with my body, let her vengeful rattle
          blind me[10] –
I'd forego my eyes to keep | all the cash I've disavowed.
Consumption, gangrenous ulcers, an amputated leg –
They'd all be worth it. A penniless champion sprinter,
If he wasn't plain crazy, a case for some smart Greek quack,
Would opt for wealth and the gout: where does athletic
          prestige
Get you in terms of cash? Can you eat an olive-wreath?
The wrath of the Gods may be great, but so is its time-lag –
And if they make it their business to punish all wrongdoers,
When will they get to me? Besides, I may find a God who's
Open to prayer and persuasion, who has a forgiving nature.
The same crime often produces quite different results: one man
Ends on the cross, but another wearing a royal crown.'
     That's how they shore up their will when they're stricken
          with guilty
Terror for their misdeeds: then when you ask them to swear
An oath at the shrine, they'll be there before you, they'll even

Drag you along themselves, plague you from pillar to post.
For when a bad case is backed by brazen audacity,
Many will take it on trust. (It's all pure play-acting,
A role like the runaway clown's in that witty farce by
        Catullus.¹¹)
But you, poor soul, meanwhile are bellowing your complaint
In stentorian tones, outshouting the Mars of Homer: 'How
Can you listen unmoved to such lies, O Jupiter? Won't you
        even
Open those lips of yours? Who cares if they're marble or
        bronze?
You ought to say *something*. Otherwise what's the point
Of our emptying packets of incense on your sacrificial embers,
Or making you all those offerings – chopped calves'-liver,
Pigs' chitterlings? Frankly, we might as well honour the statue
Of some worthy civic deadhead for all the good it does us.'
    Now accept such consolation as an individual can offer
Who isn't lined up with the Cynics, hasn't swallowed Stoic
        doctrine
(There's only a shirt between them), who holds no brief
For cultivating one's kitchen-garden, like Epicurus.¹²
A baffling illness should get top specialist attention,
But *your* complaint could be handled by a first-year medical
        student.
If you can demonstrate that no more detestable crime
Was ever committed, all right: I'll hold my peace and let you
Beat your breast with your fists, or your cheeks with the flat
        of your hand
All you've a mind to. When | you've suffered such loss, the
        doors
Must be shut in token of mourning, the household will raise
        a louder
Lamentation over your cash than they would for a bereavement
No one, on such an occasion, needs to work up fictitious
Grief, or contents himself with rending his outer garments

And forcing a tear or two – lost cash breeds honest weeping.
  But when you see how the courts are choked with
      complaints like yours,
And even though your opponent peruse the bond ten times over,
Only to pronounce it, at last, a completely worthless
Forgery (yet the handwriting's his, and the impress
Of the sardonyx signet-ring he keeps in that ivory case) –
Despite all this, you fusspot, do you *really* suppose your plight
Merits exceptional treatment just because a white hen hatched you,
Whereas we mere common pullets were born from less
      favoured eggs?
Yours is a modest loss, to be borne with moderate choler
When you set it against the big-time offences. Just think
Of the hired thug, for instance, or the fire that's deliberately
Started in your front hallway with a well-placed sulphur match.
Think of the temple-robbers, who filch big chalices
(The gifts of nations, so holy their very rust should be
      worshipped)
From some ancient shrine, or the crowns that a long-dead
      monarch
Left there in dedication. If no such prizes are going,
Your small-time desecrator will scrape off the gold leaf
From Hercules' thigh, or the very | face of Neptune, will strip
Castor of all his gilding. So why not go the whole hog, and
Melt down the Thunderer's statue, that's solid gold right
      through?[13]
Think of those who concoct and peddle poisonous drugs,
Or the man who's lugged down to the sea in an oxhide sack,
      with
An innocent ape as his unfortunate companion.[14]
Yet this is the merest fraction of the crimes on which our City
Prefect must sit in judgement every day from dawn to dusk.
If you want to find out the truth about human nature, it's all
Contained in one courtroom. Spend a few days down there,
And when you come back, see if you still dare complain

About your own misfortunes. No one's surprised by goitre
In an Alpine canton: women with breasts that are bigger
Than their bouncing babies remain quite normal for Upper
    Egypt.
A blond and blue-eyed German is something we don't look
    twice at
Even when he's twisted his greasy locks into horns:
[Why should we? All of us share the common human
    condition.]
  Down swoop the clamorous clouds of Thracian cranes, and
    out
Sallies the Pygmy warrior against them, in his diminutive
Armour; but he's no match for so savage a foe, he's caught
Up by those crooked talons, and whirled away through the air.
Such a spectacle in Rome's context would make you split
    your sides, but
There, where the fighting forces all stand about one foot high,
Though such battles are frequently witnessed, nobody ever
    laughs.[15]
  'What?' you exclaim, 'is this crook, this fraudulent swindler
To get off scot-free?' Let's suppose he's been loaded with
    chains
And hustled away, at your instance, to summary execution
(What more could your wrath demand?) – yet the loss in cash
    still stands,
You'll never get back your deposit. What does that gory
And headless trunk satisfy but pure vindictiveness?
'Ah, vengeance is good, though, sweeter than life itself –'
That's how the ignorant talk, you'll see their passions
Flare up for the flimsiest reason, or maybe for none at all:
Any trifling excuse will justify loss of temper.
But no sage would express such opinions, neither Chrysippus
The Stoic, nor gentle Thales, nor the old man who dwelt by
    sweet
Hymettus (he'd never have given his prosecutor one drop

Of the hemlock *he* had to drink in his cruel bondage).[16] Benign
Philosophy, by degrees, peels away our follies and most
Of our vices, gives us a grounding in right and wrong. It's
     always
The small, mean, weak-willed mind that takes the greatest
     pleasure
In paying off scores, and here's the proof: there's no one
Enjoys revenge like a woman. But why should you suppose
Such people *do* escape justice? Their guilty conscience keeps
     them
In a lather of fear; the mind's | its own best torturer,
Lays on with invisible whips, silently flays them alive.
It's a fearful retribution – more cruel than any devised by
Our early Republican judges, or Hades' Rhadamanthus –
To be stuck, day and night, with this hostile | witness in one's
     own breast.

  The Pythian prophetess once replied to a certain Spartan[17]
That the notion he had in mind, of embezzling the deposit
Entrusted to him, and backing his fraudulence on oath,
Would not, in the end, go unpunished. (His actual enquiry was
What the God's reaction would be, did Apollo advise such a
     deed?)
So he gave the funds back – but from fear, | not honesty. Yet
     his fate
Confirmed the oracle's truth, proved it worthy of that great
     shrine, for
He perished, he and his family, the whole house, root and
     branch,
Down to the last relation, however far removed –
Such are the penalties that the mere intention of sinning
Is liable to incur. He who secretly meditates crime is
As guilty as if he'd committed the offence he plans. But suppose
He *does* commit it: then he's obsessed by secret fears
That don't let up even at meal-times. His throat is fever-dry,
     he

Can't chew his food, it half-chokes him, and in his misery
He spits back vintage wines, the expensive cobwebbed bottle's
Not to his taste: bring out something finer still, and he'll pull
A sour face, just as though he were drinking vinegar.
At night, if his worries allow him brief respite, a little sleep,
And his thrashing limbs are still, he'll start having nightmares
About the temple, the altar, the deity he's outraged;
What's more – and this brings him out in a proper sweat of
    terror –
He dreams about *you*, you're looming over him, larger
Than lifesize, a fearful figure, he's quaking with fright, *he's
    confessing* – !
Such men blanch and tremble at every lightning-flash; when
It thunders, the first faint rumble practically makes them swoon.
For them such things aren't haphazard, or caused by the winds'
    fury:
The fire that falls on earth is a wrathful judgement
From heaven itself. If one storm does no harm, they're
All strung up for the next: this calm's a deceptive reprieve.
What's more, if they get any illness – a pain in the side, a fever
That keeps them awake at night – they're convinced it's a
    visitation
From the god they've offended: such, they suppose, are the
    arrows
And slingstones divinity wields. They dare not offer a bleating
Lamb in the shrine, not so much as a crested cockerel
To their household gods: when the guilty fall sick, what hope
Is allowed them? Have not their victims a better title to life?
  Bad men, by and large, display shifty, capricious natures:
They're bold enough in action: it's afterwards, when the
    crime's
Accomplished, that notions of right and wrong begin to
Assail their minds. But soon | they're back to the same old
    tricks
They so lately abjured – they can't change their nature: who

Ever set limits upon his programme of crime? When did
A hardened brow recover the capacity for blushing
Once it was lost? What man have you ever seen satisfied
With a single villainous action? This forsworn scoundrel of ours
Will trip up sooner or later, will find himself chained to the
    wall
Of some pitch-dark oubliette, or stuck on one of those barren
Aegean rocks that are swarming with our distinguished
Political exiles. So then you'll exult in the bitter sentence
Your enemy's serving; at last | you'll agree, with a cheerful
    smile,
That the Gods aren't deaf after all, or blind, like Tiresias.[18]

1. Again, this elderly friend of J.'s is otherwise unknown. Calvinus was the family name of a long-established branch of the gens Domitia.

2. Fonteius Capito, the only consul in the *Fasti* to satisfy the requirements of this context (see Duff's useful note, p. 394), held office in A.D. 67. We therefore have a *terminus post quem* of A.D. 127 for the composition of the satire.

3. The Nile in antiquity had seven mouths: see Statius, *Thebaid* 8.353. It might be supposed that Egyptian Thebes is referred to in this context; but Egyptian Thebes had a hundred gates, whereas Thebes in Boeotia had seven. The scholiast, correctly, ties up Thebes and the Nile mouths with the Seven Sages, which gives an extra edge to J.'s number-play.

4. This 'ninth age' is a puzzle. The longest list of the Ages of Mankind is that given by Hesiod in the *Works and Days*, 109–210, which includes five ages only: the Golden Age, the Silver Age, the Bronze Age, the Heroic Age, the Iron Age. Moreover, as Professor S. G. F. Brandon remarks, in *Creation Legends of the Ancient Near East* (London 1963), p. 182, 'this scheme of the five races or generations is truly unique; it had not been anticipated elsewhere in the ancient Near East, and in Greek literature it appears only in the *Works and Days* and its presence there seems to have exercised little influence on subsequent Greek thought.' I have sometimes wondered whether what we have here is not a mangled version of the Hermopolis cosmogony, picked up by J. during his Egyptian exile. This cosmogony was associated with a mysterious Ogdoad of Eight Divine Beings known as 'the Great Ones of the primaeval age'; J. could well have turned the eight Great Ones into eight stages of creation. For a good account of the Hermopolis cosmogony see Brandon pp. 43–52. See now below, p. 262.

5. For an idyllic description of the Golden Age under Kronos (identified by the Romans with Saturn) see above, Satire VI 1–24. But Kronos was an unpleasant enough deity; his 'country sickle' is generally supposed to have been the instrument with which he

castrated Uranus, and since both Uranus and Ge had prophesied that he would be overthrown by one of his children, he ate them as soon as they were born. But his wife Rhea smuggled Zeus (Jupiter), the youngest, away to the caves of Ida, giving Kronos instead a stone wrapped in swaddling-bands. When Zeus grew up he raised the 'Hundred-handed Ones' and the Cyclopes against Kronos, and defeated him after an Armageddon-like conflict, that lasted ten years. Professor Rose suggests that the myth not only reflects the victory of the Olympian cult over an older people and religion, but contains significant imagery of earthquakes and volcanic eruptions. This seems very likely.

6. *Siccato nectare* in line 44 is generally construed as an ablative absolute, which gives rise to some awkward and strained interpretations. I prefer to take it in the instrumental sense: *siccato* (or perhaps *saccato*, which the scholiast would seem to have read) will then mean 'distilled' or 'evaporated', and the nectar will be what Vulcan cleans the filth off his arms with – much as a modern mechanic will sometimes use surgical spirit.

7. The story of Ixion is curious. He promised a large bride-price to his prospective father-in-law, but when the poor man came to collect it, he fell into a red-hot barbecue-pit set as a trap for him by Ixion. After he had failed to persuade anyone else to purify him of his blood-guilt, Ixion sought refuge with Zeus – and promptly attempted to seduce Hera. To lull his suspicions, Zeus fashioned a cloud-double of Hera called Nephele, on whom Ixion sired the first Centaur. As a punishment Zeus bound him to a burning wheel for all eternity. The vulture, of course, is that which pecked at Prometheus's liver while he was bound to his rock in the Caucasus; the punishment of Sisyphus was to roll a boulder uphill only to have it topple back to the bottom again when he was approaching the summit.

8. All these prodigies were (it seems) of regular occurrence in ancient Italy: see Julius Obsequens' *Book of Prodigies*, now available in Vol. XIV of the Loeb edition of Livy (tr. A. C. Schlesinger and Russel M. Geer), pp. 238–319, where instances of each are recorded.

9. The translation of specific sums of money is always awkward. Sometimes it seems best to leave the original currency; sometimes, as here, to do so would jar, since the figure in sesterces would seem

very inflated. There is also the problem of shifting currency values. I have followed Highet (p. 140) in making a rough equivalent of 50 sesterces to the £. Thus the figures here are to be taken as sterling. All that I want to do is give a general notion of the amount involved for an English reader.

10. The 'rattle' is the *sistrum*, 'which', as Lewis and Short charmingly put it, 'was used by the Egyptians in celebrating the rites of Isis, and in other lascivious festivals.' It is here envisaged as an instrument akin to Athena's aegis or the thunderbolt of Zeus.

11. For Catullus the farce-writer see above, VIII 186, and n. 21 ad loc.

12. The Cynics believed that the only good was virtue, and that pleasure, if pursued for its own sake, was a positive evil: they were thus marked by an aggressively puritanical contempt for wealth and achievement, and tended to be a 'protest group' rather than a constructive philosophical sect. The first Cynic was Antisthenes of Athens; the more famous Diogenes of Sinope, his pupil, carried Cynical asceticism to bizarre lengths. The Stoics (founded by Zeno *c.* 308 B.C.) likewise believed in virtue as the supreme good, but held that action, not withdrawal or contemplation, was the highest problem for man: they thus remained in the world (many high Roman statesmen and at least one Emperor, Marcus Aurelius, were Stoics) and did not abjure material gain or luxuries: hence J.'s 'only a shirt between them'. Epicurus established a school in a garden outside Athens in 306 B.C.: his followers inclined towards political quietism, moderation, 'contracting out' (*cultiver notre jardin*). J.'s eclecticism is interesting; so is the characteristic omission of Platonic or Aristotelian philosophy, which during this period had virtually dropped out of sight.

13. At line 153 I accept D. R. Shackleton Bailey's emendation *solidum* for *solitus* (*Classical Review* NS9, 1959, 201–2); I have also sometimes wondered whether *totum* should not be emended to *totiens*.

14. For parricide in Rome and its punishment see above, VIII 214, and n. 24 ad loc.

15. The legend of pitched battles between the southward-flying cranes and the Pygmies (who lived in Ethiopia) goes back at least as far as Homer's day: see *Iliad* 3.7. Strabo, Pliny and Mela also refer to it.

16. Chrysippus (*c.* 280–*c.* 207 B.C.) succeeded Cleanthes, his teacher, as head of the Academy, and was regarded as the most distinguished Stoic after Zeno. There is a story that he saw a donkey eating a plate of figs set out for his own supper, and found the spectacle so amusing that he died of a fit of hysterics. Thales of Miletus (*c.* 640–*c.* 546 B.C.), the earliest of the Ionian 'pre-Socratic' philosophers, and one of the Seven Sages, believed that the original basic substance of all things was water. He could also predict eclipses, and made a fortune in the olive-oil business after being twitted with his impracticality. The 'old man who dwelt by sweet Hymettus' was, of course, Socrates himself.

17. This story seems to be taken from Herodotus, 6.86, where it is told of one Glaucus son of Epicydes (pp. 390–92).

18. Courtney (p. 42) queries *nec surdum nec Teresian* at line 249 and makes the attractive emendation *Drusum* for *surdum*, meaning that 'no god is either as blind as Tiresias or as deaf as the Emperor Claudius': cf. III 238.

ADDITIONAL NOTE

M. J. McGann (Additional Bibliography) has suggested that the mysterious 'ninth age' (*nona aetas*), referred to by J. in this Satire at line 28, may express a concept borrowed from the Sibylline Oracles – that human history evolves in *ten* ages, ending in utter ruin with the destruction of mankind at the close of the tenth age. J. and his contemporaries would then be in the penultimate age, just before this final *Götterdämmerung*.

SATIRE XIV

A great many things, Fuscinus,[1] of deservedly ill repute,
Things that would leave an indelible stain on the brightest
    fortune,
Children acquire from their parents. Bad examples are catching:
If Papa's a ruinous gambler, then his son and heir is bound
To be rattling a miniature dice-box by early adolescence;
Nor need the family expect better things from any youth
Whose spendthrift father, a hoary old glutton, has taught him
To appreciate peeled truffles, and the proper sort of sauce
On mushrooms; who's learnt to tuck into quails and plovers[2]
Served up with their natural juices. By the time that he's seven,
With quite a few milk-teeth left still, a boy like this has got
His character fixed for life. Set a thousand bearded tutors
On either side of him, he'll never give up his passion
For luxurious meals, or lower his standards of *haute cuisine*.

    Take Rutilus, now[3]: does his conduct encourage a lenient
Temper, a sense of restraint when dealing with peccadilloes?
Does he hold that slaves are fashioned, body and soul, from the
    same
Elements as their masters? Not on your life. What he teaches
Is sadism, pure and simple: there's nothing pleases him more
Than a good old noisy flogging, no siren song to compare
With the crack of the lash. To his quaking household he's
A monster, a mythical ogre, never so happy as when
The torturer's there on the job, and some poor wretch who's
    stolen
A couple of towels is being branded with red-hot irons. What
Effect on the young must he have, with his yen for clanking
    chains,
For dungeons, and seared flesh, and field-gang labour camps?[4]
    How can you hope, you bumpkin, that the daughter won't
    sleep around

When however fast she gabbles the list of her mother's lovers
She must stop to get her breath back a score of times and
    more?
As a schoolgirl she shared Mummy's secrets, and now she
    composes
Billets-doux on her own account – though Mummy dictates
    them –
And sends them round to her lover by the same fag go-between.
Such, though, is Nature's order: we're sooner, more swiftly
    corrupted
By examples of vice in the home, since they enter our minds
With high authority's sanction. Perhaps you'll find one or two
Youths who despise such conduct, whose spirits have been
    formed
From finer clay, with a kindlier touch in the firing; but
The rest troop off down the path where their father's
    unsavoury
Footsteps lead them, they're dragged through the ruts of
    familiar vice.
  So we've got one powerful motive at least for steering clear
    of
All reprehensible acts – lest the crimes we commit are copied
By the children we raise. We're all | too willing to model
    ourselves
On vice and depravity: you'll find some rebellious traitor
Wherever you look, in every country and clime, but
A righteous, inflexible statesman – that's quite another matter.
Let no foul sight or utterance ever approach the threshold
Of a father's dwelling-place: may this house be free from
    call-girls
And noisy all-night parties. If you're planning any misdeed,
Never forget that a child has first claim on your respect:
Don't disregard the tender years of your son, but rather
Let his presence serve to dissuade you from the sin you
    contemplate.

For if, in time to come, he earns officialdom's wrathful
Attention, and proves himself your son in more than looks
And physical build, if he's | the child of your moral actions,
And while following where you lead him, sinks deeper still in
    crime –
Then, I don't doubt, you'll revile him, you'll read him a bitter
And furious lecture, and cut him | out of your will. But how
Can you assume the mien and privileges of a father
When your old age is marred with worse indiscretions than
    his,
And the cupping-glass hasn't found any brains in your vacuous
    noddle
Since heaven knows when? If a visitor is expected,
Then none of your household's idle. 'Get the floors swept,'
    you shout,
'Burnish the columns, fetch down those spiders' webs up
    there!
You, clean the silver plate, and you, the embossed vessels –'
Hark at the voice of the master, standing over them, whip in
    hand!
You're all of a dither, poor creature: your friend's eye might be
    offended
By a dog's turd in the lobby, or some splashes of mud
Down the covered colonnade – things that one small slave-boy
Could fix with a bucket of sawdust. Then why take no trouble
To ensure that your son will enjoy the sanctity of the home
Unmarred, without blemish? Yes, | it's a fine thing to present
Another citizen to your country and people – provided
You raise him to be what your country needs, a capable
Farmer, who's equally skilled in the arts of peace and war.
    So it makes a great difference what practical, what moral
Education you give your son. The stork scours the countryside
For snakes and lizards to feed | its young ones; and when
    they've learnt
To fly, they go off in search of the same creatures themselves.

The vulture hastens home from dead cattle and dogs, or the gibbet,
Bearing carrion plunder to share with its chicks: and so
When the chick's grown-up, when it's built | a nest of its own
    in another
Tree, when it's self-supporting, it feeds on carrion still.
But Jupiter's noble eagle goes hunting hare and hind through
The upland pastures, this is the prey it brings home
To its eyrie: so when the eaglets reach full maturity
And leave the nest, at the dictates of hunger they'll swoop
Down on the self-same prey they first ate when they burst the
    shell.
  X had a passion for building: he ran up multi-storeyed
Mansions all over the place – at the seaside, in mountain resorts
Like Praeneste, on Tivoli's hillsides – done up with marble
    imported
From Greece, or still further afield, piles that eclipsed the local
Temples in splendour⁵ (just like that eunuch nabob, the
    freedman
Of Claudius, whose town house far outshone the Capitol).⁶
Such grandiose schemes made inroads | in his fortune, frittered
    away
His ready cash; yet somehow he kept a quite substantial
Proportion intact – for his crazy son to squander
On building more stately homes with even costlier marble.
  Some, whose lot it was to have Sabbath-fearing fathers,
Worship nothing but clouds and the *numen* of the heavens,
And think it as great a crime to eat pork, from which their
    parents
Abstained, as human flesh. They get themselves circumcised,
And look down on Roman law, preferring instead to learn
And honour and fear the Jewish commandments, whatever
Was handed down by Moses in that arcane tome of his –
Never to show the way to any but fellow-believers
(If they ask where to get some water, find out if they're
    foreskinless).

But their fathers were the culprits: they made every seventh
    day
Taboo for all life's business, dedicated to idleness.7
  Most faults the young pick up spontaneously: one only,
Avarice, has to be taught them, against their natural instincts.
A deceptive vice, this, with the shadow and semblance of
    virtue –
Dour-faced, gloomy of mien, always dressed like an
    undertaker,
The miser's openly cried up for his frugality:
A thrifty fellow, they say, a man who keeps closer watch
Over his wealth than the dragons who guard the Hesperides
And the golden fleece of Colchis could manage, if put on the
    job.
What's more, the men that I speak of are thought to be expert
At moneymaking: such workers forge ever-larger fortunes,
By any and every method. The anvil rings ceaselessly,
The furnace is always glowing: that's how the pile mounts up.
[So Daddy's convinced that the miser enjoys true happiness:]
The man who goggles at wealth, who can't credit any instance
Of poverty plus contentment, is bound to advise his sons
To tread in the skinflint's footsteps, to follow the same way of
    life.
Each vice has its rudiments: these he drums into their heads
From the start, they're grounded in all the pettier meannesses.
But soon they've moved up, he's acquainting them with the
    insatiable
Passion for gain. He'll pinch his slaves' meagre bellies
By chiselling on their rations – but he starves himself too, those
    crusts
Of stale bread, blue with mould, are something even *he*
    baulks at.
He'll rehash yesterday's mince in mid-September's heat and
Keep all the left-overs – beans, a tail-end of mackerel,
Half a catfish, already stinking – under lock and key, he'll even

Count up the chopped spring onions. Professional beggars
Would turn down an invitation to this kind of feast. Why
    suffer
Such tortures in search of wealth, man? It's plain stark lunacy,
Sheer craziness, living in squalor just to die a millionaire.
What's more, when your bags and coffers are crammed to the
    brim, you'll find
That the appetite for riches will expand in direct proportion
To your actual wealth: small fortunes breed less insistent
    desires.
So just one country house won't be enough, you must
    purchase
A second: you'll feel the urge to acquire more land – that
    neighbour's
Wheatfield looks bigger and better than yours, so you buy it up,
Plus his orchards, and that hillside with its rows of grey
    olive-trees.
But if no figure you offer will tempt the owner to sell, then
A herd of famished cattle, lean work-weary oxen, can somehow
Find their way, during the night, in among his green standing
    corn,
And not go home till they've munched through the whole new
    crop, so cleanly
You'd think the field had been scythed. But occurrences of
    this sort
Are so common it's hard to count them, to reckon up how
    many
Estates have come under the hammer through such outrageous
    acts.
    But think what people will say, just imagine all the malicious
Gossip! 'So what?' you reply. 'I don't give a row of bean-pods
For the neighbourhood's good opinions – especially if to earn it
Means working some meagre holding for a chicken-feed crop.'
    No doubt;
The great panacea, it seems – it'll keep you free from illness

And infirmity, you'll escape all worries, all disappointments,
Live to a ripe old age, attain true happiness –
Is to own as many acres as Rome's whole population
Had under the plough in the days of the early Kings.
Later, a battered veteran who'd fought for his country
Against Carthage or dread Pyrrhus, who'd braved the Epirots'
    swords,
Would get, in the end, a bare two acres as quittance
For all his wounds.[8] Yet none ever held this a niggardly
Recompense, less than their service of blood and toil deserved;
None charged the State with bad faith or ingratitude. This
    small plot
Was enough to support a man – not to mention his wife in
    labour,
And the other four children, three his and one a house-slave's,
Playing around the cottage: and when their big brothers
    returned
From the day's work, ditching or ploughing, a second, more
    ample supper
Of porridge awaited them, steaming hot in the pot – yet
Today we'd think the same holding too small for our kitchen-
    garden!
  Here lies the root of most evil: no human passion provides
So frequent an incentive to mix up a dose of poison
Or slip a knife in the ribs as our unbridled craving
For limitless wealth. The man whose goal is a fortune
Wants it double quick; and how much respect for the law,
    what
Decent moral scruples can such a go-getter afford?
'Be content with a humble cottage, my boy: don't look
    beyond
These hills of ours' – that's what old mountain peasants
Used to tell their sons. 'The ploughshare should furnish men
With sufficient bread for their needs: the gods of the
    countryside

So ordained it, whose generous bounty brought us the blessing
Of wheat, and rescued us from our old, crude acorn diet.
The man who doesn't disdain to wear kneeboots when it's
      freezing,
And keeps off an east wind's chill with sheepskins, fleece
      inside –
He'll never turn out a bad hat: it's these strange foreign
Luxuries, purple robes and the like, that lead to crime
And wickedness.' Such were the maxims the ancients gave their
      children;
But nowadays, when autumn is ending, a father will rouse
His drowsy son soon after midnight. 'Wake up, boy!' he'll
      bawl, 'get out
Your notebooks! Scribble away, son, mug up your cases, study
Those red-letter legal tomes! If the army's your choice, put in
For the vinestaff 9 at once, make sure your Commander-in-Chief
Takes note of your crewcut, your hairy nostrils, those broad
Shoulders of yours; destroy some Moroccan encampments
Or forts on the Scottish border; then when you're sixty
      you'll be
Centurion of the Standard – and pretty well off, my boy.
But if you're too lazy to stomach the tough routine of a
      soldier's
Life in camp or barracks, if your bowels turn to water
At the sound of bugle or trumpet, then trade's your line: find
      something
That can be resold with a profit of fifty per cent or so. And
Don't turn up your nose at the dirtier merchandise
Kept strictly beyond the Tiber,10 don't suppose there's any
      distinction
Between perfume and hides: the stink of profit is pleasant
Whatever its source. Here's the maxim that you should always
Have on your lips, a verse that the Gods, or Jove himself
In poetic mood might have framed: "No questions about the
      source

Of your wealth – but wealth you must have."' Every ancient
   nanny
Dins this into her toddlers, it's the first thing little girls master,
Long before their A.B.C. To any father who hands out
Advice of this sort, I'd say: 'Look here, you pinhead, who's
   told you
You've got to *hurry* the process? Your pupil, I wouldn't mind
   betting,
Will outshine his master. So lay off, you don't need to worry,
   you'll be
Eclipsed as surely as Telamon was by Ajax,
Or Peleus by Achilles. Go easy with youngsters:
The marrow of adult evil has not yet filled their bones.
When your boy's of an age to comb out his beard and submit
   it
To the razor's edge, yes, *then* he'll bear false witness, then he'll
Perjure himself for tuppence by any image or altar
He's asked to lay hands on. Suppose you've a daughter-in-law,
And she brings a big dowry – why then she's as good as
   buried
The moment she crosses your threshold. Whose fingers, do
   you imagine,
Will throttle her while she's asleep? The laborious amassing
Of riches by land and sea may suffice for you, but he's figured
How to make it much quicker: there isn't any hard work
In a major crime.'
            'But *I* never taught him such habits,'
You'll be saying some day. 'He never | picked up these ideas
   from *me*.'
Perhaps not; nevertheless the root and cause of his downfall
Lies within you. Whoever extols the passion for wealth
Will see his son grow up an acquisitive money-grabber –
Indeed, you're giving him licence to augment his patrimony
By fraudulent methods.[11] He's off, reins flying, full pelt: if you
   try

And call him back, he can't stop, his chariot whirls him
Away past the turning-post, indifferent to your commands.
Delinquency knows no limits: what youth will not overstep
The margin of faults you allow him? Don't they always want
        more?
When you tell a young man that only fools give presents
To friends, or relieve the debts of a poverty-stricken relation,
It simply encourages him to rob and cheat, to descend
To any criminal act – if it rakes in the wealth that excites
As great a passion in you as patriotism stirred up
In the breasts of the Decii; as great – if the Greek tale's true –
As the love which fired Menoeceus for his city of Thebes,
        where once
Armed men sprang from the furrows, born of the dragon's
        teeth,
Shields at the ready, prepared – as though the bugler had risen
Alongside them – to do battle that very moment.[12] Just so
You'll see the spark you kindled yourself now spreading
Like a forest fire, and consuming all in its path. And don't
Get the idea *you're* immune, you poor fellow: the trembling
        maestro
Will be gobbled up, with roaring, in the den of his trainee lion.
The astrologers may know your nativity: but it's a bore
To wait for that slow-running spindle: you'll die before your
        thread
Is due for shearing. Already he finds you an obstacle
To his ambitions; your stag-like longevity's sheer
Torture for that young mind.[13] You'd better see a doctor
And make him prescribe you some of the prophylactic
Mithridates employed.[14] If you're set | on surviving long
        enough
To pick one more fig, to continue | gathering rosebuds, you
        must
Take a dose, before meals, of the stuff that saves kings – and
        fathers.

What I've drawn is a first-class attraction: no theatre can
    rival it,
No smart and well-heeled praetor can outshine it with his
    games.[15]
Just think at what hazard to life men's fortunes are increased,
    what
Risks they'll run to fill up their brassbound coffers
And boost their deposit accounts! (They bank with Castor
    these days,
Ever since Mars the Avenger was robbed of his helmet, and
    failed
To safeguard the goods in his keeping.[16]) So you can forget
    about all
These lavish productions put on at religious festivals:
Mankind's commercial dealings offer far bigger sport.
What's better entertainment, the trampoline acrobat, the
Funambulist on his tightrope – or you, spending half a lifetime
Aboard your merchantman, always | exposed to each wind that
    blows,
A corrupt and compliant[17] trader in stinking burlap, who's only
Too glad to pick up a cargo of fortified muscatel
At some ancient Cretan wharfside, to travel with demijohns
From Jove's own birthplace. And yet that neat-stepping
    balancer
Makes a livelihood out of his footwork, the rope he descends
Is his prop against cold and hunger. But you take your risks
For the sake of a thousand talents, a hundred country estates.
    Look at the big ships crowding our seas and harbours:
    we've more
Men afloat than ashore now. Wherever there's hope of profit
Our merchant fleet will venture, will sail beyond Crete or
    Rhodes or
Past the Moroccan coastline, leaving Gibraltar behind them,
Till they hear the sun sink hissing in Ocean's western streams.
It's a fine return for such labours to sail back home in triumph,

Purse full, moneybags bursting, with tales to tell of the
    wonders
You encountered *en route* – not least those husky young
    mermen.
   Delusions take various forms. Mad Orestes, cowering
In his sister Electra's arms, was haunted by fiery visions
Of the Furies; when Ajax slaughtered | an ox, its bellowing
Was the death-cry of Agamemnon or Ulysses.[18] But the man
Who loads his vessel with freight to the gunwales, leaving
    only
A single plank above water, is no less in need
Of a keeper. He may not gibber and tear his clothes – yet
    think
What it is that spurs him to face all those hardships and perils:
    silver
Stamped out in tiny roundels, with portraits and superscriptions!
Storm-clouds and thunder threaten. 'Come on, cast off!' cries
    the merchant
Who's bought up a load of grain | or pepper. 'This overcast
Sky, this gathering blackness is nothing to worry about –
Just summer lightning.' Poor devil, before the night is ended
He may find himself in the water, waves surging over him,
His money-belt clutched in his teeth, or by one free hand, his
    vessel
A total write-off. Yesterday all the gold-dust
Washed down by the river-gravels of Spain or Lydia wouldn't
Have satisfied his ambitions: but now he must rest content
With a rag round his chilly loins, and a crust of bread, while
    he begs
For coppers, displaying a picture of the storm that shipwrecked
    him.
   Riches so hardly come by cost still more anxiety
And care to preserve: the guardianship of a fortune
Is a wretched chore. One millionaire was so nervous
About his Phrygian marbles, his priceless pictures, his amber

And ivory knickknacks, his tortoiseshell *objets d'art*,
That he kept a vast squad of servants with water-buckets
On duty all night. But the tub of the naked Cynic
Diogenes[19] never caught fire: if it broke, he could pick up
    another
The following day – or put some lead clamps in the old one.
Alexander perceived, on seeing that tub and its famous
Occupant, how much happier was the man who desired
    nothing
Than he whose ambitions encompassed the world, who would
    yet
Suffer perils as great as all his present achievements.
[Fortune has no divinity, could we but see it: it's we,
We ourselves, who make her a goddess.[20]] If anyone asks me
Where we're to draw the line, how much is sufficient, I'd say:
Enough to meet the requirements of cold and thirst and
    hunger,
As much as Epicurus derived from that little garden,[21]
Or Socrates, earlier still, possessed in his frugal home –
Nature never says one thing and Philosophy another.
Are those over-strict examples? Am I cramping your style?
    Then add
A dash of our latterday morals, let's compound for the legal
    minimum
Capital of a burgher.[22] If *that* still makes you frown and
Pout with resentment, double – all right, then, treble – the
    sum:
What? Not satisfied yet? Still gaping for more? In that case
Nothing will be enough, not the wealth of Croesus and all
The kings of Persia – not even that of Narcissus,[23]
Claudius' favourite freedman, on whom the Emperor lavished
Such favours, and at whose say-so he put his own wife to
    death.

Notes to Satire XIV

1. Again, the dedicatee of this satire is a person otherwise unknown.

2. The literal translation of *ficedulas* is 'beccaficoes', but I have preferred, for English-speaking readers, more familiar delicacies: the only point of the reference here is that the dish should symbolize *gourmandise*.

3. It is likely (but by no means certain) that this Rutilus is the gluttonous spendthrift of Satire XI 1–11; see n. 1 ad loc.

4. The 'field-gang labour camps' were the notorious *ergastula*, semi-underground barracks in which fettered slaves who worked the large country estates were confined. Columella condemned this system, not for its inhumanity, but because it was uneconomical: Cato, in his *Res Rustica*, recommends the dumping of worn-out harness and worn-out slaves in the same breath.

5. A passion for extravagant building was one of the main forms of what Thorstein Veblen calls 'conspicuous consumption' amongst wealthy Romans under the Empire. The tendency was satirized by Horace before J., and Martial also alludes to it. As Duff reminds us (p. 419), even people of comparatively moderate fortune, such as Cicero or the Younger Pliny, were remarkable for the number and luxury of the country houses they owned.

6. This was 'Posides the eunuch, to whom [Claudius] actually awarded, at his British triumph, the honour of a headless spear, along with soldiers who had fought in the field' (Suetonius, *Claudius* 28, p. 199).

7. J., as Highet rightly points out (p. 283), knew more about the Jews than any other Roman writer with the possible exception of Tacitus. It has been suggested that in this passage he shows familiarity with a number of technical terms: e.g. 'the *numen* of the heavens' is the equivalent of *shamayim*, one of the periphrases for the Name of God (Tacitus, *Histories* 5.5, had the same notion in mind when he said that 'the Jews worship with the mind alone'). There is a distinction between the two stages of Judaic conversion: the father is a Proselyte of the Gate, the son a Proselyte of Righteousness. Line 101 seems to parody Biblical language; and J., like other Roman

writers, emphasizes the negative and prohibitive aspects of Jewish law that would be most apparent to an outsider. Some authorities regard the request for water as an allusion to the practice of baptism; but it seems more likely that J. is attacking 'prohibitions against showing the commonest offices of humanity . . . to any but co-religionists' (Duff p. 421). Both he and Tacitus attribute the workless Jewish Sabbath to natural laziness and indolence.

8. King Pyrrhus of Epirus (*c.* 318–272 B.C.) fought several success-ful campaigns against Rome from 280 B.C. onwards: he was, amongst other things, the first general to introduce elephants into Italy. When he withdrew from Italy he remarked, with some prescience, 'What a battleground I am leaving to Rome and Carthage.' The subsequent Carthaginian or Punic Wars, in which Rome was opposed by Hannibal, were only concluded by the final defeat of Hannibal at Zama in 202 B.C. J. is thus including all the veterans of a century's campaigning in his generalization.

9. The vinestaff was the centurion's badge of office: the rank itself is difficult for a modern reader to appreciate, since it combined the func-tions of a warrant officer and a company commander. For the plebeian recruit it was the summit of his ambition to attain centurion's rank: the boy described here would be lucky to begin his service with such status, even at the bottom of the list. A person of equestrian rank, on the other hand, was obliged to serve in the army at four successive levels (of which centurion was the lowest) before becoming eligible for a post in the civil service. See Duff's useful note (pp. 427–8).

10. Certain commodities and activities (hides and tanning are an obvious example) were restricted by law to the further side of the Tiber, beyond the Janiculum.

11. At line 229 I accept the emendation of D. A. Amyx (*Classical Philology* 36, 1941, 278 f.) and read: *quippe et per fraudes patrimonia conduplicare.*

12. According to legend, when Cadmus reached Thebes, he killed the dragon of Ares guarding a spring where he had sent his followers to obtain water. Athena told him to sow the dragon's teeth, and when he did so armed men sprang up from the furrow. These were the Sparti, or 'Sown Men'. Cadmus threw stones in amongst them, and they thought they were being attacked by their fellow-Sparti: in the ensuing battle all but five of them were killed. These five

helped Cadmus build his city. Menoeceus, and his grandson of the same name, were descended from these Sparti. Menoeceus the elder was the father of Jocasta and Creon. After Jocasta's marriage to Oedipus plague struck Thebes, and Tiresias the prophet declared it could only be averted if one of the Sparti's descendants sacrificed himself for the city: Menoeceus thereupon jumped to his death from the walls. (For the magic nature of this *devotio* see above, Satire VIII 254–8, and n. 30 ad loc.) The grandson, Creon's son, either committed suicide or was killed before the gates of the city during the War of the Seven Against Thebes, when Tiresias, again, declared that Thebes would only be saved if a descendant of the Sparti gave up his life to appease Ares, still rancorous, it seems, over the destruction of the Sparti by Cadmus. The two stories may be variant versions of the same myth – but not necessarily so: they are no odder a duplication than the parallel one of the Decii.

13. Another example of the ancient addiction to outrageous tall stories in the field of natural history: the scholiast solemnly declares that some stags lived to be nine hundred years old!

14. For the prophylactics of Mithridates see above, Satire VI 660–61, and n. 49 ad loc. (pp. 152, 161).

15. For the praetor's function at the Games see above, Satire XI 193 ff., and n. 21 ad loc. (pp. 233, 239).

16. Money was regularly deposited in a temple for safe-keeping, just as we would deposit it in a bank. From this passage it appears that when J. wrote, the temple of Mars the Avenger had recently been burgled, and that the thieves had got away, not only with various citizens' cash-boxes, but also (supreme insult) with whatever they could prise loose from the god's own image. (For this practice see above, Satire XIII 150–53.) The temple of Castor was in the Forum: cf. above, Satire X 24–5, and n. 3 ad loc. Apparently a military guard was posted there – as today at the Bank of England.

17. At line 269, for the meaningless †*acullis*† or scarcely more satisfactory *ac vilis* of the MSS I conjecture *ac facilis*, and translate accordingly. Griffith, *Classical Quarterly* NS19 (1969), 386, now suggests *fatuus*.

18. Orestes was pursued by the Furies after killing his mother Clytemnestra; Ajax went mad after being adjudged the loser in his

contest with Odysseus for the arms of Achilles: see above, Satire XI 31 and n. 6 ad loc. (pp. 228, 236).

19. For Diogenes see above, Satire XIII 120 ff., and n. 12 ad loc. The text here makes it clear that his 'tub' was not a wooden barrel, but a huge pottery jar.

20. The words in square brackets are repeated from Satire X 365; and though J. elsewhere repeats a line (e.g. the doublet of I 25 and X 226) the aphorism seems very much out of place here.

21. For Epicurus see above, n. 12 to Satire XIII.

22. The 'legal minimum capital of a burgher', or member of the Equestrian Order, was 400,000 sesterces, or about £8000.

23. Narcissus was Claudius's Imperial Secretary, and a close confidant of his wife Messalina. But after Messalina contracted her lunatic 'marriage' with Gaius Silius (see above, Satire X 329 ff., and n. 32 ad loc.), Narcissus and the other Palace freedmen determined to be rid of her. According to Tacitus (*Annals* 11.30–38, pp. 240–43) Narcissus himself had her killed by an officer of the Praetorian Guard, and informed Claudius of the deed as a *fait accompli*.

Who has not heard, Volusius,[1] of the monstrous deities
Those crazy Egyptians worship? One lot adores crocodiles,
Another worships the snake-gorged ibis; and where
The magic chords resound from Memnon's truncated statue,
Where old Thebes, with her hundred gates, now lies in ruins,
    there gleams
The golden effigy of a sacred long-tailed monkey.
You'll find whole cities devoted to cats, or to river-fish
Or dogs – but not a soul who worships Diana.[2] To eat
Onions or leeks is an outrage, they're strictly taboo: how holy
The nation that has such gods springing up in the kitchen-
    garden!
All households abstain from mutton and lamb, it's forbidden
To slaughter young kids – but making a meal of human
Flesh is permitted, it seems.[3] When Ulysses, over dinner,
Told the tale of such an outrage, he shocked King Alcinous –
And some others present, perhaps, who, angry or laughing,
Thought him a braggart liar.[4] 'Won't somebody throw this
    horror-
Merchant back in the sea? A man-eating Cyclops, indeed!
Laestrygonian cannibals! Nonsense! The fellow deserves to
    drown
In his own Charybdis come true, some lethal real-life maelstrom.
I'd sooner believe in Scylla, or the Clashing Rocks, or that bag
Stuffed with the winds, or Circe turning Elpenor
And all his comrades, with one light touch of her wand,
Into grunting swine.[5] Does he *really* think we Phaeacians
Are such credulous numskulls?'

                            So might a more or less sober
Guest, who'd not over-indulged in that powerful Corfu wine,
Have justly complained: for the Ithacan's | story was
    unsupported

By any eyewitness – whereas the incident *I* shall relate,
Though fantastic enough, took place within recent memory,[6]
Up-country from sunbaked Coptos, an act of mob violence
Worse than anything in the tragedians. Search through the
     mythical
Canon from Pyrrha[7] onwards, you won't find an instance of a
Collective crime. Now attend, and learn what kind of novel
Atrocity *our* day and age has added to history.
  Between the neighbouring townships of Ombi and
     Tentyra[8]
There smoulders an ancient vendetta, undying hatred, a wound
That can never heal. What fills | both sides with such violent
     rancour
Is the loathing they feel towards | each other's gods: they
     believe
That only the gods *they* worship deserve to be recognized.[9]
So when one town had a big feast-day, the leaders and chief
Citizens of its rival decided to turn this occasion
To their own profit, to wreck the gay merrymaking
And break up the fun of the party, the tables that would be
     spread
By every temple and crossway for the day-and-night junketing
That can last a whole week non-stop. (The Egyptians may be
     peasants,
But for self-indulgence there's nothing – as I have observed
     myself[10] –
To choose between city smarties and the barbarous fellaheen.)
Besides, they reckoned on winning an easy victory over
These revellers, slurred of speech and lurching from booze, as
     they danced
To some blackamoor's piping, all greasy with rank pomade
     and
Sporting garlands galore, wreaths all askew on their heads.
This on one side: on the other, | pure ravenous hatred. Insults
Began the affray, they kindled men's too combustible passions

Like a trumpet-call: oaths volleyed back, battle was joined
With naked hands as weapons. Few jaws got through
This punch-up unscathed, hardly anyone had an unbroken
Nose by the end. Throughout the ranks there appeared
Faces half-bashed to a jelly, features knocked out of true,
Fists bloodied from eyes, split cheeks laid wide to expose the
    bone.
Yet because there were no corpses to trample on, they
    regarded
The whole affair as mere horseplay, the sort of mock-battle
That children engage in: what's | the point of so many
    thousands
Brawling if no one gets killed? So the fight grew fiercer, by
    now
They were looking around for stones – the rioter's regular
Weapon – and letting fly. But these were inferior missiles,
Not in the class of those that Turnus and Ajax wielded,
Or the one with which Diomedes shattered Aeneas' hip,[11] but
Such as our unheroic and puny generation
Has the strength to throw. Mankind | was on the decline while
    Homer
Still lived; and today the earth breeds a race of degenerate
Weaklings, who stir high heaven to laughter and loathing.
    Enough
Of this digression, and back to my tale. One side
Brought up reinforcements, continued the battle with swords
And volleys of arrows. The faction from nearby Tentyra's
Shady palm-groves now fled in headlong confusion before
The Ombite charge. But one of them, panic-stricken, pressed
    on
A little too fast, tripped, fell, and was captured. The victorious
Rabble tore him apart into bits and pieces, so many
That this single corpse provided a morsel for all. They wolfed
    him
Bones and all, not bothering even to spit-roast

Or make a stew of his carcase. Building a proper fire-pit
Was a bore, and took time – so they scoffed the poor devil raw.
  One should, I suppose, be grateful, Prometheus, that your
      sacred
Gift of fire to mankind, the spark from heaven, was spared
Such an outrage: the element has my congratulations, and you
      too,
I trust, are well-pleased. But those | who brought themselves
      to devour
This corpse, if the truth be known, never ate any meat
With greater relish. In judging | a crime of such magnitude,
Don't suppose that only the first man enjoyed the taste
Of his mouthful. After the body | was consumed, the last in
      line
Scraped the ground with their fingers to get a lick of the blood.
  Some Spaniards, history tells us,[12] once kept themselves alive
On such a diet: but here the circumstances were different –
An unkind Fortune had brought them war's harshest extremity,
The grinding famine engendered by a drawn-out siege. (This
      wretched
Instance I'm now discussing should prove no less instructive
Than my previous main example.) It was only after they'd
      eaten
All the grass, every living creature, and whatever else their
      ravening
Bellies dictated, when even | the besiegers felt compassion
For their pallor, their stick-like limbs, their emaciation, that
      hunger
Forced them to swallow the flesh of their fellows – by then,
      indeed,
They were ready to start on their own. What man, what deity
But would pardon these famished victims, after all the horrors
They'd suffered, for such an act? The very souls of the dead
Bodies that gave them sustenance might condone it. Zeno[13]
      offers

Us better advice – there is much | that's permissible, within
    limits,
For the saving of human life. But where would Iberian
    tribesmen
Have learnt any Stoic precepts – and so long ago, besides,
At the time of the Spanish Rebellion?[14] But today the whole
    world
Has its Graeco-Roman culture. Smart Gaulish professors
Are training the lawyers of Britain: even in Iceland
There's talk of setting up a Rhetorical Faculty. Yet
Our tribesmen were men of breeding; and those other
    Spaniards, who
Suffered still worse disaster (but matched them nevertheless
In honour and courage), can offer | the same excuse.[15] But
    Egypt's
Cruelty far exceeds the bloody shambles at Artemis'
Altars in the Crimea: the foundress of that accursed
Cult (if we can believe poetic tradition) ordained
The sacrificial slaughter of strangers – but nothing further:
A victim had no worse outrage to fear when the sacrificial
Knife had performed its work.[16] But what calamity
Drove *these* men to such horrors? Where was the famine, the
    siege
Severe enough to excuse so foul an abomination?
What more could they envisage to shame their lax gods, had
    drought
Parched up the land of Memphis, had Nile refused to flood?
Not even the fearsome tribesmen of Britain or Germany,
Or the fighting Poles, or the hulking Rumanians
Ever went so berserk as this useless, unwarlike rabble,
Who rig scraps of sail on their earthenware feluccas
And row with diminutive oars in painted crockery skiffs.[17]
    You could never devise a fitting punishment for this crime, or
A penalty stiff enough for a people in whose minds
Hunger and rage are alike, on a moral par. When Nature

Gave tears to mankind, she proclaimed that tenderness was
    endemic
In the human heart: of all our impulses, this
Is the highest and best. So we're moved to pity the plight
Of a friend in the dock – or a ward who's brought his guardian
To court for embezzlement, and whose adolescent kiss-curls
Make you wonder whether those tearstained | cheeks are a
    boy's or a girl's.
It's at Nature's behest that we weep when the funeral cortege
Of a ripening virgin goes by, or the earth is heaped over
An infant too young for burning.[18] What good man, worthy
    to bear
The mystic's torch, and such as the Corn Mother's priest
    would wish him,[19]
Thinks any human ills outside his concern? It's this
That sets us apart from dumb brutes, it's why we alone
Have a soul that's worthy of reverence, why we're imbued
With a divine potential, the skill to acquire and practise
All manner of arts: we possess that heaven-sent faculty
Denied to the creeping beasts with their eyes on the ground.
    To them,
When the world was still new, our common Creator granted
The breath of life alone, but on us he further bestowed
Sovereign reason, the impulse to aid one another,
To gather our scattered groups into peoples, to abandon
The woods and forests where once | our ancestors made their
    homes;
To build houses in groups, to sleep sounder because of our
    neighbours'
Presence around us, to learn collective security;
To protect, by dint of arms, any comrade down or half-
    stunned
From wounds in the battle-line; to obey one common trumpet,
Seek refuge behind the same walls, share one gateway, a single
    key.

But today even snakes agree better than men. Wild beasts
Spare their own species: when did the stronger lion
Ever strike down the weaker? And was there ever a forest
In which some boar was slain by a bigger boar's tushes?
The savage Indian tigress dwells in unbroken peace
With her fellow-tigresses: surely | bears, too, agree with their
        kind.²⁰
But man is a different matter. To have mastered the art
Of forging deadly steel on an impious anvil leaves him
Unsatisfied still. Our primitive smiths were accustomed
To turn out nothing but rakes, hoes, ploughshares and pruning-
        hooks;
On these they expended their labours, to beat out a sword
Was beyond them. Yet now we behold a people whose fury
Needs more than a death to appease it, who thinks a man's
        torso,
His limbs, his face, are for eating. What would Pythagoras
Say to such horrors? Surely | he'd run to the ends of the earth
To escape them, this man who abstained from all animal flesh
        as though
It was human, who even regarded some kinds of bean as
        taboo?²¹

Notes to Satire XV

1. Once more we have an unknown dedicatee. Bithynicus was a cognomen of the Pompeii; a Volusius Maecianus, a distinguished jurist, was in the Privy Council of Antoninus Pius (reigned A.D. 138–161).

2. Egyptian gods were supposed to manifest themselves on earth in 'theophanies' associated with specific animals. The crocodile-god Sebek (whom the Greeks called Souchos) was worshipped in the Fayyum; Herodotus (2.69, p. 129) confirms that 'some Egyptians reverence the crocodile as a sacred beast; others do not, but treat it as an enemy.' The ibis was associated with Thoth, the scribe-god of Khmunu (Hermopolis); Herodotus (2.76, p. 130) says the ibis was worshipped because it killed flying serpents. Another of Thoth's theophanies was the cynocephalous ape, and the mummified remains of these creatures have frequently been discovered. Ubastet or Bast was the great cat-headed goddess of Bubastis (cf. Herodotus 2.66–7, p.128). Several river-fish were regarded as sacred, in particular the *anet*, which announced the rise of the Nile, and the eel (Herodotus 2.72). Herodotus (2.66–7) claims that the dog was sacred, but the theophany here described is probably that of Anubis, the jackal-headed cemetery-god whose cult was mainly observed at Abydos. The contrast with Diana, in this context, is that dogs were frequently sacrificed to her (see Duff p. 440). The half-destroyed statue of Memnon at Thebes used to produce noises, at sunrise, like some sort of stringed instrument: rapid rise in temperature, it is believed, set up vibrations in the loosened mass of stone. When Septimus Severus restored the statue in A.D. 202 the musical effects stopped. The ruins of hundred-gated Thebes were a great draw for Roman tourists.

3. 'In Egypt,' the Elder Pliny tells us (*Natural History* 19.32.101), 'people swear by garlic and onions as deities in taking an oath.' Herodotus observed (2.42, pp. 118–19) that those in the province of Thebes never sacrificed sheep, but only goats; in the Mendesian province exactly the reverse was true. He also explicitly denied that the Egyptians practised human sacrifice (2.46, pp. 120–21).

4. Odysseus recounts his adventures, at length, to Alcinous and the other Phaeacians in Bks IX–XII of the *Odyssey*. In the first lines of Bk XIII we read that when he had finished, 'dead silence fell on all, and they were spell-bound throughout the shadowy halls.' The next morning Odysseus was given gifts of departure and sent on his way.

5. For the Cyclops see *Odyssey* 9.216 ff.; Laestrygonians, 10.80 ff.; Scylla and Charybdis, 12.234 ff. J. identifies the 'Clashing Rocks' of the Argonauts' voyage with Odysseus's 'Wandering Rocks' (*Odyssey* 12.59–72). Aeolus and the bag of the winds: *Odyssey* 10.1 ff.; Circe, Elpenor, and the metamorphosis into swine, 10.210 ff.

6. Here we have one of the few datable references in J.'s work. The riot took place during the consulship of Aemilius Juncus: that is, in A.D. 127. This is described as *nuper* 'recently' – though, as Duff points out (p. 442), 'recently' could stretch to a period of over thirty years. At all events, the date of the satire's composition is likely to have been about 130.

7. Pyrrha, Deucalion's consort, is chosen here for chronological reasons, as a characteristic example of a creation myth.

8. For many years it was thought that J. had got his geography wrong, and was writing on hearsay, since though the position of Tentyra (Dendereh) was not in question, Ombi had been identified with Kom-Ombo, 200 miles away on the other bank of the Nile. But in 1895 Flinders Petrie found the real Ombi not ten miles from Tentyra: see Highet, 28–9, with refs. Ombi worshipped Set, the pig-headed god of darkness, the evil killer of Osiris; Tentyra worshipped Hathor, the cow-headed goddess of love, and the Tentyrites also abominated the crocodile (Strabo 17.1.44; Seneca *Naturales Quaestiones* 4.2.15) which was worshipped at Ombi. Excavators discovered the remains of a wall between the two towns.

9. Lindsay, *Daily Life in Roman Egypt* (London 1963), devotes a whole chapter (pp. 109–21) to this incident, and the interested reader should consult it in detail. In particular he cites an apt parallel, shortly after the events here described, from Plutarch, *Isis and Osiris* 72 (380 B–C): 'Within our memory, the Oxyrhynchites, on account of the people of Cynopolis presuming to eat their revered fish, in revenge seized on all the dogs, the sacred beasts of their foes, which came their way, offering them in sacrifice and eating their flesh just as they did the flesh of other victims. This brought about a

civil war between the two cities . . .' Lindsay also cites a curious passage from Philo, *On the Contemplation of Life*, 5, in which it is asserted that the Egyptians, when drunk at a feast, 'bellow and roar like wild dogs, attack and bite each other and gnaw off noses, ears, fingers, and other parts of the body.' J. Moreau (see Bibliography) suggests that we have to do here with a magic rite designed to protect the living from the dead.

10. This is almost the only autobiographical reference in the *Satires*; it proves no more than that J. visited Egypt, but it does make the tradition of his exile there more probable.

11. For these heavings of heroic boulders see Homer, *Iliad* 5.302, 12.380; Virgil, *Aeneid* 12.896.

12. The Spanish tribe in question was that of the Vascones: after the death in 72 B.C. of the rebel Roman general Sertorius, their capital, Calagurris, was besieged by the Romans under Afranius, and the sufferings they endured became proverbial: see e.g. Quintilian, *Declamationes* 12, and other refs. cited in a valuable note by Friedländer (pp. 584–5).

13. For Zeno see no. 12 to Satire XIII (p. 261).

14. This was the war in which the Spaniards, led by the Roman general Sertorius, fought against the legions of Q. Caecilius Metellus Pius (79–72 B.C.).

15. The reference here is to Hannibal's siege and capture of Saguntum, in Hispania Tarraconensis, 219/8 B.C.: Livy 21.14–15. Though the city suffered much on this occasion (all adult males were executed), the story of cannibalism seems to be a late addition. Cf. Petronius, *Satyricon* 141 (p. 163 with note), where it is referred to, together with the sieges of Petelia and Numantia.

16. The Tauri in the Crimea worshipped Artemis (or a goddess called Opis or Upis whom the Greeks identified as Artemis) with human sacrifices of any strangers who fell into their hands: see esp. Euripides, *Iphigenia in Tauris*, passim, e.g. line 384, where the goddess is said to 'delight in human sacrifice'. J.'s point is that though they *killed* strangers, they at least refrained from *eating* them.

17. Most large Egyptian cargo vessels were made of acacia-wood, the *mimosa Nilotica* still used for this purpose; smaller rafts or punts were of papyrus reed, lashed together with rope. There is a good description of their construction in Herodotus 2.96 (p. 137). The

painted earthenware wherries described by J. seem to have been tiny craft used on the network of streams and canals intersecting the Delta: Strabo, the geographer, who also visited Egypt, mentions them in this connexion (17.1.4, C788). It is possible that the clay was laid on a wicker base, and that the boat is identical with the *pacton*, a kind of coracle, to which he later refers: cf. 17.1.50, C818, and for their painted decorations, Virgil, *Georgics* 4.287–9.

18. 'It is the universal custom of mankind,' Pliny tells us in the *Natural History*, 'not to cremate a person who dies before cutting his teeth' (7.16.72). As Duff reminds us (p. 450) this custom still prevails among the Hindus; and cremation was not universal, even for adults.

19. i.e. worthy and pure enough to qualify as an initiate in the Mysteries of Demeter held at Eleusis, near Athens. The priest, or Hierophant, would pronounce what was known as the *prorrhesis*, a warning to the wicked and profane that they should withdraw before the ceremony began, and not participate in it: see Aristophanes, *Frogs* 354–71.

20. Duff remarks on this passage, with demure accuracy: 'Moralists in all ages have pointed to the behaviour of animals to their own kind as an example to man; but the facts are not quite as the moralists have stated them' (p. 452). As should by now be apparent, a collector of natural history fallacies would do quite well out of J.

21. There are various explanations given as to why the Pythagoreans abstained from beans. The pleasantest is because they caused flatulence: the most ingenious that given by R. B. Onians, *The Origins of European Thought* (2nd ed. Cambridge 1954) p. 112. Onians reminds us of the Orphic and Pythagorean saying that 'to eat beans is equal to eating the heads of one's parents'. They were symbolic of fertility, generation, and intercourse, 'so that there is point and special emphasis in making them taboo as the heads of one's parents. The aim of these food prohibitions . . . seems to have been to prevent the eating of the *psyché* in its various abodes.' But like so many ritual prohibitions (e.g. the Jewish taboo on the eating of pork) this one may well have a solidly based original reason, medical rather than symbolic. The most convincing explanation is surely that offered by Richard and Eva Blum, *Health and Healing in*

Rural Greece (1965) p. 78: 'The disease "favism" is associated with a genetic defect in which the enzyme glucose-6 phosphate dehydrogenase is lacking. Some people from the Mediterranean basin lack this enzyme, and when they eat the fava bean (horse bean) a hemolytic crisis occurs. We may presume that this reaction had been observed in ancient times and is reflected in the Pythagorean writings.'

ADDITIONAL NOTE

At lines 85–6 I now read, with Griffith (Classical Quarterly NS19 (1969), 387), *Prometheu,/donasti,* and have modified my translation accordingly.

Gallius,[1] who can count up the rewards of a successful
Army career? If you do well during your service
[The sky's the limit, there's nothing you can't hope for.[2]]
Find me a lucky star to watch over my enlistment
And I'd join up myself, walk in through those barrack-gates as
A trembling recruit. One moment | of Fortune's favour does us
More good with the God of Battle than a letter on our behalf
From Venus, or Juno her mother, who's so fond of the Samian
    shore.[3]

  Let us consider first, then, the benefits common to all
Military men. Not least is the fact that no civilian
Would dare to give you a thrashing – and if beaten up himself
He'll keep quiet about it, he'd never | dare show any magistrate
His knocked-out teeth, the blackened lumps and bruises
All over his face, that surviving eye which the doctor
Offers no hope for. And if he seeks legal redress,
The case will come up before some hobnailed centurion
And a benchful of brawny jurors, according to ancient
Military law: no soldier, it's stated, may sue or be tried
Except in camp, by court-martial.[4] 'But still, a centurion's
Tribunal sticks to the rule-book. It's a soldier up on a charge,
There'll be justice done.[5] So if my complaint is legitimate
I'm sure to get satisfaction.' But the whole regiment
Is against you, every company unites, as one man, to ensure
That the 'redress' you get shall be something requiring a
    doctor,
And worse than the first assault. So since you've a pair of
    shins, it's
Stupidity past belief to provoke all those jackboots, and all
Those thousands of hobnails. Besides, what witness would
    venture

So far from the City, beyond the walls and the Embankment?
Have you anyone *that* devoted? Best dry your eyes at once,
    and
Stop importuning friends who will only make excuses.
When the judge says 'Call your witness', which of the
    onlookers
During that brawl will dare to stand up in court and say
'I saw it'? Find me one such, and I'll give him a place of
    honour
With our bearded and shaggy forebears. Easier find a witness
To perjure himself against a civilian than one who'll tell
The truth, if the truth's against a soldier's honour or interest.
    Now let us note some further emoluments and rewards
Of a life with the colours. Suppose some chiselling neighbour
Has encroached on a valley or meadow that's part and parcel
    of my
Ancestral estates, and uprooted the mid-point boundary-stone
To which I annually offer my cake and dish of pottage[6];
Or if a debtor refuses to pay back the sum I lent him
(Claiming his signature's forged, the document worthless), my
    case
Will have to wait, it'll be set down for the most
Crowded and popular session. And even then I'll suffer
A thousand irksome postponements: quite often the courtroom
Has just been got ready, one lawyer's taking his cloak off,
Another's gone out for a piss, when – presto! – there's an
    adjournment
And we all disperse. These bouts in the legal arena
Take endless time. But the armed and belted gentry
Have their cases set down for whatever date may suit them;
Their substance isn't diminished by the drag of a lengthy law-
    suit.
Soldiers alone, moreover, are entitled to make a will
During their father's lifetime. The law decrees that all monies
Earned by military service shall be exempt

From the bulk of property held in parental jurisdiction.⁷
That's why some regular sergeant on active service pay
Will find himself courted and honoured by his doddering papa;
He wins promotion on merit, distinguished service brings him
His just reward. And indeed, it's in any commander's interest
To see the bravest soldiers obtain the best recompense,
That they all have decorations | and medals to show off, that
    all . . .⁸

Notes to Satire XVI

1. Gallius, J.'s last known dedicatee, is as anonymous as his predecessors. Inevitably the suggestion has been made that these were fictitious pegs on which J. hung his homilies; and the practice of using such names is in fact well established by Martial (see esp. 1 *praef.*, 2.23 and 10.33). The Younger Pliny mentions the blending of real and assumed names in satire (*Letters* 6.21.5). But that J. did the same is no more than a possibility: we must not assume that Gallius, Volusius, Postumus and the rest did not exist simply because, in the deficient state of the record, we cannot identify them.

2. Jahn, followed by Knoche and Clausen, assumed – rightly, I believe – that something had dropped out of the text after line 2. I have accordingly supplied the line in square brackets as a possible approximation to the sense of what is missing.

3. Virgil (*Aeneid* 1.16) tells us that Samos stood at least second in the affections of Juno (Hera); this was almost entirely due to her great temple there, which stood at the mouth of the Imbrasos River, some four miles south-west of the modern port of Tigani. It was the fourth Heraeum built on the site (its predecessor was burnt *c.* 530 B.C.) and the largest Greek temple known to us, measuring 179 by 365 feet; it was never completed. By J.'s day it had degenerated into a kind of art-gallery and museum (Strabo, 14.1.14, c637). Lucretius (*De Natura Rerum* 1.30–40, p. 28) emphasizes Venus's ability to soothe angry Mars, in language which suggests he may have had some conventional statue-group in mind: J., as so often, debunks the concept by treating it in all too mundane terms, as an ordinary letter of commendation to Mars *qua* Generalissimo and Commander-in-Chief.

4. Highet points out (p. 287) that 'the poem seems to reflect Hadrian's own new measures to keep the army contented': the cases J. mentions are directly occasioned by his legislation. It was Hadrian who laid down (*Digest* 22.5.3.6) that soldiers could not leave their units to engage in legal activity in the civilian courts; he was also responsible for the law enabling soldiers to dispose of their property during their father's lifetime.

5. At line 18 I accept Buecheler's emendation of *exigitur* for *est igitur*.

6. Boundary-stones were worshipped as images of the god Terminus: for the ritual associated with this somewhat indeterminate deity see Ovid, *Fasti* 2.641–4. The occasion here described will have been the feast of the Terminalia, which took place on 23 February, Cf. Plutarch, *Roman Questions* 15.

7. For this privilege, and the exceptions to it, see *Digest* 49.17 and *Instit.* 2.12 pr., cited at length by Friedländer, pp. 599–600.

8. The satire breaks off abruptly at this point. No known MS contains any more of it, and the ancient commentators possessed a similarly deficient version. There are, therefore, three possible explanations: (1) the poem was censored, perhaps by Hadrian; (2) J. died before he could complete it, and the surviving fragment was published as it stood; or (3) at some early point in the tradition the end of what turned out to be the one surviving MS was mutilated or lost. The best discussion (Highet, pp. 156–9) rejects (2), the most popular theory, and is very cautious about (1). Highet makes out an excellent case for (3), pointing out that where fragments survived an author's death in antiquity his editors always tried to polish them up into some sort of completion before publishing, and that the loss of either one or two parchment quires would (at an average of 30 lines a page) produce a poem of just the right length, either 300 or 540 lines.

ADDITIONAL NOTE

At line 18 I now, with Kilpatrick (Additional Bibliography), read *agitur* for *igitur* of the MSS, and punctuate with a semi-colon after *cognito*. The translation has been corrected accordingly.

SELECT BIBLIOGRAPHY

Anderson, W. S., 'Juvenal and Quintilian', *Yale Classical Studies* 17 (1961), 3–93.

'Imagery in the Satires of Horace and Juvenal', *American Journal of Philology* 81 (1960), 225–60.

'Venusina Lucerna. The Horatian Model for Juvenal', *Transactions of the American Philological Association* 92 (1961), 1–12.

'The Programs of Juvenal's Later Books', *Classical Philology* 57 (1962), 145–60.

'Juvenal VI. A Problem in Structure', *Classical Philology* 51 (1956), 84–6.

'Studies in Book I of Juvenal', *Yale Classical Studies* 15 (1957) 31–90.

'Juvenal. Evidence on the Years A.D. 117–128', *Classical Philology* 50 (1955), 255–7.

Arnold, E. V., *Roman Stoicism*, London 1911 (reissued 1958).

Bower, E. W., 'Notes on Juvenal and Statius', *Classical Review* 8 (1958), 9–11.

Bradshaw, A. T. von S., '*Glacie Aspersus Maculis:* Juvenal 5.104', *Classical Quarterly* NS15 (1965), 121–5.

Carcopino, J., *Daily Life in Ancient Rome*, ed. H. T. Rowell, tr. E. O. Lorimer, revised Pelican edition 1956.

Clarke, M. L., *The Roman Mind: Studies in the History of Thought from Cicero to Marcus Aurelius*, London 1956.

Clausen, W. V., ed., *A. Persi Flacci et D. Iuni Iuvenalis Saturae*, Oxford 1959.

Coffey, M., 'Juvenal. Report for the Years 1941–1961', *Lustrum* 8 (1963/4), 161–215, 268–70.

Colin, J., 'Juvénal, les baladins et les rétiaires d'après le MS d'Oxford', *Atti dell'Accademia Scientifica di Torino* (class. Sci. mor., stor. e filol.) 87 (1952/3), 315–86.

'Juvénal et le mariage mystique de Gracchus', ibid. 90 (1955/6), 114–216.

'Galerus: pièce d'armament du gladiateur ou coiffure de prêtre salien?', *Les études classiques* 23 (1955), 409–15.

Colton, R. E., 'Cabinet Meeting: Juvenal's Fourth Satire', *Classical Bulletin* 40 (1963), 1–2.

'Juvenal and Martial on Literary and Professional Men', *Classical Bulletin* 39 (1963), 49–52.

'Juvenal 14 and Martial 9.46 on the Building Craze', *Classical Bulletin* 41 (1964/5), 26–7.

'Dinner Invitation: Juvenal 11.56–208', *Classical Bulletin* 41 (1964/5), 39–45.

'Juvenal's Second Satire and Martial', *Classical Journal* 61 (1965), 68–71.

'Juvenal on Recitations', *Classical Bulletin* 42 (1966), 81–5.

Courtney, E., 'Juvenaliana', *University of London Bulletin of Classical Studies* 13 (1966), 38–43.

Crook, J., *Consilium Principis. Imperial Councils and Counsellors from Augustus to Diocletian*, Cambridge 1955.

Dill, S., *Roman Society from Nero to Marcus Aurelius*, London 1905.

Duff., J. D., *Fourteen Satires of Juvenal*, rev. edition Cambridge 1940.

Duff, J. W., *A Literary History of Rome in the Silver Age from Tiberius to Hadrian*, 2nd edition, ed. A. M. Duff, London 1960.

Roman Satire (Sather Classical Lectures vol. XII), Berkeley, California, 1936.

Eichholz, D. E., 'The Art of Juvenal and His Tenth Satire', *Greece and Rome* (2nd series) 3 (1956), 61–9.

Fletcher, G. B., 'Alliteration in Juvenal', *Durham University Journal* 5 (1944), 59–64.

Friedländer, L., *D. Junii Juvenalis Sat. Lib. V mit Erklärenden Anmerkungen*, 2 vols. Leipzig 1895, reprinted 1 vol. Amsterdam 1962.

Roman Life and Manners under the Early Empire, tr. J. H. Freese, L. A. Magnus, S. B. Gough, 4 vols. London 1908–13.

Giangrande, G., 'Textkritische Beiträge zu Lateinischen Dichtern', *Hermes* 95 (1967), 110–21.

Grant, M., tr., *Tacitus: On Imperial Rome*, Penguin Classics 1956.

Graves, R., tr., *Suetonius: The Twelve Caesars*, Penguin Classics 1957.

Lucan: Pharsalia, Penguin Classics 1956.

Griffith, J. G., 'The Oxford Fragments in Juvenal's Sixth Satire', *Hermes* 91 (1963), 104–14.

'Juvenal and the Stage-Struck Patricians', *Mnemosyne* 4/15 (1962), 256–61.

Haley, L., 'The "Thou-Shalt-Nots" in Juvenal', *Classical Journal* 21 (1925/6), 268–80.

Helmbold, W. C., [see also under O'Neil, E. N.] 'The Structure of Juvenal I', *University of California Publications in Classical Philology* 14/2 (1951), 47–60.

'Juvenal's Twelfth Satire', *Classical Philology* 51 (1956), 14–23.

Highet, G., *Juvenal the Satirist*, Oxford 1954.

Housman, A. E., *D. Junii Iuvenalis Saturae*, corrected edition Cambridge 1938.

Jefferis, J. D., 'Juvenal and Religion', *Classical Journal* 34 (1939), 229–33.

Kenney, E. J., 'The First Satire of Juvenal', *Proceedings of the Cambridge Philological Society* 8 (1962), 29–40.

'Juvenal, Satirist or Rhetorician?', *Latomus* 22 (1963), 704–20.

Knoche, U., *D. Iunius Iuvenalis: Saturae mit kritischem Apparat*, Munich 1950.

Labriolle, P. de, *Les satires de Juvénal: étude et analyse*, Paris 1932.

and Villeneuve, F., *Juvénal: Satires*, Budé edition, Paris 1932.

Lawall, G., 'Exempla and Theme in Juvenal's Tenth Satire', *Transactions of the American Philological Association* 89 (1958), 25–31.

Lelièvre, F. J., 'Parody in Juvenal and T. S. Eliot', *Classical Philology* 53 (1958), 22–5.

'Juvenal: Two Possible Examples of Word-Play', *Classical Philology* 53 (1958), 241–2.

Lindsay, J., *Daily Life in Roman Egypt*, London 1963.

Lutz, C. E., 'Any Resemblance . . . is Purely Coincidental', *Classical Journal* 46 (1950), 115–20, 126.

Marache, R., 'La poésie romaine et le problème social à la fin du Ier siècle. Martial et Juvénal', *L'information littéraire* 13 (1961), 12–19.

'La revendication sociale chez Martial et Juvénal', *Rivista di cultura classica e medievale* 3 (1961), 30–67.

Mason, H. A., 'Is Juvenal a Classic?', in *Critical Essays on Roman Literature (Satire)*, ed. J. P. Sullivan, London 1963, pp. 93–167.

Mattingly, H., *Roman Imperial Civilisation*, London 1957.

Mayor, J. E. B., *Thirteen Satires of Juvenal*, 2 vols., London 1886.

Moreau, J., 'Une scène d'ant hopophagie en Égypte en l'an 127 de notre ère', *Chroniques d'Égypte* 15 (1940), 279–85.

Michel, A., 'La date des satires . . .', *Revue des études latines*, 41 (1963), 315–27.

O'Neil, E. N., 'The Structure of Juvenal's Fourteenth Satire', *Classical Philology* 55 (1960), 251–3.

and Helmbold, W. C., 'The Form and Purpose of Juvenal's Seventh Satire', *Classical Philology* 54 (1959), 100–108.

and Helmbold, W. C., 'The Structure of Juvenal IV', *American Journal of Philology* 77 (1956), 68–73.

Paoli, U. E., *Rome: Its People, Life and Customs*, tr. R. D. Macnaughten, London 1963.

Pepe, L., 'Questioni adrianee. Giovenale e Adriano', *Giornale italiano di filologia* 14 (1961), 163–73.

Pryor, A. D., 'An Approach to the Later Satires of Juvenal', *Bulletin of the Institute of Classical Studies* 8 (1961), 85 (résumé).

'Juvenal's False Consolation', *Journal of the Australian Universities' Language and Literature Association* 18 (1962), 167–80.

Ramsay, G. G., *Juvenal and Persius*, revised Loeb edition 1957.

Robertson, D. S., 'Juvenal V 103–6', *Classical Review*, 1946, 19–20.

Rose, H. J., *A Handbook of Latin Literature*, 2nd revised edition London 1949.

Ruperti, G. A., *D. Junii Juvenalis Aquinatis Saturae XVI . . .*, Glasgow 1825.

Scivoletti, N., 'Plinio il Giovane e Giovenale', *Giornale italiano di filologia* 10 (1957), 133–46.

'Presenze di Persio in Giovenale', *Giornale italiano di filologia* 16 (1963), 60–72.

Scott, J. G., *The Grand Style in the Satires of Juvenal*, Northampton, Mass., 1927.

Serafini, A., *Studio sulla satira di Giovenale*, Florence 1957.

Smemo, E., 'Zur Technik der Personenzeichung bei Juvenal', *Symbolae Osloenses* 16 (1937), 77–102.

Sullivan, J., tr., *Petronius: The Satyricon and the Fragments*, Penguin Classics 1965.

Thomas, E., 'Some Aspects of Ovidian Influence on Juvenal', *Orpheus* (Catania) 7 (1960), 35–44 (résumé in *Proceedings of the*

Classical Association 50 (1953), 29).

'Ovidian Echoes in Juvenal', in *Ovidiana*, ed. N. Herescu, Paris 1958, pp. 505–25.

Thomson, J. O., 'Juvenal's Big Fish Satire', *Greece and Rome* 21 (1952), 86–7.

Vahlen, J., 'Juvenal und Paris', in *Gesammelte philologische Schriften* 2 (Leipzig 1923), pp. 181–201.

'Quaestiones Iuvenalianae', in *Opuscula Academica* 1 (Leipzig 1907), 223–53.

Vollmer, F., 'D. Iunius Iuvenalis' (Iunius no. 87), article in Pauly-Wissowa-Kroll's *Real-Encyclopædie der klassischen Altertumswissenschaft* vol. 10, cols 1041–50.

Wessner, P., *Scholia in Iuvenalem Vetustiora*, Leipzig 1931.

Wiesen, D., 'Juvenal's Moral Character, an Introduction', *Latomus* 22 (1963), 440–71.

Witke, E. C., 'Juvenal III, an Eclogue for the Urban Poor', *Hermes* 90 (1962), 244–6.

ADDITIONAL BIBLIOGRAPHY

Anderson, W. S., '*Lascivia vs. ira*: Martial and Juvenal', *California Studies in Classical Antiquity* 3 (1970), 1–34.

Baldwin, B., 'Cover-names and dead victims in Juvenal', *Athenaeum* 45 (1967), 304–12.

'Three characters in Juvenal', *Classical World* 66 (1972), 101–4.

Beaujeu, J., 'La réligion de Juvénal', *Mélanges d'archéologie, d'épigraphie et d'histoire offerts à J. Carcopino* (Paris 1966), 71–81.

Bellandi, F., 'Poetica dell' '*Indignatio*' e del '*Sublime*' satirico in Giovenale', *Annali della Scuola Normale Superiore di Pisa*, Classe di Lettere e Filosofia, ser. III, Vol. III 1 (1973), 53–94.

Bertman, S. S., 'Fire symbolism in Juvenal's first satire', *Classical Journal* 63 (1968), 265–6.

Bodoh, J. J., *An analysis of the ideas of Juvenal*, Diss. Univ. of Wisconsin, 1966 [available on microfilm].

'Artistic control in the satires of Juvenal', *Aevum* 44 (1970), 475–82.

Brown, P. G. McC., 'Two passages in Juvenal's eighth satire', *Classical Quarterly* NS22 (1972), 374–5.

Colton, R. E., 'Death in the bath', *Classical Journal* 65 (1970), 317.

'Echoes of Martial in Juvenal's Twelfth Satire', *Latomus* 31 (1972), 164–73.

'Juvenal's second satire and Martial', *Classical Journal* 61 (1965), 68–71.

'Some rare words used by Martial and Juvenal', *Classical Journal* 67 (1971), 55–7.

Dubrocard, M., 'Quelques remarques sur la distribution et la signification des hapax dans les Satires de Juvénal', *Annales de la Faculté des Lettres et Sciences humaines de Nice* 11 (1970), 131–40.

Durry, M., 'Cosmetae (Juvénal VI 477)', *Hommages à Marcel Renard* (Coll. Latomus 101–3), Brussels 1969, 329–34.

Edmunds, L., 'Juvenal's Thirteenth Satire', *Rheinisches Museum für Philologie* 115 (1972), 59–73.

Finch, C. E., 'Juvenal in Codex Vat. Lat. 5204', *Classical Philology* 65 (1970), 47–8.

Fredericks, S. C., 'The Function of the Prologue (1–20) in the organisation of Juvenal's Third Satire', *Phoenix* 27 (1973), 62–7.

Griffith, J. G., 'Frustula Iuvenaliana', *Classical Quarterly* NS19 (1969), 379–87.

'Juvenal, Statius, and the Flavian establishment', *Greece and Rome* 16 (1969), 134–50.

'The ending of Juvenal's first satire and Lucilius, Book XXX', *Hermes* 98 (1970), 56–72.

Kidd, D. A., 'Juvenal 10.175–6', *Classical Quarterly* NS19 (1969), 196–7.

Killeen, J. F., 'Juvenal VII, 126 ff.', *Glotta* 67 (1969), 265–6.

Kilpatrick, R. S., 'Two notes on the text of Juvenal: *Sat.* 12.32 and 16.18', *Classical Philology* 66 (1971), 114–15.

Lafleur, R. A., 'A note on Juvenal 10.201 ff.', *American Journal of Philology* 93 (1972), 598–600.

Martyn, J. R. C., 'A new approach to Juvenal's first satire', *Antichthon* 4 (1970), 53–61.

'Juvenal 2. 78–81 and Virgil's plague', *Classical Philology* 65 (1970), 49–50.

McDevitt, A. S., 'The structure of Juvenal's eleventh satire', *Greece and Rome* 15 (1968), 173–9.

McGann, M. J., 'Juvenal's ninth age (13.28ff.)', *Hermes* 96 (1968), 509–14.

Morford, M., 'A note on Juvenal 6.627–61', *Classical Philology* 67 (1972), 198.

Reeve, M. D., 'Seven notes', *Classical Review* 20 (1970), 134–6.

Reinmuth, O. W., 'The meaning of ceroma in Juvenal and Martial', *Phoenix* 21 (1967), 191–5.

Settis, S., 'Qui multas facies pingit cito (Iuven. 9.146)', *Atene e Roma* 15 (1970), 117–21.

Stein, J. P., 'The unity and scope of Juvenal's fourteenth Satire', *Classical Philology* 65 (1970), 34–6.

Townend, G. B., 'The earliest scholiast on Juvenal', *Classical Quarterly* NS22 (1972), 376–87.

Waters, K. H., 'Juvenal and the reign of Trajan', *Antichthon* 4 (1970), 62–77.

Watts, W. J., 'A literary reminiscence in Juvenal (IX, 96)', *Latomus* 31 (1972), 519–20.

INDEX

Abas: 83
Abortions: 25, 149
Abydos (Egypt): 288
Academy, the: 262
Acestes: 171, 175
Achillas: 224
Achilles: 67, 71, 97, 170, 174, 175,
    186, 213, 228, 271, 278
Acilius, Glabrio: 108, 113
Acragas (Agrigento): 188
Actaeon: 129
Actium: 83, 185, 192
Admetus: 161
Adriatic: 106
Adultery: 68, 76, 82, 88, 127, 140,
    142, 145–6, 155–6, 182, 198, 215,
    254, 264
Advocates, lawyers: 54, 66, 166–8,
    178, 228, 250, 270
Aeacus: 65
Aediles: 219, 220
Aelia: 129
Aemilian Bridge, the: 187
Aemilii Lepidi, the: 156, 177
Aemilius Juncus: 14, 289
Aemilius Paulus, L.: 239
Aeneid, the (also Aeneas, Turnus,
    etc.): 41, 71, 82, 83, 118, 125, 155,
    165, 172, 175, 229, 236, 237, 243,
    244, 247, 248, 283, 290
Aeolus: 65, 211, 289
Aeschylus: 222, 248
Afranius: 290
Africa, Africans: 54, 113, 120, 121,
    168, 181, 189, 210, 211, 223, 241,
    244
Agamemnon: 152, 248, 274
Aglauros: 82

Agricola, Gn. Jul.: 12, 17
Agrippa II: 133, 154
Agrippina Minor: 73, 150, 154, 160,
    219
Ajax: 167, 208, 271, 274, 278, 283
Alba Longa: 107, 112, 155, 243, 247
Alban Sow, the: 133, 155, 243, 247
Alcestis: 151, 161
Alcinous: 126, 281, 289
Alexander the Great: 159, 211, 221,
    247, 275
Alexander, Tib. Jul.: 26, 73
Alexandria(nism): 14, 72, 106, 130,
    175
Alexis: 202
Allia, R.: 192
Alps, the: 210–11, 221, 255
Ammianus Marcelli nus: 10
Ammon: 148, 159
Amphion: 133, 155
Amyx, D. A.: 277
Anatolia: 159
Anchemolus: 171, 175
Anchises: 82, 171
Ancona: 106
Ancus Martius: 119, 124–5
Anderson, W. S.: 43, 46, 47–8, 52–3
Andros: 89
Anio, R.: 223
Antaeus: 90, 113
Antigone: 185
Antilochus: 213, 222
Antioch: 12, 100, 158
Antiochus of Syria: 221
Antiope: 82
Antipater: 221
Antisthenes: 261
Antonia: 192

307

Antonii, the: 187

Antoninus Pius (Tit. Aurel. Fulv. Boionius Antoninus): 9, 15, 288

Antony (G. Antonius Hybrida): 181, 189

Antony (M. Antonius): 209, 220

Anubis: 147, 288

Anzio: 248

Apamea: 100

Aphrodite: *see under* Venus

Apicius, M. Gabius: 105, 111, 235

Apollo: 69, 133, 155, 163, 164, 165, 172, 201, 236, 251, 256

Appian Way, the: 53, 74, 99

Appius Claudius: 224

Apulia: 106, 239

Aquae Sextiae: 193

Aquinum: 10, 16, 21, 124, 201

Arabia: 231

Arachne: 77, 82

Arcadia: 236

Ardaschan (Artaxata): 81, 84

Ardea: 248

Argonauts, the: 154, 289

Ariccia: 109, 114

Aristocracy, the: 24, 26, 177 ff

Aristophanes: 82, 159, 291

Aristotle: 75, 261

Armenia: 12, 143, 148, 158

Arpinum: 185, 192

Artemis: 133, 155, 285, 290

Arts, liberal: 163 ff

Arviragus: 109, 115

Ascanius: 243, 247

Asculum: 174

Asia, Asiatics: 119, 163, 189, 231, 238

Assuan: 231

Assurbanipal: 217, 225

Assyria: 225

Astrologers, astrology: 148–9, 159, 160, 170, 272

Asylum, the: 193

Athena: 82, 246, 261, 277

Athenaeum, the: 172

Athens: 78, 83, 170, 174, 188, 209, 261, 291

Athos, Mt: 211, 221

Atlantic, the: 17

Atlas (Mt): 228, 250

Attica: 235

Atticus, Herodes: 235

Atticus, Tib. Claud.: 227, 235

Attis: 159

Auctioneers: 92, 163, 179

Augustus (G.Jul. Caesar Octavianus): 22, 37, 40, 82, 100, 111, 117, 153, 172, 185, 192, 206, 220

Aulis: 248

Aurelius, Marcus (M. Annius Verus): 9, 37, 261

Ausonius, Dec. Magnus: 10

Aventine Hill, the: 156

Azov, Sea of: 106

Babylon: 211, 221

Bacchanalia, Bacchants: 84, 172

Baetica: 246

Baiae: 99, 236

Bailey, D. R. S.: 261

Ballet, the Imperial: 18, 129, 153, 166

Barbers: 66, 93, 102, 127, 212, 222

Bassus, P. Ventidius: 170, 174

Baths, public: 80, 84, 141, 143, 144, 158, 163, 167, 171, 227, 234

Bathyllus: 129, 153

Beans, taboo on eating: 287, 291–2

Beirut (Berytus): 101

Belladonna: 71, 205

Bellerophon: 91, 101, 216

Belloc, H.: 49

Bellona: 83, 84, 146, 159

Beneventum: 118, 124

Bentley, R.: 189

Berenice: 132, 154
Bibula: 48, 132
Bilbilis: 11, 15
Bithynia(ns): 172, 221
Bithynicus: 288
Black Sea, the: 106
Blandus, C. Rubellius: 178
Blum, R. and E.: 291-2
Boeotia: 259
Bona Dea, the: 83, 138, 156-7, 202
Bradshaw, A. T. von S.: 125
Brandon, S. G. F.: 259
Britain, Britons: 11, 17-18, 81, 109, 114-15, 205, 285
Britannicus (Tib. Claud. Caesar): 73, 154, 192
Bronze Age: 259
Browne, T.: 174-5
Bruttidius Niger: 208, 220
Brutus, L. Junius: 108, 113, 186
Brutus, M.: 118, 124, 192
Bubastis: 288
Bulgaria(ns): 200

Cacus: 125
Cadiz (Gades): 205
Cadmus: 277
Caesar, C. Julius: 37, 100, 114, 139, 157, 189, 218, 220, 224
Caesarea: 154
Caesonia: 150, 160
Calagurris: 290
Calauria: 221
Caligula (G. Jul. Caesar Germanicus): 37, 66, 72, 160, 174, 191
Calverley, C. S.: 59
Calvinus: 249, 259
Campania: 99, 197, 214
Campus Martius, the: 84, 147, 154, 159
Cannae: 169, 234, 239
Capito, Cossutianus: 189

Capito, Fonteius: 14, 249, 259
Capitol, the: 155, 157, 190, 206, 219, 266
Capitoline Games, the: 12, 142, 157
Cappadocia(ns): 159, 172
Capri: 207, 208, 219
Caria: 89
Carrinas, Secundus: 174
Carthage, Carthaginians: 133, 210, 214, 221, 223, 237, 267, 277 (see also under Hannibal)
Carus: 62
Cassandra: 214
Cassius Longinus, G.: 118, 124, 218
Castor: 273, 278
Catiline (L. Sergius Catilina): 62, 185, 192, 214
Cato (M.Porc. Cato Censorinus): 41, 230, 237, 276
Catullus, G. Valerius: 153
Catullus, L. Valerius C. Messalinus: 109, 114
Catullus (farce-writer): 183, 191, 253, 261
Catullus (?): 242, 246, 247
Catulus, Q. Lutatius: 193
Celer, Publ. Egnatius: 101
Celsus, Aul. Cornelius: 222
Censennia: 132
Censorship, Censors: 58, 203, 230, 237
Centaurs: 65, 242, 260
Centurions: 185, 272, 277, 293
Ceres: 16, 18, 21, 128, 153, 195, 201, 286, 291
Cethegus, G. Cornelius: 62, 185, 192
Charybdis: 281, 289
Chastity: 127, 138, 216
Chesterton, G. K.: 49
Children: 264 ff, 269, 271
China: 142
Chios: 224

Chiron: 94, 174
Christians: 192
Chrysippus: 255, 262
Cicero, M. Tullius: 41, 53, 153, 168, 170, 185, 192, 203, 209, 220, 276
Cilicia(ns): 180, 189
Cimbri: 223
Cinna, L. Cornelius: 223
Circe: 281, 289
Circeii: 110
Circumcision: 14
Circus Maximus, the Games: 100, 149, 187, 200, 206, 219, 228, 233-4, 239, 278
City Prefect, the: 107, 112, 254
Class-structure, Roman: 23, 25-6, 30, 34-5, 232-3
Claudii, the: 187
Claudius (Tib. Claud. Nero Germanicus): 36, 73, 103, 122, 131, 154, 157, 159, 160, 173, 188, 247, 262, 266, 275, 276, 279
Claudius (G. Claud. Nero): 237
Clausen, W. V.: 56, 125, 187, 189, 201, 202, 219, 238, 296
Cleanthes: 262
Cleopatra: 83, 192
Clients, patronage: 16, 20, 23, 28-9, 30-31, 68-70, 73, 91, 96, 117-23, 163 ff, 206, 219
Clodia: 153
Clodius, Publius: 62, 83, 139, 153, 157
Cloelia: 186, 193
Clytemnestra: 151, 153, 161, 278
Coffey, M.: 7, 18, 191
Colchis: 267
Colin, J.: 191
Colline Gate, the: 126
Columella, L. Jun. Moderatus: 276
Comedies, mimes: 90, 100
Commodus, L. Ael. Aurelius: 9, 37

Consilium Principis, the: 107 ff, 112
Consuls, consular office: 69, 156, 170, 174, 182, 185, 186, 193, 206, 209, 219, 229, 234, 237
Coptos: 282
Corbulo, Gn. Domitius: 84
Cordoba: 172
Cordus: 65, 72, 94
Corfu (Corcyra): 281
Corinth(ians): 181
Cornelia (Vestal): 111
Cornelia (mother of Gracchi, q.v.): 49, 133, 155
Cornelii, the: 187, 192
Corsica: 120
Corvini, the: 177, 187, 241, 244, 246 (see also under Valerii)
Corydon: 198, 202
Cos: 180
Cossus, Gn. Corn. Lentulus: 93, 102, 177, 187, 188
Cotta: 125
Cotys, Cotytto: 83
Courtney, E.: 132, 154, 224, 262
Courts, lawsuits: 66, 69, 77, 136, 166-8, 208, 249, 254, 293-4
Crannon: 221
Crassus, M. Licinius: 208, 220
Creon: 278
Crete: 221, 273
Crimea: 223, 285, 290
Crispinus: 26, 47, 66, 72, 105, 106, 108, 111
Crispus, Q. Vibius: 107, 108, 113
Croesus: 214, 223, 275
Croton: 31, 218
Crucified Bandit, the: 183, 191
Crucifixion: 135, 191
Cumae: 33, 87, 99
Curii, the: 177
Curius (M. Curius Dentatus): 229, 237

Cybele: 83, 146, 159, 195, 201, 202, 239

Cyclopes: 260, 281, 289

Cydnus, R.: 101

Cynics, Cynicism: 42, 253, 261, 275

Cynopolis: 289

Cynossema: 223

Cynthia: 127, 153

Cyrene: 159

Cyrus: 223

Dacia: *see under* Rumania

Daedalus: 67, 87, 99, 100

Dalmatia: 16, 17, 21

Damasippus: 183, 191

Danaids, the: 151, 161

Danube, R.: 77, 183

Day Lewis, C.: 60

Decii, the: 186, 193, 272, 278

Delphi: 148, 159, 236, 251, 256

Demeter: *see under* Ceres

Demosthenes: 209, 221

De Quincey, T.: 25, 84

Destiny: *see under* Fortune

Deucalion: 68, 289

Devotio: 193, 278

Diana: 214, 251, 281, 288

Dickens, C.: 27 ff, 34, 51

Dictatorship, the: 230

Dido: 144

Dingwall, E. J.: 8

Dio Cassius: 19, 73, 101, 174

Diogenes: 261, 275, 279

Diomede: 67, 283

Dionysus: 165

Dirce: 83

Dodona: 159

Dolabella, Cn. Cornelius: 181, 189

Dolabella, P. Cornelius: 189

Domitia Lepida: 192

Domitia Longina: 114, 173

Domitian (Titus Flavius Domitianus): 10, 12, 15, 18–19, 20, 21, 32, 34, 36, 42, 44, 47, 51, 74, 82, 102, 106 ff, 111–12, 113, 115, 153, 157, 173, 174, 190

Domitilla: 115

Dostoevsky, F.: 20

Drusus, Julius Caesar: 188, 219

Drusus, Livius: 124, 237

Drusus (?): 177, 178, 188

Duff, J. D.: 53, 56, 156, 158, 173–4, 188, 189, 191, 237, 247, 259, 276, 277, 288, 289, 291

Eclipses, lunar: 144, 158

Egeria: 87, 99

Egypt, Egyptians: 10, 11, 18–19, 20, 22, 26, 33, 41, 66, 70, 72, 73, 105, 130, 147, 149, 159, 178, 220, 223, 255, 281–92

Electra: 184, 274

Eliot, T. S.: 51, 99

Elpenor: 281, 289

Embankment, the: 122, 126, 149, 178, 188, 294

Eos: 82

Epictetus: 42

Epicurus, Epicureanism: 42, 253, 261, 275, 279

Epicydes: 262

Epiphania: 100

Epona: 182, 190

Eppia: 28, 114, 130–31

Equites, Equestrian Order: 17, 26, 69, 73, 101, 102, 112, 126, 173, 219, 275, 277, 279

Eriphyle: 151, 161

Esquiline Hill, the: 119, 125, 126, 228

Ethiopia: 210, 221, 261

Etruria, Etruscans: 102, 160, 193, 206

Eumolpus: 235, 248

Eunuchs, castration: 65, 75, 79, 141, 147, 183, 202, 242, 266, 276
Euphrates: 69, 188
Euripides: 72, 160, 161, 248, 290
Evander: 187, 229, 236
Extortion: 66

Fabii, the: 156, 177, 230, 237
Fabius (Q. Fab. Max. Allobrogicus): 187
Fabius (Q. Fab. Max. Gurges): 136, 156
Fabricius (G. Fab. Luscinus): 203, 230
Faunus: 156, 190
Fayyum, the: 288
Flaminian Way, the: 67, 71, 74
Floral Festival, the (Floralia): 136, 156
Forgery: 67, 182, 254, 294
Fortune, Fate(s): 16, 38, 39, 170, 174, 196, 200, 206, 213, 217, 219, 241, 243, 252, 272, 275, 284, 293
Fortune-tellers: 126, 147–8, 160
Fraud: 66
Freedmen: 25, 68–9, 115, 118, 164
Friedländer, L.: 187, 202, 203, 237, 238–9, 290, 297
Furies, the: 250, 274, 278
Furii, the: 157
Fuscinus: 263
Fuscus, Cornelius: 108, 114, 247

Gabii: 93, 102
Gaetulians, the: 187
Galba, Servius Sulpicius: 15, 73, 114, 159, 177, 187
Galen: 125
Gallius: 293, 296
Gambling: 68, 177, 263
Ganges, R.: 205
Ganymede: 119, 195, 196, 201, 250
Gaul(s): 168, 172, 181, 185, 192, 196, 231, 238, 285

Gazette, the (Acta Diurna): 198, 202
Ge: 260
Germanicus, Nero Claudius: 188
Germany: 155, 178, 193, 214, 223, 255, 285
Ghost, The: 183, 191
Giangrande, G.: 102, 125, 300
Gibbon, E.: 22, 63
Gibraltar: 273
Gigolos: 66, 215
Gladiatorial arena, gladiators: 24, 26, 28, 70, 80, 84, 88, 130, 139–40, 155, 157, 184, 192, 227, 235
Glaucus: 262
Gluttony, gourmandise: 70, 106–10, 111, 119 ff, 180, 227–9, 263
Gods, the: 205, 211, 216–17, 241, 244, 250, 252, 257–8, 270, 281
Gods, Egyptian: 281–2, 288–9
Golden Age, the: 35, 37, 39, 41, 48, 50, 127, 250, 259
Gorgon, the: 91, 101, 241
Governors, provincial: 66, 88, 180–82, 189
Gracchi, the: 49, 62, 155, 184, 191
Graves, R.: 173
Greece, Greeks: 20, 21, 33–4, 89–91, 100, 103, 134, 189, 192, 209, 211, 223, 238, 252, 266
Griffith, J. G.: 56, 157, 191, 246
Grote, G.: 189
Guadalquivir, R.: 242, 246
Gymnasiarchs: 103

Hades: 81, 161, 180, 250, 256
Hadrian (Publius Aelius Hadrianus): 11, 13, 14, 15, 22, 113–14, 163, 172, 296, 297
Hamillus: 212, 222
Hannibal: 84, 133, 137, 155, 168–9, 210–11, 221, 239, 244, 277, 290
Hasdrubal: 237

Hathor: 289
Hebe: 250
Hector: 214
Hecuba: 214, 222–3
Helicon: 163
Hellespont (Dardanelles): 221, 223
Helmbold, W. C.: 44, 190
Helvidius Priscus: 18
Henley, W. E.: 49
Hephaestus: see under Vulcan
Heraclitus: 206, 218
Hercules: 67, 90, 121, 161, 177, 187, 217, 229, 236, 252, 254
Hermopolis (Khmunu): 259, 288
Hermes, Herms: 188
Hero (philosopher): 20
Herodotus: 221–2, 262, 288, 290
Heroic Age, the: 259
Hesiod: 60, 259
Hesperides: 122, 267
Hiberina: 128
Highet, G.: 7, 13, 14, 16, 17, 19, 21, 27, 37, 47, 53, 60, 74, 126, 158, 159, 172, 188, 190, 201, 246, 247–8, 261, 276, 289, 296, 297
Hippolytus: 46, 224
Hispulla, ? Calpurnia: 241, 246
Historians, history: 163, 166
Hogarth, W.: 54
Homer (incl. Iliad, Odyssey): 40, 126, 144, 164, 201, 203, 213, 222, 224, 233, 248, 252, 261, 283, 289, 290
Homosexuality, homosexuals: 21, 24, 32–3, 40, 43–4, 49, 66, 75 ff, 82, 90, 124, 128, 137, 138, 139–40, 177, 181, 191, 195 ff, 215, 222
Horatius Cocles: 186, 193
Horace (Q. Horatius Flaccus): 9, 22, 36, 40, 43, 44, 50, 53, 54, 67, 103, 165, 171, 172, 248, 276
Hostia: 153

Housman, A. E.: 42, 56, 57, 73–4, 111, 158, 161, 187, 190, 201, 202
Hylas: 71
Hymettus, Mt: 255

Ida, Mt: 250, 260
Ilion: 214
Illyria: 181
India, Indians: 139, 145, 231
Informers: 62, 66, 71
Io: 147
Iphigeneia: 245, 248
Ireland: 12, 81
Iron Age, the: 127, 259
Isis: 146, 147, 159, 195, 201, 242, 246, 252, 261
Ixion: 250, 260

Jacoby, F.: 101
Jahn, O.: 56, 296
Janiculum, the: 277
Janus: 142
Jason: 132
Jerusalem: 148
Jews, the: 14, 87, 133, 147–8, 154, 182, 266, 276–7, 291
Jocasta: 278
Johnson, Dr S.: 7
Josephus, Flavius: 83
Julia (daughter of Drusus Caesar, q.v.): 188
Julia (Domitian's niece): 82, 114
Julii, the: 187
Junii, the: 187
Juno (Hera): 39, 83, 128, 150, 202, 241, 246, 250, 260, 293, 296
Jupiter (Zeus): 39, 84, 127, 129, 182, 187, 211, 214, 219, 231, 241, 244, 250, 251, 253, 254, 260, 261, 266, 270, 273
Justice: 127

Juvenal (Decimus Iunius Iuvenalis):
Life, 10 ff; exile, 18–21; as parodist,
40–41, 50–51, 276, 296; philosophy
of, 42; style, 43 ff, 51–2; structure
of satires, 44 ff, 50; imagery and
verbal effects, 7, 52–3; MSS and
textual problems, 55 ff, 73–4, 82,
83, 100, 101, 102, 111, 112, 114,
125, 153, 154, 157, 158, 159, 172,
187, 189, 190–91, 192, 201–2,
202–3, 219, 222, 224, 235, 238–9,
246, 247, 260, 261, 262, 277, 278,
279, 297; problem of translating,
59 ff; his errors of natural history,
238, 278, 287, 291

Kenney, E. J.: 36
Knoche, U.: 7, 56, 174, 201, 202, 296
Kronos: *see under* Saturn

Lactantius (Caecilius Firmianus): 9
Ladies' Day (Matronalia): 197, 202
Laestrygonians, the: 281, 289
Lambert, C.: 46
Lanista, the: 139, 157, 227, 235
Lateranus, ? T. Sext.: 54, 182–3, 190,
205, 218
Latinus: 62
Latin Way, the: 71, 74, 119
Latium, Latins: 193, 244
Latona: 214
Lattimore, R.: 60
Laurentum: 248
Laureolus: 191
Lavinium: 112, 243
Layard, H.: 225
Lays of Ancient Rome: 193
Leda: 129
Legacy-hunters: 31, 48–9, 120, 128,
212, 244–5, 247–8
Lelièvre, F.: 40, 50, 83
Lentulus: 183, 191

Lepidus: 136
Lesbia: 153
Lesbianism: 138
Leto: 133, 155
Leucippus: 218
Lex Iulia de adulteriis: 82
Lex Papia Poppaea: 153
Lex Scantinia de nefanda Venere: 82
Libya: 228
Licinianus, Valerius: 174
Licinus: 102
Lindsay, J.: 289–90
Literature, literary men: 65, 161 ff
Livia: 172
Livius (M. Liv. Salinator): 237
Livy (T. Liv. Patavinus): 35, 84,
154–5, 160, 193, 203, 224, 237, 260,
290
Locusta: 67, 73
Longinus, G. Cassius: 205, 218
Lucan (M. Annaeus Lucanus): 38,
165, 172–3
Lucian (of Samosata): 160, 173, 189
Lucilius, Gaius: 36, 65, 70, 71, 72, 74
Lucretia: 215, 224
Lucretius (Tit. Lucr. Carus): 40, 50,
59, 218, 296
Lucrinus, Lake: 110, 236
Lucullus, Lucius Licinius: 223
Lupercalia, the: 84
Lycus: 83
Lydia: 223, 274
Lyons: 66
Lysimachus: 174

Ma: 83, 159
Macaulay, T. B.: 193
Macedonia: 89, 187, 189, 220
Mackail, J. W.: 53–4
Mackendrick, P.: 247
Macrobius, Ambrosius Theodosius:
125

Maecenas, Gaius: 153, 166, 242
Magic: 88, 100, 131, 150, 158, 160, 193, 278
Marius, G.: 185–6, 192–3, 214, 223
Marriage: 127 ff, 153, 216–17
Mars: 65, 76, 79, 82, 83, 129, 190, 215, 224, 230, 237, 251, 253, 273, 277, 278, 293, 296
Marsyas: 195, 201
Martial (M. Valerius Martialis): 9, 11, 15, 16, 19, 21–2, 34, 50, 51, 83, 103, 111, 114, 155, 173, 191, 192, 239, 276, 296
Massa: 62
Maura: 138, 212, 222
Maximus: 115
Medea: 151, 160
Medullina: 139, 157
Medusa: 101
Megalesian Games, the: 239
Meiggs, R.: 247
Mela, Pomponius: 261
Melanippe: 185
Meleager: 121
Memnon: 281, 288
Memphis: 285
Mendes: 288
Menoeceus: 272, 278
Meroë: 20, 147, 159
Messalina, Valeria: 48, 131, 154, 190, 216, 225, 279
Metaurus, R.: 237
Metellus, L. Caecil.: 91, 101, 136, 156
Metellus, Q. Caecil. M. Pius: 290
Mettius Curtius: 154
Milesians, Miletus: 138
Milo: 62
Milo of Croton: 218
Minerva: 92, 95, 101, 209, 220, 241, 252
Minos: 224

Minturnae: 223
Misenum: 99
Mithridates VI: 152, 161, 214, 223, 272, 278
Moesia: 114
Moloch, cult of: 189
Montanus, ? T. Junius: 108, 109, 114
Moors, Morocco: 89, 118, 139, 210, 221, 231, 238, 270, 273
Moses: 266
Mostellaria, the: 191
Mother Goddess, the: 78, 83, 91, 101, 146, 159, 239
Mucius (G. Muc. Scaevola): 186, 193
Murder: 25, 67, 84, 150–51, 160, 184, 191–2, 198, 249, 269, 271, 275 (see also under Poison, poisoners)
Music, musicians: 142, 212
Mycenae: 245
Mystery cults: 78
Mythology, mythological allusions: 10, 39, 65, 67, 72, 73, 80, 154, 163, 174–5, 222

Naples: 173, 236
Narcissus: 275, 279
Nazianzen, Gregory: 20
Nechepso: 160
Nephele: 260
Neptune: 252, 254
Nero (L. Domitius Ahenobarbus): 15, 24–5, 36, 37, 48, 73, 83, 101, 102, 106, 109, 111, 113, 118, 124, 125, 150, 154, 160, 173, 179, 184, 187, 188, 190, 191, 192, 205, 215, 218, 219, 239, 245
Nerva, M. Cocceius: 12, 19, 22, 34, 102
Nestor: 48, 139, 213, 222, 245
Nile, R.: 66, 130, 159, 210, 250, 259, 285, 288, 289, 290–91
Niobe: 49, 133, 155

INDEX

Niphates, Mt: 143, 158
Nisbet, R. G.: 153–4, 238
Numa: 39, 84, 87, 92, 99, 101, 124, 139
Numantia: 290
Numicius, R.: 236
Numidia: 169
Numitor: 165

Oasis, the Great: 18, 22
Obsequens, Julius: 260
Ocean: 273
Octavia: 192
Octavius: *see under* Augustus
Odysseus: *see under* Ulysses
Oenone: 18
Oeta, Mt: 236
Ogulnia: 141
Old age: 211–14
Olympians, Olympus: 39, 252, 260
  (*see also under* Gods)
Olynthus: 247
Ombi: 282, 289
Omens: 79
Onians, R. B.: 291
Oppia: 212
Oppii, the: 222
Orestes: 184, 274, 278
Orkneys, the: 17, 81
Orontes, R.: 89, 100
Orphism: 291
Orwell, G.: 27–8, 30, 51
Osiris: 147, 177, 289
Ostia: 13, 27, 125, 243, 247
Otho, L. Roscius: 92, 102
Otho, Marcus Salvius: 15, 78, 83, 114, 148, 159
Ovid (Publ. Ovidius Naso): 40, 155, 222, 236, 297

Pacuvius: 82
Paetus, Thrasea: 124

Palatine Hill, the: 155, 172, 195, 236
Palladium, the: 101
Pannonia: 114, 187–8
Paris (actor): 18, 19, 74, 153, 166, 173
Paris (of Troy): 213, 222
Parody: 40, 50–51, 106 ff, 196, 198, 201, 202, 276, 296
Parthia(ns): 12, 143, 158, 174
Pasiphaë: 187
Patroclus: 97
Paul, St: 154
Paulus (L. Aemil. Paul. Macedonicus): 177, 187
Pegasus: 101, 107
Peleus: 213, 271
Penelope: 77
Perseus: 101, 187
Persia(ns): 211, 275
Persicus: 236
Persius (Aulus Pers. Flaccus): 9, 36, 43
Pessinus: 159, 239
Petelia: 290
Petosiris: 149, 160
Petronius (T. Petr. Arbiter): 30, 31, 99, 160, 173, 235, 248, 290
Phaeacia: 122, 281, 289
Phaedra: 216, 224
Phalaris: 180, 188–9
Pharnaces: 223
Pharsalia, the: 38, 173, 223
Pherae: 161
Philip II of Macedon: 220, 242, 247
Philippi: 185, 192
Philippus: 224
Philo: 290
Philosophers, philosophy: 42–3, 76–7, 91, 218, 249, 256, 261–2, 275
Phrygia(ns): 101, 147, 149, 159, 274
Pindar: 222, 248
Piraeus: 235

316

Piso, G. Calpurnius: 125, 160, 173, 190, 218
Plato: 82, 261
Plautus, C. Rubellius: 188
Plautus, T. Maccius: 191
Pliny the Elder (G. Plinius Secundus): 103, 193, 202, 238, 288, 291
Pliny the Younger (C. Plin. Caecilius Secundus): 22–3, 173, 174, 189, 246, 276, 296
Plutarch: 289, 297
Pluto: 250
Poison, poisoners: 67, 71, 150–51, 160, 161, 169, 184, 198, 205, 249, 254, 269
Poland: 285
Polydorus: 223
Polymestor: 223
Polyphemus: 197
Polyxena: 214
Pompeia: 157
Pompeii, the: 288
Pompeius, ?: 108
Pompeius (Cn. Pomp. Strabo): 174
Pompey (Cn. Pomp. Magnus): 208, 214, 220, 223, 224
Pontia: 151, 160
Ponticus, ? Valerius: 177 ff, 187
Pontus: 161, 223
Poppaea Sabina: 83
Porsena, Lars: 193
Poseidon: 211, 221
Posides: 276
Postgate, J. P.: 158
Postumus: 127, 128 f, 296
Pothinus: 224
Praeneste: 93, 102, 266
Praetorian Guard, the: 17, 26, 47, 219, 220, 279
Praetors: 68, 91, 156, 174, 192, 206, 219, 223, 233, 239, 273, 278
Priam: 139, 213, 222

Priapus: 138, 141
Priscus, Helvidius: 124
Priscus, Marius: 11, 181, 189
Probus, Valerius: 10
Procne: 151, 160
Proetus: 225
Prometheus: 109, 181, 190, 260, 284
Proserpine: 250
Prosody: 59–60
Prostitutes: 76, 89, 91, 131, 149, 155, 213, 232–3
Prudentius, Aurelius Clemens: 10
Prusias: 221
Prussians, the: 110
Psecas: 146
Ptolemaeus (astrologer): 159
Ptolemy XIII: 224
Punishment, corporal: 135, 145–6, 263
Pygmies: 255, 261
Pylos: 213
Pyrenees, the: 210
Pyrrha: 68, 282, 289
Pyrrhus, King of Epirus: 156, 237, 244, 269, 277
Pythagoras, Pythagoreans: 287, 291–2

Quinquatrus, the: 220
Quintilian (M. Fabius Quintilianus): 9, 37, 44, 137, 156, 169, 174, 290
Quirinus: 186, 230

Ravenna: 114
Ravola: 195, 201
Religion: 38–9, 40, 61, 139, 147, 156–7, 205, 241 ff, 250, 260
Remus: 237
Republic, Republicanism: 35, 39, 42, 120, 125, 230, 256
Rhadamanthus: 256
Rhea: 260

INDEX

Rhea Silvia: 237
Rhetoric(ians): 24, 36, 44, 61–2, 65,
    72, 137, 144, 156, 168–9, 173–4,
    209, 211, 285
Rhine, R.: 110, 183, 188
Rhodes: 138, 181, 273
Rhodope: 195
Rhône, R.: 170, 177, 187
Ribbeck, C.: 45
Richborough: 17, 110
Robertson, D. S.: 125
Rome: 35, 53–5, 66, 81, 87–98, 154,
    168–9, 192, 230–31, 233, 239, 255,
    269
Romulus: 35, 193, 237
Rose, H. J.: 260
Rowlandson, T.: 54
Rubrius Gallus: 108, 114
Rufinus, P. Cornelius: 203
Rufus, Verginius: 114
Rumania (Dacia): 109, 114, 155, 285
Ruperti, G.: 158
Rutila: 215, 224, 235
Rutilus: 227, 235, 263, 276
Rutuli, the: 244, 248

Sabines, the: 133, 154, 237
Sacred College, the: 190
Saguntum: 290
Salamis: 211, 222
Salii, the: 83
Sallust (G. Sallustius Crispus): 238
Samnites, the: 193
Samos: 89, 293, 296
Samothrace: 92
Sardanapalus: *see under* Assurbanipal
Sardinia: 218
Sartre, J.-P.: 49
Satire: 40, 48 f, 53, 154
Satur: 115
Saturn: 39, 127, 148, 190, 250, 259
Saturnalia: 154, 173

Saufeia: 138, 157, 199, 202
Scaurus, ? M. Aemilius: 230, 237
Schools, schoolmasters: 170–71, 212,
    222
Scipio (P. Corn. Scip. Nasica): 91,
    101, 155
Scipio Africanus (P. Corn. Scip. Afr.
    Major): 221
Scotland: 10, 270
Scott, G. R.: 83
Scylla: 281, 289
Sebek (Souchos): 288
Sejanus (L. Aelius Seianus): 7, 54,
    188, 207–8, 219
Seleucus (astrologer): 159
Semiramis: 221
Senate, senators: 69, 170, 174, 180,
    186, 203, 218–19, 228, 242, 247
Seneca the Elder (M. Annaeus Sen.):
    72
Seneca the Younger (L. Annaeus
    Sen.): 84, 103, 160, 172, 184, 205,
    218, 220, 222, 236, 289
Sentinum: 193
Sergii, the: 187, 192
Sergius: 130–31
Seriphos: 148
Sertorius, Quintus: 48, 132, 290
Servius: 10, 55
Servius Tullius: 126, 160
Set: 289
Seven Sages, the: 259, 262
Severus, Septimus: 288
Shipwreck, horrors of: 241 ff, 246,
    274
Sibyl, the: 87, 181, 189
Sicilians, Sicily: 121, 145, 171, 174,
    188, 250
Silius, Gaius: 225, 279
Silvanus: 144, 158
Silver Age: 127, 259
Sinope: 261

318

Sirens: 174, 203
Sisyphus: 250, 260
Siwah: 159
Slavery, slaves: 23, 68, 69, 93, 135, 145-6, 186, 193, 195, 199, 206, 244, 263, 265, 276
Snow, C. P.: 55
Social Wars, the: 118, 124
Socrates: 174, 255, 262, 275
Soldiers, military life: 178, 270, 293-7
Solon: 214
Sophocles: 151, 248
Soranus, Barea: 101
Sostratus (? Sosistratus): 221
Spain, Spaniards: 15, 21, 156, 172, 181, 210, 232, 242, 274, 284-5, 290
Sparta: 180, 184, 239, 256
Sparti, the: 277
Stanford, W. B.: 236
Statius, Publ. Papinius: 40, 52-3, 165-6, 173, 259
Stephanus: 115
Sthenoboea: 216, 225
Stoicism, Stoics: 23, 37, 38, 40, 42-3, 75, 91, 118, 124, 188, 191, 253, 255, 261, 285
Strabo: 261, 289, 291, 296
Styx: 80, 96
Suasoriae: 72
Subura, the: 15, 120, 228
Suetonius (G.Suetonius Tranquillus): 19, 72, 73, 82, 83, 103, 111, 113, 158, 160, 173, 175, 187, 191, 192, 218, 220, 239, 276
Sulla, L. Cornelius: 62, 65, 223, 238
Sullivan, J. P.: 8, 73
Sulpicii, the: 187
Sybaris: 138
Syene: 18, 22
Syme, R.: 15, 124
Syphax: 133, 155

Syracuse: 238
Syria(ns): 89, 100, 141, 148, 182-3, 218, 221, 229

Tacitus, Cornelius: 12, 17, 20, 38, 42, 101, 112, 187, 188, 189, 190, 191, 218, 219, 224, 276, 277, 279
Tagus, R.: 88
Tanaquil: 148, 160
Tantalus: 155
Taormina: 120
Tarentum: 138, 156
Tarpeian Rock, the: 128, 241
Tarquinius Collatinus, L.: 224
Tarquinius Priscus: 160
Tarquinius, Sextus: 224
Tarquinius Superbus: 113, 193
Tarsus: 91, 101
Tchaikovsky, P. I.: 46
Telamon: 271
Tentyra (Dendereh): 282, 289
Terminus: 297
Tertullian (Q. Septimius Florens Tertullianus): 9
Thackeray, W. M.: 28
Thaïs: 140
Thales: 255, 262
Theatre, actors: 18-19, 21, 90, 129, 184, 191
Thebes (Boeotia): 165, 250, 259, 272, 277
Thebes (Egypt): 159, 259, 281, 288
Themison: 212, 222
Theodotus: 224
Theophrastus: 159, 218
Thersites: 186, 228
Thessaly: 150, 160, 161
Thomson, J. O.: 221
Thoth: 288
Thracians, Thrace: 89, 142, 167, 255
Thrasymachus: 174
Thyestes: 185

Thymele: 62

Tiber, R.: 54, 89, 120, 125, 147, 186, 187, 193, 270, 277

Tiberinus, the: 120, 125–6

Tiberius (Tib. Julius Caesar Augustus): 111, 112, 175, 187, 207–8, 219, 220

Tiresias: 258, 262, 278

Tiridates: 85

Titans, the: 181, 190

Titus (Tit. Flavius Vespasianus): 17, 21, 154, 173

Tivoli: 13, 15, 93, 229, 266

Toga praetextata, the: 218–19, 232, 238

Tongilius: 167

Trajan (M. Ulpius Traianus): 10, 12, 13, 27, 103, 113, 155, 158, 174

Translation, problems of: 59 ff

Trebius: 30, 117 ff, 124

Tribunes: 68, 69, 173, 192, 235

Triphallus: 140

Trojans, Troy: 107, 171, 179, 184, 188, 192, 213, 223, 230, 233, 236, 243

Trypherus: 231, 238

Tullia: 138

Tullius Hostilius: 112, 119, 124

Tyre, Tyrian: 167, 206

Tyrrhenia: 243

Ubastet (Bast): 288

Ulysses: 197, 200, 203, 213, 228, 236, 274, 278, 281, 289

Umbricius (? A. Umbr. Magnus): 27, 33, 87 ff, 99

Uranus: 260

Vahlen, J.: 56

Valerii, the: 187, 246

Valerius Maximus: 218

Vascones, the: 290

Veblen, Thorstein: 276

Veiento, A. Did. Gall. Fabricius: 93, 102, 109, 113, 114

Venus: 76, 82, 106, 138, 148, 214, 224, 236, 293, 296

Vercellae: 113, 193

Verdière, R.: 239

Verres, C.: 62, 88, 100, 181, 189, 203

Vespasian (Tit. Flavius Vespasianus): 16, 21, 112, 114, 124, 156

Vesta: 142

Vestal Virgins: 105, 107, 111, 174, 222

Viminal Gate, the: 220

Vinduna: 187

Virgil (P. Vergilius Maro): 10, 40, 50, 54, 59, 83, 125, 144, 165, 171, 172, 202, 222, 233, 236, 237, 247, 290, 291, 296

Virginia: 215, 224

Virro: 32, 118 ff, 124, 196, 201–2

Vitellius, Aulus: 15, 83, 113, 114

Vitellius, L.: 236

Volscii: 185

Volsinii: 93, 102

Volusius, ? Maecianus: 281, 288, 296

Vulcan: 65, 82, 163, 186, 224, 250, 260

Wealth: 24, 26, 29, 30–31, 48–9, 68–9, 121, 132, 151, 205, 215, 228, 232–3, 245, 249, 270–71, 273, 274

Winstedt, E. O.: 58

Women: 21, 24, 47–50, 66, 76–7, 89, 127–52, 215–16, 255, 256

Woodpecker King, the (Picus): 181, 190

Xenophobia: 33, 89 ff, 270

Xerxes: 221–2

Zama: 155, 221, 277

Zeno: 261–2, 284, 290

Zeus: *see under* Jupiter